Gullah Tears

"A novel of real power and real history, *Gullah Tears* tells the story of enslavement through the eyes and lives of enslaved Gullah people. Full of heart, pain, and at times joy, the novel is a reminder of the enduring presence of the past."

—GREGORY DOWNS
Author and professor of history, University of California at Davis

"So much of the literature of antebellum America has been locked in the rut of Scarlett O'Hara and Rhett Butler. Never have we needed a more candid, insightful, and nuanced treatment of that extraordinary period than right now. Josie Olsvig's *Gullah Tears* points the way. We need to try to understand the lives of enslaved Americans (and their masters) as they were actually lived, rather than through the lens of American mythology."

—CLAY JENKINSON
Author of *Repairing Jefferson's America: A Guide to Civility and Enlightened Citizenship* and host of NPR's *The Thomas Jefferson Hour*

"Should be required reading for all students of American history. It's the story of Africans who had America forced upon them. We must all understand and have reverence for their resilience, creativity, intellect, and deep spirituality, which never did anything but strengthen throughout their many journeys, as unimaginable as they were. *Gullah Tears* helps us do just that."

—CAROLINE BAILEY
International African American Museum, Charleston, SC

"Written with the acuity of a historian and the lyricism of a novelist, *Gullah Tears* brings into sharp focus the horrors of the transatlantic slave trade and the bitter fate of African captives forced into the labyrinth of plantation slavery in the Americas—specifically in Charleston, South Carolina. Author Josie Olsvig weaves together a careful and unforgettable narrative that illuminates the interior lives of enslaved men, women, and children as they attempt to reclaim a semblance of humanity amid the consummate inhumanity of the peculiar institution."

—BRENDA TINDAL
International African American Museum, Charleston, SC

Gullah Tears:

The Enslaved Souls of Charleston

By Josie Olsvig

Published by

◤ köehlerbooks ™

3705 Shore Drive
Virginia Beach, VA 23455
800–435–4811
www.koehlerbooks.com

JOSIE OLSVIG

Gullah Tears

THE ENSLAVED SOULS
OF CHARLESTON

a novel

VIRGINIA BEACH
CAPE CHARLES

"Behold, the dwelling place of God is with man. He will dwell with them, and they will be his people, and God himself will be with them as their God. He will wipe away every tear from their eyes, and death shall be no more, neither shall there be mourning, nor crying, nor pain anymore, for the former things have passed away."
—Revelation 21:3–4

Table of Contents

Character Key

Amahle: Daughter of main character Hentie; dies on Middle Passage from Africa.

Adrian Langdon: Nephew of William Langdon, often at Twin Oaks.

Big John: Large enslaved worker who works closely with the master.

Christmas Luke: Enslaved man who shows Hentie the Gullah praise house.

Cuffee: A young enslaved man who works as a field hand at Twin Oaks.

Doll (Baby Doll): Young, biracial enslaved herbal doctor and mistress of Mr. William Langdon.

Duke: Black driver, an enslaved worker responsible for monitoring the work of the field hands.

Emily Trenholm Langdon: Wife of William Paul Langdon, the plantation owner.

Fitzwilliam: Mr. and Mrs. Langdon's son.

Hentie: Main character, brought to America by slave traders and purchased by Mr. Langdon.

Juba: A young enslaved woman brought from Georgetown, SC, to work in the kitchen house.

Lydia: Enslaved house girl on the Battery and Octavia's sister, formerly a worker at Twin Oaks..

Mattie: Irish indentured house slave who cares for the master's son, Fitzwilliam.

Mimba: Older enslaved woman who is a root doctor that practices hoodoo/conjure/root.

Nellie: Older enslaved head cook in the kitchen house at Twin Oaks.

Octavia: Enslaved house servant and lady's maid to Mrs. Emily Langdon, sister to Lydia.

Rosa: Slave doctor and herbalist. Runs the infirmary and reared Baby Doll.

Simon McBride: Overseer of both Twin Oaks and the smaller plantation, Pleasant Prospect.

Tilly: Nominal slave who lives on the Battery.

William Paul Langdon: Master and plantation owner at Twin Oaks, husband to Emily Langdon.

Prologue
Juba's Premonition

Juba awoke from deep sleep at the ringing of the morning bell. The driver shouted as he pulled the rope. "Y'all get a move on. We got fields to tend. Gots to work dey cotton fields. Harvest comin' soon. Y'all get a move on."

Juba lay on her pallet. She looked about at the early light seeping in between the cracks in the boards of her slave cabin. She could barely see in the dim, breaking daylight. She combed her fingers through her short ebony hair and over her smooth mocha shoulders, willing herself to wake up. Her body glistened with sweat. She had another bad dream last night but couldn't remember all the details. Perhaps it would come to her later. Her dreams had been troublesome lately, and she didn't know why. It was puzzling to her; she didn't understand what it all meant.

Juba was a distressed young woman as of late. To help ease her fears, she kept a charm, a talisman of sorts, for good luck. She checked under her pallet to make sure it was still there. It was a chicken foot bound up in coarse cloth and tied with a bit of twine. It brought good luck and protection. It should have kept all the bad dreams away, but perhaps it crept through because it had a message of sorts. *Who knows? Dreams can happen for all kinds of reasons,* Juba thought.

Juba thrust herself upright, although she longed for just a few more minutes of sleep. *Gots to get a move on.* She had been so tired lately. She put her feet into her well-worn shoes and shuffled across the dirt floor of the cabin. The shoes had become tight on her feet. She looked down at her swollen ankles and said to herself, *Just another thing been changin' on me.* The others around her were starting to stir as well. Seven people slept in this small cabin. It was cramped, but they managed.

As Juba crossed the floor, she felt a sudden crick in her back and yelped in pain. She jerked to one side, then tried to right herself. She drew in a deep breath and rubbed her protruding belly. It seemed to be expanding more every day.

She exhaled, then said, "Baby, me and you are gonna have to come to an understanding here. I gots to work; you gots to behave. No throwing my back out! Can't do no work if you going to behave this way. Master never go for that. It don't matter that I'm having his baby; he ain't gonna treat me any better than anyone else. Besides, his wife is trying to do me in; she all upset he visits me at night. Not my choice. Nothing I can do about it. If we gonna live, then we gots to work. I have to do what the master say. It's that simple."

Another enslaved woman called out from the other side of the cabin, "You best get used to that baby causing your back to hurt. It gonna be dat way for a long time."

"Dat's for true," another one said.

Juba shook her head, knowing she was powerless to change things. She pasted a smile on her face and nodded at the women, then grabbed a pitcher and stepped outside. She walked to a rain barrel and dipped in, drawing out a full pitcher of water. She looked around, still shaking off sleep. The rising sun bathed the trees in a soft white light. She drew in the scent of oaks and magnolias. As she made her way back to the slave cabin, she noticed that the morning air was mingled with scents of sweet yellow jasmine. Then she caught a whiff of smoke. Someone by the other slave cabins had already been up and stoked the large cooking fire. The smoke curled up, then dissipated in the trees, becoming invisible against the gray sky. Juba cringed, then mashed her lips together as the smell of smoke made her stomach jump. Lots of that going on since she had been carrying the baby.

Knowing that she mustn't dally anymore, she resigned herself to the start of another workday on the plantation. *Nothing you can do about it, gots to work. You drag your feet and the overseer will take the lash to you. Got a baby to think about now.*

She walked back into the cabin with the pitcher in hand. People were pulling on clothes. One man turned his back toward her as he started to pull on a shirt. She saw the thick, rigid scars across his back, slicing in all directions, no doubt the remnants of the overseer's lash. Workers were grabbing hunks of bread and bits of jerky before heading out. Juba poured water from the pitcher into the basin and dipped a cloth into it, wiped the sleep from her face and glided the cloth across her arms to cool off the warmth and perspiration. The moist air was still tolerable now, but undoubtedly, as the day wore on, the heat would grow more intense and become sweltering. She pulled on an ivory-colored shift made of coarse cloth. It was shabby, but it was loose and cool. Juba then donned a brightly colored head wrap, tying it securely. She would be helping out in the laundry today. She would need to be able to move about in the heat. Feeling a bit more alert now, she dabbed a bit of rosemary and lemon oil about her exposed skin to help repel the mosquitos that would surely be thick and persistent today.

Still feeling a tingling sensation over her body, she wondered what her foreboding dream might be warning her of. Something about the child she was carrying, perhaps? During the night she thought she saw small flecks or orbs of light about her, then waved it off as just her imagination. The tiredness, perhaps, or was it the spirit shrouding her? Picking up her pace, Juba walked briskly toward the laundry. The fire under the big iron cauldron was already going, and the water was heating up. Juba pulled out the lye soap used to launder the sheets and the master's undergarments. She wiped her hands on the front of her garment as she readied herself for the day.

As the hours wore on, Juba grew weak in the heat. She felt the sweat roll down the sides of her face and between her shoulder blades. She was powerless to do anything about it. *Gots to keep working.*

At one point, another enslaved woman, Patsy, put her hand on Juba's shoulder and asked, "Girl, you okay? You look a bit off."

"No, I'm fine. Just a little heat getting to me. I'll be alright," Juba said nonchalantly. The next thing she knew, she became lightheaded and weak. Juba heard a weird whining sound and detected a strong, odd odor. After that, everything went black.

Juba woke up on her pallet, an enslaved woman standing over her. She gradually came out of her haze.

"What happened? How did I get here?" Juba asked.

"You okay. You just fainted. The heat must have got to you. It's so hot, and you been standing over that boiling laundry all day. You just rest. The overseer is busy out on the other side the plantation. You just rest now."

Juba felt so tired, she thought she would listen to the woman and rest a bit. She closed her eyes and drifted off to a deep sleep. She must have drifted off for hours.

Juba woke up with a start, her heart pounding and her throat parched and dry. Her stomach was in knots. Rain was pounding down on the roof of the cabin. She heard dripping in a corner. Coolness pervaded the cabin.

What a strange dream. It felt like a memory; it was so vivid.

A man had been coming toward her and calling her name. He

said he was so happy he had found her again. He radiated love and warmth. In the dream, Juba had felt drawn to him. They were almost touching, but then a look of shock came over him. He started to stumble, then he fell toward her. Juba lunged forward to catch him in her arms. She could see the texture of his skin, the thick curls of his hair. He wore a dark woolen jacket and newer leather boots. His dark-red blood poured out of him and onto her skirt. She held his head in her lap and kept caressing him as tears welled in her eyes and flowed down her cheeks.

Who was this man in her dream? Could it be the child she was carrying? Had he been sold off and then later found her again? Juba's bilious stomach was fraught with raw nerves. It all seemed so real. The man had died in her arms. She could still feel the warmth of his body against her. His warm pooling blood seeped through to Juba's chilled, moist fingers. She remembered the intense look of the young man's eyes. They were full of love and then a startling realization he had been shot. She could see the blood pour from him into her lap as she caressed his head.

What did the dream mean? Was it a foreboding of what was to come? Juba swallowed heavily and took in a fortifying breath of the chilled, wet air. She clung tightly to the image of the man. She had felt such love for the strange man. She was afraid that if she moved, his image would slip through her fingers and unravel at lightning speed. She wanted to know who he was. Juba's fingers tingled as if she could still feel the texture of his hair and the rough, woolen fabric of his jacket. She wanted to bring him back and ask who he was. She ached to crawl back into the dream so that she could understand, but it was not to be. She had to let the dream float away on the smoke rising up from the candle near her bed.

Juba turned to see another enslaved woman standing near her. The woman touched Juba's shoulder as she set her deep-brown eyes, crinkled with years of work in the relentless sun, on the despondent young woman.

The woman said to Juba, "You okay, baby? You musta had another bad dream, but you alright now."

Juba queried, "Am I, Patsy? Am I alright? I know my dreams mean something. A man will die in my arms. I don't know who he is or why he must die. I only know we love each other very much. Is he this baby I am carrying? Who is he? How can I stop him from dying? I must find out the answer."

Chapter 1
Capture and Voyage to America

A s she lay in her small, confined space, Hentie dropped her head back and closed her eyes. She let out a sigh as she tightened her lids. Her eyes, dark and almond shaped, were once as gentle as a doe's but now had taken on a hollow cast. She cried silently in pain and sorrow for the loss of her family and for so many others she had known back in her village. The stench below deck hung like a weight around her neck, pressing her down. She started to rock to soothe herself, gripping the sides of her soiled garment saturated with human filth. To ease her tension, she wrung it till it seemed it would be threadbare. She tried to hum and think of the lullaby her mother sang to her as a child. But then a rat scampered across her, biting her hand as it passed, and the melody cracked. She yelped, yet at the same time felt impervious to the pain. Numb from all the trauma she had experienced, the bite from the rat at least reminded her she was alive.

Hentie's family was dead, and so many others from her village had died on the march from inland Africa to the ship. Many more had perished on board. In her despair she began to pray, *Nyame, creator of the world, protect me from these brutal men. They are evil. Why has this happened to me? Why did you let my daughter die? I am a good Mende woman. Why, Nyame, why don't you help me and stop this brutality?*

Hentie's chest was hollow with pain and aching; she longed to be back in her homeland. She wanted the life she had before. There she had her family. They enjoyed their land and its plentifulness. Life had been good. Now she lay confined, weakened, and famished, but unable to eat the slop presented to her. The maggot-infested gruel was repulsive. She grew weaker with each passing hour. Was death about to overcome her? Would her spirit travel back to Africa as the others from her tribe believed?

While the ship was quite large, designed to hold a couple hundred, it was filled twofold that amount. The space allotted for each human being was paltry, even before the overcrowding. The mercenaries treated the captives as if they were mere cargo, not human beings, stuffed into compartments like inanimate goods. There was no regard for their well-being, safety, or comfort. The human stowage lay between decks in cells barely more than a foot high, forcing them to cram up against one another with just inches separating their faces from planks above. The men were separated from the women and children in spaces a scintilla bigger than those used for the women.

Hentie stared at the wooden boards over her head and tried to shift her weight. She wanted to scratch her shoulder, but she was not able with the two bodies lying heavily against her. She nudged the woman to her left to see if she might roll to her side. The woman was covered in vomit and would not respond. *Is she alive?* Some souls suffocated in their tiny spaces; perhaps she had fallen victim as well. The crew pulled dead bodies from the hold every day to toss overboard without regard to the life lost.

As Hentie wiggled in her tight space, her body aches escalated and she emitted a mournful cry. Others joined in and whimpered with her. The slave driver beat on the grated hatchways between decks to silence the captives. *Whack!*

"Quiet, you animals, or you'll get even worse! Thumb screws or the lash! We'll teach you to be silent, you heathen dogs!"

Some of the crew, just released from prison, had been unable to find better employment, and enjoyed being able to now control others as they had been controlled.

When Hentie first came on board the ship, looking down as her foot touched the odd wooden boards on the deck, her head jerked up at a shrill scream of agony. Her heart skipped a beat, and the blood rushed from her head. Nothing could have prepared her for the sight of her friend, Binta, being held down on the deck by three large white men. A large mark had just been burned into her chest; steam rose from the branding iron. Hentie smelled the foul odor of burned flesh. A hot, nauseous wave swept through her body. She clutched her fists against her body as her stomach tightened into knots.

One by one, the rest of the captives were held down and branded on their chests with a red-hot iron. The iron sizzled as it sank into the flesh of another human being, always followed with that putrid smell of burned skin and hair. Her stomach churned as her fellow captives endured the searing torture, each in his turn.

Then the men grabbed her daughter, Amahle. Her long, sleek body twisted and turned as she fought the men with all her might. Amahle's deep-mocha skin was a sharp contrast against the white shirts of the sailors as they wrestled her to the ground. Poor, helpless Amahle cried and begged for them to stop. The ship's coarse captain, clad in a deep-blue jacket and white knee britches, walked over to Amahle and then reached down to cradle her face. His thumb caressed her smooth skin.

"You'll be mine, precious girl. You'll be mine," the lewd man chuckled as he smirked, revealing gray, rotting teeth. He nodded at his crew so that they understood this one would be his personal bond servant.

"Aye aye, Captain. The girl is yours," said one of the crewmen.

As they came at Amahle with the bright-orange branding iron, Hentie strained against her manacles, screaming in her native tongue, "Stop it! Please, stop it!" She staggered as she continued to wail, helpless to intercede.

The men tore open Amahle's garb and thrust the hot iron by her breast. Hentie heard the sizzle and her howl of pain and locked up her body in reaction. Amahle's suffering gripped her soul and she began to weep. At first, she tried to muffle her cry into her hand, but then she threw her head back and began to bawl, her chest heaving as she sobbed. *These ruthless animals. How could they do such a thing?*

Hentie turned away from the savagery of it all, knowing her time was coming.

Two men charged at her, grabbing her arms, and pulled her along. Hentie fell limp, fainting at the horror of what was about to befall her. It was her only means of coping.

Hentie woke lying on the deck. The intense pain of her wound radiated through her chest. When she rolled to her side, a white man snatched her up and shoved her into the crowd being led into the bowels of the ship. Little did she know that this was only the beginning of a long and arduous voyage full of pain and sorrow.

After that, whenever the captives screamed in pain or hunger, they were threatened with the branding iron. The driver would hold it up and shake it at them, then smile broadly. The captives' injuries sometimes became infected and led to their demise. Their suffering was immense.

The stench of human excrement and death permeated the ship. There was nowhere for the waste to drain; it lay stagnant. In all the dampness, the ship was crawling with disease-laden vermin, making the squalid conditions even worse. Crew members sometimes washed the cells out when the captives were taken up on deck for exercise and meals, but such efforts were sporadic. Dysentery ran rampant; others suffered from malaria and other diseases. Impending death hung like a veil. Many died under these conditions, especially the children. The dead were dumped overboard without solemnity or service, as if they were no more than trash. The crossing from the west coast of Africa to America took over a month, but it was impossible to tell time by the passing of days. It was easier to tell time by the thinning of the human cargo.

Hentie cried silently in her pain and sorrow. When the captives were periodically brought up from the ship's hold for air, a crew member would beat on a drum to "dance the slaves" and give them exercise. Those who refused were beaten mercilessly. The captain would often pull Amahle from the rest of the prisoners. He found her beauty irresistible. Amahle fought the captain but was overwhelmed every time by the captain and his minions. They would drag her from the group, behind a wall or barricade separating the crew from the captive Africans. The first time he brutalized Amahle, Hentie had been shocked by the shear violence of it all. She cowered, sucking in air and puffing it out to get through the horrific event, unable to intercede as her daughter screamed. Afterward, she saw the emerging bruises, the swollen cheek with the captain's handprint, and the blood running down the inside of her daughter's thigh, and she understood what had occurred. Amahle crumpled into a pile and sobbed.

Hentie went to her daughter's side to soothe her. Their personalities used to flow together in a calming stream, but not this day. That flow of good energy had evaporated. She said to her daughter in their native dialect, "Oh, Amahle, what have they done to you? I'm so sorry I couldn't stop those men. I wish I could take your pain from you; I would gladly do so rather than see you suffer." Tears streaked Hentie's cheeks. "My dear child, how could this happen to us?"

Hentie wrapped her arms around Amahle, clutching her body to her chest. She wanted to protect her daughter against these vile men but was unable. The ship's captain held all the authority. *We are powerless against these heartless men. Why were we seized by these animals? Help us, someone, please help us.*

Day after day, Amahle suffered.

"Dah, I don't think I can take this any longer. The men do such terrible things to me. What can I do? What can I do? Must I go on living like this forever? I can't take their brutality anymore." Her hopeless tears filled Hentie's entire being with anguish.

Their suffering on the ship had no end. They watched as the dead and nearly dead were tossed over the side to awaiting sharks that clustered about the ship, much like seagulls around a fishing boat, ready to grab the next bit of food. One of the captive men had apparently cast himself overboard. Was it a mistake? Was he shoved? Either way, he had escaped the madness, and his spirit would travel back to their homeland over the great waters.

As the days of their journey wore on, Amahle's eyes lost their light, and her smile, which previously warmed Hentie's heart, became a distant memory. She was helpless against the captain and his crew when they took turns brutalizing her. Amahle would cower and tremble as the captain in his dark bicorne hat approached her and reached out to stroke her mocha skin.

Eventually, Amahle was separated from the other prisoners and locked into a space more accessible to the captain and his crew. She and her mother were only able to speak when Hentie's group was brought up for exercise and feeding. Sometimes they were unable to converse; they could only make eye contact. Amahle's vacant look grew ever more despondent; her spirit had left her. Hentie prayed to the gods that her daughter would find a way out from her torture.

One day, an opportunity presented itself when some of the prisoners were brought up from the hull. The captain grabbed Amahle by the hair at the back of her head and pinned her against the side of the ship with the weight of his body, fondling her, biting her bare breast. Amahle had had enough. She wrapped her arms and legs around him and flipped her body backward over the railing. A look of horror passed over the captain's face, his mouth agape, his eyes wide and terrified as both plunged over the side of the ship, hitting the water at the same time. His shrieks traveled up to those on deck.

"Man overboard!" yelled one of the ship's hands.

"Damn! Poor bugger!" shouted a crewman.

"At last we're rid of the bastard," muttered another sailor.

Hentie looked over the railing to see a shark plunge toward the captain. His arms slapping the water, he disappeared under the waves. An infusion of red saturated the water.

Hentie had likewise heard Amahle shriek as she fell, the drop farther than she expected. She took gulps of water as she tried to dog-paddle and remain afloat. But it was soon over. She wailed as she was pulled under. Hentie knew that Amahle had decided she would rather die with some vestige of pride. Her daughter had been helpless to venture back to Africa in body, but her spirit would find rest in her homeland again.

⌒⌐

The day that changed their lives forever had been an ordinary day. Hentie had been well rested and happy, full of vigor. She wore a long dashiki and a colorful dhuku headwrap she had woven with her own hands. The dashiki was flattering on her shapely body, and she wore it with pride. Hentie was rather young and had lovely features. She was sturdy and tall. She glowed with a certain warmth.

As she worked, she looked about the grounds with her hand cupped over her eyes, squinting in the sunlight. Around her, everyone carried out their everyday tasks. She drew in the fresh, fragrant air as she went about her duties, basking in the sunshine. Her close-cropped hair allowed the air to flow over her face and neck. She noticed nothing amiss. She was healthy and alive. Her family was nearby, and all had seemed right with the world.

The villagers had been in a light mood, greeting one another and exchanging pleasantries. The women gathered fruits, vegetables, and nuts. A couple of women were digging up roots for medicinal use. Hentie's mother was dressed in a sage-green woven garment. She and another woman winnowed rice in a large round fanning basket. Hentie's mother delighted in her work; her mood was as light as the rice she tossed in the air. She and her friend stood near one another, bumping and touching as they joked and swayed. She nodded at Hentie and smiled when Hentie walked by. Hentie lovingly caressed her mother's arm as she passed but kept moving. Hentie was always affectionate like that—quick to share a touch or a knowing smile. She had no idea it would be the last time she touched her mother.

The men were engaged in their work and unsuspecting of the marauders closing in on them. A handful of men clustered around a couple of animals that had been downed in the morning hunt. They needed to be skinned and prepared for the evening meal. The wild game would be roasted over an open spit, and the village would share the meat. The group, which included Abeni, Hentie's husband, were in good humor due to the success of their outing. They jested and erupted in laughter as they good-naturedly tormented one another.

Suddenly, a hostile tribe surrounded the villagers. A chill ran up Hentie's back as she realized they were being ambushed. The unprovoked invasion caught them by surprise, and they froze in their confusion, just as the marauders had hoped. The attacking tribe threw nets over them, gathering the captives up like a school of fish. Villagers screamed in horror, while others attempted to escape. Abeni and a few other men tried to get away but were killed in the melee.

During the commotion, Hentie lost track of her mother's whereabouts and rushed to where she had last stood. Unable to locate her, she fell to her knees and screamed her name. Her mouth abruptly went dry as fear coursed through her body. She fell silent, frozen, confused, not knowing where to run. She was seized by two men. After their capture, Hentie had not seen her mother again.

Hentie and the other prisoners marched through the jungle like captive animals, locked into wooden neck braces and manacles, linked together with a chain, a coffle of new slaves with no means of escape. Their long journey lasted for days. They trudged through thick foliage for hours on end. Periodically, Hentie and the others received water and meager bits of sustenance, but never a full meal. Despite her injuries and fatigue, Hentie journeyed on. Those too weak to march on or in the process of dying were abandoned, left to wither alone. Dozens of the few hundred captives died or were left to perish along the way.

Once the exhausted hostages reached the coast, a ship was waiting for them at Bunce Island, just off the coastline. They saw white men wearing curious clothing and speaking a language they did not recognize. Hentie would later understand that the white men were speaking the mother tongue of England. The captain paid the leader of the capturing tribe for the new slaves, both men seeming pleased with their deal. The captain had ample funds from New York investors who sought to turn a handsome profit in marketing a human commodity.

The ship's captain shouted to his crew, "Time to load up the savages; march them out here. I want to leave this place. I hate Sierra Leone and the drudgery of this slave castle. All the bush dwellers give me the shivers. Get ready to sail."

"Aye aye, Captain," replied a crewman.

Hentie had been confused when they were rowed out to a waiting slave ship. She didn't understand what was happening to them. What value did these captives have to the heartless marauders? What did their captors plan to do with them? How could it be worth such a high human cost? She knew that warring tribes sometimes captured the hapless victims of the losing tribe and used them as slaves, but she had never heard of them being removed from their land.

After they arrived at the large ship, the captives had to go up rope ladders and then below to cramped quarters, after suffering the excruciating branding process. Tiny spaces were accorded to each person. Some people were forced to lie between the legs of another. Once in the hull of the ship, their manacles were changed out for leg irons securing the prisoners to the floor of the ship. The prisoners sobbed and shuddered with fear. Indifferent and callous, the crew shouted obscenities and wielded long whips which cut through the air and cracked loudly over the captives' heads.

It was in this setting that Hentie traveled to a strange land, bound in shackles, confined for weeks with only brief breaks, often deprived of food and water while mourning the loss of her family.

The waves rushed in on the shore of Sullivan's Island as the ship approached the American coastline. Hentie had been at sea for countless days. The day was cold and overcast, with screeching seagulls flying overhead searching for any scraps they could find. Fear rumbled through the captives as they heard the clamor of the crewmen's boots up on deck.

What, the new slaves wondered, would be the next horror they faced? The ankle shackles they wore were heavy and binding against their flesh. Would the irons be removed? Would some new tortuous device be used? Hentie had lost so much in the past few weeks. Her husband and her daughter were dead. She was yet to discover her mother's fate. What could be worth such a high cost?

Her new life began as Hentie stepped onto the deck of the ship now docked in South Carolina. She trudged forward and saw the surrounding beaches of a place she would come to know as Sullivan's Island. She had no idea which direction they had traveled. She wondered where this strange place was.

As the captives were brought up, they were given water. They rushed for it like maniacs. No threats or blows could restrain them. While Hentie focused on her new surroundings, the others shrieked and struggled for the one thing they had been deprived of for so long.

The crew continued to off-load their cargo. Hentie looked back to see bodies and debris being thrown off the ship. The seagulls clamored. Stevedores shouted and complained about the pungent and foul odors of the ship. Hentie witnessed them bring up the lifeless body of her mother. She strained against her chains, compelled to run back and gather her mother in her arms, but a harsh bark and a strike of a wooden stick stopped her.

Hentie was directed to move on. The captured slaves were slowly brought onto the soil of America and herded toward a collection of low-lying buildings. Hentie was shoved against one of the brick buildings and landed with a hard thud. No one noticed; no one cared that a bruise and lump had started to rise where she hit the ground.

As the captives were herded onward, a new ship's hand named Monahan leaned in to ask another, more experienced ship's mate, Baldwin, "Hey, what are these buildings? I thought we were taking these new slaves to downtown Charleston?"

"These are the pest houses, mate. Short for *pestilence*. These buggers can bring some nasty diseases with them, like the black vomit, smallpox, and yellow fever. In the past, scads of people died from such things. So, to avoid sharing in their diseases, they built these pest houses to keep these savages in quarantine for a couple of weeks. Otherwise, we could have an outbreak of another plague."

Hentie heard the white men around her conversing and pointing to different men of her tribe. In her haze, she noted that they were pointing out the younger, healthy men with good muscling. The white men also motioned to the younger "breeding" women. Hentie did not yet understand that the white men were picking out the more desirable tribesmen for sale in the market. After several days, Hentie's captors selected out who would be healthy enough to journey onward to market.

In the pest house, Hentie started to drift off to sleep, but she caught a chill. Her body started to shake. Was it her exhaustion or a cold breeze? Her body was shutting down from malnutrition and exposure to disease. Her head lolled and her teeth chattered. She was cold inside her bones. After hanging on to a wakeful state, she at last fell into a deep sleep, if only temporarily.

The next morning, she awoke to the sounds of waves lapping onto the beach. She smelled the salt air. For a moment, she imagined she was elsewhere, but she was soon startled by the shouting of the white men and the clinking of chains. Water and wooden bowls of slop were being passed around. Some gobbled up the mess, but she had no appetite for it. She ached for the protection of her husband's strong arms. She missed home, her precious daughter, Amahle, and the comfort of her own mother. Hentie pictured Amahle's brown face and sparkling eyes. Amahle had always brought warmth and love to her. Hentie ached to hold her and feel those emotions once more.

Hentie reflected on her times in her homeland—Amahle joking and smiling with her while they worked back in their village. The hours could be long when they worked in the rice fields, but Amahle made their labors more tolerable. She would joke and splash her with water. How Hentie longed for those times again.

The days at Sullivan's Island wore on. She wondered if they would get back on the ship and go back home or whether she would be forced to stay in the odd buildings for the days to come. After several days, Hentie was moved again.

For a moment, she had a burst of hope. Maybe she was going home. Her village and all the people in it flashed before her eyes. *It was all a terrible mistake. They have the wrong people. We're being sent back!*

But those hopes were dashed. She looked into the eyes of those around her. Fear had fallen over the group. Her heart sank, and she felt an ache in the pit of her stomach. They were not going home; they were going further into this strange land. The others whimpered and cried in terror of what awaited them. What were they about to do to them? The captives were guided back to the ship.

Monahan shouted to his mate Baldwin, "So, where are we headed this time? We going to Charles Town? Or are we making another stop along the way?"

"Nay, mate. This is a short trip. We're headed to downtown Charleston. The city used to be called Charles Town for King Charles, but the Americans got full of themselves after the Revolution and changed the name. We'll land at a big pier called Gadsden's Wharf. It's a huge wooden platform. You'll think you're in England again. There'll be several vessels there."

When they docked, the surroundings were peculiar. The buildings looked odd to Hentie, dramatically different from those in her village. Still in heavy chains, the group was led off the ship and into a holding area. The sun beat down on them as they slowly moved, dreading what was to happen next. All were weary from their long travels and from sleeping on the hard ground. Sorrow enveloped the captives at having left their homeland and lost so many people.

Hentie saw two groups of captives chained together in a circle. Some were naked; others were covered in rudimentary garments. They were eating rice at a trough. The poor, wretched victims were nearly starved and gobbled up the rice like it was their first meal in days. *Poor souls*, Hentie thought.

Hentie and her fellow captives were shoved into a room adjacent to the slave market which held dozens of others. Hentie sat there expressionless. The captors shamelessly shouted and growled at the prisoners. They seemed to believe they had a right to treat human beings as worthless creatures.

The majority of enslaved Africans who came through the Middle Passage landed in the state of South Carolina, typically the city of Charleston, just like her. Nearly half of the newly enslaved souls came to America through this port and thereby began their harrowing experience as a bondsman.

Hentie looked around at the white people surrounding her as they looked back in disgust. What were these garments they were wearing? What practical purpose did they serve? The ladies' skirts were full and billowing in the wind, dragging on the ground when they walked. Children clung to their mothers, frightened by the sight of the captives in heavy chains.

The new bondsmen were led into an open area and directed one at a time to stand on a block. Prospective white buyers and their associates circled them. Sometimes the planters discussed the virtues of the human chattel with their trusted workers, enslaved or otherwise, particularly if they would be working with them.

The new slaves up for sale were stripped of any garments or cover they had worn. A man shouted out the characteristics and virtues of each human commodity. The buyer would weigh these characteristics, mulling them over with his companion. When a prospective male slave took the block, the barker pointed out the strong back and sinewy muscle tone of each one.

Buyers circled the captives, unabashedly poking and prodding the captives, looking for signs of disease while evaluating their potential strength and endurance. Buyers haggled with the barker, trying to negotiate a better price for the human specimen. Finally, a bargain would be struck and the new slave led off.

A planter in a gray morning suit was discussing the merits of some youthful black men who looked heartier than the others.

"Isaac, what do you think of this one? Looks like an able man with a powerful build. Young, don't you think? We can use him for working in the fields for years. He must only be nineteen or twenty."

"Yes, Master. He would make a good field hand. He could work the whole day long. Best get that one."

The white aristocrat in his fine suit coat and hat nodded and approached the sales table, pulling out his billfold.

When the newly enslaved women took the block, the barker would smile broadly, point to them and say, "Look at this wench, a fine slave of child-bearing age. If you acquire one such as this, you get not only one slave, but potentially many, many slave babies. Just reward her with a new dress; she will be delighted! All of them could work your fields. Such a broodmare kept for breeding purposes could bring a fortune. Remember, the fertility of a Negro woman is an asset to the slave owner. A good breeder could bring in hundreds if not thousands of dollars to an owner. Wealth is not in the land; it's in all the slaves a planter owns that can work it."

Then a sly look would cross the barker's face as he nodded and smirked. "Not only could you use this wench in the field, but a man could use such a wench to fulfill the owner's other needs, needs not met elsewhere. The slave maiden has no choice but to comply." Following up with a wink and a nod, he made similar sexual comments with some of the children, both male and female. A few of the white men would nod at one another while raising their eyebrows, subtle smiles crossing their lips.

Hentie would come to understand the commonplace practice of white men using slave women to fulfill their sexual desires, but it was never openly spoken about, particularly by the white wives. More importantly, it was never regarded as rape, no matter how brutal or how young the victim, even if still a child. Many planters had two families—their publicly displayed white family and their hidden mulatto family.

After this, the barker would make comments about which part of Africa the future slave was from and their abilities. Captives from certain tribes or those from certain regions of Africa, such as Sierra Leone, Gambia, or the Windward Coast, were preferred due to their propensity for hard work and knowledge of rice cultivation.

One prospective buyer approached the barker and said, "I need hearty slaves for my plantation. Looking for Whydahs. They are accustomed to hard work, skilled, and obedient. I always found them to be hardy and good field hands. Have any of those?"

"Sure we do. Got some back in the slave pens. We'll bring a few out later. Wait here, sir. I'm sure you'll find a few you like," answered the seller.

Hentie was pulled out from the holding pen, still wearing part of her once colorful wrapped garment, now saturated with muck. The filthy rag was pulled from her body and discarded. She was washed and her hair was cleaned and combed. Scented oils were rubbed into her skin to make her look healthier. A used garment, beige in color, was placed on her. After a bit, Hentie was led out for sale, her turn to be offered to the highest bidder.

She was directed to stand on the block. The stand on which the new slaves were displayed stood on the street corner in the open air with no form of barrier or concealment. The barker tore off her wrap. She stood naked and ashamed in front of the large crowd, most of whom were men. The barker reached up and squeezed her large breast, then prodded her hips. He commented as to the potential uses such a slave might have for her master. Hentie bit her lip so hard she drew blood as she endured the humiliation of the spectators leering at her.

In time, a well-groomed man in colorful garments approached the block. She would later come to know this man as William Paul Langdon, a local, wealthy planter. He circled Hentie as he inspected her. He had his trusted bondsman with him, Big John, a tall and broadly built dark-skinned man. He had features similar to hers but spoke a language she did not understand. Some of the sounds and gestures were the same, but his words were blended with another language or dialect. Although he was as huge as a mountain, he seemed kind and gentle.

Mr. Langdon continued to circle and ponder. He asked the barker to open her mouth so that he could examine her teeth. While he did this, Hentie looked at the man's eyes. She had never seen such pale eyes; they were a striking shade of light blue.

"Hmmm," Mr. Langdon mused as he caressed his fair beard and continued to eye her. "She'll do," he eventually muttered. He nodded at the barker and gestured toward the table handling the purchase of slaves.

Smiling kindly, Big John made some gestures to Hentie, then uttered a couple of sounds she understood. This helped soothe her a bit. Hentie followed his direction to step down from the platform and follow him. She snatched up her garment from Big John's hands and covered herself. While smoothing her garment, she followed the men.

A price was struck between Mr. Langdon and the slave merchant. He walked to the table where his paperwork was prepared for his records. As shameful as the transaction was, the paperwork was a lovely scrolled document. The large sheet of parchment looked similar to a deed for land, much of it penned in a beautiful calligraphy. The bill of sale delineated the purchase price of a human being: $600. Big John glanced down, repulsed at the transaction, and tensed his body. Although he did not read the words on the document, merely glancing at it, he understood its meaning. After the new owner collected his document, he strolled away with his merchandise.

Big John guided Hentie to the back of a plain wooden phaeton wagon loaded with crates and barrels. With gestures, he instructed her to sit among the other goods purchased that day. He appeared friendly and helpful, wanting to make her comfortable for the ride. Hentie complied, not understanding what was happening to her and where she was being taken. As her new master mounted the wagon, he reached for a chain and wrapped it around Hentie's wrists, binding her to the wagon and securing it with a heavy metal lock. As it snapped shut, Hentie looked to Big John; he dropped his head in response, unable to intervene. Her master tugged on Hentie's chain to make sure it was secure.

Early in their journey, they rolled through the streets of Charleston, past strange-looking buildings and white people in odd clothing. Eventually they approached a waterway, and their wagon rolled onto a flat-bottomed craft. Big John got out of the wagon and guided the horses onto the craft. He held them still so as not to concern the other passengers. Apparently, this ferry was the only means of getting to their destination. It took them to the other side of the Cooper River. As they approached, the vessel bumped against the dock. Big John held the horses as the other passengers readied themselves to debark. Ropes were thrown to secure the craft. Once the ferry was secured on the riverbank, people started to move out. Big John waited for all the white folks to get off, then led the team of horses over the wooden ramp onto the grassy landing, checked the back of the wagon to ensure everything was still secure, and mounted the rig. He nodded and gave a sorrowful glance at Hentie when he tugged at her chains.

Hentie's new owner then nodded to Big John, saying, "Ready to move on? Homeward!" He shouted, "Ha!" as he snapped the reins and the wagon jerked forward.

They were traveling to a local plantation in the town of Mount Pleasant several miles from the shopping district of downtown Charleston. On the bumpy ride to her new home, Hentie saw unfamiliar sights completely outside her realm of experience.

There were a variety of homes, some very grand, others quite small. Mr. Langdon gestured up to a nearby house. The ceiling of the porch, the door, and the window frames were all painted blue.

Mr. Langdon queried Big John, "Do the Gullah people really believe that painting their doors and windows pale blue will ward off evil spirits?"

"They sure do. Haints can do evil things. They are the restless spirits of the dead. They have all kinds of powers. But you can fool 'em. They think the blue is the sky and go the other way."

Moments later, Big John smelled delicious odors emanating from one of the cabins. It was the edge of Mr. Langdon's plantation.

"Must be Rosa's cabin; it sure do smell good. She must be making a stew."

Far from the big homes were small wooden shacks, or slave cabins, all lined up in a row. Dark-skinned people stood outside. Smaller trees and shrubs were nearby. At one cabin Hentie saw an older black woman with several small children near her. She saw a small garden near the cabin with different plants throughout it. *What is she growing?* she mused.

They rode past neat rows of small trees. Big John commented to Mr. Langdon, "Look like another good year for the pecan trees. They are doing good, real good." The grove of trees was heavy with pods containing the delicious nut.

Big John turned and pointed to a cluster of orange monarch butterflies roosting in the trees. "Look! The butterflies are migrating. Have you ever seen anything look so pretty?"

Hentie was jolted from her musings as the driver slowed the horses down for a turn into the drive of the plantation. It was a long lane lined by tall oaks on either side. The trees dripped with what appeared to be a peculiar hair. She would later learn it was Spanish moss. Hentie thought it was quite odd; she had never seen anything like it in her homeland. As the wagon rolled down the lane, Hentie noted all the activity and people milling about. Nearly everyone had ebony skin like hers. She found comfort in that.

The wagon pulled past the house, and the plantation's enslaved workers approached. Hentie wasn't sure what they would do. Would they speak in her language? She quickly discovered that they spoke a language she did not fully understand, although its cadence and accentuations sounded familiar. Later she learned it was Gullah, a creole language born of African dialects and British English. The language also included expressions, certain body postures, and hand gestures.

A dark-skinned woman approached her and waved her toward some small buildings. She guided Hentie to one of the shacks. It was from there that her new life began.

Chapter 2

Hentie's Life in Her New Home

O ver time, Hentie began to adjust to her new life as an enslaved worker on a large plantation. Her days became a bit more routine. The plantation, Twin Oaks, was owned by William Paul Langdon, a tall, fair-haired white man with a trim beard. He was a wealthy planter of English descent, the third generation since immigration to America.

She drew in a deep breath and smoothed her dress as she glanced out the kitchen-house window. Her calloused hands caught on fibers of the coarse shift. The low gray clouds, filled with moisture, were beginning to roll out overhead. In the distance Hentie heard a dog barking at the rumbling thunder, but the dog's sounds trickled down to a whimper as the storm moved away. The recent rain made the air thick with moisture and brought up the heady mustiness of wet dirt mixed with the sweet scent of saturated flowers. Standing there, Hentie paused to admire the view under the leaden skies. The sun winked out from behind the clouds, conjuring rainbows from puddles and a nearby pond until they gleamed. Then Hentie shook away her thoughts, reminding herself there was much to be done and the master was an impatient man.

Hentie reached for her worn white apron as she readied herself for another workday. There was a lot to do in the next two hours as she set about to prepare the morning meal. She laid out the flour, butter, milk, some mixing bowls, and a tin to bake muffins in. She felt her stiff muscles begin to loosen as she stretched to reach for various items.

As Hentie pulled together her baking needs and tossed them into a large mixing bowl, a lower overseer known for his incompetence and penchant for cruelty suddenly walked through the kitchen-house door to check on the work being done. Over the clunk of the cast iron pots, she heard his boots clunk across the kitchen floor.

The overseer seemed to ignore Hentie, but his indifference was a sign that he trusted her and approved of what she had done thus far. Sometimes the missus would pass through too, but not today. Hentie breathed a sigh of relief as the overseer breezed back by her and out the door. He went on about his morning trek, inspecting work going on throughout the grounds. The terror Hentie held following her capture and enslavement had begun to diminish. She used to freeze in fear when a white man approached her. She was fortunate to be working near the main house. Being a bit more mature, with comely features, a quick mind, and a pleasant disposition, Hentie was chosen to work in the kitchen house to prepare the family's food and execute general household duties.

Hentie quickly learned commands spoken in English and other essential household terms. She acquired the new words from another kitchen-house worker, a middle-aged woman named Nellie who was plump and nearly toothless. In addition to English, Nellie was patiently teaching Hentie a second language called Gullah. This creole language was spoken by all the enslaved workers. Nellie would smile and nod when Hentie pronounced a new word correctly and would sigh and cluck her tongue against the roof of her mouth whenever she misspoke. The gentle shaping of her new language skills proved effective. Hentie, being totally immersed in the language by all those around her, was able to catch on rapidly. Being such a quick study proved helpful to her as the master and his wife had little patience for dawdling enslaved houseworkers.

Later that same morning, the two women served the morning meal to the master and the missus in the dining room. Hentie waited at attention for the two to take their seats at the long, impressive, polished wood table. She tried to make herself invisible and listen to all that went on around her. The missus came in first, looking lovely in a rose-colored dress and recently coiffed hair. Her petticoats rustled as she crossed the rug to take her chair at the table. She stopped briefly at the Hepplewhite sideboard set under a large window where she selected a boiled egg and some cold, smoked fish, setting the items on a blue china plate. Then the master strode into the dining room and, without greeting his wife, took his seat at the head of the table. His black boots, polished to a high sheen, thudded across the room. He was dressed in a simple but well-tailored suit with a crisp white linen shirt. He pulled a gold watch out of his watered-silk waistcoat and looked at it a moment before replacing it, then glanced up.

The missus's face grew pinched at being ignored by her husband without so much as a nod. She looked down at her pale, thin fingers as she plucked at the sturdy fabric of her dress, contemplating whether she should speak.

First Hentie poured tea for the missus and said, "Mornin', ma'am," and gave a hasty curtsy. Mrs. Langdon murmured, but never looked up. Hentie then stepped over to the master. As Hentie poured the master his tea, she noted the delicate bone china cup in his large, long fingers. They seemed incongruent with such a small, fragile cup. Hentie observed the power in the muscles and bones in the back of his hand and wondered if that was what he used to strike disobedient house slaves. Suddenly, Hentie heard a rapid rattling of china and looked down to see the missus's hands shaking badly. Hentie feared that she might drop it and antagonize the master, so she moved quickly to extract the Wedgwood cup and saucer with a calm and steady hand. The missus responded with a jerk of her head and briefly upturned lip.

A few moments later, Nellie entered the room with a platter of grillades and a bowl of steaming hominy grits. She laid them both down on the server and then took the platter to the missus's side and began to serve her. Nellie then stepped over to the master, but he held up a hand to halt her and firmly said, "No, just grits for me and a small bowl of fruit." Nellie quickly laid down the platter. Her skirts swished about her as she scurried to the adjacent room to fetch the fruit.

The master suddenly grabbed Hentie's arm, shaking her from her momentary trance. "More tea, you twit!" Hentie's heart thudded in her ears. The master glared at her with taut, blistering eyes. Something about this man pushed at her blood, making it rush through her veins in a hurried torrent. She quickly poured the tea as he demanded, nodded with respect, curtsied, and took a step back toward the sideboard. She remained motionless so as not to disturb him; her chocolate-colored eyes flickered up to the master, then back down. She studied the floor while the utensils tinkled against the fine china plates. Nellie returned with the fruit requested by the master and nimbly served him. In a matter of minutes, the master and missus quickly and quietly consumed their meal, laid down their cloth napkins and exited the room. Barely a word had been shared between the two, striking Hentie as odd. Nevertheless, she went about her business of clearing the dishes and returning to the kitchen house to start preparations for the midday meal and supper.

Upon exiting the room, the master had announced that he was going into his study to review his ledgers. He spent a good deal of time in there each day. He transacted business affairs of the plantation and recorded everything in his detailed account books. This took a fair amount of time each day, but his records were said to be meticulous. Sometimes he would review them with the overseer, Simon McBride, and other times with his brother. The missus said she didn't have a head for such matters. Hentie was sometimes called into the study and overheard bits of conversations. She inconspicuously took in as much as she could so that she could better understand what made the master tick and the inner workings of the large plantation. She hoped to one day understand what all the writing meant in the ledgers and correspondence that lay on his desk. If she could understand how to read, maybe one day it would help her to become free. She tried to follow bits of conversation, and through that she learned of business and politics. She even heard the master's concerns about secession and the coming war with the Federals.

The kitchen house was a smaller building located behind the main house. It was constructed with bricks that had been formed and fired on the grounds of the plantation. If one looked carefully, one could see the fingerprints of the enslaved laborers who formed those bricks; some were men and others were children. Maintaining the kitchen house as a separate building was necessary to prevent kitchen fires from spreading to the main house. Since an open hearth was used to prepare meals, it was a constant risk.

The interior of the kitchen house was modest but functional, with two rectangular tables made of wood, one larger than the other. There was an open hearth on the wall opposite the door, with an oven recessed into the brick adjacent to the fireplace. Nellie made her famous corn bread muffins that the master loved so much in that oven. She also made some wonderful grain breads in there—their delicious aroma wafted all over the plantation grounds. Hung beside the hearth were all of Nellie's fireplace and cooking utensils. Nellie had a place for everything and believed in keeping things well organized. This high level of efficiency kept the kitchen house running in good order with food production humming along.

Over the kitchen house was a large dormitory area where Nellie slept. She shared this large room with several other enslaved workers. They were all crammed into the space, which offered no privacy or relief from plantation life.

Not far from the kitchen house was the outbuilding for the blacksmith and his open fire. He used it to forge a variety of items, but particularly all the horseshoes. He also made some lovely ornamental items, like gates, lamp posts, and boot scrapers for the men to remove the mud and dirt from their shoes. Behind the blacksmith were the stables. It was used for the horses, the tack, and the different buggies and wagons. The master had three men to keep up with running a smooth operation in the stables and maintaining the animals.

There was also a laundry house behind the main house. There wasn't much to it, mainly a fireplace with a caldron for boiling the white sheets, nightclothes, and undergarments with lye soap. On an adjacent wall stood a folding table on which clean items were folded and neatly stacked. Outside was a second caldron and a bar to hang the wet items on to dry. As simple as the operation looked, it was hard, backbreaking work lifting the hot, heavy bedclothes. There were two women devoted to keeping this work going, along with the starching and ironing. A rotation of children helped them out as well.

The master's clothes and those of his family of course came first for the laundresses. But following this, they sometimes helped with washing clothes of some of the skilled laborers. Their garments were made of a different type of fabric from those of the white slave owners. Most shirts were made of natural color or white Negro cloth or osnaburg cotton, and the trousers were crafted out of linsey-woolsey or kersey twill. They were typically darker, solid colors.

To the rear of the laundry house was the infirmary, a kind of a small hospital or medical clinic for the plantation's sick and injured workers. There were a handful of beds neatly lined up to take on patients who sustained significant injuries or illnesses. There were two skilled women, herbal doctors, assigned to this building. They provided medical care and comfort to all the enslaved Negro workers and, on occasion, to white Langdon family members.

Rosa, the older of the two enslaved women who worked in the infirmary, saw Hentie approaching and yelled out to her, "Hentie, how's your hand doing? That was such a nasty burn you got the other day. Let me take a look." She reached out and grabbed Hentie's hand and turned it over as she carefully examined it. "You gots to be careful hoisting those big pots over the fire. A bad burn can be hard to heal. I'll give you some good oils for it; just follow me."

"Thank you, I appreciate it," uttered Hentie as she dutifully followed Rosa.

Once inside, Rosa reached up on her shelf of various oils, balms, and salves. "Here, show me your hand, Hentie." The skilled healer put liniment oil on her. "There you go. That should help it heal up just fine." Rosa nodded and gently squeezed Hentie's hand.

"Thank you again, Rosa. You're very kind. My hand was bothering me something terrible for a while." Hentie squinted as she remembered the initial pain from the burn. "I best get on with my business now."

Hentie came into contact with all of the family members and many of the enslaved Negroes who worked in the main house or the grounds immediately around it. She had to carry food prepared for the family from the kitchen house to the warming kitchen located on the first floor of the main house. Hentie had a sweet demeanor, and most of her fellow workers adored her. She was kind and always considerate of others. Over time, she developed a network of friends among the other enslaved workers.

One woman, a lady's maid, became a close comrade; her name was Octavia. She was of medium height, had large, expressive brown eyes, and was a bit younger than Hentie. They often had contact on the first floor of the big house. Octavia tended to Mrs. Emily Trenholm Langdon, the master's wife, and did her bidding. Mrs. Langdon was a very flighty, temperamental woman, so Octavia had learned to do whatever she asked and to do so quickly without question. Octavia was a good soul who took the brunt of Mrs. Langdon's nastiness. Poor Octavia was often seen flying around the house, sprinting up and down the steps, scrambling for the missus's latest request. She would bolt up the steps, sometimes briefly leaning on the banister to catch her breath, her heart hammering in her chest from the exertion and anxiety over the missus's ill-tempered behavior.

Mimba was one of the older enslaved servants, a small-framed feeble old woman who worked as a seamstress in the house. She sometimes watched the children or did other household tasks. Mimba was also an old herbal doctor and sometimes practiced hoodoo. Hentie learned that hoodoo was a kind of black magic.

Mimba could be a sly one. She was so light and diminutive she could slip around the big house without the master or mistress noticing her. Since she had such a variety of duties, she could legitimately be anywhere in the house. She loved to take little token items from the missus, like a button or thimble. It was her way of playing a prank on her. She also used to snatch sweets from the missus, too, especially her shortbread cookies. She would just slip one off her plate and quickly stick it in her pocket. She didn't keep them for herself but would pass them along to Octavia, since the younger woman had such a sweet tooth and loved them.

One time, Mimba put a hex on Mrs. Langdon for her mean disposition and ill treatment of the house staff. The missus would have enslaved workers whipped for small infractions like accidently dropping food or a dish when clearing the table. Once, the master asked a house girl to wake up Mrs. Langdon and bring her to him. The enslaved worker did as she was ordered. Nonetheless, Mrs. Langdon had the servant beaten for awakening her. Mimba took personal items from Mrs. Langdon's bedroom, things like special hankies, hat pins and hair from a brush. She used these personal items to cast her spell. The hex Mimba had put on the master's wife caused her to have fits. She would crawl around the floor, barking and howling like a dog.

Mr. Langdon called the local white physician, Charles Hayes, to examine his wife and determine what was wrong with her. He entered her room and surveyed her, then removed his black frock coat and placed it over the back of a wooden chair. He examined her carefully and spoke with her briefly. Following this, he asked more penetrating questions of her husband. After pacing a bit, he stopped and turned to Mr. Langdon. Dr. Hayes said she was suffering from the blues and some form of anxiety. He gave the master a small bottle of opium to treat his wife's condition. The master passed along the bottle to Octavia, to give her a few drops when the missus seemed most anxious, but her fitful behavior continued.

After about a month, Mr. Langdon asked for an outside root doctor who practiced hoodoo, Dr. Tiger Lowe. The root doctor made the missus two conjure bags of ground rattlesnake rattles and directed her to wear them under her armpits. Within a week the fits stopped. Mimba would laugh behind Mrs. Langdon's back, amused at the frustration she had caused the missus.

The missus seemed to recover after a time, but she still was temperamental. Octavia came to Hentie when she couldn't take another moment of the missus's hysterics. When Octavia and Hentie were alone in the kitchen house, Octavia would vent her frustrations and pray to God for the wherewithal to persevere. Octavia's full figure would quake as she gyrated with emotion and attempted to shake off the frustration. Mrs. Langdon's craziness was sometimes just too much for her. When Octavia came to the kitchen house to unload her irritation, Hentie got so tickled at her antics that she would cover her mouth and giggle as the two shared a moment of mutual understanding and compassion.

"These damn crazy white folks! How can they talk about *our* needing their guidance and correction? That missus can't guide me or give me no direction. She is as crazy as a bedbug!"

For years, Octavia was made to sleep on a pallet outside the missus's bedroom. The missus had insisted that Octavia be available to her twenty-four hours a day, seven days a week, since she had a multitude of needs. On a whim, Mrs. Langdon often had Octavia run frivolous errands late into the evening. Some of the requests were nonsensical, like fetching a feather she had found earlier in the day. Other times she would send the staff searching for a doll she carried as a child or a cameo brooch her mother had worn shortly before her death. She would just want to hold it. Once clasped in her hand, her body would relax and she would snuggle down into her bedsheets, drifting off to sleep. She seemed to need those tangible things to confirm or soothe memories from earlier in her life. Once validated, she was calm and peaceful. While such antics seemed to calm the missus's anxieties, it drove Octavia and the other house servants crazy.

One time, Hentie accompanied Octavia when she went to the missus's bedside. Octavia preceded her through the doorway while Hentie stood paralyzed in the threshold. Octavia cleared her throat in an attempt to prod Hentie. In response, Hentie shook loose her fear and attempted to compose herself.

The missus seemed half crazy; in her delirium she was moaning and thrashing about on her mattress. While she had periods of lucidity, most of her words were garbled. She lay pale and fragile as a porcelain doll. Although the woman had been a great beauty in her day, her allure had dimmed. Her ennui and dark mood had seized hold of her. The small woman looked diminutive on her expansive bed, a magnificent mahogany frame with an elaborately carved pediment hung with heavy draperies. It seemed to dominate one entire side of the room. Bed steps led to the immense, soft mattress made of goose feathers. Above her head was an intricate ceiling medallion surrounding the crystal chandelier. The mosquito net that was sometimes drawn over the bed was tucked behind a dresser. On an opposing wall stood a marble-topped dressing table with graceful cabriole legs situated between the two floor-to-ceiling windows. Fancy fretwork topped a large mirror above the dressing table. A striking armoire towered toward the ceiling at one end of the room. It held many of the missus's accoutrements, such as dressing gowns, corsets, and petticoats.

There was a faint aroma in the room, a trailing scent of tea rose perfume that seemed to waft up as the missus thrashed in her bed. Hentie felt nervous seeing the missus in such a state; fidgety thoughts darted through her mind, much like a squirrel running on the branches of a tree. What could make her act this way? Once she and Octavia stepped out of her bedchamber and into the hallway, Hentie's agitation faded away.

It seemed as though the missus was haunted by the master's first wife, a strong-willed woman named Virginia. One time, Octavia had run across Virginia's daguerreotype kept in a demure silk-covered case and had shown it to Hentie. It had been tucked away in a small drawer in a dropleaf table in the main sitting room. Virginia had been a beautiful woman with dark hair and large eyes. Apparently, the photo was taken shortly before her marriage to the master. Lying nearby it was a small wooden music box; if you opened the lid you could see the working mechanisms inside underneath a clear glass cover. The lid was slightly dented with a mild watermark, but it still worked. When Hentie opened the lid, she smelled the strong scent of roses, just like she had smelled in the missus's bedroom. Perhaps it was the essence of her spirit? When the music box lid was open, a familiar song began to play, its tinkling noise soothing to the ear.

Octavia had heard that Virginia, although a robust woman, died during the summer fevers a few years after their marriage. She had been pregnant with their first child at the time. Reportedly, it was yellow fever that got her. So many had been lost that year to the dreaded scourge. Virginia had loved the outdoors and tended to her flower garden on a near-daily basis. She particularly loved her rose bushes and the exquisite colorful varieties she was able to cultivate. It was her constant exposure to the out-of-doors and the waters which nourished her beloved flowers that led to her demise.

The missus believed that Virginia's spirit lingered in the house and was somehow watching her. It disturbed her dreams when she slept, and it led to her frequent sleep-deprivation. Her melancholy produced mood swings and tantrums. Consequently, the missus took this out on the person most accessible to her, Octavia.

Octavia grew exhausted from the ongoing need to be persistently wakeful. While Mrs. Langdon was occasionally able to enjoy tranquil, serene sleep on her mattress made of goose feathers, Octavia became hypervigilant, tense and ready to jump in response to her owner's constant demands. Over time, this took a toll on Octavia. She grew so pale and weak that one day she fainted as she descended the steps, rolling down the stairwell and landing in a heap at the bottom. Fortunately, the reverend was present at the house for a luncheon engagement with the master when it happened. The reverend was able to assist her up, but she became unsteady on her feet and appeared ready to swoon once again. Worried for her, he called for a damp cloth and someone to assist him. Octavia was taken to the plantation's infirmary and was tended to there. The reverend intervened on Octavia's behalf, although whether it was because he was concerned for her as a human being or a plantation commodity wasn't clear. Nonetheless, he insisted on Octavia gaining some real rest. After that she was given a bed in a cabin, which she shared with a handful of other enslaved house servants.

Octavia was also periodically permitted to travel to the nearby city of Charleston to visit with her only local family member, a sister, Lydia. At one time Lydia had been owned by the Langdons and lived at Twin Oaks, but was abruptly sold to the Simmons family. Lydia had committed some misdeed and was removed from the plantation without warning. The two sisters being torn apart so unexpectedly nearly broke both of their hearts. In the past year, they had grown to accept the change. Lydia was actually in a much better situation with a more benevolent mistress who lived in large mansion house near the harbor. Her mistress's stability and more tranquil demeanor helped ease Lydia's adjustment and afforded her a better life.

There were other house servants, one of whom was Mattie. She was nursemaid to the young master, the Langdons' son, Fitzwilliam. He looked much like his father, with golden-blond hair and sparkling blue eyes that showed a bit of the devil in him. He was full of energy and often seen running through the house on his way out-of-doors, making sport out of all kinds of odd things. Fortunately, Mattie was a young woman with the energy to keep up with him. She was a white indentured servant, and somehow her enslavement worked differently than Hentie's. Mattie would be released after a period of years. She had been with Fitzwilliam since his birth and had forged a strong bond with the boy. While Hentie had contact with Mattie, it was very limited due to Mattie's commitments with her charge. Mattie said she was Irish. She had bright-red hair with an abundance of curls. Mattie tried to keep it tucked up tightly with hairpins, but inevitably little wisps of curls fell out as the day went on. Hentie had never seen anything like it before. Mattie also had very fair skin and freckles. It all seemed quite odd to Hentie.

Hentie sometimes stood near Fitzwilliam and Mattie when he practiced his letters and started to read certain words by sight. Hentie took in all that she overheard to make sense of it in her head later on. Sometimes Fitzwilliam would read the cans and crates of foods in the warming kitchen and say words like flour, salt, sugar and such. Hentie tried hard to remember what he said.

Another key figure in Hentie's life was Big John. Although he was a strong, hulking man, he possessed a kind soul and was endearing. Big John had dark skin and kind eyes that soothed all those around him. He seemed to be trusted not only by the master, but by all the enslaved workers as well. Big John was brought to Charleston from the West Indies rather than Africa like most of the other enslaved workers. Big John was a good man, and Hentie found she could rely on him. He was becoming a good friend.

Chapter 3
Gullah Religion

Hentie woke up in a terrified state from her usually sound slumber. She was sleeping in the main house. Someone, a man, pressed down on her, leaving her unable to move. His hand was cupped over her mouth. "Don't make a sound," he said calmly. "Do not move until I tell you to."

Dread skittered down her spine and pushed away the last tendrils of sleep. *Please no! Not me,* Hentie thought as a knot tightened in her belly. *Please no. Stop. Leave me! Make this an ugly dream and go away. Protect me from this man. I can't take any more pain.*

Hentie had heard many stories about late-night visits from white men who brutalized helpless enslaved women. She couldn't stop it; the moment was here. Hentie shut her eyes tight and in her mind called out to the protective spirits of Africa. She shook with fear, and her fingers clutched the worn, thin blanket draped over her. Her breathing hitched in starts and stops as she prepared herself for the heinous act about to befall her. She bit the inside of her cheek until the tang of iron spilled onto her tongue. She knew it was just the first of the blood to be spilled that night.

But when the man spoke, he said, "My name is Christmas Luke. I mean you no harm. I want you to come with me. It is time you learned about our faith here. You need to see the praise house. But don't you make a sound. The master mustn't hear a footfall. Don't let a floorboard creak. Glide your feet careful-like along the floor. The master don't like us going out in no woods at night."

Pushing back the thin covering, Hentie disentangled herself from her pallet. She put her bare feet onto the wooden floorboards and felt the early autumn chill on her legs. Pushing her feet into worn, simple shoes she acquired from the missus when she was about to discard them, she and the man glided soundlessly down the hallway.

As her eyes adjusted to the dim light coming through window, she could make out the outline of his face. Hentie watched him for a few heartbeats. He was an enslaved worker, a field hand perhaps. He looked older and worn. In profile, she saw a strongly curved jaw and large eyes. It appeared as though a portion of his right ear was gone, perhaps as punishment for some misdeed. His eyes were focused ahead, and he listened carefully to see if anyone was about.

The two quietly made their way out of the house, sneaking down the back stairs and into the darkened space by the butler's pantry. Then they glided across the floorboards and out the rear door without detection. They hastened toward a wooded area between the fields. Christmas Luke held her hand and pulled her across the field, with which he was clearly familiar. Gusts of air tore across the brow of the woods, shaking branches and whipping Hentie's worn shift. An owl hooted in a tree above Hentie's head, and she jerked her gaze up at the sound, looking up to a nearby tree to spot the stoic bird observing them. Hentie's shift caught on brambles and dead twigs, so she eventually hoisted her garment up toward her thighs, exposing her bare legs. She willed her heart to slow down as she gulped down air. Moonlight softly illuminated the way and guided them toward their meeting place. They remained in the shadows, which concealed their crouched bodies and provided protection.

When they reached a very small, dimly lit building situated in a clearing encircled by thick woods, Hentie heard chanting from inside. "What they doing?" Hentie asked softly. She couldn't make sense of the sounds. She could tell that the small amount of light escaping through the single window was from candles that flickered from movement inside. The ghostly light slashed through the mists surrounding them, giving an ethereal feel to the setting.

As they entered the small wood-framed building, Christmas Luke told her they were in a praise house. A group of people in the center of the large room stood in a circle swaying rhythmically. Hentie scanned the room and saw that the plain, backless benches had been pushed back against the walls, as had a makeshift altar. The walls and the furniture looked as though they had once been whitewashed. Most of the other colors were neutral as they were items taken from the land or the seashore, but there were bits of color, such as turquoise blue or a deep red. Some of the items were handmade Christian artifacts, like crosses, while others were mementos of their African homeland.

The encircled group slowly moved in a counterclockwise direction. An older woman seemed to be charged with keeping the rhythm of the group going. She would call out shouts, to which everyone replied. Big John led the replies. His deep, booming voice helped to garner a strong response from the others. At first the group gently flowed around and around, shuffling their feet and clapping their hands. The woman calling out spoke of the hardships the others had faced and their hopes that God would lead them to the Promised Land. She also thanked the Lord for his good grace. Although the road was rough and they were weary, they realized that God was with them. Despite their present troubles, they would one day pass on and enjoy his glory in heaven. And God will wipe away every tear from their eyes. No more pain, no more hurt." One man, separate from the group, was down on his knees. He prayed with his whole body, his hands raised over his head, fingers extended, head thrown back, and eyes closed.

The man shouted, "Praise Jesus! Show us the way, Lord!"

As time went on, the sounds grew louder, sending reverberations throughout the room. The foot pounding became stomping, and the clapping grew into something almost feverish. The stomping seemed to replace the drums that were so familiar in Africa. Hentie was both excited and frightened by the intensity of it and the energy in the room. For just a moment, she got confused about where she was, losing herself in thoughts of home. As the rhythm ended, Hentie was jolted back to reality. She wasn't in her homeland but back in Charleston. The people around her had stopped clapping. They were talking with one another, smiling and happy. She shook herself from the trance.

One of the members, a woman with kind brown eyes and a smiling face, said, "This is our ring shout, our holy dance that keeps us Gullah connected to our home back in Africa. You just follow what the others are doing. You will feel the spirit move you. Here the material world and the spirit world blend. It is the Holy Spirit that moves us." Hentie smiled back at the gentle woman as she glanced down at her pale ivory muslin dress and the cross necklace around her neck.

Big John approached Hentie and looked affirmingly at her. He was dressed in a loose, oatmeal-colored shirt and worn trousers. Big John's upbeat mood buoyed Hentie. "This is how we praise the Lord! With the white folks, their religion all in their head; with us, we feel it in our spirit."

Another woman Hentie recognized as one of the field hands said, "This is how we worship on plantations. We ain't got many things, but we got a lot we can't hold in our hands. We got a lot in our hearts. Jesus and our families hold us together. You sneak off here to the praise house so you can remember the promises of Jesus." Her faded and frayed beige dress hung from her; nonetheless she glowed with pride and hope.

While everyone's spirits were still high, they started to sing gospel songs like "Down by the River Side," "Swing Low Sweet Chariot," and "Every Time I Feel the Spirit." The words of the songs held special meaning, a meaning white folks didn't know or understand. Only the Gullah could appreciate it.

It was Hentie's first exposure to the faith. It seemed to be a blend of African customs and some of the white man's Christian religion. Hentie was somewhat acquainted with the Bible and the teachings of Christ. The other enslaved people helped her to understand that Christ was a man who was unfairly persecuted, just like she was. He was beaten and hung on a cross to die for acts he did not commit. Hentie also learned about the Egyptian people who were treated so unfairly. Moses and the children of Israel were forced to act as slaves. They later went searching for salvation. Hentie thought that it seemed similar to their own experience and the oppression they suffered.

After leaving the praise house, Hentie felt imbued with a spiritual feeling that was new to her. It filled her up with happiness and sheer exhilaration. Over time, the secret religious meetings fulfilled her need for fellowship. She enjoyed the warm feelings and the bond she felt with the people there. Octavia gave Hentie a small cross that she had made when she was a child. Octavia said it was a keepsake; it gave her warm feelings and comforted her. Octavia wanted Hentie to have it so she felt more at home at the praise house.

Hentie learned that part of becoming a Christian involved being baptized. It was best to use the salt water of the ocean rather than the fresh water found in streams and rivers. One's baptism needed to be timed so that your sins could be carried away with the outgoing tide. One seeking baptism wore a white gown and stood in the surf while they were submerged as a special blessing was said. Hentie submitted to the ceremony several months later.

Hentie later learned that the Gullah religion had evolved over time. Most slave owners did not allow formal religious practice. Slaves were not taught to read or allowed access to a Bible. In most circumstances, they were not permitted to attend church. She heard that occasionally kind slave owners taught Bible passages to those they enslaved, but the practice was rare. Most of the white people who let their slaves worship were either Baptists or Methodists. In towns south of Charleston, such as Beaufort and St. Helena Island, some of the churches had special services for enslaved black people. Over time, a similar practice was permitted in Charleston. The Anglicans, who became Episcopalians, did not recognize this practice.

Later Hentie discovered that the African Methodist Episcopal Church, originally established in Philadelphia, had formed a parish in downtown Charleston named Mother Emanuel a few decades earlier. A man from Philadelphia named Richard Allen, along with Rev. Morris Brown, had formed the local church. It was too far to travel to on a weekly basis. Some people got to go to their services at Easter or Christmas, but the master wouldn't let everyone leave at once.

Mr. Langdon claimed to be Christian and to pray to the same God. While he made gestures, he was violent to those around him, particularly the colored folks. Hentie didn't understand how he could talk about practicing charity with his neighbors and then brutally beat his enslaved workers, cut off fingers and hack their feet. Hentie had seen Mr. Langdon direct McBride, the overseer, to whip a disobedient slave held captive in a stockade for a few days. The victim's head and arms were locked down so that the subject of the master's violence could only move his lower body. How could he consider himself a man of God? Hentie could not make sense of this disparity.

In the days following, Hentie learned that there was more to Gullah spirituality than was expressed at the praise house—that there were loathsome spirits that many people feared called boo hags or haints. Some of these notions were taken from African tribal customs and beliefs. They were thought to be female spirits. During the day, they might seem to live normal lives and go about their regular household chores. But an evil streak lurked within them.

It was said that hags would come into homes at night, perch on a bedpost, and pounce on the chests of their sleeping victims. Entry was gained by way of keyhole, chimney, or door. There was no chance of keeping hags out. Once inside, hags would ride the people to utter exhaustion. While victims thought they were screaming, they remained frozen and mute. This might persist for several nights, leaving victims sleep-deprived and horror-struck. Some became frantic and hysterical.

Some sufferers would cut off bedposts to keep the hags from roosting, to no avail. Others thought to distract hags by placing numerous items by their bedsides to keep the hag occupied until the light of day. Hentie took note of these beliefs. She wondered if some type of evil spirit had seized her and that was what led to the death of her family. Just to be safe, she placed an open jar of salt and one of sand on the floor by her pallet. She changed the jars frequently. Hentie's hope was that the hag would stay busy counting the granules all night long. As the sun started to rise, Hentie would quickly pop on a lid, capturing the haint so it couldn't harm her or those around her. Hentie was told that the hags would be trapped in the jars this way. To ensure that they could not harm her, she quickly buried the jars outside. She did this repeatedly for several months, then started to feel safer, as if she and the spirits around her were at rest.

Some folks tried to protect their homes by hanging an inverted horseshoe over their doors. Hentie learned that roaming spirits were afraid of the color blue because it reminded them of heaven. To ward off the spirits, enslaved Negroes used leftover indigo from the boiling pots to make blue dye to color their doors and windows. However, by the 1800s, when the indigo cultivation started to wane, the slaves began to use a light turquoise paint as it was most like heaven.

⌒

Hentie learned that many things were taught to young children through the use of old Gullah customs and folktales. The Gullah community had brought very little with them when they were captured in Africa, but they brought their memories of these folktales and continued to tell them to their children. Many African stories had a clever animal able to outwit bigger and stronger opponents. Tales of the "trickster" tactics sometimes took the lead character into perilous situations in which he ultimately prevailed. Writer Joel Chandler would later popularize these Gullah stories in his tales of Uncle Remus.

⌒

From the enslaved Gullah servants, Hentie learned that many herbal medicines that had been used in her homeland had been adapted for use in America. The Deep South had some similarities to Africa in terms of access to salt water, climate and certain vegetation. The land was moist and verdant. Some, but not all, of the plants, trees, and roots that were plentiful in Africa could be found here as well. For other remedies, they just had to watch and follow what others did locally. Sometimes it meant watching Native American customs. Males who had been medicine men in Africa became root doctors in America. Since enslaved Negroes usually had no access to medical care, they came to rely on this type of medicine. It was through women in the infirmary that Hentie began to understand some of the remedies available.

Often the enslaved would hide their symptoms from their masters and overseers as they feared white-man medicine. It was unreliable and often deadly. Black workers avoided their masters' practices of bloodletting, purging, plastering, and blistering, and instead sought the help of trusted herbalists. The Gullah root doctor was an herbalist with special skills who not only understood the healing powers of the herbs, but also the spiritual implications. Even white folks understood the great success of herbal remedies and published books about their healing properties. Rosa, the plantation herbal doctor, provided comfort and care to the enslaved at Twin Oaks, including Hentie as she continued her life there.

Chapter 4
Learning About the Lowcountry

As Hentie became integrated into life on the plantation, she began to develop a bond with the other enslaved workers, particularly Octavia. Hentie felt like she could trust Octavia and rely on her when she needed to do so. She could ask Octavia questions about the plantation and surrounding area. Hentie also learned about the regional trees and vegetation, often from Nellie. Much of it looked so different from her homeland. She had been impressed by the avenue of oak trees, draped with their strange hairs, that lined the road up to the house.

One Sunday afternoon when the enslaved were allowed to take some time away from their duties, Hentie and Nellie sat under an old oak tree. It was a massive tree with gnarled roots extending out. Hentie asked Nellie about it; she had not seen such a tree in her native Africa.

"This old tree has been here for ages. Folks say it's hundreds of years old. I bet it would have a lot to say if it could talk. You see that tree hair hanging from it? That's called Spanish moss. I don't know why they named it that. It's not Spanish. Big John say it's not a moss either."

"Then what is it?" asked Hentie.

"It's a special plant that can live on just air; it wraps itself around tree branches and sucks the water right out the air," Nellie explained. "The Indians, they use it in all kinds of ways. They made clothes out of it and used it with their babies. They put it under the baby's bottom in the papoose, then threw it away when the baby dirtied it. They a wise people, sure enough."

Nellie nodded as she spoke.

"They also made horse blankets out of Spanish moss. They were careful when they handled it, so it didn't pick up chiggers off the ground, because they make you itch real bad."

The two continued to sit under the tree and breathe in the fragrant air and enjoy the shade. It sure was nice that day.

Hentie continued to learn more about life on the plantation and how to cook food the master liked. Under Nellie's guidance, Hentie emerged as a thrifty and efficient cook, making good use of fruits and vegetables grown on the plantation, most not far from the kitchen house in their little garden. Some of the things she prepared were foods brought to America from Africa, such as yams, okra, and field peas. Hentie learned special Gullah recipes. Okra was a vegetable that could be prepared a variety of ways with special seasonings. Everyone seemed to love it. Stewed okra and tomatoes were a staple served with numerous meals.

Hentie learned through Big John and others that rice had been the principal crop in the region and very important to South Carolina. It came to America in the 1600s and served as a cash crop from the 1680s through the 1800s. It proved to be a key element in the development and prosperity of coastal South Carolina. Red rice, a dish made with tomatoes, onions, spices, and local rice, was often served with supper. Ham and greens was another favorite. The master's family loved it. At her cabin, Hentie and the other enslaved servants would eat lesser foods. They received limited rations on a weekly basis, typically on Saturdays. The enslaved were given such foods as corn meal, lard, peas, and flour. They also got about one to two pounds of meat a week, which they supplemented as best they could. The workers made a boiled corn paste served in leaves, similar to the *adidi* they ate back in Africa. They also made a thick porridge of wheat flour called *fufu*. Sometimes an old enslaved woman would make up a large batch of stew with peas, beans, turnips, and potatoes seasoned with a ham bone and whatever they could pull from their own small gardens. It was cooked up in a big iron kettle and shared among all of them.

In the kitchen house and the big house, Hentie saw and heard a lot of things about the family, the master, and all the things he owned. Over time, she learned how the plantation worked and how the master made his money. Sometimes she got to go out to the fields with food or water for the enslaved farmworkers and observe what was happening in other parts of the plantation. Hentie learned about all the different things the plantation grew. The big crops were rice and indigo, but there were other things, like vegetables, peaches, strawberries, and pecans. Indigo had started to wane when Hentie arrived at the plantation, but rice was still vital. Nellie and Octavia helped explain to Hentie the significance of what she overheard. Hearing different terms and seeing what they were helped her to integrate the information. As her fluency in English grew, so did her understanding of how the world around her worked.

Rice was very complicated to grow and extremely labor intensive. Sometimes Hentie got to see the whole process in action when she and Big John drove a wagon out to the fields. It was during such a ride that Hentie learned that Big John could read. He once mentioned what was written on the side of a few crates.

Hentie, surprised by the revelation, asked, "How you know so much?"

Big John spoke in hushed tones when he said, "Don't tell nobody, but I learned my letters and how to read a bit when I was with my first owner, down on the island of Jamaica. Down there, some black folks learned to read. I also learned a bit from my first master's wife, who gave me Bible passages. I still try to read things. I always look over the boss's shoulder to see what he is reading. It makes me feel good when what I read is the same as what they say. But I don't let on that I can read; law don't allow it." Big John's big eyes and cautious demeanor urged Hentie to keep the confidence.

"Don't worry, Big John; your secret is safe with me. I won't tell," Hentie said.

"That's good. I thank you for that. Maybe someday I'll teach you your letters and how to write your name. But you can't let on to the white folks; you'd get the lash for sure," Big John warned.

In some dust on the wagon, Big John drew the letters *A*, *B*, and *C*. "See this? This is the first three letters, *A*, *B*, *C*. The letters make up the alphabet, and from them you make words."

"Oh, looks hard. I don't think I could ever get all that. I try to pick up things, particularly when Mattie's schooling little Fitzwilliam, but it's more than I can understand."

"Sure you can. You a smart woman; you know lots of stuff." Big John pointed his large finger at her to emphasize his point. His finger was so full and plump it looked like a small sausage.

Hentie just shook her head. "I'd never understand all that. It's too much for me!" Hentie sighed, and then the two both turned and went back to work. But first Big John rubbed out the letters he had formed.

Hentie learned a lot through Big John; he understood so much about the plantation. The master let him go everywhere and be involved in so much.

"Hentie, you will understand how everything works here at Twin Oaks and in Charleston too. It's important you understand it all and the place colored folks have here. We're important in running it all, but we gots to remember our place. The master and missus, they both very moody people. What they want can change with the wind." Big John looked carefully at her to make sure she understood.

Hentie shook her head. "I always try my best, Big John. I know that the missus can be a crazy woman. I watch myself real careful," Hentie confided.

"We used to grow rice as our principal crop here. But that's changing now. Cotton is the big crop now. Rice was hard to grow, lots of steps to it. We had to flood the fields with the fresh water we got from the rivers. Couldn't use the salt water from the Atlantic Ocean. We had to be careful. The tides influenced how the river water flowed, but the salt water tapered off. Years ago, they converted the swampy lowlands into fields that they planted, and they built dikes, canals, and trunks. The trunks were small floodgates."

Big John looked down and shook his head. "It was hard work. Hard work on everyone. Some of the field workers got sick and died. We had two plantings every year. Once in late March or early April, and then a second time in early June. By September, we had to harvest right quick. Not just 'cause of the crops, but 'cause the hurricane season. Field hands had to work real fast cutting the rice stalks before they lay them back into the mucky waters."

"Oh my, it must have been hard work. Them poor folks must have hurt bad," Hentie murmured.

Big John went on to say, "It's a long process with the rice. It first went to the threshing yard, where the rice was separated from the stalk. Hands had to work right quick and send the rice on to others, so they could do their part. Next, they use a large standing mortar and pestle and pound it to remove the hulls. The pestle is real big, about four feet tall. It almost looks like a big butter churner with a big pole that go right down the middle into a deep, hulled-out wooden bowl. That mortar is real heavy and hard to use for all the hours it took to pound. It be hard work, real hard.

"From there, the rice gets passed along to another worker for the winnowing. They mostly women folk who do that work. They use big round sweetgrass baskets. Those baskets were specially made by their hands. They use different special grasses like bulrush, palmetto fronds, and sweetgrass that they collect down by the water. It makes them real strong." Big John looked down at Hentie to make sure she understood his words.

"Big John, it all sounds so hard. So much to it all. How you get to know so much?"

"I got to watch myself real careful around the master, but I ask lots of questions. I do my best to keep him happy. I never say nothing he'd get mad at. But I think he trusts me. He lets me see a lot. He let me hear a lot too. The master, his brother Charles, and the overseer, McBride, let me come with them when they have their meetings. They talk about how they can increase productivity. How they can make the slaves work as hard as they can but not die on them. They have two plantations. One here, one up north."

Hentie, mesmerized by all Big John knew, nodded to show her understanding.

Big John went on. "They've done different things to control the size of the group of workers. Mr. Langdon and McBride found that they couldn't really manage a group of slaves any larger than about one hundred. So once the gang got so big, the master split the group into two and put the smaller group on the other plantation up north."

Big John held out one hand, then the other to model the two different estates owned by the Langdons. "We're on Twin Oaks. The other plantation, Pleasant Prospect, is run by the master's younger brother. They got about fifty of the slaves. It's up in the village of McClellanville, up the road quite a ways. I think it has two hundred acres. They don't do as much farming up there as they do here. That area known more for fishing, shrimping, and oystering, but there still lots of farming.

"Us black folks, we work from 'day clean' to 'first dark.' Some of us slaves have chores before we get to the fields. Master, he works us all real hard. Even the prime hands, the young men, just can't keep up."

"I know, I see workers come in from the fields. They dead tired. Even young men, they just fall into bed in the slave quarters. Too tired to eat." Hentie shook her head as she thought about it.

Big John explained how the labor was divided. "The master, he schemes with McBride and the black driver, Duke, to work us all as hard as they can. They tried different things to get as much labor as they can. First, they tried using the 'gang' method. An entire group or gang of slaves perform the same task at the same time, such as picking cotton. But then they were thinking that certain men might be setting the pace of the work and forcing the others to slow down. With such a big group of slaves, the driver might start on horseback at one end of the line, then by the time he reached the other end, the first end started to slack off."

Big John shook his head as he spoke. "Some men hate the master bad. They real angry about being a slave, and they do other things to resist the master, things in their own way. They pretend they are sick, maybe break some tools or somehow foul up things. I just try to look the other way when I see them doing things like that. I don't want to take part, but I don't let on I see it. I gots to work hard for the master, but the slaves, those folks are my family."

"That's wise of you, Big John. I don't like being a slave either, but I try to do my best. I hope I have freedom someday, but for now, I just do what the master say," Hentie grumbled.

"So, since the gang method didn't work so good, they use another way, the task system. This way, they assign a special area to each field hand. He works a certain area, or he have to pick so much cotton or peaches to make quota. They use it with folks with special skills too, like a trade or something. Or sometimes they give a man a special chore, like chopping wood, splitting fence rail, or making barrels. Once their part of the work is done, they free to do other things. Most days still real long, but sometimes folks get time to work on they own garden or maybe work for hire on another plantation. McBride say it make the slaves work hard without so much supervision. You gots to keep working until it done."

"I didn't realize they do it that way. All I know is the field hands work real hard." Hentie flared as she spoke.

"Mr. Langdon said to McBride, work them hard, but don't work them to death. He thinks we just a number in his ledger, just like his horses and his tools. He don't really think we people, you know. I hear some of the other plantation owners even worse. They treat them bad and let them die. It just like getting a new cow, that's it." Big John's ire rose as he spoke.

He picked up a small branch and tossed it as he paced. "The master, he can be a cold man. I know lots of white folks like that. He keeps a ledger for each year. He writes things in it every day. All kinds of details, about all the things he owns. He keeps a list of the black workers just like the list of his cattle. I saw where he listed the name of every slave, the age and what he does. Then he put a figure of what that man is worth. Skilled slaves worth more. Both plantations have the same system for keeping their ledgers."

"That seem like an odd thing to do. Listing people like that and putting a dollar figure on them," said Hentie

Big John went on to explain the rating system. "Workers are rated by their age, skills, strength, and health. They note if you are lame, if a woman can still have babies, or she a wet nurse. He even rates the little youngins'. He calls children a quarter-hand or half-hand, depending on their age, how smart they are, and what they can do. When they are real young, just babies, they can't do all that much. They are not sent to the field until they are older, maybe ten or eleven. When a worker reach age seventeen or eighteen, he becomes a prime hand. He usually works in the field all day. Your dollar value changes from year to year, so master changes it in the book."

"How can they think of people like that?"

Big John hissed, "One time I saw my own name in the book.

When the master bought me, I was a big, tall boy, maybe thirteen. I knew a lot about ships, things about trade, and getting the crops out to other places. He paid five hundred dollars for me. I also saw the listing for Octavia, bought as a ten-year-old child along with her brother, Ezra; he a year younger. Both were listed as a half-hand—value two hundred dollar each. Over time that value changed."

"Big John, I had no idea that's how it all works. Sure don't seem right," Hentie moaned.

Big John and Hentie made their way back up toward the house, and Hentie continued to think about all that Big John had shared with her. Shortly thereafter, Hentie asked Octavia what happened to her brother, as Octavia had never mentioned him before.

Octavia said, "One day my brother Ezra went crazy when they sold the woman who raised us. She was a house girl and her name was Liza. She had been a good house slave that had borne the master lots of babies. Then one day the missus wanted her gone right away. I didn't understand why at the time. When the overseer drug Liza away to be sold at Ryan's Slave Mart, Ezra cried and wailed, then ran after her. First McBride told him to hush and stay put, but Ezra kept screaming and running. Then McBride pulled out his pistol. He shouted, 'I said shut up, boy!' Then he shot Ezra square in the chest."

Octavia's eyes welled up with tears. "There was nothing I could do, and I was afraid to make a sound," she said. "McBride might shoot me too. So, I just turned around and walked back into the house. I held in my sorrow the rest of the day until I got into my bed that night. I just cried and cried as quiet as I could manage. I wanted to wail and scream with anger, but I didn't dare. I lost Liza and Ezra at the same time. I'll never forget that day. We were so helpless."

Hentie, not knowing what to say, just squeezed Octavia's hand. "I'm so sorry," she said. "I know he must have been a good boy and you loved him very much."

"I did, Hentie. I did. He was too young to die like that. He was shot down like he was nothing. Ain't right, Hentie." Octavia just shook her head and wandered away, wiping a tear that had rolled down her cheek.

Hentie thought, *No, it ain't right. How can a child be shot down like that because he was missing the woman who raised him? How can a human like Liza be drug off and sold on a whim? Ain't right. No, ain't right.*

Living conditions for those enslaved were obviously harsh, but what she learned from Big John and Octavia showed her how truly evil slavery was, and the lengths some enslaved servants would go to escape it. Physical labor in the fields pushed workers beyond their limits and sometimes into premature deaths, often as young as thirty years of age. Toiling for as many as eighteen hours a day in hot, semitropical conditions, coupled with brutally abusive overseers and a poor nutritional base, was too much. In order to deal with the constant stress of the situation, some sought refuge away from the plantation in the region's woods. Some harbored thoughts of heading north to freedom, a hard task to accomplish, indeed. Others spontaneously made a break with no real plan and merely chose to live in the woods, sometimes for the long term and more often for the short term. These deferments sometimes acted as a safety valve.

In the woods, the runaways largely relied on their own wits and survival instincts. Sometimes they could arrange for drop-offs of food from other enslaved workers, but this was very risky for all involved. Runaway slaves had also been known to join local Native Americans and be absorbed into their tribes. Over time mixed-race groups emerged, and these multiracial tribes remained in the region for generations.

Chapter 5
Renting Out Skilled Slaves/Slave Badges

Late one evening, some of the enslaved were down by the slave quarters sitting at the outdoor tables enjoying a moment of rest and camaraderie. A few people left and went to their quarters, exhausted from the day. Big John moved down to be closer to Hentie. She felt this was an encouraging sign, that he might want to be a friend of hers, but her pulse began to pound in her throat, making it hard to swallow or even speak.

"How you doing, Hentie? How have you been getting on?"

Nervous, Hentie noticed the intense look in Big John's eyes. "Fine," was all she could emit. She quietly took in a breath, hoping to quiet her pulse.

"Well, that good, Miss Hentie. I hope you feeling more comfortable round here. I hear the other folks around here like you, they like you a lot. I know you got so much to learn about this place. I know it's hard, but I'm here to help you. I know other folks are willing to as well, like Octavia and Nellie.

"Maybe someday you won't just work in the kitchen house and sometimes help in the main house; maybe you'll get to move to the big house full time. The master might let you learn a special skill. You might be a lady's maid one day. If that happen, maybe he allow you to be rented out to rich white people. He gets most the money, but you get to keep a few coins for yourself." Big John looked carefully into Hentie's face, watching for her response.

"What does that mean, 'rented out'?" Hentie queried.

"Well, the master, he has a good business head. I heard people say that about him. He's smart about how to run this place. He diversifies his crops and encourages a few of the colored folks to learn a new skill or trade. We have some men who learned carpentry. Jed, he makes beautiful things for the main house. He learned to copy European styles and make furniture white folks like. He makes tables, dressers, and desks. They're just beautiful, carved all nice like with a smooth finish.

"Another man, his name Sam, he works with metals and iron. He gone from shoeing horses to making fine wrought iron gates. Mr. Langdon figured out that if he rented out his slaves, he could earn more money. He learned there were a bunch of trades he could rent out—the folks that make the bricks, the fishermen, the bricklayers, the blacksmiths, all kinds of workers. Most of the money, it goes to the master, but a small amount goes to the slave worker. Sometimes he rents out the women too. It depends on what another white man might need. Sometimes womenfolk go and work at another plantation around here, sometimes for a few days, sometimes longer."

Hentie stammered, "Oh my, Big John, I don't think I could do that. I'd be afraid to leave here. It's not for me."

"Hentie, someday you might want to do this. The master has to agree to it. First McBride, he would have to get you a badge. He would go into Charleston, register you with the city and get a special metal worker to make you a metal tag and pay some kind of fee. You gots to wear the tag on you all the time or else the City Guard might think you a runaway." Big John looked to Hentie to see if she understood.

Then he went on to say, "If you work hard, save up your money, some colored folks finally buy their freedom. That don't happen very often. But if it does, you get a different badge. It says you're a free person of color and you live out on your own."

"Oh, I can't imagine a woman doing anything like that. I couldn't live on my own." Hentie curled her fingers into tight balls around the folds of her skirt and shook her head.

"Well, you might not want to, but some others do. I guess most are men. Jed got to rent himself out to some of the wealthy white folks in Charleston. Sometimes the master arranged for Jed to carve furniture for the white folks, but more often Jed arranged it on his own. He real lucky."

Big John reached up and pointed toward the waterfront. "From what I hear from the men who work on the boats, we're the only city that does this. No place else has the special badges. We also got more black folks than other cities, so things work different here," Big John explained.

"I think I remember seeing one of them special badges, Big John. I was in town with you, Octavia, and the missus. I remember seeing a Negro man wearing overalls and an oil-stained shirt. He had a heavy bag of tools slung over his shoulder. It seemed like he had his mind set on where he was going. Like he was fixing to go his job. He nodded at me as he passed and said, 'Mornin', ma'am.' I remember nodding at him as he walked by. As I passed him, I noticed the diamond-shaped badge he had on his overalls. The metal flickered in the sunlight and caught my eye. I saw words on it and a number. I didn't know what it meant at the time."

Big John's eyes lit up. "Oh, I think I remember that day. I know that man; his name is Lucas. He works on machinery around the city doing all kinds of repairs. Lucas does good work. I hear from the men down on the docks that men like Lucas are in demand by the white businessmen and shipowners down on the wharf. But he has to watch himself. Some of the white German and Irish immigrant workers don't like him because they think he takes work away from them. They get real resentful at times."

Hentie nodded in acknowledgment. "I think I heard about that. Some of those white folks who come to America trying to make a living, some of 'em are real poor. But it's not our choice to be here working for the white man. It's not our fault; we got no choice," Hentie insisted.

"It can be hard, but we gots to make it as best we can. All the colored folks have to watch themselves, all the time. The rented-out slaves gots to be even more careful about where they stay and the hours they keep. Most can't tell time, don't have no timepiece to keep track of it. They have to be concerned about travel time and work hours. There is a curfew for Negroes: nine at night in the winter and ten in the summer. Right before the top of the hour, a city worker starts to beat a drum. About that same time, the bells of St. Michael's Church start to ring. That tells the colored folks they best get a move on. When the drum starts to roll, black folks gots ten minutes to clear the streets or they might be taken to the Work House by the slave patrol—they like the police. They been around for a hundred years. They got guns and whips they use all the time. They don't care if they hurt you or end up killing you. Colored folks don't matter to them. But usually they take black people to the slave Work House. Bad things happen there. Real bad."

"Oh, Big John, that all sounds terrible. How Negroes supposed to get around? No matter what you do, you always got to worry about something happening to you." Hentie scrunched her forehead as she scowled.

"The Work House is a terrible place, just a horrible, scary place. It's an ugly old building near the marshes. Kind of looks like a castle with a high wall around it. It used to be a sugar refinery, so people call it the Sugar House. If a slave runs away or he cross his master, he can be snatched up and taken there 'to get a bit of sugar.' They whip colored folks there and maim them all kinds of ways. It's like a torture chamber. A master can take his slave there and have him whipped for twenty-five cents. But usually it's the slave patrol or City Guard that take the colored people there. They can haul you off for all kinds of things—being out after curfew or even looking at a white woman the wrong way. No matter what you done wrong, they beat you all the same." Big John rested his forehead in the palm of his head as he pictured the horror of it all.

After a moment, he drew a breath and went on. "I talk to men who have been in there. Some are crippled from what they did to 'em. One man lost an eye. They say there's lots of whipping posts there to tie you up and lash you. Other black folks are forced on a treadmill with their arms shackled to an overhead rail. They make a big waterwheel go around like a grist mill. They tie your feet to a plank so you can't get off. They don't let you rest all day. If you trip or fall, your foot might get between the rollers. Might even be killed. If you make it through the day, you can't walk for days. Leg muscles too damaged."

Hentie drew one hand up against her chest, aghast.

Big John expanded on the depravity. "The white man uses the treadmill to grind corn or wheat at the Work House. Then they sell it to folks in the city. I walk by there sometimes and hear men screaming for them to stop, but they never do. I'll never forget their screams. It breaks my heart to think about it." Big John hung his head and let out a deep sigh.

Hentie would come to know the Work House as a truly abominable place, but it only hid atrocities that were frequently meted out elsewhere, and in public. Many slaveholders thought that the Work House was vital to keep order and manage recalcitrant slaves. There were a variety of whips used, generally of multiple strips of cowhide. When in motion, the sonic momentum could cut through the air, then land a blow that cut the skin with razor-like precision. Victims would often lose so much blood that they fell into a state of shock. Periodically, residents around the Work House would suspend their neighborly visits with those in their social circle as the lingering smell of drying blood and mangled flesh was too putrid. On those occasions, genteel ladies would refuse to even walk through the area due to its offensive odor.

The whipping was so brutal that it sometimes resulted in death. As a result, it was not uncommon to not only hear the anguished screams of pain, but also the grief-stricken shrieks of the newly widowed Negro women. For those who survived ruthless whippings, their back might be left with flesh-knotted scars.

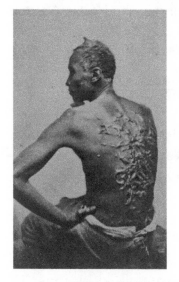

Sometimes, Negroes were tortured and killed quite publicly in other sites around the city. Some Negroes were mutilated, then lynched, while others were hung by a hook and chain to a pole in White Point Gardens. The hook was fastened to the third rib through an incision in the abdominal cavity. The victim would then be whipped or beaten with a stick while swinging from the chain, and would hang there until his death, up to three days later.

One couple, both servants in the same household, were unable to explain the sudden death of a white infant in their charge. As a result, they were publicly set on fire and burned until dead. The horrid odor of charred flesh could be smelled for days. Their scorched remains, intended to strike fear within the colored community, lay where they burned for days until they were unceremoniously disposed of by a white city worker. All that remained of the wrongly accused black couple was dumped onto a trash heap and forgotten.

Chapter 6
Nellie Working in the House Garden

"Hentie!" Nellie shouted, "I'm going out to tend to the garden. Can you start snapping the peas for tonight's dinner?"

"Yes, Miss Nellie. I sure can," Hentie replied. "Is there anything else I might do for you?"

"No, now go on. Don't let the master see you idle. Keep working at all times," Nellie cautioned.

Nellie went out to the garden, out past the kitchen house and the laundry house, where sheets and nightclothes were boiled. Big John walked by with an armload of wood for the laundry-house fire. He was such a big man it looked like he was carrying little matchsticks.

Big John hollered to Nellie while he was passing by, "Hey there, Miss Nellie! Fine day, isn't it?"

Nellie shouted back to him, "It *is* a fine day, John. By the way, I noticed you already loaded up my firewood. I thank you for that. I sure do appreciate it when you load up the wood for me!" Big John nodded graciously and strode on to the laundry house. Big John was such a friendly, good-natured man. A man his size could snap another man in half if he wanted, but that was not his nature.

Nellie called out, "Hey, Big John, tonight after supper, why don't you sing to us? You have the most powerful voice on the plantation. And it's so beautiful too!"

John replied, humbly turning his head downward, "Well, I don't know. Gots to see what the master wants me to do. But I'd love to sing a few spirituals for y'all. It will help raise us up."

Nellie nodded and said, "I hope you can. We all need to be raised up. We need to be reminded that the Lord is here with us."

"Sure enough," said Big John as he nodded in agreement. "You have a good day, ma'am."

Hentie was walking through the work yard to the kitchen house with some items from the spring house. She first shouted a greeting to Nellie, then turned to Big John. He almost tripped when he saw Hentie.

"Watch yourself there, Big John! You're too important to us for you to get hurt, now." Hentie smiled.

"Uh, I'm important?" Stumbling for words to say, he just flushed and looked down at her.

"Yes, Big John, you're important to us. Now, you have a good day." She smiled and walked on.

Big John stood briefly, still taken by the interlude. *I'm important to her?*

"Big John, you best keep moving. Lots to do today," Nellie hollered to stir him into action.

"Oh yes, best get moving." He broke his gaze away from Hentie and jerked into action. "Yep, best get a move on."

Nellie chuckled at Big John's fascination with Hentie, then turned and began the tedious work of pulling weeds, plucking ripened vegetables, and cutting back unwieldy plants. This had been her job since she was just a child. Her calloused hands kept moving in her labors, but her mind drifted off to days, years ago, when she worked the garden with her mama.

Nellie could see her mother in her mind's eye, shouting at her, "You best hurry up, now! The master don't like lazy children. Now, no long mouth. Master don't like that! You best get a move on it!"

Nellie remembered that she had an ivory work dress made of Negro cloth. It was from a length of fabric her mama had been given the previous Christmas. It was like a light muslin, a nice weight in the summer months. That Christmas she received her first real shoes because she ran so many errands for the folks in the main house. Her little feet almost froze without them. Before her first shoes, she wore moccasins her daddy had made with his own hands from animal skin. She felt so fortunate. So many slave children had no clothes or shoes at all. Usually children were five or older before they gained a garment—they had to earn the right. They had to be working to somehow support the plantation. Otherwise, the adults were clothed first, and children were an afterthought. If children were lucky enough to have clothes, they wore a coarse sackcloth or tow linen made into a sort of shirt that hung low, reaching down to the child's knees. Enslaved children wore it night and day, as it was their only garment, changing it once a week. If all else failed, mothers made a garment from a gunny sack with holes cut for the arms and head.

The holidays were a happy time of year for the enslaved workers. They might get an additional food ration or special holiday food—a real treat from their severely limited food rations. They usually got a day off from their labors on Christmas. All the enslaved workers also got their one pair of shoes for the year and fabric to make themselves a garment. They looked forward to these pleasantries all year. What they got for Christmas depended on the success of the harvest. Particularly generous masters might give fabric or shoes at other times, but such kindnesses were rare. However, there were limits on what enslaved servants could receive.

There were laws in South Carolina which mandated what was permissible clothing for blacks to emphasize social stratification.

Materials suitable for their clothing were only the cheapest fabrics made of lesser quality, such as Negro cloth, duffelds, coarse kearsies, blue linen and checked linen, coarse garlix or calicoes. Enslaved blacks could not wear fine clothes unless they were well-worn, cast-off clothes of their masters. These laws were enacted in response to whites complaining about seeing Negroes in fine garments in downtown areas. It never occurred to slave owners or lawmakers that Negroes could have feelings or take pride in how they dressed, or if they did, it seemingly didn't matter.

Nellie must have been about five years old when she got her shoes. She remembered how lucky she considered herself to be helping her mama in the kitchen house and to have a beige shift or shimmy and something on her feet. Things were easier for house servants than for field hands. Nellie and her mama had nicer clothes because they worked in the kitchen and were up and around the big house. They were also given a nicer cabin that was closer to the main house than the others.

Their food was rationed, just like for everyone else, but they had the opportunity to nick an item here or there. Sometimes Nellie would sneak an egg to her mama, and she would cook it. Nellie would hide under a willow tree and eat it so the master wouldn't see her. Other times she could sneak a piece of fruit or pilfer some salt for cooking at home.

Nellie stood, straightened her back, and wiped at a piece of dirt clinging to her cheek, smearing it across her skin. She then wiped her brow and sullied cheek with the red-and-white kerchief that her husband, Samuel, had given to her shortly before his death. She liked to carry that kerchief with her every day. Nellie frowned as she shielded her eyes with her hand and the brim of her worn sunhat, a special hat her grandmother had made her out of hand-sewn sweetgrass. She adjusted it to block the bright sunlight.

It was only midmorning and already the heat was nearly unbearable, covering the land like a wet blanket. It had rained earlier, but it didn't do much to relieve the heat. The mosquitos were out and biting. Nellie slapped her leg to rid herself of the pests. No use complaining; she needed to get the work done. The master was very particular about how the kitchen-house garden was to be maintained. The sweet aroma from the few nearby Osage orange trees drifted up to her in the rain-soaked air. The master had installed these few, along with a couple of lemon trees, for fruit and to discourage flies and rodents.

She bent again toward the sodden ground, down among the ridges, and resumed deftly pulling up weeds from the garden plot. The plantings were spices, herbs, and vegetables like cucumbers, tomatoes, eggplant, cowpeas, okra, broad beans, and squash, along with a few tubers like red-skinned potatoes that Nellie used for the master and his family—they loved them. Further out she had an area planted with sorghum that she made sorghum molasses from every year. The tall rows of it looked like corn stalks.

⌒

Later on that evening, Big John sang to them as Nellie had requested. The other enslaved workers gathered around him down at the outdoor wooden tables near the slave cabins. It seemed incongruent that such a big, musclebound man could have the voice of an angel. His baritone was deep, strong, and steadfast, and his songs were heartfelt. At first, they were all mesmerized by his captivating voice, unable to interact.

But as the evening wore on, and Big John began singing more gospel songs, others joined in, responding to his melodic voice by calling back or clapping. It left Hentie breathless and shaky, nearly dizzy with delight. She and the others came alive with the music, some playing percussion instruments. An effervescent ardor rose from those surrounding Big John. As the singing persisted, the energy continued to percolate and spread over the crowd. That energy pulsed with a healing quality. It seemed to make the crowd forget their sorrows and their weariness. The late hour did not seem to matter; the closeness they shared with one another kept them there. The music and the mood of the crowd was magic, like sunshine made audible. At last their joyous song raised to a crescendo, held for a few moments, and then fell to earth. Everyone was full of warmth and joy from their glorious experience. And so the night ended, and those gathered strolled off to their cabins. The spirit of the Lord God blanketed them all and tucked them safely into their quarters.

Chapter 7
Lydia's Mistress on the Lower Peninsula

Hentie woke to the gentle sound of a woman singing. The room around her was cold, and the blanket covering her was thin and laden with holes. In her half-awake state, she imagined that it was her mother singing, vaguely recognizing it as a lullaby she had once sung to her own daughter, Amahle, but the voice was different. She suddenly felt the sob in the back of her throat for the loss of her mother and of her daughter. She knew she would never hear them sing again or feel their touch. Hentie's eyes snapped open, fighting her sense of loss; she couldn't allow the grief to swallow her in its easy embrace. She had to shake it loose and let go of the memories. She had another day to face and couldn't let these wounds overcome her. She looked about her room and saw the faint blue of breaking day casting shadows over the walls of her small wooden-frame slave cabin, a two-dwelling building with a shared chimney. Her dream of Amahle still clung to her bones.

Hentie sat up, trying to orient herself to the new day. Her small, cramped cabin contained a little worktable and a stool. A crate held her few clothes and prized possessions. The other slaves lying on their low platforms and pallets were just starting to stir. Hentie felt weary and dull. Perhaps it was the winter season. But she was heartened; it was warming up, and she remembered that today was Sunday and she would be going into the city of Charleston with her friends Big John and Octavia. The image of the three of them on the open road put a spark into her. She threw her legs over the side of her bed, drew in a deep breath, and decided to ready herself for the day.

The long hours she had spent laboring in the kitchen house the previous day left her sore and stiff. She smelled of smoke, pork fat and perspiration, a remnant from working in the intense heat.

Hentie pulled on her worn Negro shoes as a fleeting image of the missus's fine new leather boots skipped across her mind. She stretched out her sore torso and placed a shawl over her shoulders and stood, urging her body to awaken. She shuffled to her door and stepped outside. Following the sound of the singing to the kitchen house, Hentie saw several of the other enslaved up and starting to move about the grounds. Hentie jumped into the mix, and her energy rose.

As Hentie turned the corner, she saw a small boy wearing a one-piece beige osnaburg garment sprinting toward a willow tree with something in his hand. He ducked under the long tendrils of the tree and then sat under the spreading crown of it, propping himself against the scaly gray trunk. Having readied himself, he then spread open his hand. He had a piece of corn bread tucked in a small cloth. Cook must have given it to him as a treat. He unwrapped the food and gobbled it all down in four large mouthfuls, nearly choking on it twice. Hentie paused, ready to intervene and pound his back should he need it. He looked up at her, leaking tears from his near choking. Crumbs clung to his small, smooth cheeks, and bright gratitude lit his eyes. He brushed the remnants from his cheeks, capturing each crumb, then licked his hand to get every last morsel. He grinned and waved at Hentie. Smiling, she nodded back at him. He was the picture of sheer delight at his good fortune.

But his joy was abruptly swept away when the overseer passed by, noticed the contented and seemingly angelic child, and barked, "Hey, you! Damn pickaninny black child! Get a move on it! Start watering the garden and pulling the weeds. Don't sit there eating the master's food!"

Hentie jumped at his jarring tone and arched her back, but then quickly calmed herself when she realized she was not the target of the attack and walked onward into the kitchen house. *Poor child, didn't get to even enjoy a scrap of bread before being thrown into his work. He's not even five years old.* Of course, black children started working around the plantation as soon as they could understand directions. Many had assigned tasks by age four and a regular work assignment by age five. Some worked a full day by then. They would perform tasks like gathering wood chips for the fire, tending livestock, churning butter, preparing and scattering manure and fertilizer. Sometimes small youngsters would work in children's gangs, where as a group they would perform tasks under the direction of an enslaved adult. They might do things like sow a turnip patch, clean slave quarters, water plants, shuck corn for the hogs, dig potatoes or pick peaches. However, they were not permitted to eat what they picked.

As Hentie entered the kitchen-house doorway, she heard Nellie humming the lullaby she had heard earlier. Nellie was smiling to herself and spooning batter into muffin tins. The sight of her lightened Hentie's heart.

"Morning, Miss Nellie!" Hentie said. "Fine day, isn't it? I get to go into town today with Big John and Octavia. We're gonna visit Octavia's sister in the city."

"Oh, that's nice. Lydia, she a nice woman; you'll like her," responded Nellie. She had known her before she was sold off to the family in Charleston.

After completing her morning work, Hentie headed back

to her cabin to freshen up and change her clothes. It was a fine, sunny morning, and a typical February day, mild and warming up nicely. New growth poked up through the ground. While the Deep South had intense heat in the summer, it was blessed with temperate winters. Hentie had heard the master say temperatures were hanging around the sixties. She thought that was good, but didn't fully understand what it meant. The warm weather of South Carolina allowed the master to enjoy a nearly year-round growing season. The Lowcountry had three planting seasons; the first would be starting soon.

Rain had fallen periodically over the past few weeks, but this morning was fine. A fierce rain swept through overnight and the air was cool and fresh. Petals from the early blooms floated in the rain puddles. Since the planting season hadn't started yet, Hentie and Octavia were given the afternoon off and permitted to travel into Charleston to visit Octavia's sister, Lydia, on the Battery on the lower peninsula in Charleston. They were given travel tickets in the form of cursory letters written by the master to ensure their safe passage. The slave patrol and City Guard carefully controlled the movements of Negroes, free and enslaved, all around the city. A black person must have a badge or a ticket to be away from his master. The Black Code, which had been in effect since colonial times, mandated it.

The Black Code controlled nearly every aspect of a black person's life. They were forbidden from smoking cigars or pipes and could not carry canes. They were restrained from carrying on loud conversations and assembling on street corners or other places. Negroes were mandated to give way to all white persons of any station in life, no matter how lowly, so that they might pass. Most gave a quick bow or a curtsy.

Big John would take them most of the way from the plantation in Mount Pleasant to the City of Charleston in the dray wagon. He, too, had a travel pass that allowed him to leave the plantation and travel into the city. He needed to drop off some parcels with a businessman on King Street. The proprietor needed the items for the start of business on Monday morning. From the shopping district on King Street, the ladies would walk to the lower peninsula.

Big John was already standing by the dray when Hentie approached him with Octavia following behind her. His face cracked wide open in a broad smile as he looked at Hentie.

"My, this sure is a fine morning. And you're looking mighty pretty in that dress, Hentie." Big John beamed as he spoke.

"Thank you, Big John." Hentie looked down as she flushed. She was radiant and glowing in her fresh, celery-green dress with long sleeves. The missus had grown tired of it and given Octavia the frock, along with a light woolen jacket. The items had been far too small for Octavia, so Hentie managed to acquire them. She was so grateful for the clothes, particularly now that Big John seemed to like them.

Yeah, I'm looking real fine too, Big John, Octavia thought, feeling a twinge of jealousy at Big John's overtures toward Hentie.

After the three had settled into the wagon, Big John nodded to the two ladies. "Ha!" he shouted at the horses, and the wagon lurched forward. As the three of them started out in their rig, down the avenue of oaks, their spirits were high. A light breeze rushed over their faces. The tall oak trees bearded with Spanish moss shaded them from the bright sunlight. They laughed and chattered as the team of horses cantered down the lane, pulling them to the main road.

Hentie sat back in her seat, feeling any tension wash away. She would be far off from the grounds and the meanspirited disposition of the master, as well as the flighty bidding of the missus. Having Big John in control made her feel safe and allayed her worries. Having him nearby was like having a wall of protection. As he handled the reins, Hentie found herself mesmerized by his strong hands and unable to turn away.

Their trek would take a while. They were only about a dozen miles from their destination, but they had to cross the Cooper River before reaching the peninsula on which the city lay. The crossing there was sporadic, and one never knew how long the wait would be for a ferry. But their spirits were high, and the trek, no matter how long, would be a welcome break from the tedium and labors at Twin Oaks. Hentie stared at the scrubby trees along the road and tried to take in the newly cleansed air. The road was full of puddled ruts, the air still dewy with moisture. The pounding of the horse's hooves became rhythmic, pacing out the miles as the wheels rolled through the sandy mud. Navigating the rough road took most of Big John's concentration. The wagon jumped and bumped. The ladies, thrown together, clasped one another tightly, Hentie's arm tucked under Octavia's. After a time, they reached the water's edge. The wagon climbed the road to the levee, with the deep waters passing by beyond it. Chunks of leaves and bits of debris from the recent storm dipped and twirled in a watery dance. They made the crossing without incident and traveled on, down from the neck into the lower peninsula.

Once they reached town, Big John pulled up the rig in the alley adjacent to the shopkeeper's store. He helped the ladies to the ground, and they approached the front of the store. Big John tapped on the door, attempting to gain the shopkeeper's attention. No one responded. "He must be back in the supply room or busy in his office," Big John said.

In that moment, a handful of passing dockworkers yelled at the trio and started making derogatory remarks. Their words included sexual comments about the women.

One who looked to be no more than a teen said, "I ain't had myself a black woman before. Hey, you in the green dress, you lookin' mighty fine. Might give you a taste of what a white man can do."

Then another of the young men shouted over him, "No, you never know what diseases that bitch might carry. Just a nasty carcass. Why does this beautiful afternoon have to be sullied with the view of stinkin' niggras anyway?" The rest of the group erupted in laughter.

Hentie looked up to Big John and saw him struggle to curb his emotions. His hands clenched and unclenched at his sides while he took deep breaths in and out. His jawbones worked furiously. Hentie had never seen Big John so worked up; perhaps he was thinking of what he might need to do to defend himself and the two women should they be attacked. While attempting to rein in his anger, he turned his back to the young men, so as not to cause a confrontation.

The dockhands paused as if debating whether or not to start something and start sparring, but then thought better of it. The one who appeared to be the oldest of the group yelled, "I don't want to waste my time with that ape! I'll just dirty my hands with him."

The group continued to shout demeaning remarks but moved on. Hentie breathed a deep sigh of relief. She had heard horrid things of what might happen to Negroes traveling into the city.

Sounds came from the door to the store. The shopkeeper, peering through the glass, unfasted the lock and opened the door.

"Oh, John, so glad you could come." The amiable man smiled broadly and nodded at Big John in greeting. His kind gray eyes had flecks of brown in them, and their warmth seemed genuine. The two men talked about the bundles Big John had brought with him. The shopkeeper was delighted with the shipment and quickly opened the side of the building to receive the new items. They took care of the transaction quickly while the women looked around the street. The windows were full of colorful goods and fashionable garments Hentie had never seen before.

Big John finished his business with the merchant, then joined Octavia and Hentie back on this street.

"Well, let's move on down to your sister's house. I'll make sure you get there safe, then I gots some things I need to do. I'm meeting a friend later."

They left the dray parked by the shop and walked down the street, the rumble of buckboards and carriages about them. The cries of enslaved vendors called out. The loud, discordant voice of a woman rose up: "Red roses, beautiful red roses." The din of commerce clamored on all about them.

As they walked toward Lydia's home, they passed two of the city's flower ladies, part of a common trade carried out by Negro women from outlying areas. One older woman sat on a wall with flowers in her hand and a basket of produce by her feet.

"You want any flowers for your mistress? I'm sure she'd love 'em," said the older flower lady in the worn dress as she exposed her toothless grin.

"No, thank you," Octavia said as she passed the woman. "We're just in the city to visit my sister down on the Battery."

"Oh, she must be a lucky woman to live down there. The masters treat their black folks better down on the Battery," the old woman said, nodding while she spoke.

"Yes, she sure is lucky. I hope you don't have to spend your whole day there selling your flowers. You best get home soon. It's Sunday, a day of rest." Octavia smiled kindly at the woman as she continued down the walkway.

"Yes, I plan to be here jus' a short time. Catch the white folks as they leave the church, then I'll go home." The old woman nodded again and smiled at Octavia and Hentie. "You ladies enjoy your visit."

The second flower woman was a younger girl. While trying to master the art of balancing a basket on her head, she rose to her feet. She tentatively moved down the street, carefully keeping her head erect with the heavily laden basket of vegetables and flowers on her crown. She was going to make a couple of deliveries down on Rainbow Row. Some of the white folks that lived there planned to use the vegetables for their Sunday supper and decorate their foyers with the fresh flowers.

As the young flower woman moved down the street, an elite, white couple walked toward her. They were dressed in fine attire, the woman wearing an olive-green silk dress with puffed sleeves adorned with forest-green trim. Her large hoop skirt swayed to-and-fro as she progressed. She shielded her face from the sun with an ornate folding fan she carried in her gloved left hand. The elegantly attired white woman held her right hand on the arm of her husband, who walked on the street side, as they progressed toward the Negro woman. The gentleman puffed out his chest as he strolled along with his cane. His auburn hair was pomaded back, leaving a rather shiny expanse of forehead, partially covered by his top hat. As the couple continued toward the flower lady, they maintained their position on the walkway, clearly expecting the Negress to give way. But the flower lady did not notice the couple, keeping her eyes focused downward on the walkway, careful not to step on a stone or in a hole. As the aristocratic white couple was upon the young flower girl, the man's face drew up in a rage, his brows furrowed together.

"Here, here, Negress, you are to give way! You stupid niggra!"

He pulled his cane out to the side of his body and brought it hissing through the air to crack hard upon the backs of the flower woman's knees. The young woman gave out a sharp cry as she pitched forward, sprawling onto her front, the vegetables and flowers flying in all directions. She landed with a thud, her cry piercing the late-afternoon air. Hentie, appalled by the sight, covered her mouth in horror. Octavia, more accustomed to such acts, threw her arm across Hentie's chest to hold her back and calm her.

"Girl, we best cross to the other side of the street. This white buckra fit to be tied!" Octavia made eye contact with Hentie, then tipped her chin to the other side of the road. The two ladies scampered swiftly across the roadway. Big John pulled back against a building and stayed behind.

The flower lady struggled to make it to her feet. As the couple passed, the man kicked a couple of vegetables and glared down upon the stunned woman with disgust. He then regained his composure, straightened his back, and strolled on. The young woman, still dumbfounded by the incident, got on her knees to gather her items. Her knees and elbows had been skinned and were bleeding. The blood ran in bright-red rivulets against her dark skin and onto her worn, pale-colored shift, which became saturated with her blood. She tried to recover emotionally from the incident, but tears ran down her face. She knew some of her flowers and produce were too damaged to pass along to her customers. She might very well face the ire of her first white customer, a sadistic old widow, once she reached her home. Then she'd fall victim to yet another violent walloping. All of her work and the special trip for a few extra coins would be for naught.

The more the young woman contemplated her plight, the more profuse her tears. Octavia and Hentie, seeing the young woman unable to regain control of her emotions, crossed back over to assist her. In her motherly and tender way, Hentie seemed to find just the right words to lend comfort to the woman. As they were picking up the items, Big John caught up with them. He reached down to assist her, and she looked up at him, stunned by his immense size. He was well over six feet tall and broad. He looked upon the still-shaking young woman, bent down, and in one effortless and smooth motion had her on her feet.

He looked into the woman's face and calmly said, "Now, you don't never mind what the stupid white buckra do. He just a white fool. One day God will make sure that he gets his comeuppance. He do bad, bad come back to him. God will dry all our tears. You'll see."

The young woman, still speechless, bobbed her head up and down in understanding.

"You be alright now. Don't let that man ruin your day." His dark face suddenly split open into a white smile and a gentle look.

Hentie and Octavia watched as Big John spoke to the woman. Hentie was particularly moved by his tenderness. *He is such a big man but can be so kind.* They remained nearby to support the young woman, who still seemed distraught.

In that moment, the young woman was overwhelmed by all the harshness and brutality that controlled the lives of the city's black citizens. There were laws, edicts, and customs that controlled every moment of an enslaved woman's life. There was the City Guard, the curfew, the passes, the searches, the night watch, the vigilante committees, the slave catchers, the Work House, the constant demeaning acts and humiliations doled out by the white folks. She felt helpless against them. Constantly controlled, demeaned, and abused—the sheer viciousness of it all was too much.

"I just wish I was dead. Let the good Lord take me. I can't do this no more. I's been hit and beaten too many times. I can't do it no more!"

Hentie put a calming hand on the woman's shoulder. "Yes, honey, you can. I know sometimes it seems too much. But we can do it. We gots to. We gots no choice. We have to look at the good in each other. Us colored folk is your family. We gots to support one another; that's how we make it." Hentie locked eyes with the young woman to lend assurance.

As the young woman steadied herself, she sniffled loudly and passed her forearm under her nose. She forcefully exhaled and straightened her back. "You're right. I gots to go on. Ain't got no other choice."

Hentie, Octavia, and Big John put every last bit of fruit and vegetables in her basket, laid the flowers on top, and handed her the bundle. "Here you go," Big John announced.

Hentie touched the young woman's arm. "You'll be alright now. Wipe away those tears. We're here to help you, and so are all the other Gullah folks around here. You'll be fine."

The young woman took the basket, nodded, and said, "Thank you. Thank you so much. I appreciate your kindness. Lord God will somehow repay for what you done for me."

The young woman smiled at the trio and started her descent down the peninsula, the others headed to the wharves. Big John, with his long legs, kept out in front of Octavia and Hentie, progressing with determination to keep his appointment. The sun momentarily peeked out from the clouds, and the warm sun shone down on their faces. They breathed in the briny and soothing harbor breezes floating up from the waterfront.

About five minutes later, the trio came upon an egotistical, aristocratic white man who lived in the area. This white man always carried a huge stick over his shoulder and was known to strike black folks who did not scamper out of his way quickly enough. On at least a few occasions, Big John himself had been on the receiving end of the stick. Well, on this day, he would not accept the intimidation of this white fool.

Today, as the pompous white man approached Big John, he froze in the middle of the walkway. The white man, awestruck by Big John's challenge, pulled back his stick to strike him.

Still filled with ire from the last confrontation, Big John shouted, "Not today, old man. Not today!"

Big John knocked the stick out of the white man's hand and grabbed him up with one hand on the front of his suit coat and another hand on the seat of the dumbfounded white man's breeches. Big John tossed him facedown in a large mud puddle in the middle of the road and held him down with his booted foot. After a moment or two, Big John allowed the cantankerous old man to roll onto his back.

"You've done hit me for the last time, old man!" Big John pointed his index finger sharply at his face and held it there for a few beats, ensuring that the man understood his point, then turned and strolled off.

Laughter burst forth from some passing Irish laborers. "Good for him! I've always hated that old man. He's just a hard-hearted old bastard, he is. He tried to cheat me once when I did some work for him. He got his due!" shouted a red-haired Irishman.

Two other white workers in the group nodded in agreement. One spat on the ground near the dumbfounded old man and shouted, "Time that old crow got his!"

The workers strolled on, gawking at the mud-covered man. Other passersby nodded approvingly. It seems that the egotistical old man didn't have one friend on the street this day.

While typically white society folks would have been appalled by such an act, and black folks would have cowered at the possible outcome of such a confrontation, on this day everyone seemed to support the act. Later, his black friends quietly applauded Big John's boldness. Even white men laughed as the story was told again and again in the local public houses and taverns. The old man, having been humbled, was far more cautious and peaceable going forward.

"Ladies, I best make myself scarce. These white folks seem happy about what I did to that evil white man, but they may change their minds. They might kill me for that, even though he deserved it. I'm going to run on to my friend's house and hide out there for a while. I see y'all at the end of the day," said Big John.

"You're right. The slave patrol like to string you up for gettin' a white man like that. You best get a move on!"

Hentie, disappointed to see her friend go, was more reluctant. "Big John, I hate to see you go, but you best keep safe. You never know what the crazy white folks might do. I see you later on?"

Big John reached out and gently touched Hentie's hand. "Don't you worry none; I see you later today. We all ride back together to the plantation. We'll have a nice ride home, you'll see."

Their eyes lingered on each other just a moment longer, both smiling with a kind, affectionate look. Octavia looked from one to the other. *Hmmm, I think these two might be sweet on each other. He doesn't touch my hand like that.*

Without glancing at Octavia, he turned and started back to the store on King Street to get the rig and move it up to the neck. He was headed north to the neighborhood above the neck of the peninsula of Charleston, to Boundary Street, later called Calhoun Street. Many of the free people of color and hired-out enslaved Negro workers who lived independently resided in that area.

Octavia and Hentie chattered and laughed as they progressed down the peninsula to Lydia's house. Their mood had been buoyed by the spectacle of Big John leveling the irritable old white man, and, somehow, they were more assured following the incident.

Upon reaching Lydia's house, Octavia said, "We can't enter here. We needs to go around to the back. That's where the colored folk enter." The two walked around to an alleyway and spotted a heavy wooden gate. "That's where we go in." Octavia motioned.

As they passed through the back gate, they saw several enslaved workers milling about the grounds carrying out a variety of tasks. Hentie gently touched Octavia's arm, her eyes wide and mouth agape, bowled over by the sights and smells going on before her. It was like all the work of a plantation was compressed into a city block. Behind the elegant mansions was a work yard where many of the tasks involved in running the home occurred. This backlot was much different from the mansions in front, where the white aristocrats dwelled. One would never guess the odd assortment of activities that transpired behind the noble walls of the mansions, nor would one guess at the conditions and the odors that emanated there. The backlot was dirty and smelly. While it was tolerable on this mild day, one could only imagine what it must be like on a hot, humid summer day. Twenty or so bondsmen were busy doing the work to support their slave masters, everything from trimming the grape arbor and pear tree to cleaning out horse stalls. Hentie had never seen anything like this.

The work yard ground was made up of sandy soil, with some inlaid brick in certain portions of the yard. Some of the buildings were made of wood, while others were brick. At the very back of the yard were two outhouses, lined up squarely against the back fence.

Adjacent to one of the outhouses was a blacksmith's shed and a large hearth with iron thongs, rakes, and pokers leaning against it. Opposing it was an iron stand to support a horse during shoeing. Hentie noted one of the enslaved men had just tidied up the farrier's box with multiple shelves and organized boxes of tools and nails. The box held an assortment of interesting items, like the metal rasp used to scrap the hoof. She had seen one used at the plantation. An anvil, forging hammer, and cross peen hammer lay nearby. Close to this was a wood and coal house; no doubt it provided the fuel to keep the fires going.

Livestock sauntered through the work yard, and chickens clucked as they scurried. There was a cow house adjacent to the stables and the carriage house, but one cow must have gotten loose, as it roamed around with a goat. There was a modest-sized garden toward the back of the lot that held a variety of vegetables and herbs. A few fruit trees were nearby, including a peach, an apple, and a fig tree. Closer to the mansion was the kitchen house, with good smells emanating from it. It seemed the back lot had everything necessary to make a large and genteel household hum with efficiency.

Hentie and Octavia looked up toward the house and saw a cheerful black woman waving to them from the back porch. The woman was shouting, "Octavia, you're here!"

Octavia shouted, "Lydia!"

Lydia scrambled down the back steps and rushed to greet Octavia. The two shared a warm embrace, then Lydia stepped back and said, "My, am I happy to see you! And who do you have with you today?"

"Let me introduce you to my good friend, Hentie. She works with me for Master Langdon."

Lydia grinned broadly at Hentie, saying, "I'm happy to meet you."

The three women walked over to a long wooden table under a large shade tree. It was where the enslaved ate most of their meals. The women sat and talked about their respective lives, laughing and chattering away. The warmth and friendliness between the women flowed freely.

While Lydia had been heartbroken when she was sold to the Simmons family and separated from her sister, she was grateful that she periodically had contact with her. Lydia also grew fond of her current mistress and her life in downtown Charleston. This slave-owning family was far more reasonable in their treatment of Lydia. The master had rarely used the lash. Negroes were seemingly treated better in the city than in the outlying plantations.

In Lydia's new life in the city, she had a variety of duties as an enslaved domestic in the main house and was gaining close instruction from an older worker about her developing role as a seamstress. She had made progress honing her sewing skills and had started to create a more complicated dress just that week. This was a skill she might someday use to earn money to support herself, should she ever be free. That was her dream, to no longer be owned by another human being. No one to tell her what to do, no fears of being sold off to another family. Seemed like such a simple idea, but the reality of it was so far away. The women sat and pondered what life could be like if they were free, a dream seemingly out of reach.

Chapter 8
City Life for Black Charlestonians

Lydia, Hentie, and Octavia chatted for over an hour. They shared confidences, told of their hardships, and laughed about lighter moments. Eventually the women decided to go for a walk toward the Battery down at the end of the peninsula. There was the beautiful city park and the harbor just beyond it.

"Come on, y'all, let's go down to the waterfront," urged Lydia. "You can't come this far and not take a gander at the sea close up. You can see the topsails moored in the harbor and some of the nearby islands!"

"Oh my! That would be fine, real fine. I've never seen the waterfront from down here," said Hentie. A horrid memory of the slaver ship landing on Sullivan's Island popped into her mind, but she shook it loose, not wanting to think of that grisly time.

The ladies walked down to the waterfront and enjoyed the view of the ocean. They took in the intense smell of fish and oysters and the briny air about them. As they looked out, they saw pelicans dive straight as blades into the water. Ships moved about in the harbor. They listened to the sharp whistle of steam engines and the slap of sails and boat lines in the wind. The cool breeze wafted over them as they took it all in.

Lydia shouted, "Look, you can see the new Fort Sumter! See the flag?" This installation would later play an important role for the South. Lydia suddenly suggested, "Let's walk up to Rainbow Row! The houses are so pretty up there. They're pretty shades of pink and blue."

So, the ladies turned northward to view the houses, casually strolling and talking, Lydia pointing out sites as they walked.

Lydia said, "My mistress told me that this is how they paint their houses down in the Caribbean. The white men who founded Charleston were sugar plantation owners down there and brought enslaved blacks to the city. Those slaves built these houses and painted them the same colors used down there, pink, apricot, and yellow. Some of the black folks say these colors help them to remember which houses to make the deliveries to; the different colors makes it easier for them."

At the tip of the lower peninsula was the most beautiful section of Charleston, where lovely gardens were maintained. Much of the land had originally been marshland and was filled in so that mansions and a park could be constructed on this valuable real estate. Initially it was called Oyster Point, then later White Point. In the 1830s the city would have gardens installed, as well as beautiful pagodas and broad and serpentine walks along the Battery. It was a lovely promenade for Charleston's wealthy citizenry to stroll. Charleston's social pyramid, almost like a caste system, was vigorously enforced by the white aristocrats, such as the Middletons, Grimkés, Pinckneys, Heywards, Draytons, Manigaults, and Alstons. Laws had been enacted forbidding Negroes from walking in the area from five to ten in the evenings so as not to stain the view. While Lydia resented the restriction, she was able to walk in the park with her mistress in the afternoon and enjoy the sea air.

On this day while on their walk, the three companions passed another enslaved worker, Josiah, who was also owned by the Simmons family, the same family that owned Lydia. He stayed in the slave quarters behind the mansion house, but he was rented out to assist with mining phosphate rock on Wadmalaw Island. He earned six dollars a month, and the master let him keep one dollar of it. It was hard, dangerous work that he performed. Phosphate, a naturally created, potent fertilizer, was used in the city's gardens and in the fields of the surrounding plantations. Phosphate was a steady and reliable source of income for some of the families around Charleston and the Lowcountry. It supplemented the inconsistent income from cash crops. As the ladies passed him, Lydia noted that the pale residue she typically saw on his hands and work clothes was absent this day; he also didn't carry that odd odor that usually accompanied the mining of the rock. As he approached, Lydia nodded and smiled brightly at him.

"Hey, Josiah, how you doin'? I'm glad you're out enjoying the sunshine today."

"How you doin', Lydia? You lovely ladies just brightened my day." Josiah smiled as he looked over the three women. "The mistress let you leave the grounds with yo' company?"

"Yes, my sister comes and visits me as often as she can, sometimes once a month, other times not so often. The missus lets us visit and walk in the area. Let me introduce you to my sister, Octavia, and her friend Hentie. We're just going for a walk down around the harbor."

"You ladies keep safe. You know the white folks sometimes don't like us black folks down around here," Josiah urged as he tipped his cap to them.

"We'll be careful. It helps that there is three of us, instead of just one or two," Lydia pointed out. The ladies moved on and waved goodbye to Josiah.

As the women made their way through the city, they passed an array of people with differing skin tones and dress, reflecting the diverse mix of people who lived in Charleston. Most notable were the fair-skinned city dwellers of English extraction; these aristocrats controlled much of the goings-on in the city. But there were other immigrants and their kith as well. Among them were French Huguenots who left their homeland to escape religious persecution, as did Eastern Europeans in the area. There were Scottish, Irish, and German immigrants, who formed most of the working class, along with the free Negroes, often referred to as "free people of color." The enslaved black workers and free people of color seemed to make up most of the population, more than half, something that stood in stark contrast to other American cities. Most enslaved Negroes who lived in the city were domestic servants of a kind. Some two-thirds served in this capacity, which put them in close quarters with their masters. Most were well groomed and spoke proper English. They comported themselves in a mannerly fashion. The remaining one-quarter worked in a wide variety of occupations, including mechanics, blacksmiths, masons, and seamstresses.

The presence of the enslaved Gullah workers throughout the city was vivid and indispensable; they were the lifeblood. They lived and worked in close proximity to elite whites, and no Charlestonian could imagine the city functioning without the benefit of its enslaved workers. Northerners who visited were often impressed by the visually profound impact the Gullah had on the intercourse of the city. Young Negro children romped in the streets, the women wore colorful headscarves, and the men worked to the rhythms of gospel songs, hollering to one another in their own special Gullah language with its melodic tones.

In the short time since the friends had started their walk, heavier clouds had moved in. The sky grew dark, tinctured with an approaching storm. The Battery was no longer the welcoming place it had been earlier in the day; it became more foreboding. Wind blew in their faces, bringing with it the smell of rain and oleander. The clouds dripped halfheartedly. Flecks of white foam drifting off the whitecaps, waves crashed against the Charleston Bar, a series of submerged shoals. The marsh grass pitched wildly around the edges of the city. The steeples of Saint Philips and Saint Michael's tossed dark shadows. In the distance, they heard the lonely whistle of an incoming train.

With bad weather on its way, the three returned to Lydia's house, quickening their step as they progressed up the street to home.

Chapter 9

Nominal Slaves and the Saint Cecilia Society

After the three women returned to the Lydia's home, they entered the slave quarters to dodge the incoming rain. The rain splattered the outdoor tables and equipment. The chickens started to cluck and scurry to the henhouse. The ladies spoke briefly with some of the other enslaved servants who lived on the grounds and quenched their thirst with cool water. Lydia brought out dried apricots and leftover bread for them to enjoy. As they sat and broke bread, they heard the raindrops hit the hard-packed ground outside.

After they settled in a bit and began to chat, Lydia brought out a quilt she had been working on. The chocolaty smell of the oleander leaves streamed in through the door. At times the odor was sickeningly thick. Disregarding the scent, Lydia displayed her impressive needlework; the bright array of fabric scraps she had used was striking. Since she was doing a great deal of sewing in the big house, she had access to an assortment of fabric scraps. The quilt was a wedding-ring design she hoped to use one day.

While sitting at the table with the quilt spread out, a friend of Lydia's stopped by the slave quarters. Tilly was considered a "nominal slave" and was given a fair amount of freedom despite being an enslaved woman. She was permitted to freely walk throughout the city, but she still had to observe the curfew for Negroes.

A minister at a local Methodist church technically owned her; he paid one dollar to hold ownership and agreed to care for her. He arranged for her to have a room in the home of a parishioner. She lived in a small house in the Neck, a neighborhood on the Charleston peninsula's northernmost end. It abutted the original city wall. Nearly every day, Tilly walked southward to the city's Battery and surrounding shopping district. She ran a small business of sorts; she was a talented dressmaker. All the white ladies on the Battery loved her work. Tilly was able to copy the latest fashion garments and sew beautiful embellishments. She had become quite successful with her business and gave pointers to Lydia about the trade.

Her owner, the minister, took his cut of her income. While it was kind of him to sponsor her as he did, he still made a tidy profit from her skills and standing in the community. Tilly sometimes resented the cut he took from her profits, but she dared not offend him as her life circumstances could change in an instant if she aroused his ire. She could lose her business, be forced to turn over all her savings, and be sold to a different slave owner.

Most of Tilly's customers assumed she was a free person of color. Having a somewhat lighter complexion, she was able to fit into the middle social strata of Charleston. The city had formed three social levels. At the bottom tier were dark-skinned enslaved workers. At the top were white elites. In the middle were the brown-skinned free people of color who were generally educated, were trained in a skilled trade, and presented themselves with white, genteel social graces. Tilly fell into that middle tier.

Tilly spoke with enthusiasm when she told her friend, "I'm designing three gowns for a rich white woman, Mrs. Theodore

Gourdin, who lives on East Bay Street. I am using a pattern as the foundation, but I'm adding a lot of my own special touches. I think they will turn out real nice. I hope they are happy with the gowns. It could really help my sewing business."

"Oh my, how exciting for you!" Lydia said.

Tilly went on with eyes wide. "I know them white folks want all kinds of fancy dresses for their cotillions. There's two for the missus, then one for her teenage daughter. They're making such a fuss about it all. I guess it's something real important for all the rich white folks around here."

"Um, um, um. They have time for all them fancy affairs just to show off. They all tryin' to outdo each other," said Lydia.

"The first gown I'm making is for the missus to wear Easter Sunday. She wanted a pretty spring frock, she said. She picked out some pretty fabric, a lemon yellow with green trim. Ordered it from England. Then there's the upcoming spring ball hosted by the St. Cecilia Society. It's a real big deal for white folks in Charleston. Only certain people can be a member."

Octavia chimed in to the conversation. "I think I heard about that, Tilly. I think only men can be a member of the society if their relatives were from England or something. Gots to be rich with a good family name. Women can come as a guest but can't be a member. I heard Master Langdon talk about it. He and the missus go to it."

"I think you're right about that. Some fancy rich folk's thing. Anyhow, Missus Gourdin's daughter is to be presented as a debutante at the ball. That means she is coming out a woman for the first time and can get married to someone. She really has to look beautiful that night, so she can get some wealthy man with land. I am using a real elaborate white silk with Venetian lace for her gown. She'll look like an angel from heaven. Sure will. They're fixin' to hold this dance down at the Hibernian Hall. Them white folks sure know how to throw themselves a fancy party!"

⌒⁀

The dark-cobalt skies seemed to pass.

"We best get a move on. We have a ways to walk until we reach our meeting point up by the market. I hate to leave you, but I'll see you next month. I promise," said Octavia.

"I best be going too. I gots lots of sewing to do tonight. Can't disappoint them white folks," said Tilly as she moved toward the door. "I'll try to stop by sometime next week. It was nice meeting you ladies." Tilly waved and walked out the back gate, leaving the three enslaved women by themselves.

"Yes, don't want to leave Big John waiting," said Hentie.

Lydia walked them to the door. She gave Octavia a long, warm hug and teared up. "I miss you so. I wish we still lived in the same place."

"I miss you too," Octavia said, her warmth shining through. She squeezed her sister's hand and said, "At least we get to share times like these together."

Lydia reached into the pocket of her dress and pulled out two objects. "Here, take these stones with you. These lodestones are for you and your friend."

"What is it?" Hentie inquired, looking down at the reddish-brown stones. She glanced over at Octavia with a quizzical look.

"They are special stones with unique powers, lodestones. They pull in good luck while pushing away the evil. I got them from a lady down by the market who practices good hoodoo. They will protect you on your travels."

A chill tiptoed up Hentie's spine. Speaking of dark spirits this way made the fine hairs on the nape of her neck bristle. Hentie had heard others speak of hoodoo, a form of folk magic, but usually it referred to dark practices, not protection. She knew of its practice in Africa and then heard of it at Twin Oaks through Mimba. She knew of others putting a "fix" or a curse on someone they disliked, but she had never really understood the full extent of its power. Hentie also heard of measures one could take to allay evil, but she wasn't sure what to make of it all.

They took the stones, thanking Lydia for her kind gift. Hentie quickly tucked the stone in her dress pocket, then patted it from the outside. After the confrontation with the dockworkers near the store on King Street, she thought they could use extra protection.

Hentie and Octavia met with Big John later that afternoon, as agreed, on the corner of Bay Street and Market, near Market Hall. The ladies were tired from their walk, but happy and fulfilled from their visit with Lydia and Tilly. Big John was giddy as he had just spent the afternoon with friends and had won several hands of cards. He happily jingled a few coins in his pocket. The skies were cloudy and continued to sprinkle a bit, so the friends decided to hastily head back to Twin Oaks. Big John helped the ladies climb into the wagon, his hand lingering on Hentie's back just a moment longer. Then everyone got settled. Hentie checked her pocket to see if the lodestone was still there. She ran her hand across its smooth surface and hoped the stone would surround them with a cloak of protection during their travels.

The friends chatted as they rolled along the streets toward the ferry. In the center of the city, the streets were paved and lined with pride-of-India trees, but the streets away from the city's center were crushed shell mixed with sand. Apparently, the crushed-shell mixture was a remnant of the city's Caribbean heritage, founded by English descendants from Barbados. As the wagon pulled up to the levee, Hentie glanced over at Big John and noted his firm grip on the reins. The friends loaded their rig onto a flatboat that took them slowly but surely across the Cooper River back home to Mount Pleasant.

Upon reaching the other side of the river, the three settled back into the wagon and rolled down the levee to the main road. The rhythm of the horses' harnesses jingling along with the clop of their hooves was hypnotic, and Hentie was almost lulled into a trance.

The friends chattered about their day and the lovely things they had seen in the city. Big John smirked as he talked about his card-playing friends who so generously gave him their money.

Hentie popped her hand into her pocket again. This time the stone felt hot; it almost seemed to burn in her hand. She let it loosely roll around in her palm, wondering what had caused such a difference in its temperature. A bolt of lightning struck at a distance, and a few beats later the thunder rumbled through. Big John announced, "We best get home. Looks like the skies are gonna open on us!" With that he gave a snap of the reins and hollered to the horses, "Giddy up!"

The two mares picked up speed, but then abruptly pulled to the left, and one reared.

"What they doin'?" hollered Big John, puzzled by their actions. He looked down on the road, then saw a cottonmouth snake edging out onto the roadway.

"Ah Lord, it's a snake!"

Octavia shrieked and grabbed Hentie's arm. Hentie froze with fright and gritted her teeth. Big John stepped down from the wagon and approached the horses to soothe them. He spoke calmly and carefully paced out his steps. The snake paused, then wriggled further onto the road, rearing its triangular head, exposing its fangs. Hentie saw the pits between its eyes and nostrils. Its eyes had a cat-like elliptical shape and an evil look to them. Its long, muscular body powered across the roadway.

"Oh God, it's about to strike! Dear Lord, help me. Help me now!"

Hentie reached into her pocket and furiously rubbed the stone. Another bolt of lightning lashed out, followed by thunder. This time the lightning struck a nearby tree, causing it to explode and split. The boom jolted Hentie from her seat. A branch went flying, and a sizeable prong of the branch pierced the head of the snake, crushing its skull and nailing it to the ground. It wriggled in death throes a while, then lay still, dead.

Big John sprang back onto the rig and said, "We best get out of here!" With a hasty snap of the reins, the horses sped off. The wagon bobbled hectically down the lane as Big John urged the horses onward. The hysteria continued until the trio reached the front of the plantation and turned onto the avenue of oaks. Home at last!

Chapter 10
Denmark Vesey and the Uprising

O ne day, word about a planned uprising of black men, enslaved and free, came through the community like wildfire. Lydia heard the news while shopping in the market. She was browsing over the fresh produce while keeping her coins safely tucked into her skirt pocket.

The open-air City Market was a bustling place; black vendors, known as higglers, sold fresh, good-quality fruits, vegetables, meats, and seafood to the residents of Charleston and surrounding areas. It could be a dodgy place, though. Butchers threw out fat trimmings that were quickly scooped up by waiting vultures, birds protected by a city ordinance as winged collectors of refuse. Women pushed their way through stalls, trying to snap up the choicer selections of beef and pork, while others tried to snag a free loose peach or a handful of pecans. Then there were those unsavory characters who with sleight of hand could lift a purse or pouch full of coins. For many of them, it was a means of survival.

Lydia was looking for hearty vegetables and a good cut of meat for the evening meal. As she rifled through a stack of mustard greens, her friend Tilly sidled up beside her and greeted her in hushed tones.

"Follow me down this alley so we can talk. Keep your voice low."

The two tiptoed away, eventually finding sanctuary under a broad, craggy oak tree. Tilly's eyes darted about as they tucked themselves between the oak and a crepe myrtle, the sagging blossoms helping to conceal them.

"Did you hear of the planned slave uprising? The white buckra found out about it and they are all worked up. They got a Negro man named Denmark Vesey down in the jail. He's a big man round here. God only knows what they will do to him," Tilly said.

"Where is he from? Why he so big?" asked Lydia.

"He lives in a nice house up on Bull Street. He came here from the Caribbean," said Tilly. "He's been important round here, over at the church. He does some of the preaching. He knows the Bible inside and out—quotes it all the time. He's educated; he can read and write. He can speak all kinds of languages. He can even speak French."

"What church is that? The black folks church?" asked Lydia.

"Over at the Mother Emanuel AME Church. He preaches over there. He gets the folks all worked up." Tilly's eyes grew wide as she spoke, and she raised her arms. "He supports them and raises the people up. He's a free man; he makes everyone want to be free. He stirs them to want more in their lives. He teaches them about resistance to the white buckra and tells them to learn to read. Vesey, along with his men, Peter Poyas, Monday Gell, and Gullah Jack, talk about liberation, saying we're like the Israelites. We need to find our freedom just like they did."

Tilly went on to explain, "Vesey won a bunch of money in the lottery, then he bought his freedom. He been working as a carpenter ever since. He's a big brawny man and saw some ugly things as a child. As a boy he had been working on a sugar plantation in Haiti when he was picked up and put on a slave ship. His master thought he was a quick-witted, good-looking boy and kept him as a cabin boy. He worked on a slave ship for a long time with his master. Working that way made Denmark real mad. He saw too much ugliness."

"Ah, that poor man," murmured Lydia as she shook her head.

"Months ago, the white folks burned down his church. It meant so much to him. It was just one too many heartaches. Denmark couldn't stand the white folks taking yet another thing from him. He was free, but he couldn't stand what they were doing to the black man. He had to do something," huffed Tilly.

"Oh my. I heard his name before, but I never knew all this about him," said Lydia.

"The uprising was going to happen on Sunday at midnight, but someone told the damn white buckra about the plan. You know, there were thousands of men involved with this plot. All the names were kept in a black book by Denmark and his men. The police, they got a house servant to tell them about the scheme. They tortured that poor man for hours before he gave up what he knew." Tilly paused, looked down, and shook her head before going on.

"But now they are fixing to hang ole Denmark. They got him and dozens of other black men locked up at the Work House. I don't want to think of what they might be doing to them. For sure they are going to hang. But you best watch yourself. All the black folks here in danger. The City Guard and militia all over town. They are fixing to do something, just don't know what yet. Lord God, protect us now!" Tilly gasped as she spoke. "Them poor men! It's gonna be ugly. They are planning a special hearing. Ain't no hearing at all; there's no jury, there's no real evidence. They are just planning to hang them all! It be making all the white folks crazy." Tilly had sweat beading above her lip, her eyes wide, her movements frantic.

Tilly looked deep into Lydia's eyes with worry. "How the white buckra gonna treat all us?"

Lydia's mind raced with thoughts of the slave patrol, the city jail and the wailing of black men. She worried how planters might treat their slaves with this discovery. Masters on the plantations were often more brutal than those in the city. Lydia thought of her sister, Octavia, back on the plantation, and the others who had been so kind to her. She looked around the market for someone from Twin Oaks Plantation.

"I best go, Tilly. I want to see if my sister might be near, or someone from Twin Oaks."

"You watch yourself, now. Try to be safe." Tilly grabbed Lydia's arm, her eyes narrowed, and she said, "Hear me now?"

"I hear you. You keep safe too. Lord only know what can happen to the colored man now," Lydia said as she turned and walked away.

Struggling with her basket and parcels, made more cumbersome by her layers of skirts and worn button-up boots, she searched the crowd, darting in and out and nearly turning over a vegetable cart. Then she spotted Big John, who stood well above the rest. She should have known he would be there. He typically accompanied the master and his family to the market.

"Big John! Big John!" she shouted when she spotted him.

Big John's head swung about when he heard the panic in Lydia's voice. Then he saw the concern in her eyes. He gently touched her shoulder and said, "What's wrong? You okay?"

"Oh my!" Lydia replied. "Terrible news! There's been an attempt at an uprising against the white folks. The Negroes planning it was caught. God only knows what they will do to the poor men!" The two went on to discuss their fears, not only for the men involved in the plot, but for themselves and the others on the plantation.

"What can we do, Big John? White folks gonna be crazy about this!" exclaimed Lydia.

"I don't know. We gots to be calm. Don't draw attention to yourself. Don't give the white man any excuse to strike out. Can't have no uprising. Besides," Big John added, "even if we kill all the white folks, what we do then? Where we go? Gots no money. Most black folks can't read nor cypher."

As the two stood by the market trying to figure out what to do next, they heard the steady clomp of boots in the distance, then the shouting of men, startling them. They drew up, tense and alert, and turned toward the commotion. Three slave women broke past them, scampering across the road as they held their skirts above the mud puddles. Marching toward them was a cluster of South Carolina militia, sabers drawn, some pistols drawn too. The formation was flanked by the City Guard, looking stern, carrying muskets. Horrified, Big John quickly pushed Lydia against the side of a building. They stood stick straight and frozen in place until the clamoring guard had passed.

Big John clamped onto Lydia's arm with fear in his eyes. "You best get home. Now! You take to the back alleys. You duck into doorways and get home quick. Don't walk on the streets. God know what they might do." In a moment, they parted. Flashing a look back at John, Lydia saw that he was watching as she scurried down the street.

Once Big John was back at the plantation, he shared the news with the others. Everyone was fearful for the captured men. What would they do to them? Undoubtedly, they would face a brutal death. There was talk that the men would have a trial, but everyone knew that there would be no justice. The judge, the white planters, and others had already made up their minds.

The long-harbored fears of the plantation owners and other townspeople seemed well founded. Ever since the Stono Rebellion in 1739 and the San Dominique slave rebellion in 1796, whites held a deep-seated fear of another uprising.

The apparent instigator of the plan, Denmark Vesey, was a free person of color. When he won $1,500 in a lottery, he paid his owner, Captain Vesey, $600 for his freedom, even though he was worth more than that. Denmark was just thirty-three, healthy, smart, and physically fit when he gained his freedom. He had always had a powerful build and was very energetic, walking miles every day. He had numerous wives, as many as seven, at various ports. He had two sons and several stepchildren. He was known to be unkind to them at times.

His influence in the black community was due to his good looks, intelligence, physical agility, and bold force of personality. Over time he became a beacon of hope. He presented himself as a black minister and even the black messiah, with his superior knowledge of the Bible. Vesey combined Christianity, Islam, and elements of African religious beliefs into a moral crusade for black freedom. While he was free to leave South Carolina and travel to other regions of America or other countries, he chose to remain in Charleston. He wanted to stay "and see what he could do for his fellow creatures."

Word rumbled through the black community that Denmark had carefully planned out the uprising over a period of years. Every detail was considered, and recruits from miles away were committed to the plan. Men of color were carefully chosen for their loyalty to the cause and their emotional distance from their masters. House servants were rarely trusted due to their close alliance with their white owners. Women were not recruited, not so much because they could not be trusted, but because they did not want their children to become motherless in the event of violent death.

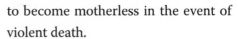

The scheme was to be kept a safely guarded secret. The uprising had to unfold with complete surprise, otherwise the white slave owners would surely quell the plan. Those involved were warned that plantation owners would use the services of the Work House and, perhaps, the brutal hanging hook as punishment.

Weapons had been stockpiled for

three or four years; some were stolen, others were handcrafted. Pikes and cartridges were made at meetings, then hidden for later use. Those in on the plan met monthly at Bulkley's Farm, selected because a lower-level overseer on that plantation was one of the initiated. The farm was accessible by water, so members could elude the City Guard when traveling there.

Clusters of black conspirators had planned to seize the arms in the arsenal and the guardhouse in the city and around the Neck. The others would come from islands surrounding the city of Charleston and assemble near the Battery. Armed men from the countryside were to advance from the Neck, the northernmost part of the Charleston peninsula. This legion of men made up six infantry and cavalry companies. The combined forces were to join and commence their slaughter of whites throughout Charleston, thereby gaining their freedom. On their way from the bloodbath they would seize whatever money, goods, and firearms might be to their advantage. The city was then to be burned to the ground with explosives and incendiary devices. The men would then leave the city by boat. They hoped to travel to Haiti, perhaps even Africa. The plan was to unfold at midnight on the appointed day. However, the conspiracy was uncovered days before its planned execution, and the plot was thwarted.

⌣

A hearing was held for the charged men in a small, cramped room of the second story of the Work House. There was no jury; typical courtroom and evidentiary protocols were suspended. Common law principles were waived. The bench was composed not of sworn judges, but a pro tempore panel of freeholders who themselves were slave owners acting as hearing officers. Most had no legal training whatsoever. Among those who took the bench in this case were James Legare, James R. Pringle, and William Drayton. They acted as both prosecutor and judge.

Black men under arrest, both free and enslaved, gave testimony against Vesey. Oral evidence was often conflictual, some seemingly coerced. Throughout the proceedings against him, Vesey was unmoved and detached. Often sitting with his arms crossed, he looked down, concealing his thoughts. Vesey was permitted to conduct cross-examination of those black men who testified against him. He used sound judgment in the delivery of his penetrating questions, picking up on the line of argument used by the court.

One associate justice of the US Supreme Court, William Johnson, anonymously made a submission to the *Charleston Courier*, which was then printed. Johnson suggested that the proceedings and execution were nothing more than legal murder. Clearly, the trial had not been an impartial court proceeding which implemented equitable and legal principles. It was a mockery.

There was uncorroborated testimony of one prosecution witness who testified Vesey had spoken of seizing weapons and rising up against the white man for freedom. There were no details to this assertion. There was no tangible evidence, such as the list of alleged coconspirators, stockpiles of weapons, incendiary devices, guns, ammunition, or any other items which might have shown motive or intent. During the course of the trial there were no defense witnesses whatsoever. Sometime later it would be suggested that the planned uprising was nothing more than disgruntled men engaged in loose talk. Perhaps a scapegoat was sought due to concerns about the stability of the price of cotton, which was fluctuating as much as four cents a pound. Cotton controlled the entire economy of the Deep South, and it had people nervous.

Despite his sound defense work, Vesey and numerous others were ultimately found guilty and sentenced to death. A total of thirty-five were executed. Twenty-two codefendants were hanged on Line Street in a depressed black area on the west side of the city. They were left to swing in the wind for days, intended as a brutal reminder of how uppity blacks would be dealt with in the future. This gruesome site was intended to strike terror in the heart of every slave so that they would never take such action again.

Denmark Vesey's hanging was surreptitiously performed just blocks away from his twenty-two cohorts, probably from the Ashely Avenue oak tree, later known as "the hanging tree," from which black victims would be lynched for decades to come. The tree, which at one point was chopped down, was replanted and remained on the streets of Charleston into the following millennium. Vesey's subsequent burial was secretly performed under the cover of darkness so the grave site would not be used to glorify his martyrdom. Whites harbored fear that the black community would use his death and suffering as a rallying cry. Surprisingly, however, Negroes were permitted to wear black to signify their mourning.

In addition to those hung, a large number of alleged coconspirators were banished from South Carolina. Those dispelled included one of Vesey's sons. They were ousted from the entire United States. The Vesey affair sent shock waves across the South, and it prompted Charleston officials to crack down on its African American population by tearing down the Mother Emanuel AME Church, curtailing the few liberties afforded free blacks, and tightening slave supervision.

After the incident and while the hearings were going on, not much was printed in the local papers, but tongues wagged with details and fears of the local citizenry. After the hangings, two publications were printed, one by the two justices who presided over the hearings, and a second by the mayor of Charleston. Both gave a cursory overview of events, emphasizing what they considered to be poor management and supervision of the slave population. An accusatorial finger was pointed at those Negroes who were hired out and lacked accountability or supervision. It was thought that most of those involved were laborers of some variety who had been rented out and who had certain allotted hours at their own disposal, during which they could meet and share conspirator ideas.

Following the foiled uprising and the criminal proceedings,

white citizens were chastised for their lax ways. Conservative and proslavery leaders called for a harsh and unequivocal response to the affair. Secretary of War John C. Calhoun quietly relocated military officers and troops sympathetic to slaveholders to the Deep South to better manage activities.

Numerous laws and protective measures were put into place to guard white Charlestonians against another such occurrence. The City Guard was given six horses so that mounted patrols could cover more territory searching for potential Negro attackers. This force, and the armed men dressed in uniforms who made up the armed guard, were attached to the Citadel. They maintained careful vigil to keep the city's Negroes completely subordinate. The guard enforced the city's expansive Black Code, which became even more restrictive.

Shortly after this, Charles Pinckney rose to the defense of slavery in an address on the floor of Congress. He contended that South Carolina needed to move away from nationalism and toward extreme sectionalism. He was opposed to federal tariffs that were geared toward federal improvements and protective tariffs that predominately benefitted Northern and Western states but were detrimental to South Carolina, with its slave-based economy. Thereafter, Robert J. Turnbull, in a series of articles in the local newspaper, the *Mercury*, noted the growing strain between the federal government and the state of South Carolina. He promoted what he termed "disunion," or breaking away from the rest of the union. He introduced the concept of a state being able to nullify an act of the federal government that was detrimental to it. Another Charlestonian, James Hamilton Jr., a former intendant (mayor) and soon-to-be governor, first coined the term "nullification" as he protested a tariff imposed by the federal government on international trade, the Tariff of Abominations of 1828. Following this, the South Carolina state legislature adopted the Exposition and Protest, secretly written by John C. Calhoun, now vice president, who, like Turnbull, argued that the protective tariff was unconstitutional. Calhoun would later become the champion of what was termed the Nullification Crisis, contending that the state of South Carolina could determine within its state court system whether or not they needed to follow federal law. It was his position that the matter need not be determined in the United States Supreme Court, a proposition without legal merit. This line of thinking seemed to spark secessionist ideals.

The hysteria about slavery and maintaining the South's peculiar institution persisted. With the distribution of literature promoting abolitionist ideas banned, even talk of it was quashed. It seemed all discussion about fairness and equality for Negroes was quelled. Those who harbored such ideas kept the notions as closely guarded secrets for fear of reprisal. It remained this way for decades to come.

Chapter 11
Planter Summers Away

The horse-drawn carriage came up over a hill, and in the distance Hentie could make out a row of white cottages.

The carriage driver shouted, "There she is, that beautiful lady!"

Finally, they had arrived at White Sulphur Springs, the resort that would later be known as the Greenbrier. The sight of it was overwhelming. All neat and tidy, there in the middle of dark-green foliage were a series of well-kept buildings. Hentie drew in a deep breath, taking in the enchanting place.

"Oh my," she murmured.

Hentie glanced across the carriage to Octavia to see her expression; her brown eyes had grown wide, and she broke into a broad grin. Even the missus started to giggle and gently bounce in her seat, much like a young child. Hentie had never seen anything so grand in her entire life. It was such a contrast to the wild thickets and trees she had seen over the last hundred treacherous miles. Hentie was weary. They had been traveling for days, first by train, and then they toiled along in horse-drawn carriages over rough mountain roads, stopping in taverns and roadhouses.

Now May, the high crest of spring, the day was mild and sunny, with cornflower-blue skies that served as a beautiful backdrop against the impressive white buildings in the complex. The air was free of mosquitos and other flying creatures so endemic to the Deep South, and fragrant with the intoxicating magnolias, camellias, and crepe myrtle. Hentie was overwhelmed by the beauty of the grounds: the trimmed hedges, the huge white oak shade trees, along with an assortment of spring flowers. The blossoming trees and bushes were at the height of their color, creating stunning shades of coral, fuchsia, violet, and pale pink.

Dust kicked up under the carriage wheels, and Hentie felt grimy with it. She glanced over to the mistress and saw her try to beat the road dirt from her skirt, then sigh as she gave up the battle. Hentie knew not to complain—not of grime, not of hunger, not of anything else, particularly after the long, arduous journey. The mistress saw this trip as a special treat for her enslaved help, and she frequently reminded them of their good fortune.

As the carriage drew closer to the resort, rows of scarlet-red rose bushes came into view. She took in the vivid colors and noticed a bursting red rose on the doorman's lapel that must have come from one of the bushes. He tipped his hat to the occupants of their barouche as he reached for the carriage door. The women inside glanced at one another and drew in a collective breath, the missus making an audible sound of relief when she heard the metallic *click* of the coach door; at last their long trek had concluded. The carriage door swung open, and the missus rose out of her seat. The skirts of her traveling suit rustled as she moved toward the gaping coach door. Taking the hand of the footman, she glanced about the grounds as her booted foot touched down, feeling the front walk of the hotel.

Although the journey was long, Hentie felt blessed to ride in the coach with the missus and Octavia. It was taxing and at times terrifying due to the perils of the roads, but now it was over. The family could relax and be pampered for the entire social season. The Langdons and their enslaved workers had made it to White Sulphur Springs, the most spectacular of the numerous sulfur springs hotels in western Virginia. These resorts, nestled into the Allegheny Mountains, were a refuge to many elite Southerners and to a few wealthy Northerners. This Virginian haven was a getaway that many looked forward to all year. It was also the most critical venue for one's social standing. It was *the* place to see and be seen.

Mrs. Langdon was followed out of the carriage by Hentie and Octavia, her lady's maid. In a coach that followed the women was Mr. Langdon, his young son, Fitzwilliam, his nephew Adrian Langdon, and Big John. Mr. Langdon had briefly ridden in the front coach but was driven to distraction by his wife's giddiness and excitement over their pending arrival. Therefore, he chose to ride with the other men in the second carriage. This second rig carried most of the trunks and bags loaded with Mrs. Langdon's fine gowns and accoutrements, as well as the personal belongings of the rest of the party. Two fine steeds tied to the second rig were for the men to ride into the mountains while they were on their holiday. At times, Mr. Langdon and Adrian had chosen to ride horseback rather than be shaken up in the carriages, thereby giving the horses a bit more exercise and freedom of movement.

Mister Langdon strolled into the main building of the Old White Hotel and tapped the bell on the counter. A darkly clad gentleman came out from the office adjacent to the guest registration desk and smiled broadly at Mister Langdon and his party.

"The name is Langdon. We have reservations in our cottage up on Carolina Row. I believe you should have received our correspondence about it some time ago," he blared out with authority.

"Oh yes, sir. I noticed that you would be arriving today. We've been expecting you. Your cottage has been freshened for you and your family." He nodded and smiled at him.

The desk agent then went on to say, "I believe you have stayed with us before, so I will just briefly remind you of the layout of the resort. Here in this building we have a number of guest rooms upstairs; a gentleman from Charleston, Mr. Charles Pinckney, is in one of those rooms. He wanted to see you sometime after your arrival. Then we have the parlor, a dining room, and the ballroom. I'm sure you and your wife will want to visit with friends at our evening cotillions. But you will be staying in your quarters in one of the Carolina cottages. One of the finer ones, I must say."

Mister Langdon nodded in agreement. The check-in process completed, the family went on their way. Mister Langdon took great pride in having a stately cottage commensurate with his station in life. He had built the dwelling a few seasons before; it was more akin to a small, elegant house than a cottage, situated further back on the resort. The family traveled through the well-manicured grounds past clusters of other cottages and outbuildings, all in perfect condition. The missus rolled her eyes as they passed Young Bucks Row, where the bachelors stayed, and Wolf Row, where drunken late-night parties were known to occur. She thought it unbecoming that such activities were permitted on the grounds.

At last the Langdons arrived at their own home situated on one of the more exclusive sites. Securing a room at the resort was a very competitive process. Many hopeful travelers were turned away without proper credentials and recommendations from other known guests. Wealthier families sometimes chose to build their own accommodations. The Langdons' cottage was one of a limited number constructed for select aristocratic families who could afford this indulgence. While the Langdons paid for the component parts of the cottage, the resort controlled the style, location, and specifications of the dwelling, thereby assuring continuity of architecture and consistency of style for the neat rows of similarly designed cottages. These cottages would continue to be the most exclusive accommodations for generations to come.

The opulent surroundings of the bungalow were breathtaking. The luxurious cottage was strategically situated in the middle of verdant, manicured lawns, skillfully shaped topiary, and pruned rose bushes. Wisteria vine webbed the windows with branches as thick as Big John's arm, and lovely blossoms dangled. The porch provided an astonishing view of the surrounding grounds and the mountains which hugged the expansive resort. Hentie and the other members of her party took in their surroundings, feeling blessed to be away from the heat and bustle of Charleston and the plantation in the spring. Here they could relax in the cool mountain air and enjoy a respite away from Twin Oaks. As the Langdons directed the unpacking of the carriages, other Carolinian guests strolled past to their cottages.

Colonel Richard Singleton and his family were just returning from taking in the waters at the main springhouse and greeted the Langdons.

"Langdon! Moving in for the season?" shouted Richard Singleton as he waved with delight. His brusque voice carried over the cluster of cottages.

Mr. Langdon shouted back to him, "Yes, we just arrived. A long journey it was. Some of the roads were washed out by the spring rains. Broke a wheel on the way; it got caught in all the muck and mud. Thank God my darkie Big John thought to stow tools and extra parts in our wagon. He was able to fix it rather quickly."

"Damn lucky, Langdon! Some people can waste a day or more on things like that. It always is such a chore to get here, but I love the mountain air. Does a body good. My wife swears by the spring waters. She goes to the bathhouse nearly every day."

"Good for her! I hope she enjoys it," Langdon replied. "Think my wife will be doing much the same. She has a problem with her nerves. The waters will do her good."

"The waters do everyone good. We must drink a dozen cups a day. I feel so healthy when I'm here. I feel safer here, too, away from the disease of the humid Charleston summers. I know the coloreds can tolerate it, but we white folks can't. Our blood is different from theirs. I need the cool air and healing waters. I feel so alive here!" Richard Singleton beat his chest with both fists to demonstrate his vitality.

"We trust we'll feel the same. I'm always so afraid my delicate wife or our son will fall ill in the Lowcountry. Disease and sickness seem to roll over the land with the great heat. I'm glad to be away from it. Look at all the epidemics we've endured in the Carolinas: yellow fever, malaria, cholera, and typhoid. It's like those illnesses lay in wait like a wolf waiting to pounce on an unsuspecting victim. It could be one of our children playing on the grounds of our home or one of our slaves in the field. It can strike anyone! Malaria killed thousands just a few years ago. Thank God we're here and away from it. We can enjoy the social season in safety. It's such a load off my mind." Mister Langdon looked down and shook his head as he spoke.

"Some just go the short trek to Sullivan's Island or the Isle of Palms and stay in a beach house there, but I much prefer it here. It's like a different world. The smells, the air, everything is different. Not to mention the fine service and wonderful waitstaff."

"Well, the one thing you can get here that you can't get on Sullivan's Island is the mineral waters. That's the deciding factor for me. My wife and I ride the circuit out here and take of the waters at all the surrounding resorts. Even my sinuses are better when I'm here!" Langdon touched his nose and breathed in the air. "I'm looking forward to a fine meal tonight. Will you be in the dining hall?"

"Wouldn't miss it for the world! Staying for the dancing and all the falderal?" chuckled Singleton

"Of course, my wife wouldn't let me slither out of that! Then I'll see you at dinner tonight." Langdon strolled off wearing a cheerful smile.

The family entered their cottage, grateful to have finally ended their journey, and began to relax. Emily Langdon was thrilled to be away from the rather remote plantation where she only had house servants to interact with. At last, she was at her favorite place with other likeminded Southern ladies where she could socialize and gain the latest gossip. Staying there was like being in a fairyland. She could eat in well-appointed restaurants and watch ladies parade by in the latest fashions. Moreover, she got to people watch some of the most famous citizens in the country, including presidents, wealthy entrepreneurs, congressmen, and military leaders. Some of the guests would stay a matter of weeks, others for months.

As soon as they started to settle into their accommodations, the missus yelled at Octavia in a shrill voice. "Start unpacking my gowns and airing them out! I simply must look proper at dinner. I'm sure all the ladies will be judging me. How about that yellow gown? I have beige satin slippers I can wear with it."

"Yes, ma'am. We'll pull that out straightaway and air it out. Hentie can comb over it with some herbs I brought. Why don't you lay down a spell while we ready things for you?"

"I'm not a child! I can wait before I nap. I want to make sure all my precious things are going in the right spot." The mistress stamped her foot and clutched her fists. Although she said she wasn't a child, her behavior indicated otherwise.

Hentie exchanged a glance with Octavia. They had grown used to the missus's tirades. Best to just nod in agreement and stay calm. To do otherwise might have disastrous results. As the enslaved servants pulled out gowns, hairpieces, and ribbons, they exchanged comments. Octavia let out a loud grunt as she lifted one of the missus's big trunks. Her aging back found the work difficult, but nonetheless necessary to appease the fussy woman.

"Big John say there are some important people here, big people from Charleston and all over the South. The missus is going to be a nervous wreck. That woman always worried what others think." Hentie spoke in hushed tones to Octavia as she laid out a silver mirror and brush on the dressing table.

"You got that right. She loves to be around these rich white folks, but it makes her crazy. Did you remember to bring her drops?" Octavia eyes widened and her raised brow creased.

"Octavia, would I forget the most important thing the missus owns? The master would have us both lashed if we forgot those drops!" Hentie hissed as she spoke; then they both broke into a chuckle. "You know that woman is as crazy as a bedbug. What you thinking? I already gave her drops twice on this trip. Let's hope the mineral waters help her nerves."

"Lord God, let's hope that helps!" Octavia jerked her head and turned on her heel to keep up her pace.

A number of wealthy families from the South would travel to White Sulphur Springs for an entire season. Several were from South Carolina. One was Colonel Singleton, who was an enormously wealthy man, owning a 12,000-acre plantation. His principal cash crop was cotton, and to a lesser extent peanuts, but he was also a respected horse breeder who raced his thoroughbreds at the Washington Race Course at Hampton Park, an annual horse race held in February that all the elite of Charleston attended. (The park was named for Wade Hampton, who would later act as a Confederate general.)

Richard Singleton was very popular on the grounds of not only Hampton Park, but also of White Sulphur Springs. It had become much like his second home, and on more than one occasion he lent his money to the resort owners, John and James Caldwell, to ensure the vitality of the retreat.

Along with well-known South Carolinians like Wade Hampton and John C. Calhoun, many other famous men came from all over the country: Henry Clay; Daniel Webster, a congressman from New England; and Presidents Zachary Taylor, Millard Fillmore, and Martin Van Buren. W.W. Corcoran, the Washington, DC, banker who founded the Corcoran Gallery of Art, was a frequent guest and owned one of the Colonnade cottages. Future Confederate president Jefferson Davis frequented the resort. Likewise, future Confederate officer Robert E. Lee visited and often stayed near Baltimore Row.

On the family's third day at the resort, the young Adrian Langdon spied a lovely young woman from New Orleans named Antionette Denault. She was a fresh-faced beauty with dark, raven hair. Her father was a wealthy shipping entrepreneur. As with many of the other young single ladies, she had come to the resort with a trunk full of ball gowns and a headful of dreams, hoping to meet her true love.

The summer season at White Sulphur Springs was a matchmaker's haven. For the young women, this was a paradise rife with possibilities. The place brimmed with young, wealthy, eligible bachelors ripe for the picking. Young ladies arrived to the mystical place with a bevy of frocks designed to allure a potential husband. The fragrance of rose water collected and seasoned for months prior to their arrival would draw the bachelors like bees to nectar. Young women cultured with a classical education of ancient and romantic languages, music, and the arts received intensive instruction as to mannerly behavior and appropriate topics of conversation to politely engage a suitor.

Young bachelors traveled from various Southern cities to enjoy the company of well-bred young ladies. These youthful men, including Adrian Langdon, enjoyed a variety of sports at the resort, such as falconry, horseback riding, golf, fox hunting, billiards, and badminton. Most enticing was the gambling that transpired in the cottages on Bucks Row where the young men stayed. Here the youthful vitality pulsated. They stayed up until the wee hours of the morning smoking cigars, playing cards, and sipping port and fine scotch. The lads would try to outdo one another with their finesse at playing cards and talk of the fair ladies they had danced with that evening.

The transition these young men went through during the course of a day was stunning. During the day they wore attire appropriate to the sport they engaged in and bantered with fellow comrades while at play. In the evening they would be dressed in tailored jackets and the finest accoutrements of the landed gentry. Adrian, a tall, well-muscled young lad, fell into the cluster of sought-after men. He was well educated and well bred, having been trained extensively on the social graces of a Southern gentleman.

As dinner ended, the musicians struck up a popular dance tune. Guests looked to one another and smiled, as they knew the evening would now transition to glamour and romance. Adrian Langdon looked across the room and noticed that Antionette's eyes had gravitated to him. Caught admiring him, she lowered her eyes and blushed. He laid down his napkin and excused himself from the table. He strolled across the grand room and bowed as he approached her.

Antoinette looked up into Adrian's face; her eyes widened.

"I believe my name is the first on your dance card. Would you do me the honor of accompanying me to the dance floor?"

Antoinette glanced down at her stiff parchment card and said, "Why, Mister Langdon, I see you are the first listed on my card. I would enjoy the opportunity." She flushed as she spoke, then gracefully rose from her chair, offering her hand as she did so.

"Why, don't you look lovely tonight? Let me see you. Such a lovely gown. Is it from Paris? Spin round for me."

Happy to allow him and the rest of the room to take in her new gown, she floated off a few feet from him, then obliged him by slowly turning, full of grace and glamour. She held out her arms and twirled, the long skirts swishing around her. Adrian smiled admiringly at her, taken by her charms and elegance. Gently taking her hand, he guided her to the dance floor. As he looked about the room, he saw guests bending over to one another behind their fans, undoubtedly gossiping about the two lovebirds.

The two danced for several numbers, their eyes locked on one another, oblivious to those around them. They made their way around the floor for the better part of an hour before finally taking a break at the punch bowl.

"Miss Denault, might you accompany me on a stroll of the grounds?"

A half smile appeared on her face, knowing what he was asking.

As she responded, a new light appeared in her eyes. "Why, sir, I would greatly enjoy joining you on a walk." She flipped out her fan and fluttered it nervously.

As Adrian Langdon offered her his arm, she switched the fan to her other hand, drew in a breath and placed her small hand on his forearm. As she did so, she thought she heard whispers rise from a cluster of young women. *Ladies, you have missed out again. Adrian Langdon is my beau,* she thought as she squeezed his arm. He looked down at her and smiled affectionately. The two were on promenade for all the guests. They glided out the door and headed to Lover's Walk, where seclusion gave privacy to the young couple.

The walkways at White Sulphur Springs had been carved out of the wooded area stretching across the hills at the rear of the grounds. The paths had been specifically designed and incorporated into the grounds in the mid-1800s to accommodate the resort's annual collection of sweethearts. Differing sections of the paths had different names, which became legend. At the front of the walkway was a section called Hesitancy Row, aptly named for those who only wanted a brief stroll and were not prepared to go on. Other sections included Lover's Leap, a point which overlooked a steep cliff, then Courtship Maze, which transitioned into a dead end called Rejection Row. The largest and most inviting part of the pathway was called Acceptance Way to Paradise. Not surprisingly, this path led up to Paradise Row, a section that honeymooning couples often enjoyed.

While Adrian floated off with his new love, the rest of the family enjoyed the gaiety in the parlors of the main building. Mr. Langdon and his family had come here for years, as his parents had done. His wife looked forward to seeing her dear friends and having tea in one of the large gathering rooms in the main building. Some of them she had seen at Race Week, the height of the social season in Charleston, when the Jockey Club and elite planter families hosted dinners and balls.

However, most of all, Mrs. Langdon looked forward to the bathhouse. Following the evening meal, she and Hentie strolled over to it while Octavia readied her bed. The thermal baths offered a luxurious and sensual experience unknown elsewhere. As most other guests of this era, the Langdons did not possess a full-sized tub. Typically, one sufficed with a sponge bath. But at the White Sulphur Springs and the other nearby resorts, guests were offered a unique opportunity to be fully submerged in the buoyant waters.

As they entered the bathhouse, they were directed to a special room where ladies changed in privacy and quiet. The well-appointed room had a reclining lounge chair and two elegantly upholstered high-back chairs, two vases of fresh flowers, and dressing gowns for guests. Fresh towels were laid out as well as dusting powders and a crystal bottle of scented rose water. Hentie assisted Mrs. Langdon in removing the many layers of undergarments so that she could slip into the robe she would wear to the pool. Mrs. Langdon giggled to herself in anticipation of the bubbly waters.

"Oh, Hentie, don't worry with folding everything now. I want to enter the waters. I've looked forward to this all day. It is so sinfully delightful. It's the best part of being here at the resort!" Mrs. Langdon smiled broadly, something she rarely did but had done with greater frequency since arriving at White Sulphur Springs. The resort truly soothed her troubled spirit.

"Yes, ma'am. I know you want to get in the bathing pool. I'll sort this out after you're in the water."

"Thank you, dear. I want to hurry on."

Dear? She called me dear. That woman don't even call her husband dear.

With that, the two hurried out to the pool. Mrs. Langdon tittered with elation. She was finally where she longed to be all day. She approached the water, first dipping her toe, then stepping down into the pool. She closed her eyes and exhaled in relief.

Ladies could frolic in waters that bubbled up on them like champagne, a glorious indulgence that transformed the mind, not only while one languished in the waters, but on into the evening and night, thereby impacting one's dreams. The bubbling waters offered in the mineral, thermal baths were like a seductive lover, an experience the nineteenth-century woman would not encounter elsewhere. The buoyancy of the water made one as light as a feather. The soft waters rolled over the flesh, creating a titillating experience that some considered so sinful they refrained from it on Sundays.

The type of minerals a particular spring possessed could vary from one location to another in a nearby site and might include sodium, sulfur, aluminum, calcium, magnesium, potassium, and even traces of arsenic. As a result, resort springs developed reputations for addressing differing medical conditions. While one might be known for its curative powers for women's ailments and uterine diseases, another might be reputed to help with kidneys and gallstones or another ailment. Mrs. Langdon went to a neighboring resort to try their spring known to diminish nervous conditions.

Most guests not only frolicked but also drank of the waters. Often a particular regime was followed which started early in the morning, before breakfast, to take of the waters and then continued until evening. Guests might drink upwards of fifteen to seventeen glasses of mineral water in one day. It offered a type of internal cleansing of the body.

White planters took of the waters and so did their enslaved servants. Negro bondsmen, of course, gained access to the waters through different means and used different drinking vessels. Sometimes the servants traveled to the resorts with their masters, as Big John, Octavia, and Hentie had on this social season. Other times, enslaved servants might travel on their own with papers and then reside under the supervision of the proprietor for a period of weeks or months. Planters saw this as a way to preserve their investment and to enhance loyalty. While accommodations for these individuals was often of a lesser quality, such as a space in the barn or their owners' coach, their stay was generally far more pleasant than life on the plantation. In this instance, Hentie and Octavia stayed on pallets in Mrs. Langdon's anteroom. Big John was permitted to sleep outside Mr. Langdon's door, also on a pallet. Not all enslaved servants fared so well.

The Langdons ate their evening meals in the grand dining room. It was an impressive place with high ceilings, white pillars, and plush furnishings. Enslaved servants wore starched alabaster jackets and bleached aprons tied at the waist. They kept one arm at a right angle with a white towel crisply and neatly folded over it while standing ready to assist. The servants' agreeable nature and polite manners assured the waiters of good treatment from the diners. However, it was the guests, more than the waitstaff, who had to be concerned. This was one place where a person's name, wealth, or power did not necessarily matter. Everyone at White Sulphur Springs was rich. People did not automatically get what they wanted when they snapped their fingers. Kofi, one of the resort's enslaved workers, was keenly aware of this.

There were other things Kofi was aware of as well. He had been fortunate in that he had been taught to read along with his master's children. Kofi could read portions of the black newspapers circulated around the Northeast and Mid-Atlantic that came in with some of the servants of the resort's guests. A handful were printed daily, including ones from Washington, DC, and Baltimore. Kofi read about a variety of topics, typically those matters that most affected black Americans. It served as a means to communicate notions of resistance and freedom from slavery. Kofi became friendly with Big John and sometimes shared the news with him. Likewise, Big John shared with Kofi matters he had heard on the waterways from stevedores and dockhands along the Wando and Cooper Rivers, as well as the Atlantic. These men frequently acted as conduits in sharing news about the lives of the enslaved and the efforts of abolitionists.

The personal slaves had to toggle with the hotel's enslaved staff in providing comfort to their masters. However, in the dining room it was a firm rule that the diner's own slaves got to remove the plates and have the first opportunity to eat the leftovers. While the white diners ate lavish meals of fine foods, the enslaved black servants consumed smaller amounts of more humble cuisine. In order to bolster their intake, they swiped leftover food, much as they did on the plantations.

Big John was charged with attending to the family while in the dining room. He looked handsome in his new clothes, a livery suit made of a dark cloth with a crisp white shirt, sewn by a tailor in Charleston to wear while at the resort. Every family of importance had its own liveries with different colors, well known and easily distinguished. Elite Charlestonians did not want to be waited on by servants in shabby dress; moreover, elite whites knew that public scrutiny was often focused on slave attire. It was a sign of wealth to keep one's enslaved servants well groomed and formally attired. Hentie also assisted the family and was given attire appropriate for the dining room and other parts of the resort, including a newly made dark-blue dress for formal affairs and two used garments formerly worn by the missus suitable for other parts of the grounds. Octavia likewise gained new garments for her stay at the resort, including a new dark, forest-green, coarse cotton gown.

It was important that Mrs. Langdon and her husband look their best. They went through at least three changes of clothes each day. Early every morning, guests met up at the springhouse and took of the waters. Visitors typically drank one or two glasses of the mineral water before breakfast, socialized with others, and then went on to the morning meal.

Resort guests took of the waters again after breakfast and then danced "the German," a traditional dance done in a wheel or spoke formation. The dancers would form lines three or four abreast with partners of the same sex. They would also dance a variation of the German, the schottische, and the quadrille. Since it was daytime, the ladies wore hats and dresses which covered their shoulders. It served as a preview of the young, available ladies one might meet at the cotillons later in the evening.

After a handful of days at the resort, the men decided to go riding. The air was cool and fresh, acting as a lure to the picturesque mountainsides.

"Big John, go down to the stables and have the livery ready our horses for a ride after lunch. Adrian and I will both go. You shall go as well. See if anyone else from the resort cares to join us. Pull out our riding outfits and see that they are properly brushed." Mr. Langdon spoke in short, curt sentences as he meted out his directions to his valet.

"Yes, Master, sir. I'll pull out the clothes first, then get down to the stables." Big John smiled brightly in an attempt to soothe his master.

Big John went into the trunks and pulled out the new riding clothes they had ordered from a merchant up on King Street in Charleston. The garments were finely made in deep colors made of sturdy fabrics. Big John thought the master would be pleased with them.

After Big John hung up the garments, he headed out to the stables. He dared not tarry, as the master was sure to check on his progress. As he crossed the grounds, he ran into Kofi, the waiter from the main dining room.

"Blessed day to you, Kofi!" Big John grinned as he strode up to him.

"Your people down in Charleston gone crazy! They startin' bonfires in the street down there! Burning pamphlets sent by abolitionists in Philadelphia. I think one of them abolitionists is originally from Charleston, Sarah Grimké." Kofi's eyes were wide as he explained what happened. "They burned those pamphlets right out in front of the post office. Didn't even let the mail go out."

"Oh my, what set them off? What exactly is an abolitionist?" Big John tilted his head.

"It's folks who want to end slavery, to abolish it. There a lot of those folks up in Philadelphia, but they are other places too, mostly up north." Kofi held up a pamphlet in one hand as he explained the work of the abolitionists to stop slavery.

"Sarah Grimké, huh? I think her father a big man in Charleston. A lawyer, I believe, but they hold lots of land, big plantations outside the city."

"Well, I don't know who she is, but she been chased out the city. People warning her to stay away or sheriff will get her. Her life has been threatened." Kofi made a fist and shook it at Big John.

"My, I didn't know white folks have to worry about the sheriff getting them too. I thought it was just us black folks have to worry about it." Big John shook his head at the idea of it.

"Yes, sir. Anyone who talk against slavery is risking their life down in South Carolina. No one can talk about ending slavery, black or white. They kill you and burn down your house."

"I best get on. My master might lash me for dithering." Big John pulled away from the conversation and moved on quickly.

Mr. Langdon had brought his own mount and one for his nephew. Others found it too cumbersome and rented a mount at the resort's stables. Mr. Langdon and the other men looked forward to such excursions. They would ride over the thousands of acres of grounds, then up into the nearby mountains and spend the better part of the day there. They enjoyed the camaraderie of their fellow riders and the friendly banter. The mountains were honeycombed with riding trails. Guests enjoyed the vistas of the Allegheny Mountains and the smell of the fragrant woods with vibrant green trees, a special sanctum to them. This special haven had trees the Langdons typically did not see at home: sugar maple, white oak, red oak, tulip poplar, white pine, Virginia pine, and so many more up in the forests surrounding White Sulphur Springs. The enslaved servant who accompanied the party brought a basket with sherry and small cups for them. This helped to lubricate their good humor.

Once high into the mountains, the party dismounted and stretched their legs. Meanwhile, Big John readied the crystal glassware and uncorked a bottle of sherry. After a bit of chatting about the fine weather and enjoying a couple of glasses of spirits, a sudden turn in mood transpired. The tone became dark and pessimistic.

The recent price of Sea Island cotton was brought up by one of the resort's guests. It had dropped in value since other countries were able to undercut the price of American cotton. The recent trend had the Southern planters frightened. This, coupled with the impending war between the states, had them all dismayed.

Cotton was king in the South. It had replaced Carolina Gold rice as the leading crop of the region and bolstered the great wealth enjoyed by Southern planters. Once the cotton gin was developed, production soared. With the advent of this machine, the processing of raw cotton bolls skyrocketed, allowing tons of this commodity to be quickly cleaned and sent off to market, making it extraordinarily profitable and the impetus for soaring wealth. It also greatly impacted the textile mills in England and elsewhere, affecting the world market. Cotton as the United States' top cash crop would lead the economy for generations. It was critical for world stability.

A fellow rider lamented, "I hope this year's crop of Sea Island cotton performs well. The value of cotton has become so unstable as of late. I'm worried about the price I'll get at harvesttime. I've gone into debt to expand my plantation and make improvements. I need a successful growing season so I can make a good return."

"I've done likewise," chimed in another rider. "Everything rides on the performance of the cotton crop."

Mr. Langdon complained, "It's the fault of the damn cotton growers in India. Who knew that they would be clever enough to invent their own cotton gins? On top of that, they have had the ingenuity to develop superior cotton plants. I wonder if they somehow stole our process. How else could they have come up with it?"

Mr. Langdon's nephew Adrian became heated and said, "We

grow some of the best crops in the world. Definitely the best cotton and the best rice. The Indians must have stolen seeds from us! Their envy must have driven them to it."

"Don't worry; they will fail. Those coloreds don't have the know-how and mental capacity like we do. Over time, they will fail. You'll see. Our American breeding and superior intellect will win the day," assured Mr. Langdon.

A silence fell over the group. They all became lost in their respective thoughts. Mr. Langdon and his nephew climbed back on their horses and headed back to the resort. The rest of the group followed. They needed to ready themselves for the evening. They took a more direct route back to the resort, maintaining a steady gait.

By the time they reached the stables, Mr. Langdon's horse was gleaming with exertion, his dark flanks heaving like bellows in the intense heat. Langdon's dismount was heavy as he dropped to the ground from his handsome steed. The master's hair was swept back from his forehead, and his cheeks were rosy from the sun and the wind. Adrian was just behind him, also pink-cheeked.

A stable hand retrieved the horses, nodding to the men and saying, "I'll rub them down and give them oats and water. They will rest and look beautiful later on, sir."

Mr. Langdon nodded and, without so much as a word, strolled off. Big John remained behind to make sure everything was handled properly.

Meanwhile, inside the resort, many were enjoying various activities at the spa and on the sporting fields, such as croquet or ground billiards. Mrs. Langdon enjoyed a thirty-minute mineral bath after lunch and a bit of lounging with friends. This was followed by a warm, snuggly nap in which she enjoyed a deep sleep that left her well rested with good color in her cheeks. Her health was coming back to her.

Elsewhere on the grounds, guests readied for feasting and dancing later in the evening. Dressing in preparation for dinner and the evening cotillon was a chore. Hentie helped the missus with the selection of her gown. The missus seemed relaxed and excited about socializing with other ladies at the ball. She had developed more confidence around others, and Hentie hadn't seen the missus using her drops lately or shaking like she had before. Nonetheless, Hentie noted that the missus kept the drops close at hand in case she needed them. Hentie ran across the familiar small blue bottle when she was looking for combs and hairpins to embellish the missus's chignon.

"Ma'am, this one looks so flattering on you. It brings out those big blue eyes of yours. I notice the master can never take his eyes of you when you wear it." Hentie smiled broadly at Mrs. Langdon as she held up the gown.

Mrs. Langdon flushed while fluttering a small hankie. "Oh, my dear, I'm sure you're wrong. I thought about wearing this pink one. I have so many things I can wear with it."

The debate went on for several minutes as to what complemented Mrs. Langdon's coloring, what the other ladies were wearing, what others had already seen her wear, and what was the latest fashion.

Mrs. Langdon whined, "It's just that some of the ladies can be so vexatious. They are so belittling with a single glance. There are ladies here that get their gowns from Paris, France! I know some women who wear jewelry passed down through royal bloodlines. How can I compete with that?"

Hentie tried to be courteous and only rolled her eyes when her back was to Mrs. Langdon, but somehow her frustration and impatience must have leaked through.

Mrs. Langdon became agitated, spewing out her words. "Hentie, you have to help me! Where is Octavia? She should be here to assist me! The ladies here fuss so much over what they wear and gossip terribly about each other. I don't want to make a misstep. These women are brutal here!"

Hentie responded quickly, "Octavia is tending to Master Fitzwilliam right now. He had asked for her. She will be here shortly.

I am sure you will look beautiful. You always do. I hear the others comment about how lovely you look."

Mrs. Langdon tilted her head in disbelief. "Oh, really? Why didn't you tell me earlier? I would have been so much more assured."

Hentie lowered her eyes. "I'm sorry, ma'am. I should have thought to do that."

Hentie didn't want to disturb Mrs. Langdon. She had been doing so well.

Mrs. Langdon quickly changed the subject and said, "I understand that Jane Caroline North, another South Carolinian, is here with her aunt and their family. She is new to this resort and we should make her feel welcome, or the wolves with eat her up. Please keep an eye on her for me and let me know when she might need me to come to her side."

Hentie obediently acknowledged her request. "Yes, ma'am." She bobbed a quick curtsy.

Then the missus walked toward the dressing table and sat down before it, looking at herself in the mirror. Hentie quickly joined her. Hentie drew in a breath and stretched out her hands, splaying her fingers to rid herself of the arthritis that seemed to have set in. She then reached for Mrs. Langdon's golden hair and started unfastening the missus's coiled locks, shaking it out and running the fine bone comb through.

"How would you like me to do your hair tonight, ma'am? I know you will want something special," inquired Hentie.

Octavia entered the room with a few freshly cut flowers to tuck into the missus's hair. "Here, let me do that. I brought these flowers special for you, ma'am." Octavia stepped toward the missus, holding out a couple varieties of lovely white flowers, beautiful and fragrant.

Moments thereafter, they started the long, arduous process of dressing, starting with foundation garments, a chemise, and calf-length cotton drawers. Both Octavia and Hentie helped with the ordeal. They started with her drawers. They were split in the middle from the front to the back and only attached at the waistband. This was to make it easier for a lady to relieve herself amidst all the layers of petticoats and skirts. A chemise was pulled on next. Then came a pair of white cotton knee-length stockings, supported by ribbon garters. This was followed by the most difficult step, the corset with stiff whaleboning. Octavia took in deep breaths as she exerted all her strength in tightening the corset so that the missus had a waistline of a mere child. The next garment almost resembled a cage with a framework of flexible steel hoops joined by vertical bands of fabric tape. The missus stepped into the hoop and Hentie tied it at the waist. Following this, Hentie applied drops of rosewater upward through layers of slips and petticoats until the gown was finally pulled on and buttoned.

Despite all the wrangling and complaining, Mrs. Langdon looked beautiful standing there. Although a bit older, she looked gorgeous in a golden taffeta gown highlighted by topaz jewelry and her golden-blonde hair. She filled out her hairdo with a hairpiece she had made from her own hair, carefully collected from her hairbrush for nearly two years. She looked magnificent.

A few minutes later, Mr. Langdon stood in the doorway and said, "Why, dear, you look simply ravishing! You'll be the belle of the ball!"

Mrs. Langdon looked down and blushed. It was probably the kindest thing he had said to her in ages. She walked toward him and took his arm as they went to the main building for that evening's dance.

Hentie followed at a distance. While her dress was nowhere near as grand as Mrs. Langdon's, it was clean and pressed and a pleasing shade of deep green. Hentie had carefully combed and braided her hair and put it in a taut circular bun. Once in the dining room, then later in the ballroom, she would quietly take her place against the wall.

The Langdons enjoyed a scrumptious evening meal in the grand dining room, then progressed to the adjacent rooms for an evening of dancing. Upon entering the ballroom, a buzz of high energy permeated the room, with much happiness and gaiety. Laughter rang out. No one was stoic or aloof. The more removed individuals must have been out on the piazza or back in their rooms.

All the ladies, no matter their age or condition, looked beautiful that night. Their high energy and happiness brought out their inner beauty. Vividly colored skirts swirled throughout the room as the dancers circled the floor. Many were enchanted young couples, but there were also older married couples and uncles taking nieces out for their first spin on the floor. As the Langdons entered the dance floor, it was as if they floated back in time to their youth. As they looked into each other's eyes, they remembered those first years after they met and how deep their love was back then. In the rush of varied colors and the flow of energy, they felt transported back to those special early years. Not forever, but for an evening.

Chapter 12
Charleston's Great Fire

Lying on her pallet outside her mistress's bedroom door, Lydia was restless as she tried to sleep. She stared out the hallway window at the twinkling stars and crescent moon. It was a mild night and the window was open. The lace curtains moved gently as the cool breeze circulated through the second floor.

Lydia missed her sister, Octavia. Lydia lingered on the memories of her most recent visit and what it was like when the two lived together at Twin Oaks. She missed the closeness and companionship the two had shared there. They had been through so much together: the loss of their mother and the death of their young brother, who had been gunned down by an overseer. Lydia could always cling to Octavia when she needed to and rely on her for support. They had always been that way for as long as she could remember. Lydia pictured the slave cabin the two shared as children, her pallet next to Octavia's in the crowded room where eight other enslaved workers slept. They would pass a doll their mama made for them one Christmas back and forth. As their mama was able, she added little embellishments to the doll, like a scrap of cloth or a bit more hair. As children, most of their evenings had been spent outside at the wooden tables umbrellaed by craggy oak trees. It was much too crowded in the one-room slave cabin to play. Out by the trees there were fragrant odors and room to move and patches of soft grass.

Lydia drew in a deep breath as she reminisced about playing out-of-doors as a child, seduced by the sweet smell of honeysuckle. But she was suddenly jarred from her thoughts; she detected the smell of smoke. Lydia twitched her nose as she sniffed the air to take in the pungent, woody odor. It wasn't the type of odor she recognized as being from a cooking fire. It smelled more like lumber or an outbuilding. She was seized with panic as she realized there must be a house fire nearby.

Moments later she heard the fire bell ring and people shouting. Lydia sprang to her feet and rushed to the window. She stuck her head out, looked up Bay Street, and saw great flames reaching skyward. The nighttime wind seemed to whip it, driving the flames from building to building. The low, monotonous clang of the fire bell persisted as people poured onto the street. Men bounded from their homes in their nightclothes, stopping momentarily to pull on boots.

Lydia grabbed her wrap to cover her shift and pulled on her shoes. She knocked on the missus's door while frantically pulling on her wrap.

"What? What is it?'" inquired the missus. "What time is it?"

Lydia's curt reply was "Fire!"

Lydia bolted back to the window and saw the flames enlarging. A sick dread settled in her stomach as she caught sight of the mighty flames engulfing the buildings in the business district. Lydia ran back to her missus's side and helped her into her wrap, then quickly grabbed her shoes, laying them by her feet. She darted down the hall to wake her master, who was sleeping in a different room. Lydia found that he was already up and pulling on his clothes.

Her panic felt electric. She fought her emotions, trying to decide what to do. A prickling sensation ran down Lydia's back as she wondered how the blaze had started. She sped out of the house, looking north toward the flames. A crowd of men and women grew. Some ran up to the burning buildings with a bucket in either hand. As she wandered into the street, Lydia's eyes stung from the smoke. She searched the crowd for the other enslaved servants and the whereabouts of the master. She saw him run down the street with a bucket of water in hand. Lydia looked back to her mistress, drawn in a panic for some signal as to what to do. She motioned for Lydia to go on. People were swarming everywhere, and their panicked voices shouted out to one another. The air was heavy with smoke, making it difficult to see.

She overheard a neighboring man shout at his wife standing at the threshold, "Wake up the children! Start rounding them up. We need to get away from here!"

Another neighbor from an adjacent house hollered, "Get all the buckets you can find! This is a big one. We'll need all the water we can get!" When he saw Lydia on the street, he shouted, "Hey, you there! Girl, get a bucket and fetch some water! Don't just stand there!"

She hurriedly looked for a bucket and ran back to the water pump in the yard. With the pail in hand, she ran toward the flames. Her heart lurched as she began to grasp the dire magnitude of it all. Women were screaming and wailing. One woman dropped a baby down to her husband's waiting arms. The pungent odor of burning wood wafted over the crowd, grabbing them like immense fists. Lydia struggled as she carried the heavy pail of water, splashing it all about. She moved as fast as she could, hoping to help in some way. Fear and panic grabbed hold of her as she realized the city was engulfed in the flames of hell. Citizens and the members of the mainly Negro volunteer fire brigade fought valiantly, but the flames were too intense.

Suddenly, there were explosions. Unable to discern what was

spurring them, Lydia wasn't sure which way to run. It could have been coming from the powder magazine or another stockpile of gunpowder and ammunition. Only God knew what it could be; all Lydia knew was she needed to get away from it. She saw people in panic running blindly in all directions, then an eruption, and all sorts of debris went flying. Lydia gazed at the pandemonium, stunned. At a momentary standstill, she saw a small white gown fly by her, and a flash of blonde hair followed.

When the concussive blast waves temporarily stopped, she heard an odd yowling sound, a low, guttural, keening cry, almost like an animal in distress. It made the hair on her neck stand on end and caught the breath in her throat. She turned to discern what the noise was, then realized it was coming from a young mother, bent over her small blonde-haired daughter wearing a white linen nightdress with blue ribbons. Her legs were gone. The mother had her hand over her mouth trying to contain her horror. Lydia moved toward the woman but, unsure of what to do, simply stood next to her, barely touching her shoulder with her fingers, unable to say a word. All the women could do was stand frozen. The child was obviously dead—blood poured from where her legs used to be, with bones sticking out from under her nightdress. Her tiny slippers lay nearby. Lydia watched mutely. Minutes later, two men with a stretcher shuffled past. They lifted the small, limp body onto the stretcher and covered her with a blanket. One man nodded to the now wailing mother, saying, "Sorry, ma'am."

Lydia glanced at the child's diminutive slippers, a body blow that stole the breath from her, thinking of the great loss this woman just suffered. Unable to do more than squeeze her shoulder, she moved on.

The crescendo of explosions climbed to a heart-stopping pitch. Lydia froze in place, waiting, bracing herself and praying that the explosions would stop and not reach her. *Not here, not tonight.* She gritted her teeth, waiting to feel the concussion. But the explosions ceased. After a few heartbeats, she ran on, wanting to get out of the area.

Lydia found her mistress and stayed with her throughout the night. They huddled in an area away from the fire while chaos unfolded all around them. Lydia's sorrow was indescribable; her body ached with emotion. She worked to keep her composure so that she could comfort her mistress, who just sat and sobbed.

Lydia kept saying, "It's okay, ma'am; we'll be okay. We done made it through the night. We'll be okay."

Lydia kept telling herself that they had to believe they would be okay, or they would go crazy. The city and its people would survive. They would endure this horrendous event.

Despite the valiant efforts of the fire brigade and the citizens, the fire burned on throughout the night and into the following day. It finally dissipated around daybreak. Lydia, her mistress, and others nearby started to make their way home at the first light of dawn. Moving slowly, they warily passed smoldering embers and small fires still burning. They moved south with others crowded along the sidewalks and streets. It was almost impossible to see anything beyond the backs of those in front of her and the rubble on the ground. Far above, the sky was still burnished red from the fire. Where Lydia's favorite store had once stood, a general dry goods store, was a smoking ruin. *Oh my, what else has been destroyed? I hope I still have a home to return to.*

As Lydia made her way down the street with her mistress by her side, she heard some church women yelling, "Mrs. O'Brien, did you hear? Saint Mary's Catholic Church burned down! Where are we to go? It was the only Catholic church in Charleston and all the Carolinas."

A woman responded, saying, "Where will they hold Mass? Where will we get our communion? That was the second church we had built. We just built it! How could God let this happen?"

Lydia felt hopeless moving along the street. Women wailed, children cried as fathers looked on, lost in a daze. Just hours ago, this grand city beckoned to visitors with its heavy green foliage and tropical uniqueness, inviting with its exotic smells and unique offerings. Jovial and exuberant people walked streets lined with some of the stateliest mansions on the Eastern Seaboard. This thriving port was full of hard-drinking seamen and elite businessmen, all patronizing local public houses and clubs. Charleston's markets were thronged with a cosmopolitan population where a mix of languages could be heard within the same city block: French, German, Portuguese, Gullah, and, of course, English.

Lydia wandered the soot-coated street. Smoke seemed to cover the whole city like a dark veil. Drawn to the promise of light and the possibility of refuge, she kept moving. She urged her mistress to continue toward their house. As the smoke cleared, Lydia could see her home still standing. She touched the arm of her mistress and said, "Look! Look! Our house is still there! Thank you, Lord! Thank you!"

A week later, Octavia came to see Lydia. This time she and Big John traveled by water on a boat the master had secured to deliver some goods at the wharf. It was a rather large shipment of produce and other goods that the master didn't want jostled around on the country roads.

As they approached the city's waterfront, one of the crew disembarked to check in with the harbormaster to discern which wharf the ship would be permitted to dock at. Such a matter always changed depending on a variety of circumstances. The fire in the city had made matters even worse. The devastation had stopped just a short distance from the waterfront. After nearly thirty minutes, the crewman stood at the end of one of the wharves waving a large white cloth. The vessel approached and at long last moored at the landing. Eventually, Octavia and Big John were allowed to leave the ship and travel to the end of the peninsula.

The two walked to the estate where Lydia lived with the wealthy Simmons family. They were stunned by all the devastation. Some people wandered the streets, seemingly lost. It wasn't clear if they were looking for family, for their homes, or perhaps something entirely different. Big John maintained a protective stance and stayed closer to the ash-covered street, hoping to guard Octavia from harm. Big John walked with Octavia to just inside the back gate of her sister's home. They agreed on a place and time to meet. Once Octavia assured Big John everything was okay and she would be fine, he departed.

Lydia peered through a window in the slave quarters. She was delighted to see Octavia standing outside and rushed out to her. Octavia opened her arms wide and Lydia collapsed into her, sobbing and broken.

"Oh, Octavia, it was terrible. Just terrible. I didn't know if I would survive it. I saw people die and a little girl blown to bits. So much was burned to the ground. It's just rubble now. This city never gonna be the same, Octavia, never, never. That fire went all the way down through the business district to the Cooper River wharves. Like to burn us all to the ground, right down to our sandy dirty ground!" Lydia shouted in anger and pain.

"Oh, sweet baby girl, we'll rebuild. All them rich white planters, they'll make sure it gets rebuilt. They have to send out those crops and all the cotton up north. There will be public houses and taverns for the men to drink in, shops for the white ladies and a brand-new marketplace. You'll see!"

"I suppose you're right. The white folks gots to have ports and train yards. How else will they make their money?"

"Anyone know how it all started? What caused such a big fire?"

"Well, no one exactly knows. At first, they were thinking someone set it on purpose. But after a while folks figured that wasn't it. Most think the fire broke out late in the evening in a paint store up on King Street. Some big winds fanned the flames across King Street, and from there it spread throughout the city. Scary how it just jumped from building to building."

"I can't imagine what it was like for you, seeing all those buildings burned, and there you were, trying to take care of the missus right in the middle of it."

"They say the fire burned half the city. Nearly all the stores done burned up. Acres and acres, nothing but ashes. Master says that more than five hundred properties burned, at least eleven hundred buildings altogether, including houses, stores, stables and such. Lots of poor souls died in this fire. And what an ugly death so many faced. Some mamas had to watch their poor babies burn up in the house because nobody could get to them." Lydia shook her head, tears in her eyes. "Those poor babies . . ." Her voice trailed off.

"Makes you wonder what the Lord could be thinking. Why he let such a terrible thing happen?" Octavia murmured.

"And that new hotel burned down. I heard it was such a beautiful place. It hadn't even opened up to the public. Just the workmen and the owners got to go in it. Completely destroyed, they say. What a waste! And then the churches, all burned down. People can't even go to pray. The time you need the Lord the most and can't go and worship! It's just a mess! I tell you, sister, don't know what we gonna do. Just don't know." Lydia's frustration leaked through as she spoke.

"I hear that because so many wood buildings burned, they ain't gonna let so much timber be used when they rebuild. They gonna make people use brick. It's gonna be expensive to build houses all out of brick. Don't know how some folks gonna afford it. But they are starting to clean things up already. They renting slaves from some of the outlying plantations to get the work done. Most the labor being done by black men. They do all carpentry, masonry work, painting, you name it."

"I bet they do. Black man built this city. They done it once, they can do it again. They got some talented craftsmen here. They can do it." Octavia nodded, assuring Lydia of the truth of her words.

"The missus says she gonna rent me out to make some of the workmen's clothes and some for the shopkeepers too. I suppose I'll be busy keeping clothes on their backs. But I gots to do my part. Thank the Lord Jesus that I still have my few belongings and a home still standing. There so many not so fortunate."

"Thank the Lord you made it through. I don't know what I do without you. It near broke my heart when the master sold you off. I cried myself to sleep at night for days." Octavia looked down as she remembered the great sorrow she suffered when her sister left Twin Oaks.

"Don't look so downhearted. I ain't gonna leave you again. The master I have now is a good man. He not like Master Langdon and all those other plantation owners. He's a city man; he's different. He is more kindhearted. He has his moments, but he never lashes people until they bleed to death or cuts their fingers off. He's not like that."

Octavia looked at her, then nodded, knowing she was probably right.

"Now come on, let's sit down and have some lunch. Sit and tell me about your life at Twin Oaks. How's that Hentie doing?"

They sauntered down to where the cook was preparing a big pot of stew over an open fire, stirring it slowly with a large stick. It had fish and vegetables and a thick broth. It smelled delicious.

"That sure do smell good." Octavia's eyes grew large. Lydia chuckled as her sister took in the heavenly aroma. "Let's go over to the kitchen house and see if the bread's done. I can smell it from here. That goes really good with this fish stew."

Octavia's eyes flashed even wider. "Fresh-baked bread, you say? Mmm mmm."

⌒

Time went on. Lydia worked hard to help the city rebuild. Streets were cleared and new buildings went up to replace old ones, and this time most were made out of brick and stone. Lydia's mistress rented her out to other families and businesses. She made new clothes for those who had lost so much. The dresses she made, sometimes in conjunction with her friend Tilly, lightened the hearts of the city's wealthy white women. Lydia also made work clothes, shirts, trousers, and breeches for Negro workmen and white shopkeepers. She touched the lives of so many as the city strived to recover from the catastrophe. Throngs of workers poured into the city to revitalize it. The skills of enslaved Negro laborers were vital to the redevelopment of the city. Over time, the city of Charleston emerged as the phoenix from the ashes, more beautiful than ever. Many residents decided to rebuild their homes and churches in the Greek Revival style, making the city one of the foremost places to view spectacular architecture.

Lydia persevered through it all and felt relieved when much of the rebuilding was over. With time, she overcame the trauma of the event and all that she had witnessed. She was bolstered with the support of the other enslaved servants and her sister. They grew to regard the tragedy as simply another hardship they had to endure, and they rose above it, knowing that they would receive their reward for all their struggles here on earth when they were called home to the Lord.

Chapter 13
The Death of John C. Calhoun

S ometime after the city faced the horror of the Great Fire, it faced another devastating loss, the death of John Caldwell Calhoun. The church bells at Saint Michaels rang out, signaling the arrival of the steamer carrying his remains from Washington, DC, to the bosom of his native state. Calhoun was a highly regarded statesman and beloved son of South Carolina. His body had been transported from the nation's capital to Wilmington, North Carolina, on a train. The coffin was then placed on the steamer ship, the *Nina*, which made the somber trip to Charleston.

Although Calhoun was born in the upcountry, city leaders from Charleston had lobbied hard for him to be buried at Saint Phillips Church, located in the center of town. He had lived here for at least part of his life. John C. Calhoun was the pride of Charleston, even though he didn't care for the city.

While it was originally decided that no formal assembly would receive Calhoun at Smith's Wharf, spectators and military officers gathered. A great admirer of Calhoun's, the master had brought his family to stay at the Planter's Hotel in town, and Big John and Hentie had accompanied them. Mr. Langdon and Big John stood on the street overlooking the harbor watching as the steamer came into the city. Langdon was joined at the wharf by his wife and son, Fitzwilliam. The misty salt air wafted over them as they stood waiting. Mistress Langdon was cloaked in black. She wore a high-necked heavy cotton dress with a bustle and covered her head with an onyx-colored sunbonnet. In her gloved hand she clutched a small Bible, which she had been given as a child. Behind them stood Hentie and Big John. The incoming ship sounded its horn in short bursts, signaling its approach. The group shuffled restlessly in anticipation. They were blessed with mild temperatures on the late April day, which made the waiting more tolerable.

Big John pointed with his chin and excitedly said, "He's here! His ship is here!"

"Good Lord! He has arrived!" The master spoke in hushed tones, but his stiffened posture and large eyes revealed his excitement.

The American flag on the edge of the harbor was displayed at half-staff in honor of its fallen son.

As Master Langdon watched early for the ship's approach, he spied another planter from the area and leaned over to speak to him. He was an older gentleman outfitted in an expensive, tailored suit, charcoal gray in color. He carried a cane and dove-gray gloves in his right hand.

"Sad day, isn't it? South Carolina has lost a good man," the master said.

"It's not only the State of South Carolina, it's the whole country who will miss this man. He was such a brilliant asset to all Americans," the older gentleman offered.

"True. We were lucky to have such a statesman of good breeding, and so well educated, leading this country," the master replied. "A Yale man. Received sound instruction from his youth. Attended the

Willington Academy. A fine school, I understand. Boy could have had an impoverished life. Lost his father quite young, I believe. He had to take over running the plantation in the upper state as just a teenage boy. Thank God he had the assistance of his brothers."

"Damn lucky, yes indeed." John Calhoun's story was well known. His father had died when John was just thirteen, and his mother died suddenly when he was eighteen. His brothers had sent him through his university education while they ran the family's plantation and business endeavors. Their commitment to their younger brother's education was a good investment of their time and money. Their father was a poor Scotch-Irish immigrant and wanted more in life for his sons. He had high hopes for them all, and wanted one of them to follow in his footsteps and develop political ambitions. Abbeville provided rather humble beginnings, but with John's education and the contacts he made, he went on to lead this entire country. "Damn fine example of what a Carolinian can do." The older man nodded and popped his cane on the ground to punctuate his point.

"Poor Calhoun, I understand he had a rough time of it in the last few years. Up in Washington all by himself. Got to be too much to take the entire family with him to serve in the US Senate. I thought I read in the paper that he died alone in a boarding house. Succumbed to tuberculosis. Poor man, such a pitiful, lonely end. He didn't deserve that. He was such a fine Southern gentleman. He was the biggest champion of our peculiar institution of slavery and the Southern way of life. Such a damn shame he passed as he did. Damn shame."

"Well, the country is recognizing him now. All of his comrades and those who loved him are here. They recognized him up at the nation's capital, too. Did you hear how many days he laid in state in the Capitol rotunda? At least a couple days, wasn't it?"

"Yes, something like that. But at last he's home, back in the bosom of his own state."

"People around here have done a fine job of honoring him. I think every house and business is draped in black bunting. Did you see that the Rhetts have a bust of Calhoun in front of their house all draped in black with green wreath? I have seen other displays like that too. Everyone loved him so. He may not have been born here in Charleston, but we certainly adopted him as our own." His head bobbed as he stressed his words. Calhoun had moved to Charleston after he attended law school at the Litchfield Law School in Connecticut. He joined the best law firm in the city at that time, and made a lot of good connections that way.

As the steamer coasted into the harbor, it labored and belched, carrying not only the body but perhaps also the very heart of South Carolina. A somber military procession gathered to honor him. While the men spoke, cadets slowly moved the casket onto an assiduously decorated wagon. The special soldiers moved with taut discipline. As they moved Calhoun's casket, Big John and Hentie drifted closer to the water. Hentie looked up to Big John and rolled her eyes.

"That man is no honorable saint; he the devil in wool tweed," she muttered.

"Word down on the waterfront has been most of the Mid-Atlantic and Southeastern United States is celebrating that he gone. He was such a hateful man. Calhoun says slavery a good thing, a positive good. Beating your slave just something you have to do to keep him working. Keep him respectful. It's a terrible thing. I'm glad the old man is dead!"

"Hush now. Don't let the white folks hear you. They think he God and the angels all wrapped into one!" Hentie's eyes grew wide as she darted a look to Big John.

"Look at all they doing for this man. He never even liked Charleston. He thought it was full of too much foolishness. He was too serious for this town. He always laughed behind their back at all their high society airs." Big John chuckled.

"I suspect he was right about that much. Everything else he got wrong. If he got his way, he would have made all the black folks and all the Indians in America into slaves. He relocated those poor Indians and made them walk all the way out West. How can a man do that?! He was just evil." Hentie's body quaked at the thought of him.

"We best stroll back over to the master. This ain't no day to upset him."

Hentie nodded and tapped Big John's arm with her elbow.

As they made their way, the military officers marched in unison carrying Calhoun's remains. The coffin was flanked by an honor guard commanded by Captain A. M. Manigault and accompanied by distinguished pallbearers, including Jefferson Davis. Federal and state troops were assembled at Marion Square in front of the Citadel (then at its original location on the square) to lead the procession as it moved through the city. The wagon was drawn by six black horses, each attended by a groom. They moved mournfully through the streets of Charleston to city hall. Minute guns were fired along the route in honor of the man so many had adored. The façade of city hall was draped with black bunting and ribbon. Stoically, and with full military aplomb, the heavy sarcophagus was carried up the white marble steps into the multistory redbrick building, which would later be covered in a white stucco.

The casket was placed inside an elaborate catafalque which had been set upon a raised platform. Heavy drapes of black velvet surrounded it. The display was illuminated by huge candelabras. The body lay in state in the council chamber until interred at Saint Phillips Cemetery the following day. The funeral itself was tremendously elaborate. Modeled on Napoleon's, it manifested every bit of grandeur. A fine ending to the life of one of South Carolina's brightest stars. Or so those in attendance believed.

Chapter 14
Introducing Doll and Rosa,
the Herbalists at the Plantation's Infirmary

Twin Oaks was lucky to have its own young herbalist named Doll. Everyone loved to be nursed by her. She was a beautiful young woman. One young man once commented, "Just look at her; that's enough to lift your spirits and make you feel better!" She was only in her teens but had the same basic knowledge as her grammy, Rosa. Although Rosa wasn't Doll's real grandma or "dah," she had raised her and groomed her to take her place one day as the herbal doctor.

Doll's mama died during childbirth. Doll had been told that she got all twisted up and backward. It was a long delivery and more than her mama could endure. The events of that day were vivid in Rosa's memory, and she shared the story with Doll.

When Rosa found Doll's mama in her cabin trying to birth the baby by herself, she rushed in and knelt down by the bed. The scent of blood, old straw, and musty bedding hit her as she leaned in. She called for help and left the straining mother for just a short time to get items from the infirmary. When she returned, blood had spilled, and the slime of afterbirth had spread, seeping through the bed and onto the dirt floor. Rosa tried to help Doll's mama and the newborn baby. She yanked off her apron and scooped up the newborn, cleaned Doll with the pinafore and wrapped her in it. Rosa looked down and saw the blood pooling between the new mother's legs. There was nothing she could do to stop the bleeding.

Doll's mama gasped and raised herself up on a shaky elbow. "Please help my baby. Save her, Rosa," she pleaded. She extended her arms out to Rosa and the newborn baby. Rosa caressed the newborn's soft scalp as she passed her over to her mama. The new mother cradled the tiny baby in her arms and kissed her head. The baby squirmed, and a weak cry slipped from her. The wilting mother rolled her head, weakened by the pain and blood loss, sweat saturating her forehead.

"Rosa, promise me you'll care for my little girl." Her breaths came harsh as she pointed to a blue, beaded choker lying on a crate. "Make sure you give this to my baby girl. It will protect her always. It carries her grandma's spirit and will carry mine too. Promise me you'll be her mama, her dah, raise her to be a good woman." She gasped, knowing she didn't have much time.

"Shh, shh, don't worry none. You'll be here to raise her. You're her mama." But Doll's mama had lost too much blood. As it became apparent she wouldn't make it, Rosa's heart softened.

"I'll take her. I'll love this baby as much as you do. I promise." The words spilled out from deep inside Rosa, and she knew she was making a lifelong commitment to a dying woman. It came from the deepest pocket of her soul.

The dying mother pulled Rosa's hand to her mouth, kissed it and pressed it to her pale, wet cheek.

Rosa pulled her hand back while gently holding the hand of the fading woman, raised it to her lips and kissed it back. Rosa then reached down and touched the newborn's chest, saying, "Promise."

Other enslaved workers came to help attend the dying mother. Although she couldn't really eat, some food and drink were brought in, as was the custom in such situations. She took a few sips but didn't have the strength to swallow, and it ran down her chin.

Rosa then squeezed her eyes shut and began to pray. She started to make promises to God, if only he would let this young mother live. She said one prayer, then another. She was ardent in her devotions. Others came by and looked in on the scene, then held vigil outside. They sensed the Lord was calling her home. They sang gospel hymns in an attempt to restore the spirt and vitality of the mother, or, if it was God's will, to send her into his glory.

Rosa silently urged the woman to make a comeback. At one point the dying mother said, "Do you hear them? It's the angels. Their voices are so lovely. I've never heard anything so beautiful."

Tears welled up in Rosa's eyes. Eventually, the mother's hand fell limp. Sorrow filled Rosa's heart and a sob rushed up through her chest. Unwilling to abandon the woman, she prayed to God for her revival, hoping to somehow bring her back, but after a spell, she reconciled that she was truly gone. Rosa climbed on the bed beside the young mother and held the sleeping baby between them. She put her long fingers on the mother's eyelids and drew them shut. Rosa then curled up beside them, curling her arm across them, and began to weep. Eventually her quiet tears turned to a howl directed at God; the heartache was just too painful. The other enslaved servants standing outside realized the woman's spirit had left her body. A shriek went up, and the cluster raised their voices in sweet, harmonizing gospel song, hoping to guide the spirit on a good passing.

Another enslaved woman eventually entered the cabin and lifted the baby off the bed, then urged Rosa to get up. "You helped this new babe into the world. A new life. Almighty God in his wisdom called her mama home. Now we best care for the baby she gave us."

Still unwilling to fully accept what had just occurred, Rosa hesitated. Then, pulling herself up, she said, "Yes, you right. Best take care of the baby and my responsibility. That's the best way I can serve her mama."

Planting her feet on the floor, Rosa stood. She turned and looked down upon the young mother one last time. Then she took the newborn into her arms and walked to a nearby table. Rosa bent over and brushed her lips against the newborn's soft head, then gently kissed her crown. She held up the baby's small hand and splayed her tiny fingers, kissing each one in turn. Laying the baby down on the table, she exposed her middle. Rosa then carefully cut the cord and wrapped the stump in a spider's web. This would help the umbilical site heal.

After a spell, Rosa fixed in her mind that she was a new mama now and had a tiny baby girl to care for as her own. That was the custom among the Gullah. Frequently others stepped in as caretakers, committed for life. Doll's mama had referred to Doll as her "baby doll," so she was given the basket name of Doll in those last few minutes that she was alive. Most folks were given a proper name in the days following their birth and their basket name became secondary, but not Doll. Her basket name stuck. Similarly, Christmas Luke was born on Christmas Day, so he was given the basket name of Christmas. Then a week later his mama gave him the proper name of Luke.

Many of the enslaved workers continued to linger near the cabin. The driver and overseer had heard what happened and allowed a group to care for the woman's body and hold vigil. They realized the importance of the custom.

Her mama had been supported by the enslaved community during the death watch and afterward as well. Singing and praying went on around her for about an hour after she passed. Some just talked about her passing on and being with the Lord. The vigil was intended to strengthen her as she passed. People waited to hear if Doll's mama spoke of a heavenly visit or some sort of vision. When Rosa reported that she had, all were comforted that she had been called home and had a "good dying." She was at peace and there was no concern of her returning as a haint.

Doll's mama was buried in the slave cemetery, with a service for her the day after she died. As they prepared her body and carried her to the burial plot, those around her were told not to look at her face. They wrapped her in cloth and tied the fabric down. The black cemetery was in the far back end of the plantation, out by a marsh, away from the white family cemetery and all the main buildings. The Gullah buried their dead near the water so that their spirits might cross the ocean and return to their home in Africa. It was mainly the duty of the older enslaved workers, with the help of young children, to tend to the black cemetery. They went from time to time to pull weeds and maybe add a new plant near a grave. For the most part the cemetery was left undisturbed. Most thought that one should not intrude on those who had departed but rather respect them from afar.

On the day Doll's mama was buried, the master allowed all those enslaved to attend her burial after sundown, when their daily chores were finished. Since the skies were darkened, some carried an uplifted torch to light the way. The master even brought out some food and drink for them after they returned. There were rumors that the master was Doll's daddy and that was why he showed such kindness. Doll's mama didn't have much, but they tried to put the things that she would want or need the most in the afterlife around her grave. Some of the last things that Doll's mama had touched were also included. These items had her imprint and would soothe her spirit. They gave her the chunk of wood she had been biting down on during her labor. They tore a piece of the fabric Doll had been wrapped in at delivery and laid it by her right side. There was a small button from her dress and a lock of Doll's hair. They also decorated the grave site with other items important to Doll's mama, such as a china cup she loved, which was broken into small pieces, showing the breaking of what had been useful in life but was no longer needed. It symbolized the ending of things in this world.

Since she had a good death, unaffected by evil spirits, they thought her spirit would stay near her place of burial, while her soul would go to heaven.

There was no headstone, as was the Gullah custom. Her grave wasn't outlined with stones, as white folks often did, but with conch shells that represented the ocean crossed from the Gullahs' homeland in Africa. "The sea brought us, and the sea shall take us back," said one of the mourners.

There were no flowers, but there were two small yucca plants and a small tree near her grave. The tree's roots would journey to the other world, just like the deceased. They acted as a type of marker. A few grave sites had headstones, but no one could read what they said. The master had those stones made, as an enslaved servant would never have had the money to create such markers. In the Gullah tradition, it was believed that the spirit traveled like the sun, from east to west; therefore, the body was oriented eastward.

The Gullah kept a bottle tree near the graves for the spirits. The spirit was earthbound, while the soul went to heaven. The "trablin," or troublesome, spirit was restless and roamed the area where it once lived, disturbing all who were there. A bottle tree was made by inserting the small branches of dead trees into the necks of empty bottles, preferably blue, to attract roaming spirits to the bottles. The bottles were especially attractive when the sun struck them, causing the special glass to flash and glitter. In the spirit's excitement, it would rush inside and be trapped, thus rendered harmless to those living around it. Some believed that the spirits were eradicated with the first rays of the morning sun.

All of the young black children on the plantation were brought to the funeral for Baby Doll's mama. Following the formalities of the graveside service, each child was passed back and forth over the grave. Doll was the first one to be passed to-and-fro over her mother. Observers were concerned that since the death was sudden and occurred during childbirth, Doll's mama might try to visit Doll or another child, perhaps worry her in her sleep, causing her to become restless. This passing of children over the grave would forestall such an occurrence. After all the children had been passed over, the body was lowered into the grave, and a spiritual song was sung.

Doll grew up knowing the love of Rosa and many other enslaved workers, and she became a beautiful woman and a reliable assistant.

The two herbalists handled all the ailments and injuries of the enslaved field hands on the plantation, those in the big house, and even some of the neighbors. For the most part, the Langdon family used white doctors to address their illnesses, but white medicine was unreliable at best. They knew Rosa and Doll had the skills and quick wit to swiftly address any situation.

The clinic was just one large room with four beds adjacent to the laundry room. Doll and Rosa boiled the white sheets in a large cauldron and changed the sheets on the beds with some frequency. They did their best to maintain a degree of cleanliness for their patients.

Then that terrible night came when Mr. Langdon's son, Fitzwilliam, became deathly ill. Big John came running with the boy in his arms. Mr. Langdon trotted behind him, tears welling in his eyes. The boy had a serious case of the flu. He was still quite young and was a sickly child. The missus was near hysterics. They had tried a doctor from nearby, but the boy only grew worse when he treated him. Finally, Mr. Langdon saw no option but to ask for Rosa and Doll's help. He had lost his first wife, so he knew what it was like to lose a loved one. He did not want to go through that again.

It was at that time he first really got to know Doll. She touched his hand when she took the young lad from him. Mr. Langdon saw the kindness and concern in Doll's eyes. Her warm touch and loving care comforted him. Doll examined the child in Rosa's presence. The boy was racked with fever and ague; he lay limp and motionless on the bed. Doll listened carefully to the boy's shallow breathing and noted that his eyes were sunken into his head. Doll took the boy's hand and pulled up a bit of his skin. The flesh stayed pinched up in a fold for a bit before lying flat against his hand again. Doll glanced up at Rosa with deep concern in her eyes.

Rosa nodded and said, "Dehydration has done set in. This boy needs liquids right now. Doll, go get me some water with a bit of salt and sugar in it. We gots to get some liquid in this boy or he won't survive."

Stunned, the master turned toward Doll; his look bored into her. He knew the situation was dire, and he felt the claw of fear take hold of his heart.

A few minutes later, Doll returned with the concoction. She sat on the bed, and Rosa helped to situate the child against Doll's chest by picking him up under his arms, hauling him up and leaning him into Doll. Rosa parted the boy's lips, then stood back and watched. The master leaned in to watch Doll proceed. Initially, the boy fell back, and the liquid rolled down his chin. Doll reached around the boy's chest, grabbed his chin in one hand and directed the spoon into his mouth with the other. This time the fluid successfully ran into this mouth. She held the boy's head against her shoulder with her chin and continued the process. After getting most of the fluid into the boy, she laid him on the cot.

Rosa prepared some tea. She tossed in dry ingredients and used a mortar and pestle to grind it to a fine powder as she kept her eye on Doll and the boy. She ordered Doll to wait a bit, then give the boy more fluids: first her special preparation, then later tea from life everlasting. Doll nodded her understanding and followed her directions.

As the hours wore on, the boy seemed to grow worse. He twitched and moaned, and his small angelic face went ashen. His bright-blue eyes stared at Doll, but he did not seem to see her. As she touched the boy's cheek, it nearly burned her fingers. Mr. Langdon's eyes grew wide with alarm. He stayed with the boy, carefully watching, tears leaking out of his eyes. He gripped the bedsheets and moved closer.

"Papa, Papa. I'm so hot," said Fitzwilliam. In response, the master looked deeply into his son's eyes and brushed the sweat-soaked golden locks off his head.

"I know, son. I know. We're doing everything we can to help you. I'm right here by your side."

Doll looked at Mr. Langdon and saw his despair. She touched his hand to comfort him. Mr. Langdon looked back at Doll, grateful at her kindness, and then rested his eyes on the boy.

In the meantime, Doll made cold compresses for Fitzwilliam's forehead. She followed this with a camphor rubbed onto the boy's chest. Rosa kept checking him and continued with the compress, the tea, and prayer. Eventually, Rosa gave the boy valerian root. This helped him to sleep and to ease his pain. The night lapsed into the following day.

Master Langdon continued that second day with his vigil at the boy's bedside, watching for any small change, his thin hope dwindling. After several hours, he asked Doll, "How is he?" Panic permeated his words.

"No real change, Master. But your boy is fighting; he wants to live." She sat on the edge of the bed and looked helplessly at Fitzwilliam's sweat-soaked face.

Master Langdon sat transfixed, afraid to leave his son even for a moment. By the end of the second day, he had grown weary. Dark circles formed under his eyes, and a beard had started to grow on his squared jaw. Clearly, he adored this little boy with a deep and special love. Worry weighed heavy on his heart and depleted him.

Finally, at the end of the second day, he sought rest on a nearby cot. The boy remained listless and sweaty throughout most of the night. Rosa and Doll changed the bedclothes and the sheets, helping to comfort him. The missus was periodically updated about the boy's condition; word was conveyed though the enslaved house staff back to her, but she never came out to see her son.

The boy lingered in a feverish delirium for two days. He could not hold down food but could manage droplets of liquid. His fever remained unabated, and Rosa continued to slowly drip a tea made from mullein leaves into the boy to ameliorate the fever. The hours wore on and Fitzwilliam remained frail and flushed, lying in his bed.

On the third day as daybreak came, Mr. Langdon jolted awake in a panic. "Is he—?"

"Your boy is coming around nicely, Mr. Langdon. His fever broke a little while ago. I think he will be fine. We gave him a little more tea just before you woke. He has started to speak again."

Mr. Langdon collapsed against the cot. "Oh, thank God! Oh, thank God!"

He was so grateful not only to God, but to Rosa and Doll. He bent over and kissed Doll's cheek and instinctively grabbed her hand in his, locking eyes with her, staring into her beautiful green eyes. He then found he could not let go of her hand. He watched in fascination as his fingers slipped between Doll's like keys of a piano, her caramel skin against his ivory fingers. The heat of her hand and the small bones made a shocking contrast against his much larger hand.

Doll's head grew light as she realized she had not drawn a breath. The air seemed so still. She tore her eyes away from their linked hands and looked up at Mr. Langdon. He was equally mesmerized. For a moment his grip grew tighter on Doll, who suddenly remembered her social position and the impropriety of touching a white person. She drew her hand free but smiled at the master as she did so, not wanting to offend him. Doll stood and avoided looking at her master, not sure what to think of the exchange. He suddenly scrambled to his feet and muttered, "Thank you. Thank you so much. You saved my son."

Doll's face throbbed with mortified heat. She drew in a gasp and let the words "You're welcome" roll softly from her lips. She wasn't used to a white person thanking her for her labors.

The two locked eyes again and held them upon each other for what seemed like minutes, and then the master turned to leave. "Well then, I bid you farewell." He strolled to the main house.

Doll tried to discern what to make of the exchange, then shook off the notion of a romantic interlude as she went about her work. But she found thoughts of the master seeping back into her consciousness again and again.

After that experience, William Langdon started paying a great deal of attention to Doll. He would sometimes bring her small gifts. Occasionally, the gifts were flowers that had been cut from the house garden, and at other times he presented small trinkets he purchased in Charleston or elsewhere on his travels.

From there a romance of sorts started to blossom. Rosa warned Doll to keep her distance from the master, as you never knew when a snake would turn on you. But Doll couldn't see any evil in William Langdon. She thought him a kind man. She had seen such tenderness in him when his son took ill. He waited by his son's side for more than two days. Surely, he was a good man.

On a couple of occasions, Mr. Langdon took Doll into town with him under the guise of getting a few medical supplies and items for her clinic. Big John went with them to keep appearances up, but he spent most of his time on his own while in downtown Charleston. Mr. Langdon even drafted a pass for Big John so he wouldn't be questioned.

In the meantime, the master and Doll went shopping. Some of it was for the plantation, but much of it was to impress Doll. He bought her a nice calico dress and hat. At another store he bought her a lovely hatpin. These pins, sharpened by hand, were incredibly expensive, but a planter such as Mr. Langdon could afford such gifts, and he loved showering them on Doll. He also planned to build Doll her own small cabin on the grounds of the plantation or perhaps a small house in downtown Charleston. Having her own dwelling would make sneaking away for their trysts even easier. And so it went, the much older planter, Mr. Langdon, acting like a blushing schoolboy, trying to impress the apple of his eye, the young and beautiful Baby Doll.

Chapter 15
Purchase of Enslaved Girl from Georgetown

D oll pulled on her light-green calico dress and smoothed back her hair, readying herself for the day. She slipped on her shoes and contemplated what tasks she must accomplish first. She stood at the window of the small cabin the master had built for her. The sturdy brick walls gave her a sense of safety and protection. She breathed in deeply, and her spirits were lifted by the potent aroma tickling up her nostrils. Most of the enslaved lived in cramped, wooden shacks, but not Doll. The master had a brick cottage built for her. The bricks had been fired right on the grounds of the plantation. Big John had pressed his thumbprint in a brick right by the doorframe with a double XX so she would know it was him winking at her. Leaning out slightly, she looked over the lovely row of gardenias growing below, their pristine petals luminescent in the early-morning sun.

There was a soft rapping on the door, and Doll turned to look as the full figure of Rosa entered the room. Lately they had been busy with an assortment of injuries, everything from snakebites to broken arms. A few of those who came in were enslaved workers who defied either the overseer or the driver and suffered hideous injuries for their impudence.

Rosa nodded at her, then said, "Mornin', Doll. You best get a move on. The master is in a mood today. We have one of the field hands in the infirmary. He back-talked to McBride. I got him all bandaged up. No one else has been to the infirmary, so we best help out in the laundry house. Lots to do."

Doll sighed, then shifted her weight, saying, "Oh, again! It seems like he is in a bad mood nearly every day now."

"Now you carryin' that child, his mood has changed. I expect it will be that way for a while."

Doll rolled her eyes and followed Rosa out the door. She knew Rosa was probably right. This had become a prickly situation. Doll reached up and touched her neck to make sure she still had on her mother's blue choker. She believed that this necklace had special powers and could protect her throughout the day. The two trotted down the path to the laundry house and passed another enslaved woman dressed in a taupe-colored shift and dark-blue head wrap, picking ripened vegetables from the garden. The women acknowledged each other before they swiftly moved on to their duties.

⌒

Inside the big house, Hentie dashed down the steps of the main staircase in a frenzied state, trying to focus on her next task. She grabbed the newel post at the bottom of the steps and spun around it, heading down a hallway. Suddenly she slammed right into a wall. Initially, all she saw was a man's broad chest, her palms planted in the center to protect her face from the impact. She looked up and saw the frantic face of Big John. He was so tall and so immense that she couldn't see around him. They both suddenly took a step back and paused. Hentie shook off her intense concentration to focus on the man before her.

Smiling, Hentie nodded and said, "Morning, Big John!"

Big John broke out in a broad grin and said, "Morning, ma'am!" He chuckled at their folly, his gentle essence caressing her soul. She briefly closed her eyes and let it flow over her, then caught herself. Tensing, she blinked to shake off ardor. They ever so briefly locked eyes.

Big John stepped back a few inches, put his giant hands on her shoulders as he steadied her, and said, "Gots to get that special platter for Miss Nellie. She be wantin' it, and I gots to hurry. She said to make sure we're using the special Chinese porcelain."

"It's right over there, Big John. Best be careful with it. Missus have you lashed if you break it," Hentie cautioned.

"I know. I know that for sure!" he exclaimed.

As Big John hurried on his way, Hentie shook her head. The kitchen and main houses were abuzz with activity. The missus had the enslaved house servants running like chickens with their heads cut off. Who would think a few houseguests could cause such a fuss? But the house staff had been in high gear for days now, preparing the family's abode for their guests, who were to stay for a month. Mr. Langdon's cousin from Virginia, Thaddeus Langdon, was coming with his wife and two daughters. Thaddeus was also a plantation owner, but his principal crop was tobacco. Thaddeus sold his tobacco to markets in the United States and in England. This aristocratic Virginian was an enormously successful planter and had accumulated an inordinate amount of wealth from his landholdings, tobacco, and other cash crops. This allowed Thaddeus Langdon and his family to enjoy a rather lavish life, even more opulent than that of William Langdon.

Having guests stay at the house for an extended period of time was rare, and it had thrown the missus in near hysterics. Life in rural Charleston was typically very boring and lonely.

The missus was having the whole house turned upside down so it would look statelier and more luxurious for the master's cousin and his family. The staff rushed around the main house changing bedding, freshening drapes, and renewing the furnishings. Heavy cleaning was undertaken, and the whole house was being aired out. It seemed like Hentie spent hours every day with the bristle brush. Chairs and tables were moved so that the house looked more elegant, and a few paintings and works of art had been borrowed to enhance the surroundings.

As their arrival approached, a feast was planned. A pig was chosen for butchering. Hentie had never really watched the process before. Big John and two other hands cornered a pig. Big John blocked the pig and yelled, "Jed, you hit the pig in the head with that mallet, smash her head!"

Jed yelled, "You block her, Big John. You stop her if she runs. Damn, she can move fast!" Then Jed reached out and delivered a stunning blow to the rotund sow, Gertie, with a wooden mallet. Having subdued the pig, they carried it over to a broad, wooden bench with buckets already set up to catch the blood.

"Here, Jed, help me hold this here sow on the bench. Duke, you take the knife to her." Big John hoisted the pig on the bench as he nodded to Duke. "This pig is gonna be good eatin'!"

Big John and Jed held the pig down while Duke reached under the animal's neck and deftly sliced its throat. The heavy smell of fresh blood flowing from is neck permeated the air as Gertie bled to death. Expertly tying the pig's hind feet together, the men hoisted it to an awaiting hook. This was to prepare the beast for scraping the bristles off its hide before it was disemboweled and halved. Nellie would not waste any part of this animal: bristles would be used for brushes, fat would be used for lard, and the small intestines would be made into sausages. Other parts the master would let the enslaved workers eat, like feet, jowls, ears, tails, and heads. Nellie would also make up chitterlings after carefully cleaning out the intestines, a vile job. A Christmas ham would be prepared and smoked, and then fresh roast pork would be prepared for the following day. Every bit would be used in some manner or fashion.

"Okay, we gots to finish this job. I'm fixin' to line the pit," Big John announced to the men. He strolled over to the well and dipped a hollowed-out calabash gourd into a bucket of fresh water. "Best get your drink now, boys."

Big John yelled to Duke, "Now help me finish off this fire pit to smoke the meat. I dug it all out, but we gots to finish lining the pit with rock. Then we gots to stock it with wood and coals." He pointed with his chin to a stack of wood and a pile of coals nearby.

The two men started the work while Jed and Nellie worked on the sow. After lining the pit, they stacked the wood and coals nice and thick so the fire could go for hours. Then they laid poles over it to support the pig. The pig would be slowly roasted for nearly fifteen hours. It was seasoned with special herbs and garlic.

"Hey, Big John, I got your sow all fixed. I put little holes in her and stuffed them with garlic pieces. Takes out that gamey taste. Makes her taste real good. Now you gots to soak this beast with sassafras and pressed tea leaves. It makes it taste even better. It's gonna melt in your mouth," Nellie said.

The missus came out to inspect the goings-on to make sure everything would be up to her standards.

"Now, Big John, I want you to make sure this pig is roasted until it's tender, no matter how long it takes. Do you understand?"

Big John's head bobbed up and down as he said, "Yessum. I sure do. I'll make sure it done real tender."

The other enslaved servants helping Big John held their tongues and bobbed their heads accordingly. They knew the missus was all tensed up and wanting everything to be perfect for her guests.

Big John and two other enslaved servants went down to the beach to dig up sea turtle eggs. They would be cooked by tucking them into the ashes. Nellie would also stick apples in the ashes to slowly bake them after covering them with honey, cinnamon, and lots of butter. Such a treat! Big John was dead tired from all his labor preparing the pig, but his efforts were sure to be worth it.

The missus was near delirium urging the old plantation seamstress, Mimba, and another apprentice seamstress to finish two special dresses for her. One was for the picnic, a bright, cheerful, saffron yellow of fine cotton, and a second dress was a silk, multicolored dinner gown with extra whalebone corseting. The missus hoped to wear both during her guests' stay. The missus was so excited about the frocks; she hadn't had a new dress in a while. The fabric had been shipped from England, along with all the special trimmings and a newly designed book of patterns. The missus hoped that she could present herself as fashionably and as lovely as her houseguests.

After her fitting, she dashed down the steps to check on the progress being made with fresh cakes and scones for the afternoon tea. She knew her guests expected nothing less than perfection. As she swung into the warming-kitchen doorway, she saw one of the house servants snatch a scone, break off a piece, and pop it into her mouth. The poor servant girl was caught with the pastry still in her mouth, and her hand slapped over her lips to hold it in. The girl's eyes grew wide, knowing she had been caught and would surely face the missus's ire.

"What! What are you doing? You know that food is for our guests! Are you out of your mind? You are forbidden to eat this food!" Mrs. Emily Langdon shouted. Her voice reverberated throughout the house.

The house girl was trapped, unable to do or say anything to stop the flood of emotion pouring from her mistress. She swallowed hard and choked down the bit of scone.

"Ma'am, ma'am, I'm so sorry. I must have lost my head. The scones smelled so good and I was so hungry. We've been working hard for hours—"

"Of course you have been working for hours. We all have been working for hours. We have very important guests coming. You are expected to act accordingly."

Her rant continued, "Don't we give you food? We gave you the dress on your back and a roof over your head. This is how you repay us? You steal from us? You're a thief! A thief in our own home. I cannot tolerate a robbery like this under my own nose. I simply cannot tolerate such behavior," shouted the missus.

"But, ma'am, it was only a piece of a scone—" the servant murmured.

"You stole from us, you thief! God only knows what else you have stolen. I will not tolerate a thief in my home. Hentie, go get the overseer. He must take care of this insolent behavior straightaway!"

Hentie, stunned by what she had overheard, was frozen for a moment; then she jumped when the missus shouted, "Hentie! Hentie! Are you deaf? Go get the overseer, Simon McBride! I want this girl punished for her stealing, straightaway!"

With that, the missus harrumphed and turned on her heel. She walked into the front sitting room and paced back and forth.

Five minutes later, McBride rushed into the house, blustery and anxious to please the missus and to calm her down.

"McBride, I want that slave girl punished. She stole from us! I have guests coming, and she is eating all the food intended for our honorable guests. I won't have it! I won't have a thief in my own home! Do you hear me?" Mrs. Langdon shouted. "I want you to use the iron muzzle on her. I want that bit in her mouth so she cannot eat the food she stole or any other food!"

"But, ma'am, she won't be able to eat or drink anything. I believe she is with child. We could lose not only one, but two darkies. They are inventory important to the master. I know he was just reviewing his ledgers." McBride tried to understand her intention.

"I don't care if she and her bastard child both die! That is none of my concern. She is a thief and stole from me!" the mistress shouted.

"Yes, ma'am. I understand." McBride bowed and nodded, then turned and left the room.

A short time later, Hentie looked out a window down onto the work yard and saw the young house girl being manhandled. McBride punched her in the face and knocked her to the ground. He and the driver, Duke, restrained her as they continued to assail her. An awful medieval-looking contraption was forced upon the enslaved girl while she was chained to a pole. A flat iron piece, or bit, went into her mouth, and a type of mask went over her face. McBride forced the contraption down onto her head and clamped it shut and locked it at the back of the neck. The poor girl screamed, but she wasn't able to articulate, only make guttural sounds. Hentie's body tightened as she listened to the terrified girl shriek in agony. Hentie bit her lower lip so hard she tasted blood. She could only think of the blood flowing into the helpless enslaved girl's mouth. Hentie's pain was nothing in comparison. *Oh, how horrid! How can a person do this to another human being?*

While the torturous device was being applied to the girl outside, the rest of the enslaved servants continued to scurry about the house carrying out preparations.

Mr. Langdon had left the fracas for calmer surroundings, driving out to inspect the smaller plantation in McClellanville and visit with his brother, Charles.

The master left before dawn and spent most of the day at the property up north. While there, he and his brother visited the neighboring town of Georgetown to get some supplies at the dry goods store. They delivered fresh produce and sweetgrass baskets woven by Negro plantation workers to a local merchant. Following this, the two went on to visit a local public house for some libations. While the food was good, the beer was even better.

After indulging at the pub, the brothers strolled down the main street. They passed a barker with a young Negro woman on a sale block. The barker was pointing out her attributes, including her fertility and sturdy frame. He was offering her for the special price of just 500 dollars. The barker said the owner needed to liquidate some assets and this was a particularly good bargain. Mr. Langdon, having just reviewed his plantation ledgers that week, knew that the price was a more than fair. Feeling flush at the time, on a whim he purchased the girl.

The master did not return to Twin Oaks until after dusk on the fourth day. When he arrived back home, he had the new enslaved servant in tow. This young woman had a medium complexion and short-cropped hair. She was of average height with a sinewy, well-muscled build. The slave girl's typical caramel complexion looked a bit pallid in the well-worn mustard-colored calico dress that hung from her frame. She appeared apprehensive of her new surroundings. When asked a question, she was unable to respond. Fear and dread rushed up her throat, and her tongue, a feeble instrument, lay in her mouth like a slug in its crevice. She tried to move her lips, but nothing came out. Only a silent mouthing. Her eyes grew wide at her own shock of being unable to speak.

The master barked at Hentie, "Take this girl. Get her cleaned up and settled in. Make haste with any pleasantries. Just get back to work straightaway."

Hentie calmly guided the new girl, Juba, toward her cabin. On the way, she passed by Mimba's sewing area and looked for a garment Juba could wear. She found a dress that might fit among the remnants of fabric Mimba had accumulated to make quilts. It had belonged to a teenage slave girl who ran from the plantation and was later killed for her misdeed. While it had a couple of holes, it was much better than what Juba wore.

Hentie retrieved a washbasin that Juba could freshen up with, then stepped out of the cabin. Juba had barely made eye contact with Hentie; she seemed so spiritless and dejected. She acknowledged Hentie's directions with nods and guttural sounds. On one occasion her downcast expression altered, and she murmured, "Yes, ma'am."

Before Juba undressed and washed herself, she looked out the window of her new home. Juba's first impression was the grayness of it all. It was mid-autumn and late in the day. The half-seen sun withered by degrees as it sank into the western sky. Juba could make out some of the surrounding outbuildings and the expansive fields that lay beyond. Juba lamented that she was now truly alone in a new town and with a new master. She was completely powerless to control her destiny, where she lived, or even the garments she wore. She was helpless against the power of her white master and her destiny. She exhaled and momentarily shut her eyes tight, letting herself rest for just a moment before she tackled the task before her. With that, she mindlessly disrobed and dipped her hands into the cool water.

After Juba cleaned herself and changed her dress, the two walked to the main house. Despite the new girl's aloofness, Hentie tried to start a bit of conversation with Juba, but the dialogue went nowhere. As they approached the mansion, a strip of dark-blue shade draped over the two women from the roofline, darkening as they fell silent. The palmetto trees clacked in the wind, the only sound about them. After a brief void, Hentie gave up her efforts to lighten the mood. Juba continued her sad, aloof demeanor and did not utter a word. As they entered the big house, Hentie introduced the new girl to Octavia and a few other enslaved household servants. Octavia was outgoing and friendly in a warm, friendly way. Hentie thought she would make a good first acquaintance. Octavia sensed the young woman's trepidation and tried to comfort her with words of welcome. As Octavia reached out to touch Juba's hand, Juba instinctively jerked back like a scared animal. Octavia's eyes widened as she glanced over to Hentie to see if she had caught Juba's response.

"Well, you'll do fine here. We get along well with one another. I know we do our best to help you get on here." Octavia made sure to maintain her distance but stood in front of Juba and looked directly into her eyes. "Now, you best get to work. The missus is in a tizzy."

Juba was quiet and swift in her work for the remainder of the day. She seemed to try very hard to please everyone around her, but she remained cowed. The only time Juba spoke up was to assist the laundress in taking up the missus's clothes to her bedroom. She meticulously laid the cotton items, the chemises and drawers, flat in the bottom drawer of the linen press. Juba was careful to smooth them out as she did so.

Octavia instinctively tried to soothe Juba the remainder of the day and make light conversation, but it never went very far. Hentie likewise made efforts to engage Juba, but the new girl remained aloof. As a sign of welcome, Hentie quickly made a palmetto rose of palm leaves and laid it on Juba's pallet. She hoped it would help ease Juba's transition to her new home.

The following day, the Langdons' guests arrived. Hentie was preoccupied as she busily tidied up the dining room and set out fresh flowers on the table. She heard a commotion in the foyer and a loud voice reverberating down the hallway. Deep and clear with staccato accents, it rang with authority. It was Thaddeus Langdon with his family. He was a well-groomed gentleman with a robust disposition. He had an ebullient presence and a loud voice. The master took note of his firm handshake and take-charge personality; although something often characteristic of wealthy planters, it initially made the master take pause. Thaddeus Langdon carried a lit cigar in one hand while he punctuated his points with the other. His wife was a good-natured Christian woman of exceptional beauty. She was immaculately dressed in the latest fashion, as were her daughters.

The missus invited her guests into the sitting room to rest after their long travels. Hentie offered the guests light dragoon punch—a blend of black tea, sugar, brandy, Bermuda rum, orange slices, and lemon wedges. The girls, of course, were only permitted a half glass.

The ladies of this family were well mannered and refined. The eldest daughter, Hannah, was a gifted pianist and had obviously practiced long hours developing her skill. Her younger sister, Sarah, had a strong singing voice and would accompany her elder sister at the piano. During their stay, the two entertained the entire family and any guests who joined them with a variety of musical renditions. Despite their exceptional skills, the girls were modest regarding their accomplishments and humbly accepted praise from others.

After several days, Thaddeus Langdon and his family began to integrate into life on the plantation. They would enjoy a formal breakfast in the elegantly outfitted dining room with eggs, smoked sausages, and bread. Then they went for walks on the grounds and lingered in the gardens. The two girls often read books or wrote in their journals under the large oak trees.

The master's wife seemed to come out of her depressed mood and relied less frequently on the use of her opium drops. Her mood had been lightened by the company, and she was far friendlier. This seemed to impact how she treated the house servants, including Hentie, Octavia, and the others. Her cruelty dissipated, and she was even kind on occasion. The missus and Thaddeus's wife, Elizabeth, often sat on the davenport and chatted as they worked on their needlepoint. Elizabeth guided Emily through her callow attempts to design a more elaborately embroidered tablecloth. Through their time together they seemed to forge a bond. The two took tea nearly every afternoon and would prattle on about their husbands and friends. Their giggling, much like young girls, could be heard throughout the first floor of the main house. Master Langdon would just roll his eyes and head for the nearest door when he overheard their cackling. On these afternoons, Octavia took the opportunity to snatch a scone or shortbread; the missus was so oblivious she never suspected a thing. Octavia loved all the treats, and her wayward behavior served as her own form of slavery resistance. It made the afternoon special for her and the missus.

As the weeks wore on, Hentie tried to befriend Juba, performing small gestures to put her at ease. Hentie did not want to intrude, yet she wanted to somehow allay the young woman's suffering. She really was quite pretty, but the dull pallor of her skin and depressed affect diminished her appearance. Over time, Hentie invited Juba to share meals at the kitchen house and told Juba she was welcome to put her pallet on the floor of her small shack to sleep.

After a couple of months, Juba revealed to Hentie the horrors she had endured at the hands of her previous master. When she began to recount the trauma, a cold chill rolled over Juba; she shook and grabbed a broom to steady herself, lacing her fingers around it and waving off Hentie's look of concern.

Juba murmured, "It's okay. It's of no matter. I'm used to it. I just get a chill when I think about it all."

Juba's eyes fell. Her face crumpled at the memory, but she recovered her composure. The timbre of her voice dropped into a softer register. "It's hard to talk about. Sometimes I can't believe I lived through such torment. But I did. I remember at first, I could hardly sleep at night. Now I can sleep, but at times I wake up and I think someone is over me." She twirled her hand and shook her head. "It gets all confused at times. It's so hard to trust, to open myself to share what happened . . . There was so much pain."

She had been owned by a planter who owned a huge plantation up in Georgetown. "There were a number of big plantations like ours with hundreds of slaves. We had nearly four hundred. My master, he grew about the same crops as we grow here, cotton and such." Juba drew in a deep breath and paused. "It was such an awful place. A bad, bad place."

Hentie saw in Juba's eyes all the pain she had been carrying. "I'm so sorry, honey. I know that it must have been hard." Hentie's kind heart went out to the troubled young woman. *This poor child. What did they do to her?*

Hentie only meant to commiserate, to show sympathy with her new friend. But something in her words had struck at Juba, as sharp as a deep and painful stab. Every vestige of color faded from Juba's face. Hentie reached out to Juba and touched her hand, just for an instant. This time Juba accepted the kindness.

"I'm so sorry, Juba. I didn't want to upset you or make you relive your pain."

Juba took in a deep breath and then broke with emotion. She sobbed out loud without regard for her surroundings. "He made me do things. I didn't want to . . . but he forced me. I was just twelve or thirteen. At first I fought him, but he had me whipped. The lashings were so brutal that I passed out. I lost so much blood, they didn't think I would live . . . So, I started to give in, whenever he wanted."

Hentie said, "It must have been awful, being treated so badly by such a devil. I know you were powerless to stop him from hurting you. I'm so sorry."

Juba went on. "I was all by myself, no mama, no family. My whole family had been sold, except me, and I wasn't sure where they went. I was so scared. Being so frightened, I could hardly sleep at night. I used to have bad dreams, real bad. One time I had this terrible dream while I was pregnant about a man dying in my arms. It was so vivid and real. I still don't know what it meant. I thought I might have been cursed." Her voice was so soft that Hentie had to lean forward to hear her. "I just felt so dead inside. My body hurt so much."

The master continued to press relations on Juba. To no one's surprise, she subsequently became pregnant with her master's baby. Once his wife found out about her husband's trysts with Juba, she became enraged. She would seek out Juba on the plantation grounds and spit in her face. Other times, if the two passed, the missus would demean Juba and berate her with accusations. One day, the missus erupted on Juba and threw a dish at her.

The missus grew ever more enraged at her husband's frequent absences and went into a tirade. She shouted at Juba, "You harlot! I know you lured my husband off and seduced him. You are merely your master's courtesan, nothing more. We offered you a home. We treated you with paternal kindness and offered you shelter. We gave you the clothes on your back. You have far more here than you would have ever had in the jungles of Africa. Under our kind hand you were offered protection and the guidance you needed to survive. We offered you the benefit of slavery and living on this plantation. We did you a great kindness and offered you a good life on earth. Through our Christian benevolence you had the hope of salvation for eternity. Otherwise you would have been a heathen savage destined for damnation. Now you will face the fires of hell for the seduction of your master, the very man who tried to save your soul. You whore! You wretched whore!"

Over time, the missus became more erratic and violent. As Juba's stomach grew prominent, so did the wife's ire. One day the wife became enraged and attacked Juba in the kitchen with a heavy stick, striking her repeatedly on her stomach. She called Juba a whore and cautioned her to stay away from her husband. Juba protested, saying that she had no choice but to submit to his demands.

The mistress then grabbed a pot of boiling water on the stove and threw it directly at Juba. Most of it missed, but some still splashed on her and badly burned Juba's arm and shoulder, which Juba had raised to protect her face. The master ran into the kitchen when he heard Juba's screams of excruciating pain. In an instant, he reached out and struck his wife. The blow was such that it slammed her into a wall and onto the floor. As she struggled to stand, he shouted, "No more!"

The blow to Juba's stomach and the shock of such a traumatic event must have thrown her into labor, as it started later that afternoon. It was a long and painful ordeal for her, especially with the severe burns. She lay alone in a small slave shack with a wood-framed bed. The bed had belonged to a house slave who recently passed away. The bed and its surroundings were dusty and barren, but it was the best Juba could hope for that day. It was terribly hot outside; the humidity made the sweltering heat even worse. After a while, Juba barely noticed the annoying flies and mosquitoes that buzzed around her. The shack was adjacent to the barn, so the smells of hay and animal excrement wafted into the room. At times, the cloying odors and pressing air overwhelmed Juba and caused her to gag. But she just swallowed hard as she separated her mind from her body and made herself think of times under the great oaks when the jasmine was in bloom.

Unbeknownst to the master, his wife had sent word to the enslaved servants that they had better not provide any comfort to Juba during her childbirth, or they would suffer severe consequences. The master's wife hoped Juba and her unborn baby would both die during the ordeal. She ignored the fact that an enslaved woman was powerless to resist her husband's advances and chose to believe that Juba had seduced him. She wanted vengeance.

It took the better part of the day and hours of pushing, but eventually Juba delivered a premature baby boy. She knew at first glance that he had been born too early to live on his own for very long. Nonetheless, Juba immediately fell in love with her baby. Doll-like due to his tiny body, he had a pale complexion and brown hair, much like his father. He struggled to breathe from the outset, and after a brief period, Juba felt him shudder and fall lifeless. There was nothing she could do besides hold her dead baby and sob. Although other slave women peeked into her cabin out of curiosity after hearing her screams, none helped her out of fear of floggings ordered by the master's wife. An older enslaved woman quietly crept in while the missus napped in the big house and took the baby from Juba's arms, hiding it in her apron as she walked toward the woods. She feared that the master's wife would see the small body and find yet another way to hurt Juba. The tiny baby was buried later, with other enslaved women in attendance.

After she gave birth, the master and overseer saw to it that Juba was given some respite. She acquired salves and ointments from other enslaved workers on the plantation. One woman brought her pokeweed salve with lavender in it. It helped bring down the swelling and mend the burns. In time, her wounds started to scab over and heal.

A couple of months later, Juba was taken to town with other forsaken souls and sold from a sale block in the market building in the heart of downtown, like a farm animal would have been sold at auction. There was no regard for her as a human being or grieving young mother.

Master Langdon bought Juba without knowing her history. He had been unaware of Juba's recent pregnancy and the debilitating abuse she suffered at the hands of her master and his wife. Her burns had been covered by a sack cloth shift. He merely saw her as a sturdy young girl who could help out at the plantation and birth new slave babies.

Juba sobbed as she told her tragic story to Hentie. She had just been separated from everything she knew, and now she was alone on a new plantation. She revealed the scars on her upper arm and shoulder and the initials that had been burned into her thigh, a standard branding at her former plantation.

Juba told Hentie that the slave owners in the Georgetown area used differing methods of marking their chattel slaves in order to identify runaways. The runaways' unique markings were described along with other characteristics in posted billets demanding their capture. Various methods were used to create these markings, such as cropping ears, creating hash marks around the head or neck, and branding, like Juba had on her thigh. Slave owners thought it an important and necessary measure to maintain dominion over their bondsmen.

Juba swiped her hand down her dusty skirts and looked off to the lowering sun. Tiredness and disappointment spread across her face. Her very personhood projected sadness and pain. This poor young girl had endured so much. She had been mercilessly terrorized at the hands of her master and his wife. She grieved the loss of her son. Juba had no family to provide comfort or support. She didn't know what was to become of her. Would this master treat her the same? Hentie, with her unselfish and compassionate spirit, decided she would help Juba as she would have helped her own daughter, Amahle, had she not died by suicide on the transatlantic journey.

Hentie said to Juba, "Loss of a baby hurts. It's like it bleeds and aches in your heart. I know he seems to call your name in the middle of the night. You can't be alone; you need to come with me." Hentie gently held her hand across her heart to signify the deep hurt of a mother who had lost her child.

Juba moved in more permanently to Hentie's shack, and the two started sharing most evening meals together. Hentie encouraged other enslaved workers to extend themselves to Juba and be sympathetic to her plight. Octavia stepped up her efforts. She gave Juba an old doll that she had held as a child. The small, homemade keepsake helped to comfort Juba at night when she lay on the low platform that served as her bed and thought about the baby she had lost.

Juba started to integrate into life on the plantation. Her mood lightened and she carried herself more upright when walking through the grounds. Juba put on a bit of weight, and her complexion appeared healthier. Loud noises no longer terrified her. Juba became more confident in carrying out her daily duties and walking about the plantation. She interacted with others on the plantation and acknowledged people when they passed her.

Master Langdon's kin remained at the house. The two Mrs. Langdons continued to enjoy each other's company and share most afternoons together. During the evenings, they would do their needlepoint and compliment each other on their work. Elizabeth also had her daughters doing needlepoint. They worked on items for the trousseau, such as napkins and pillowcases. One had made an elaborate sampler with all the letters of the alphabet and a Bible verse. Their mother was very stringent with what was considered acceptable work. She thought it imperative that they get their stitches right. She stressed to the girls that having such skills was part of being a good wife and finding an acceptable husband.

As Emily and Elizabeth grew as friends and close comrades, they shared confidences with increasing frequency. While the teenage girls, Hannah and Sarah, were out on the grounds during the day, the two older women often gossiped and shared some of their pressing concerns. One afternoon, Sarah was practicing her scales as Hannah performed her quick fingering of the keys. Outside the window, bees buzzed around the jasmine. The women clinked delicate china teacups while enjoying the afternoon sun from the comfort of the brocade davenport.

Hentie stood in the butler's pantry and listened to the faint ticking of a clock. Its soothing sound lulled her into a daze. While she stood folding napkins on a counter, she overheard Elizabeth Langdon share that their house girl, Jennie, had been born just two months after her youngest daughter, Sarah. She was concerned that they were too close; she wanted her daughter to maintain her distance from the house slave and have a firm grasp on her proper place. She thought it imperative not only for Sarah's well-being, but also when she became the wife of a planter and ran her own household.

"Our peculiar institution of slavery demands that we keep our Negroes at arm's length and not become too close. While we must guide and discipline them appropriately and treat them in some ways as if they were a family member, it is important to remember they are Negroes, part of an inferior race that can never be a real family member," said Elizabeth Langdon.

"Oh, I heartily agree. While our role as a mistress is to guide with a firm hand and act with benevolence, we cannot be too close. They are not our equal and never can be. They are like dogs of a lesser breed; they will never have our intelligence and means. Slaves are children who need our guidance to survive. To emancipate them would be entirely unfair to them as they would be helpless."

"Oh my, yes! Why, Sarah raised the question of manumission for Jennie. I'm sure it is because she had developed a fondness for her Negress. Jennie is so fair that Sarah thought that she might be able to pass as white out in society and have her own life." Elizabeth shook her head at the wrongminded thinking.

Elizabeth went on to say, "Well, our Jennie has been a part of our estate and even our household since her birth. Her mother, Ceceilia, used to work in our house as well, but then I discovered that Ceceilia had been, let us say, rather close with my husband. I thought it was best to have her moved to another location." Elizabeth Langdon looked upward, then glanced into her companion's eyes for assurance.

"Oh, I fully understand. These things do happen. Men have certain needs that must be satisfied; they are different creatures from us. I am sure Jennie's mother was flattered by her experience with Mr. Langdon, but she had to be moved. Did she have other children?"

"Ah yes, well, Ceceilia had eight children in total. Most were sold to other estates. They all had a similar look and build, a lighter complexion and almond-shaped green eyes. Very bright and skilled in different trades. We were able to garner a good price for all of them." Elizabeth smiled as she spoke.

"Oh, I see," replied Mrs. Emily Langdon.

As Hentie stood in an adjacent hallway listening to the discussion, she was stunned. *How can these white women think we slaves are stupid and incapable? We run this plantation! We do all their work, fix their meals, sew the clothes and run their households. The missus would be curled up in a corner whimpering to herself if not for Octavia and me! That stupid crazy woman! Maybe we should hide those special drops from her for a week; then we see who's incapable!*

Hentie remained stupefied in the hallway, looking down momentarily, unable to fathom it all. *Those white folks and all they do to the people they hold captive. Did Juba's missus think she was "flattered" by the master's attentions too? Ain't right, just ain't right.*

Hentie was still staring at the woodgrain in the floor when the heavy wooden front door suddenly opened. Mr. Langdon and his cousin sauntered into the hallway.

Mr. Langdon breezed past Hentie, nodding in her direction and saying, "Afternoon, Hentie."

Hentie nodded back and gave a short curtsy. "Good afternoon, Master."

The master's cousin followed and nodded in Hentie's direction. It was then that she noticed his eyes and gasped: almond-shaped green eyes. *Did Thaddeus Langdon have eight children by that poor slave woman? Almighty God, he had more children by his slave girl than his own wife Why, Jennie must be his daughter too. Born just two months after his younger daughter. No wonder his wife thought it was important to sell her mother.*

⌇

One day, after the harvest season was over, several of the enslaved workers were sitting at the outdoor tables near the slave quarters. They were sharing their midday meal and taking a few minutes to relax. Hentie noticed one of the prime hands, a young man about twenty years of age, when she saw Juba suddenly look over at the young man as if her head were jerked by a string. He was very handsome, well-muscled, and seethed with virility. Juba's eyes brightened as she gazed at him, her eyes lingering for a few minutes.

Then he slowly turned toward Juba as if he could feel her eyes upon him. He flashed a smile at her. Hentie watched the two young people as a magnetism took hold.

Juba wore a pale shift, and as she rose the sunlight poured through the muslin dress, revealing her curvaceous form. A light turned on in the young man's face as he absorbed her feminine figure. *Men are such simple creatures,* Hentie thought.

The young man pulled back his powerful shoulders and smiled broadly at Juba as he walked toward her. His well-worn clothing and calloused hands from years of physical labor betrayed his life as a field hand. His deep-brown eyes were bright with excitement as he stammered his first words to her. Juba blushed and smiled at him in a coy manner. Her reaction seemed to encourage the young man to take a step closer and engage Juba in conversation. Their interaction was brief but meaningful. Hentie smiled to herself at seeing the young man's interest in Juba. *A spark of romance might just be what Juba needs to pull out of her depression*, she thought.

Hentie and Juba whispered about the young man at a communal meal later that evening. They learned that his name was Cuffee. He had come to the plantation in the past year. The master had chosen to rent him for the year from a neighboring plantation as he needed more field hands to handle the ever-increasing cotton crop. He came on New Year's Day after the annual announcements were made about who would be rented out. Traditionally, the enslaved were given a brief respite during the Christmas holidays, but then sometimes torn from their families the first of the New Year. After a period of months, the master bought him outright.

"Cuffee," Juba mused. "Hmmm, Cuffee. He sure is fine." Juba flushed as she spoke the words and gazed at him. Cuffee, at first oblivious to her stare, looked over briefly at her. His face lit up when he realized she was looking his way. He smiled back and gave her a nod. It was like a small bolt of electricity; as she caught his gaze, her body gave a subtle jerk and she smiled back. Titillating sensations crept up Juba's spine as she eyed the young man. He seemed so different from the other men on the plantation. Their gaze lingered a few moments before it was interrupted by the driver, Duke, speaking to Cuffee. The connection broke, but Juba continued to tingle. She was captivated by him. *He sure is handsome*, she mused. *He sure is handsome.*

Chapter 16
Dinner at the Big House to Talk about Their Peculiar Institution of Slavery

One evening, the master planned a dinner for two important gentlemen friends vital to South Carolina's looming plans to secede from the Union and perpetuate slavery. The enslaved domestic workers who were tending the house were told to make sure everything was in its place, and only the best ingredients were used for that night's dinner. The master even sent his oldest and most trusted house slave, Amos, down to the wine cellar to retrieve two bottles of fine wine and one of port.

The master made sure that the front of the grounds and the adjacent formal gardens were swept and meticulously groomed. Out front, a fountain gurgled into an impressive marble basin. Surrounding the fountain were the boxwood hedges which an enslaved topiary craftsman had carefully sculpted. The fragrance of the boxwood lilted through the air.

Hentie tilted to extend her stiff back, then pulled out some of the finer linens for the long dining table. She then snapped the linen over the dark wood and smoothed out the damask cloth, careful not to leave a single wrinkle. She topped it with a pretty arrangement of flowers.

What if one of the men don't like Nellie's dinner dishes? What if a server accidently spills something? The master would be fit to be tied.

The master ordered that the house attendants use the "whistle walk" as they carried food from the kitchen house to the main house. This protocol required the slaves to whistle the entire time they walked from where they picked up the prepared food in the kitchen house until it was delivered at the main house, thereby ensuring that the server did not spit in the food as they walked. Apparently, some enslaved had been known to sully the food as recompense for bad treatment, an offense that might be disciplined by twenty stripes, no matter how much the master might have deserved it.

Nellie passed Hentie in the dining room, and sweat was beading up on Nellie's forehead. Hentie noticed her nervous demeaner and how she kept fretting. Hentie smiled at her tenderly, carefully cradled her hands, then said, "Don't worry none, Miss Nellie. Your dinner gonna be fine. You makin' everything the master love. The guests always love it too. We just got to get through the evening. That's all."

Nellie continued to shuffle the china and silverware, trying to speak over the clatter. Then she let the remaining silverware in her hand drop on the mahogany table as she went to her friend. "Hentie, you don't know the master like I do. He can be a mean man. One thing goes wrong, he blows up!"

"Nellie, it'll be fine." Hentie patted Nellie's arm. She knew what Nellie was talking about. The master could be unbelievably cruel at times, and you never knew when he would erupt. His mercurial temper could flare in an instant, causing him to lash out. The women returned to their chores, focusing on all that needed to be done, and didn't speak again until the meal was served, so as not to risk the master's annoyance. Hentie inwardly harbored the same fears as Nellie.

When Hentie heard horses clop up the lane to the house, she glanced out the front window and saw a buggy advance down the avenue of oaks. The heat inside her rose; her stomach tipped. The first guest was arriving. Hentie wiped her damp palms on the skirt of her pinny, took a deep, steadying breath, and with a cheerful countenance entered the warming kitchen from the front hallway. She wanted to make sure that the beautifully displayed dishes could be carried out on the master's signal.

One of the invited guests came from Charleston, although he maintained a second home in Beaufort for his family. He arrived in a stately cabriolet coach made of black leather pulled by two fine steeds. The horses were beautiful, well-maintained animals; their shiny coats glistened in the descending sunlight. The passenger in this fine rig was Robert Barnwell Rhett. He was a plain-looking man, plump with balding hair. Despite his bland appearance, he comported himself like a peacock. He wore a charcoal-gray woolen suit with a fine white linen shirt complemented by a burgundy silk cravat he had purchased in London.

Regarded by many as a crank, he was surprisingly vain, blustery and arrogant, full of self-importance and narcissism. Loudly announcing his presence, he presented fine cigars to the head butler to be circulated to the men following the meal. As the butler placed the cigars on a nearby table to be distributed later, Rhett took in his surroundings. He noticed the finely carved moldings, the thick mahogany doors with leaded-glass transoms, and the heavy brass door fittings. The entry had a tall ceiling and a crystal chandelier imported from England that glittered. Rhett's feet tapped on the black-and-white marble floor, heralding his arrival. He nodded as he thought with satisfaction that Langdon was truly a member of their "club"—the wealthy, elite planters of Charleston.

Rhett was a zealot known for his extreme views and bigotry; a man of conviction, he was the epitome of intolerance. He was a member of the South Carolina Southern Rights Association, an organization which promoted secession and the perpetuation of slavery. Rhett spewed support for the institution of slavery and the white elite way of life. Rhett was dubious in his reasoning but steadfast in his stance. Argumentative, loud, and rabid, he shared his views with anyone who would listen. Acknowledging the sometimes brutal treatment of slaves, he contended that planters were actually providing a godly service to the Negroes in their commitment to provide the poor wretches with training, shelter, and food. Never minding the black man's skills with ironwork, carpentry, masonry, and rice production, he contended they were hapless, feebleminded and inept.

Rhett was a disciple of statesman John C. Calhoun and would later follow Calhoun into public service, having taken his seat in the US Senate following his death. When speaking of Calhoun, he did so with reverence, as if speaking of a deity. Rhett never mastered the art of compromise and consensus-building, a skill necessary in Washington. This failing contributed to his mixed success as a politician. Never able to fully realize his high aspirations for political office, he became dejected and left his Senate seat after a short time.

Despite Rhett's aristocratic tone, he was actually of rather humble beginnings. Born with the surname of Smith in the town of Beaufort, south of Charleston, to parents of modest means, Rhett was frustrated by his simple lifestyle and minimal opportunity for fame. Thus, he positioned himself as an aristocrat, holding himself out as having been the heir of honorable British bloodlines derived from colonial governors. In the early 1800s, he adopted the surname of his great-great-grandfather, Colonel William Rhett, who had acted as the British governor of the Bahamas. Robert Rhett's voice was an octave higher than most other men of his breeding; he compensated for it with a feigned British accent. He always waved off questions about his slight accent as a consequence of his family's strong British influence.

Many of Rhett's views were published in his brother-in-law's newspaper, the *Charleston Mercury*, a paper of limited circulation.

Select articles penned by Rhett were widely circulated in other rags, including the *New York Times*, which brought him some notoriety. He proudly used this distinction whenever possible.

The second gentleman who came to the house that night was in an even finer rig, one made in London and shipped to America. This brougham was of impeccable finish, a deep red in color. The enclosed body of the carriage kept its rider shielded from the elements, inevitable insects, and the view of onlookers. When the carriage reached the front of the mansion, the driver set the brake and soothed the horses. Then the coachman descended, opened the door, and the occupant stepped down from the coach. His name was William Lowndes Yancey.

Yancey had darker hair than the first guest, sort of a salt and pepper. He too owned a plantation, but it was situated in the neighboring state of Alabama. He had come to Charleston to enjoy the luxurious lifestyle the city offered and to meet with other likeminded men, eager to perpetuate slavery and secede from the Union if necessary. Both owned numerous slaves. They were known as "fire-eaters," ones who inflamed passions about South Carolina leaving the Union. Yancey had the distinction of being the prince of the fire-eaters. Much like Rhett, he was rather nondescript in appearance, a compact little man with no discernable characteristics. Perhaps that was why he became so ferocious, to compensate for his otherwise unremarkable countenance. He was finely dressed in a brocade waistcoat and well-tailored dinner jacket.

As Amos, the butler, guided Mr. Yancey into the house, he bowed and lowered his eyes as a sign of respect. Yancey harrumphed at the gesture and walked by the humble enslaved man. Meanwhile, Big John approached the fine rig and directed the driver to follow him back to the stable, where the livery boy would tend to his horses. The animals would be fed, watered, and brushed out.

As Mr. Langdon's guests settled in, two more people were announced. They were the British relatives of Mr. Langdon's wife.

Lord David Turnbull and his wife, Rose, had written to Emily about their tour of the American Southeast and their plans to visit; however, due to her "spells" and chronic use of her special elixir drops, Mrs. Langdon had forgotten the matter. Lord Turnbull had previously acted as a newspaper correspondent while in Cuba and had observed the harsh reality of slavery. Little did this great abolitionist know that he was stumbling into the lion's den of slave owners. He had once written a letter to Lord Palmerston, the British foreign secretary, of his observations of slavery in Cuba, calling it "the greatest practical evil that ever afflicted mankind." He did not support the institution of slavery, but was cautious enough to hold his tongue while in the home of a Southern planter.

Hentie was anxious about the whole ordeal. Amid the clatter of china and silverware, she thought, *Oh Lord Jesus, why does he need to have this big party anyway? What is the master making a fuss about? Some wealthy white men he need to impress?*

In the main room a violinist and his accompaniment serenaded the guests during the sherry hour. They mixed and chatted, exchanging pleasantries, and started to relax after their travels. Hentie stepped outside for a few moments to calm herself. She stood by the railing and took in the scents from boxwood and recently pruned rose bushes. She stared at the figures moving past the windows inside the room. The music behind the windowpanes soothed her. As she felt the wind rise and began to shiver, Hentie decided she had best return to the festivities. The missus would be vexed if she found her out there. She strolled back in, drew in a deep breath, and prepared herself to face the rest of the evening.

Hentie and Nellie went on with their preparations. They tried to anticipate every need to keep the dinner moving along and keep things in good order. Their perturbed state intensified as the evening progressed. Hentie exuded anxiety.

At one point, Hentie brushed the flour from her apron, wiped her dark hands on a cloth, and silently walked toward Mimba, the older enslaved house servant who practiced hoodoo and loved to play tricks on the white folks who visited the big house. Mimba was a tiny woman, bent at the waist, her frame contorted from years of labor. No longer sturdy enough for work in the fields, she had been retrained as an enslaved house girl and seamstress. Mimba looked up at Hentie as a child might before being scolded, knowing what Hentie was about to say. The small troll-like creature was notorious for her wicked practices and had been chastised on many occasions before this night.

Hentie made Mimba swear to God that she would behave herself while they entertained the house guests. Hentie, in her firm but gentle manner, managed to solicit a promise from Mimba that she wouldn't tinker with the occult; no hexes and no conjuring. Mimba promised to stay in her quarters and away from the house, refraining from any hoodoo on the white buckra. Hentie was relieved when Mimba strode away from the house toward some other servants walking toward the slave cabins at the rear of the plantation.

Hentie kept checking in on the master and his guests to make sure they were enjoying themselves. Hentie overheard the master speaking companionably with his guests, nodding in agreement with them. Fortunately, all went well. The master looked his best; his tall frame filled out the new suit of clothes he wore, and the pale-blue shirt and tie complemented his captivating blue eyes. He kept nodding at Hentie and smiling when he was able to do so, his pale aquamarine eyes flashing at her. Hentie would nod back at the master and give a hasty curtsy as she backed out of the room. Her manner always seemed to soothe him.

As the diners completed their meal, Hentie's worries dissipated. Everyone enjoyed the foods served, and their appetites were satiated. The fine wines served by the master seemed to lubricate their spirits. As the evening progressed, some of the others began to peel off and leave the room. First, Fitzwilliam rose to retire to his room accompanied by his valet. Then Mrs. Langdon, their nephew Adrian, and Lady Turnbull left the dining room, leaving the four men alone to talk, drink port, and enjoy their cigars. The discussion changed from pleasantries about their families and reminiscing about the days when they were young men to a topic of a more serious nature.

The men rose from the table and strolled to an adjacent room, the master's library. The room was a very masculine setting with a large, hand-carved desk and leather desk chair. On the wall opposing the desk were three club chairs covered in a blue damask fabric and a burgundy silk settee. Drapes in a deep-wine shade complementing the settee were made of an imported brocade. Well-organized books lined the shelves, with an occasional memento for decoration. Two portraits in gilded frames hung from opposing walls.

Hentie entered the room with a tray of fresh crystal glasses for the bourbon and port. Included was an array of cheeses and sweets plated and garnished in a visually pleasing manner. Hentie set them on a side table and assumed a position by the wall, taking care to be inconspicuous.

Yancey approached the box of hand-rolled cigars brought to the dinner by Rhett. After critically examining each one for shade and color, he plucked a choice specimen from the case. He deftly clipped the end of the cigar with his personal silver cigar cutter. In one flowing motion he then struck a match on the heel of his boot and lit the stogie, blowing out a plume of smoke.

Taking a deep breath, Yancey opened the discussion by saying, "The question involving our peculiar institution of slavery is one the whole nation is grappling with now. It's not just us who wonder what may happen. The importance of slavery weighs more heavily on the areas of the South where cotton is grown. It's more critical in the Lowcountry; the labor slaves provide keeps our production going and our crops bountiful."

Robert Rhett settled upon the settee, cleared his throat, and responded in his assumed British tongue, "Managing slaves can be a precarious matter. We not only have to contend with those

Yankee agitators, but uppity blacks as well. Look at what occurred in Barbados with their slave uprising. In the middle of the night a whole army of slaves attacked their white masters and their poor innocent families. The bastards slit their necks while they were sleeping. How do we protect ourselves from such an event here? There are far more Negroes than white men in South Carolina. We will always have to be on guard against them."

Rhett went on, pacing his comments in his disguised accent. "Look at the Stono slave rebellion in the last century. They didn't just talk about killing their masters. They rose up and did it. They slaughtered about thirty whites outside Charleston. It was horrid, absolutely horrid!"

Langdon added, "Those recalcitrant slaves were enticed by the Spanish down in Saint Augustine promising to give them aid and comfort. It was like dangling candy in front of children."

Langdon raked his fingers through his thick flaxen hair and went on. "Look at what happened with the Denmark Vesey planned uprising. Had that bastard's scheme gone as planned, we'd all be dead. That hasn't been that long ago. Thank God the authorities found out in time and shut it down. Vesey had recruited legions of men all over the city and throughout the countryside. That snake had connections all over the entire black community! First at that damn black church of his, Mother Emanuel, and then through his carpentry business. He got all the slaves riled up. There are still reverberations because of his agitation. Slaves couldn't handle freedom even if they were granted it. The poor wretches don't realize they are much better off under our care and supervision."

Yancey rose to his feet, his short frame full of rage as he pounded his fist on the large mahogany desk. He pulsated with agitation as his voice quaked. "We should be able to do whatever we want to keep our slaves scared and under our thumbs! Don't let them challenge our authority. The slaves outnumber us here by some incomprehensible number. The ratio between whites and blacks had been two-to-one;

I understand it's now three-to-one. Up in outlying towns like Goose Creek, it's as much as four-to-one! One man there claimed it was actually more like ten-to-one. Who knows?"

Rhett chimed in, his high-pitched voice almost jarring. "Thank God we've taken on safeguards in this city with the City Guard and the slave patrol. Those charged with managing the city of Charleston aren't afraid to do whatever it takes to maintain order and keep the Negroes in their place. I think hanging an insolent darkie up in chains in White Point Gardens was one of the best things we ever did. He dangled there for days so that all the coloreds could see, especially those passing on Charleston Harbor. We have to keep them scared and keep them in their place. Hang their damn bodies for all to see!" His grating voice lingered in the room for a moment.

Langdon added, "How would we ever run our plantations without the help of the slaves? We're not like the Northern states. We don't have factories and machines that can do our work. We need their labor and lots of it. Big John, McBride, and Duke tell me when to plant the rice, when to flood the field, and when to drain it. They do the same thing with the cotton. It's too labor intensive; I could never do it all without them. Nor could I afford to pay hired help."

Langdon thrust out his arms in dismay. "For the cotton I grow, I have to have my field hands to pick it all. I couldn't do it without them. The bolls appear all at once and have to be picked within days. Those shards would cut your fingers to pieces! What white man would do that work?"

He toyed with a paperweight on his desk, his long fingers knocking it to-and-fro as he spoke. "Labor is our most precious commodity. It's not the land, really. It's the manpower, the labor of our slaves, that's so critical."

Rhett dropped his voice an octave and tucked in his chin. "Langdon is right, you know. Planters just put new plots under cultivation if they need to. Land we have; it's the labor that keeps it all going. This rich land of the South is just asking to be harnessed.

I think we are just the men to capitalize on it. We will form a new gentry more revered that those damn Yankees ever dreamed of!"

Rhett became red in the face, all splotchy and scarlet, and jabbed his arm outward, then slapped his hand on the table. "States were promised that they would always keep their rights when we formed this union! The federal government has to stay out of the business of South Carolina. My dear friend and mentor John Calhoun emphasized that to me. Maybe just our state should secede from the Union. We could function on our own, you know. This state has to remain a proslavery state, no matter what happens. We need the labor of our slaves too badly."

Rhett recited the contention of many Southerners with the slow-paced authority of the King's English: "We all know that a black man is a lesser being than a white man. One doesn't ever want colored people living fully in our society; it would sully our race. They don't have the intelligence to survive on their own. We do the black man a favor by offering him a place to live, giving him clothes on his back, and teaching him a trade. It's not just a necessary evil, it is a benevolent act done with the blessing of God himself."

Rhett took in a deep breath, then tugged with both hands on the bottom of his waistcoat and continued. "After all, we are good-looking men of wealth, descended from English gentlemen. Look at the global strength of the British Empire. Our ancestors gave us distinctive breeding and looks. Take our host, Langdon, for instance. A dashing tall man with broad shoulders, fair hair and sharp blue eyes like a wolf. That's how Charlestonians came up with the term 'master race'—not only based on our looks and our superior intelligence, but on the fact that we are a race of masters."

Yancey then mused, "Rhett, you're exactly right. We are meant to carry the wealth of the South, if not the country. God bestowed this superior ability on us, and it is our duty to fulfill His plan. Our social order has worked for generations. We inherited our wealth and have kept it in our planter families. We are the ones who are fit to rule the land, with our superior intellect by breeding and fine classical education. Physical labor could kill the intellect a man possesses; he would become a mere animal. That is why the black slaves are charged with performing the toil of the fields. It is their place as God devised!"

"The Church supports what we do," said Langdon with steadfast certitude. "All the local clergy speak of our role as benevolent caretakers. This is a way of life sanctified by God. We have mutual responsibilities and affections with our feebleminded slaves. We treat them like family and provide a sound home to them."

Rhett, with his chilling voice, chimed in, saying, "Slavery serves to elevate the character of the master and the society he inhabits. Maintaining such a social order makes the probity of the white master stricter, the pride of character higher, and the sense of honor stronger. Being free of physical labor and toil, we have the leisure necessary to pursue art, literature, politics, and the refinement of our mind, our physical being, and our community as a whole. It results in a more cultivated man and society. Just look at the societies of Egypt and Rome and the everlasting works created by the labor of slaves. For eons sophisticated societies have flourished with the use of slaves. How can it be wrong?"

"We are merely the master class as God intended. I for one am not about to fight the will of God!" shouted Langdon.

With great reverence for his idol, Rhett retorted, "Thank God we had a good man like John C. Calhoun that helped bolster our way of life and guide our thinking. He was one of the best men who ever lived. Look at all the posts he held, both here in South Carolina and at the federal level. Who else accomplished all that? The man was brilliant."

Rhett went on to explain, "Calhoun understood slavery; he interacted with those darkies most of his life. While some hoped that the institution of slavery would gradually fade away, Calhoun bravely defended our peculiar institution. How could it be wrongheaded if John C. Calhoun believed it? Southerners trust in his words; it defines our way of life."

Rhett shook his head as he continued, "Well, some held a few unfortunate incidences against him. You know, the Nullification Crisis and the Petticoat Affair. He was right in both instances; it was just an unfortunate turn of events for him."

Lord Turnbull, having been noticeably quiet, finally spoke up. "What was the Nullification Crisis all about, anyhow? I'm not sure I understood it all."

Rhett explained, "Calhoun believed his home state was unduly burdened by federal taxes. Back several years ago, the Federals set a tariff of a sixty percent tax on most imported goods to the United States. Sixty percent, can you believe that? Calhoun thought it would discourage trade between Great Britain and the Carolinas. Cotton was, and still is, the lifeblood of the South. We need to export the cotton overseas, and Britain needs it for its booming textile industry. It was a symbiotic relationship, really; we both got something out of it. If the tax was perpetuated, foreign trade would have been interrupted, and God only knows how it could have impacted the price of cotton. Planters and the South as a whole could have been ruined. Calhoun believed a local court could declare the tariffs null and void within our sovereign boundaries. He didn't think they should be bothered with a US Supreme Court review."

Rhett continued to speak in sympathetic tones of his mentor Calhoun. "Well, I believe that's what led Calhoun to call for secession back around 1830. He wanted to defend states' rights. We couldn't let the Northerners decide everything. How could they know what was best for Southern interests? They had all that heavy industry; our interests were different from theirs. But the Nullification Crisis eventually came to a head and there was a compromise, otherwise South Carolina might have broken off from the rest of the country. Fortunately, it all worked out in the end."

There was a break in the conversation as the men refreshed their drinks. Hentie poured generous amounts of liquor for the guests. Lord Turnbull remained silent throughout the conversation, appalled by what he was hearing. He reflected on those things he had seen while in Cuba—the brutality of how slaves were treated.

One of his neighbors, a lawyer, took pride in the fact that he "disciplined" his own slaves. He didn't pale at the unsavory job of whipping a servant. Lord Turnbull saw him execute a lashing of one of his servant girls. She had bumped him while he was eating, causing him to slosh his soup and burn his lap. He had sprung to his feet and grabbed the girl by her hair, dragging her to an adjacent room. He directed his family to stay at the dinner table while he executed his duty. He directed Turnbull to follow.

After shutting the door, he ordered the young girl to disrobe and stand before him. While fondling her, he asked if she had experienced a man yet. She hesitated at first, not quite understanding what he was asking. She then blushed and said no.

The master burst out, saying, "Well, girl, it's high time you did!"

Then he savagely beat her and then bit her breasts. Once she fell to the floor, he pulled her up and entered her. The girl screamed with pain, but he persisted and said it was time she was broken in. Following the act, he dropped the girl like a rag doll. He then pulled out the lash made of cowhide and beat her. Too overwhelmed to move, she lay helpless. Her skin split open, and scarlet droplets ran down her back. Lord Turnbull remembered how disturbing it was to see the girl's blood spattering the white walls. Some even marked the dinner host's white shirt. The moment was a stain on Turnbull's mind.

His mind turned to another incident in which a house girl made the mistake of accidently soiling a ledge with ashes while cleaning the hearth. She was whipped for marking the mantelpiece with a dead coal. The slave woman's mistress forced her mammy who had reared her to lash her bare back, a particularly painful task since she had raised the girl from a newborn.

Turnbull had seen so much cruelty in Cuba and more in America. He was aware of the harsh laws impacting the lives of Negroes in the United States. Pursuant to a slave code from the late 1600s, a black man was forbidden to strike a white man, even if he was being attacked. He could only hit a white man if defending his master. Punishment for hitting a white man could be severe and included death for a second or third offense.

Much to his horror, Lord Turnbull witnessed many of these acts of discipline. Slavery did seem to blunt a man's moral sense of what was right or wrong. The abominable injustice of the law of South Carolina, much like Cuba, was zealously enforced by self-righteous men who considered themselves Christian and deserving of their position in life. *How wrong,* he thought. He saw Negro men shot dead in the street as if they were mongrel dogs. *How can these men talk about human life as if it had no value whatsoever?*

He turned his attention back to the conversation at hand.

"Gentlemen, is this really the only way you can live, standing on the backs of black men and women? Human beings are being tortured and killed." Turnbull's query burst forth like a foul odor in the room.

Rhett reared up and barked in his shrill voice, "The Negro man is not a concern. They are not people; they are a lesser being!"

Turnbull was taken aback by Rhett's venom. Slavery perverted the natural feelings of the human heart. He rethought how much he should say. He was already on tentative grounds with the crown and British monarchy over his reporting in a British newspaper, the *London Times*, of the horrors of slavery in Cuba. In addition, Turnbull had written a book documenting the abominable condition of the enslaved and was subsequently expelled by the Cuban government. He had been indicted and convicted in absentia for allegedly promoting a slave rebellion. The latter fact was apparently unknown to his host and Mr. Langdon's guests.

Hentie began clearing away the fine crystal glassware as

she carefully passed through the room, trying to make herself inconspicuous as she moved. She held a small round tray in her left hand and reached down with her right to clear the stemware and small dishes.

Yancey yammered on about the expansive plantations near his home. "Fields of cotton go on for miles and miles. You can watch the Negros workers as far as the eye can see." He abruptly swept his hand out just as Hentie approached, knocking off one of the small pieces of stemware. It hit the hard wooden floor and exploded into a hundred pieces, scattering shards everywhere along with a fine white dust.

Stunned, Hentie jumped back. She had never had an accident with dishes or glassware. Her jaw dropped as she touched her fingers to her cheek in horror. "Oh my! Sir, I'm so sorry. I didn't mean to get in your way. I'm so sorry!"

"You stupid wench! You clumsy buffoon! How could you so carelessly smash your master's fine crystal!" Turning to Langdon he said, "You must have this careless Negress whipped! Look at what she did." He waved his hand over the broken glass.

Knowing what a good and reliable worker Hentie was, the master hesitated for a moment. In all her time at Twin Oaks, she had never committed a transgression. "Certainly, I will send for McBride straight away. He will ensure she is punished. I think twenty lashes should do it. Amos! Go get McBride, now!"

Turnbull jumped to his feet. "But, sir, the fault is not with your servant. Yancey is the one who knocked over the glass. Why should your slave girl be punished for your guest's error?"

"Because she broke the glass! It fell from her tray. She alone had control over it. We cannot blame Yancey for her carelessness," shouted Rhett.

"Sir, you whip her only because she is a Negro, not because she committed a wrongful act." He turned and picked up an imported crystal carafe with an amber liquor in it. He carefully lifted it up, then held it momentarily before him. "What, then, shall you do to me?"

And he dropped it from chest height onto the floor, smirking as he did so. It hit the floor and broke into fragments.

"What are you doing? You idiot! That carafe belonged to my father!"

"Then surely if my transgression has wronged you, should I too be flogged?"

Yancey clucked his tongue against the roof of his mouth and turned away, shaking his head. Rhett harrumphed and paced to the other side of the room. Meanwhile, Hentie remained motionless, terrified to move.

As Amos entered the room, the master said, "Amos, take Hentie to her quarters. Tell McBride I will speak with him later. Hentie, we will talk in the morning."

The master, feeling caught in a ticklish situation, stepped back and drew a deep breath.

As everyone returned to their chairs, they avoided eye contact. They straightened their jackets, swirled their drinks and knocked the ash from their cigars. Looking about the room, a deadly silence fell over them. It continued for a few minutes.

Turnbull rose to his feet as anger rose inside him. "Gentlemen, you don't *have* to do this. You don't have to perpetuate slavery and your brutal treatment of Negroes. We are a civilized society. Men are free to rule their lives and their society as they see fit. We can rise above this and function with greater humanity."

Yancey abruptly lifted out of his fine upholstered chair and said, "Sir, you are not an American, let alone a Southerner. You do not understand our way of life here. Slavery is vital to us!"

Turnbull took a step toward the man and look down upon his short frame. "I understand far more than you do. I am a worldly gentleman. I have traveled extensively. I have seen more than you will ever see in your lifetime. As a journalist working internationally, it was my job to understand humanity. You can't see beyond the end of your nose, man," Trumbull huffed, then returned to his seat.

Langdon swung his head, glancing between the men, not sure what to do. Trumbull was kin; his other guests were mere friends, but vital to his interests. *Damn, how shall I handle this? I must tramp down the hostility here.*

Yancey, inflamed by the words, stamped his heeled boot on the wooden floor. "Why, you vile bastard! How dare you challenge me while on American soil! You are a mere guest here. I can ensure that you will be sent out to sea by dusk tomorrow, you fool! The British are not to tamper with our affairs here. We've thrown your stinking hides out once, by God; we can do it again!"

Turnbull seethed with anger but held his tongue, at least momentarily. He knew that Yancey had a point. He was a powerful man and Turnbull was on thin ice being on foreign soil. He squirmed in his seat a bit, looked away and rolled his eyes.

A moment later a thought occurred to him. "The framers of your constitution spent days debating the slavery question. They knew it was wrong, but they were being courted by rich men of greed, much like yourselves. Those planters were worried about keeping their pockets lined with money garnered by the sweat and blood of unfortunate Negroes. No morals, no scruples, just sheer greed. The men who wrote the Constitution just crossed their fingers and hoped this horrid institution would fade out. Men would eventually see reason. Your minds are too small to have reached that conclusion."

Rhett sprang to his feet, slamming down his crystal tumbler of scotch whiskey, spraying the liquid across Langdon's desk. He stomped toward Turnbull and spoke so forcefully his spittle sprayed his opponent's face. "You pompous ass! What do you know of our constitution? The Brits have gone around the globe conquering people and snatching up land for centuries. What does your country know of freedom? How do you think most of these slaves got here? It was through the damn British slave traders. Don't speak to me of your righteous notions!"

Turnbull jumped from his chair and moved toward Rhett. He came inches from his face and drew back his hand to strike the smaller man. Their stare was fierce. Rhett refused to back down, standing his ground and stiffening his body, preparing to be struck. Turnbull, knowing his options, let out a forceful puff of air and turned toward the door.

"Gentlemen, you are wrong. What you are doing is depraved and evil. One day you will realize that. I blanche at the thought of what your country will go through to rid itself of what you call your peculiar institution of slavery. You poor fools, I will pray for your souls. I bid you good night." With that he turned on his heel and exited the room.

Rhett shouted, "That man Turnbull is a fool."

In exasperation, Langdon huffed, "I can't imagine a Southern gentleman without his slaves. They are essential to us."

Rhett rose and paced the floor as he rubbed his balding scalp, his truncated physique obvious in the large room. He added matter-of-factly, "It would behoove us to reinstate international slave trade. If we had fresh slaves directly from Africa, their heads wouldn't be so full of ideas about freedom. But international slave trade has been illegal for a while now. A lot of countries support that. That would be a hard one to fight."

"Maybe we get it started again, but we don't tell all those other countries," Yancey suggested with raised eyebrows and a mischievous smile.

Following the evening meal, port, and cigars, most everyone retired to their respective rooms, as the guests would be spending the night at Twin Oaks. Lord Turnbull had exited out the back of the main house and decided to take a stroll and contemplate the discussion he had just heard.

Charleston was such a city of contrasts, with gaiety and splendor, yet misery and degradation. He walked past the balustrade at the rear of the main house and out onto the grounds of the plantation.

A warm, moist breeze caressed his face as he strolled. He looked out on the well-manicured, rolling lawn and gardens. The evening dampness had started to roll in, and he could detect the fragrant green grasses surrounding him. The scent from the magnolia tree with its deep-green, leathery leaves wafted over him. A partial moon peered through an opening in the cloud cover, a shadow taking a portion of the edge. The skies foreboded darker times to come; the thought sent hairs prickling up his back. As he progressed through the gardens, he continued to draw in the heady scents. The constant whirring of the cicadas comforted him.

Lord Turnbull noted the enslaved servants who were still walking about the grounds, carrying out their duties. It was such a long day for them. He looked out to the slave cabins in the distance, where delicate floral blossoms in pastel hues hung against the deep, charcoal gray of the decrepit hovels. Such beauty surrounded the dark, dank pits of existence. Such a dichotomy.

The perplexed Englishman tucked his hand into his waistcoat pocket and pulled out a small case of tobacco, his pipe, and a match. He struck the match on a retaining wall enclosing a large bed of roses. A small flame flared, birthing a smoke tendril that curled and plumed. He lit his pipe and puffed until the light took hold, then flicked the match to the ground as he strolled along. As he sucked on his pipe and puffed out the smoke, he wondered how the human mind could be so twisted as to believe that the brutality of slavery was a good thing for enslaved Negroes.

As a British subject, Lord Turnbull was fully aware that the queen and Parliament were troubled by the slavery question in America. The Commonwealth wanted to maintain good relations with the rebellious young country, but it was a diplomatic nightmare. By this time, all European countries, including England, had abolished slavery. Wanting to maintain diplomatic ties, England and the British Isles walked a narrow line in upholding their own legal mandates while recognizing the racist practices of the United States.

The city possessed a preponderantly black population. Being so dramatically outnumbered, white elite Charlestonians were terrified of the thought of a Negro insurrection. They began reinforcing the fence tops of the walls that surrounded their stately homes, installing spikes and *chevaux-de-frise* as ornamental armor. The legislature was pressured to enact laws which impacted Negroes, both Americans and nationals of other countries. Free black British seamen were being jailed upon landing in Charleston. Under the laws of South Carolina, if the seamen went ashore or even came into Charleston Harbor, the sailors would be thrown into the city jail. The conditions of the jail were horrific. As the ship was about to depart, the Negro seamen would be put back on board the vessel—that is, if the local constable felt like it. Some were kept, perhaps on a whim, perhaps because they argued that they were free and should not be subject to such foul treatment. The only basis for their incarceration was that the sailors were black. While at the jail, these foreign Negroes faced the same harsh treatment and brutality as local people of color. They could be beaten, starved, and raped.

The ostensible reason for the confinement was the fear that the black seamen might have a subversive influence on South Carolinian citizens of color. White Southerners lived in constant dread that their enslaved Africans might be inspired to rise up and kill their masters. Liberated blacks were seen as carriers of an insurrectionary plague that must be quarantined. The pronounced racial imbalance in the Lowcountry heightened the fears.

The British consul in Charleston seemed much like a sinking boat in a fetid swamp. It was difficult for Her Majesty's consuls to maintain diplomatic rapport, protect British interests, yet challenge the unreasonable actions of the local police. What to do? The Americans needed to sort this out, and the Brits had no power to intercede. They could be thrown out much as they had during the Revolution.

Lord Turnbull knew that, unfortunately, the African slave trade was surreptitiously occurring as the fire-eaters hoped. While a slave ship rarely made landfall in Charleston, newly captured slaves sometimes made their way to the city after arriving elsewhere, such as Cuba. Traders then took them to the United States and other countries to eagerly waiting buyers. Human trafficking was a lucrative business. No matter where the ship was registered, they often flew the flag of the United States so that they would not be boarded while on the high seas. Often the underwriters were wealthy investors, such as New Yorkers or those living in Newport, Rhode Island, with deep pockets. Some saw it as a more predictable, stable investment than industry or the stock market. These wealthy moneymen were guided and abetted by men like Robert Barnwell Rhett, Jr., and other fire-eaters.

Recently, a slave ship named *Echo* had been captured in Cuba and subsequently moored in Charleston Harbor. The ship was seized during an antislavery patrol in the Atlantic conducted by an American warship—the first victory in the slave-trafficking struggle.

The captured vessel was moored at Gadson's Landing. The foul smell of vomit, blood, feces, and urine emanated from the ship, hanging in the hot, humid summer air. The slaver was laden with disease and vermin. A screen teeming with fleas and gnats covered the ship. Cockroaches poured out of the vessel in a moving black sheath. Some of the townspeople had never seen such a sight. The Middle Passage had been outlawed for some time, so most had never encountered a slave ship. The squalid vessel contained about 300 naked and diseased Negro captives who were mere skeletons. About 100 of the original 471 Negroes had died on the journey. Of those who had survived the passage, sixty were women, and each and every one of them was pregnant. Articles about the incident and the atrocities committed on board appeared in Charleston's local newspapers, the *Mercury* and also in the *Courier*.

The captain of this ship and his crew were arrested and locally imprisoned. It was rather an odd sight to see the vessel's crew paraded through the streets of the city en route to the jail, since slavery was something that had gone on in the city for over 200 years.

The captive Africans experienced a different fate. Much discussion went on as to whether the enslaved should be parceled out to plantation owners or maintained in a neutral environment. Ultimately, it was decided that the 300 or so African captives who had survived would be housed on the grounds of the newly constructed Fort Sumter. There they would await a decision following the prosecution of the ship's captain and his crew. The weeks wore on with the Africans waiting in this rather precarious situation.

The defendants were represented by lead attorney Leonidas Spratt, a vocal advocate of the revival of the African slave trade. He owned a local newspaper named the *Charleston Standard* that not only defended slavery but glorified it and promoted the life of the white elite. Spratt contended that slavery was a natural condition of the Negro and should be perpetuated.

While there was an abundance of evidence that the captain and his crew had in fact transported newly enslaved humans from Africa, the Charleston jury refused to indict. It seemed no justice could be had in the city.

Thirty-five captive Negroes died at Fort Sumter while awaiting the outcome of the marauders' criminal proceedings. Those who survived were later transported by ship back to their native Africa. Another seventy-one died while en route. While indelible trauma, heartache, and pain was inflicted on the Negro victims, the white perpetrators were let go without consequence. The fire-eaters such as Rhett and Yancey pushed on to reopen the African slave trade as the feckless citizenry despondently stood by, afraid to act or even speak against the proslavery advocates.

White Charlestonians were fearful of even showing kindness to a Negro. To do so could bring reprisal. Such actions had been known to result in people being attacked and beaten. Some had their homes or outbuildings burned. It was a precarious situation in the city and environs.

And so, the brutal institution of slavery continued on without interruption while the debate continued to percolate throughout the country.

Chapter 17
Fall Harvest:
Long Days of Labor and Eventual Celebration

Hentie picked up her basket of feed and made her way to the kitchen-house door. Now that she and Nellie had the kitchen in order for the morning meal, she needed to tend to some of her other chores. Nellie could finish baking the buttermilk biscuits for the master and his family. Hentie stepped out in the work yard. The warm sun shone down on her, and a gentle breeze swept across her face. Clucking sounds from a handful of hens and a rooster drew her attention. As she turned to toss the feed out to them, the fragrance of the late-blooming honeysuckle wafted by her.

The pleasant odor was such a lovely blessing. It mellowed Hentie's spirit and enlivened her. She would need the energy not only today but for a few weeks to come. Summer was coming to a close, and harvest would commence soon. With the field hands doing extra labor, the kitchen-house staff would be called upon to work even harder.

Twin Oaks produced a variety of crops. To the gold rice, indigo, tobacco and cotton were added limited numbers of fruits and vegetables, particularly peaches and pecans. Recently, the master decided to add a fig orchard. The fruit produced could be dried and shipped anywhere. Certain crops drained the soil of its nutrients, so a rotation of crops was incorporated. Other nearby planters did not bother with rotation and trying to build up depleted soil; they just moved on to another plot of land. Certain crops could have more than one planting in a year, such as strawberries—they had three plantings, starting in February. In contrast, cotton took the entire growing season.

When growing season ended, everyone was charged and eager. It meant long, grueling hours in the hot sun, but once it was over the enslaved workers were usually rewarded with a day or two off from their labors. It was the only time of year that such a reprieve occurred, other than Christmas.

As the day to commence the fall harvest neared, enslaved workers geared up. McBride, the white overseer, encouraged Mr. Langdon to increase the food rations of the enslaved workers. Mr. Langdon agreed and added a modest amount of food to their meager rations. While generally the enslaved only got about a pound of meat a week, the master sometimes allowed one and a half to two pounds and extra starches like rice, corn, or potatoes. Although it was a direct benefit to the slave owner to keep his workers healthy and properly fed while they worked eighteen-hour days, it was nonetheless viewed as a kindness by most of the workers. Even planters themselves considered it a benevolent act.

During this time when harvest was crucial, as many hands as were available went to work in the fields. Overseer McBride rode on horseback to monitor the workers. Duke, the plantation's black driver, traveled sometimes on horseback and other times on foot to maintain a closer view. The work was arduous as field hands picked cotton and other crops by hand. The air hung with the moisture, swelling and emulsifying with the humid weight, even beyond what one typically endured in a Carolina summer. The temperatures soared from around ninety to one hundred degrees. The sun beat down relentlessly on the workers during the workday. Their dark heads glistened with sweat as their strong bodies repeatedly bent and straightened, moving in lines down the fields.

However, as the days passed from August into September, something in the air started to change. In the morning the skies were saffron in color, but the setting sun was more turquoise, garnet, and sapphire. Nearly every afternoon was baptized with roiling thunderstorms, full of electricity, thunder, buckets of water, and the power of the gods. As damning as the thunderstorms were, they did bring down the oppressive temperatures a bit. It went from blistering, sweltering heat to thick, sultry humidity you could wade through in hip boots.

The rain and blustery winds often sent a chill skittering up Hentie's back, bringing back memories of the turbulent seas she had endured on the slaver ship. The rocking ship on the steep waves of the open ocean was such a horrific memory. All the captives had been so sick and unable to quiet themselves in the tight, cramped spaces of the hold of the ship. She always tried to push such memories out of her head.

Around this time of year, veteran workers would point out special clouds called "mares' tails," cirrus clouds that warned of tropical storms heading toward the mainland. Usually within a week after witnessing mares' tails clouds, a tropical system would pass through.

On this day, Hentie, Nellie, and Juba brought food and drink out to the workers. Big John drove a wagon for them to carry all that they needed. They brought with them young children old and sensible enough to manage water and properly dispense it to the parched workers—usually around age four or five. This was one of the most crucial times of the year, and everyone was called upon to do their part. As they approached the field workers, Hentie heard the low rhythmic melodies of field songs.

Juba was always eager to help by passing out food and water. Cuffee, the young man she had her eye on, worked in the fields. She pined for him and was at the ready to take nourishment to his team. It allowed her to have contact and to share a few words. While long conversations and any intimacy were out of the question, Juba was thrilled if Cuffee touched her hand and smiled when taking food from her. As Cuffee caught Juba's eyes, excitement seized her. She quickly jumped down before the wagon came to a full stop.

"Slow down, child!" exclaimed Octavia as she chuckled her warm, treacle laugh. "That boy ain't goin' nowhere." She shook her head and smiled, then turned toward Hentie and rolled her eyes. Hentie, catching her look, smiled back.

From where they stood, Hentie saw dark figures standing in the waist-high cotton, dipping and rising like waves on the ocean as they tended to their work. Traditional songs and gospels floated through the air. Their harmonies helped them endure their labors and get through the day.

When Cuffee looked up again and locked eyes with Juba, her heart thumped erratically in excitement. Juba carried the food to Cuffee and the others. She felt a bead of sweat trickle down between her shoulder blades as the heat beat down on her. Juba didn't mind, not if it meant she might be able to see Cuffee; she would wait all day in the sun to do so.

The enslaved workers were happy to see Hentie and the others; they had worked up an appetite. The harvest was going well, and they were starting to see the light at the end of the tunnel. The feeling that morning was that they were all part of a united team and excited as they pursued a common goal of bringing in the harvest. They knew it would be followed by some much-needed rest and celebration.

As Juba had hoped, she got to speak with Cuffee briefly. As she passed him a piece of corn bread, the air above their hands sizzled with electricity. That spark would stay with her for hours; it filled her with jubilation. She was now like an empty vessel that had been filled with fine wine. She was suddenly brimming with happiness. Once they got back onto the wagon, she would take in a deep breath of air, hoping to capture some of Cuffee's essence to last her the rest of the day.

During the harvest, their hours were even longer than usual. The workers were not allowed to leave the fields until long after "first dark." They used torches to light the fields. When the workday ended, they slowly trudged back to their dwellings. Depending on which field they were assigned to, it could be a walk of some distance to reach their quarters. Some of the field hands lived in a larger dormitory; others lived in smaller cabins with a handful of others. Some were so weary they just fell into bed. Others assembled at outdoor tables where an evening meal was brought to them. Nellie would stand over a large, suspended pot, stirring constantly. She served up stone-ground cornmeal seasoned with hog's lard and some salted pork. They would also have greens cooked with fatback and onions. Nellie made her tasty corn bread; most everyone loved it and gobbled it down. Hentie cut up watermelon and cleaned strawberries. She had the smaller children pick berries up around the big house and bring them to her in sweetgrass baskets. The evening meals were much heartier than usual.

Some of the more elderly women, ordinarily charged with laundry, child care, and seamstress chores, had shifted duties. They helped out with the kitchen and any other duties needing tending. Everything was focused on the work of the field hands. As progress was made, the mood of the group started to lighten. Although the work was grueling, the enslaved workers knew they were making headway as the hand-picked cotton and fresh produce piled up in barns and storage sheds, bushel after bushel lined up. It was a colorful sight with the differing hues up against the stark wood of the barn. It filled the workers with happiness and gratification to see the stacks.

Mr. Langdon was always anxious this time of year, wondering what the outcome would be. Often vile and stressed, he had no tolerance for wasted time and effort. The results from the harvest would predict the financial outcome of the plantation for the entire year. Their labors were paying off with a seemingly abundant harvest. As a result, Mr. Langdon's humor improved as he saw the stockpiles rising. Everyone stayed on task and did as they were told by the driver and overseer. They worked efficiently and steadily.

One day Mr. Langdon rode out to the fields in a wagon with Baby Doll at his side. They were laughing and smiling. The master had on a white shirt, a pale-gray waistcoat, and breeches; his ensemble looked new. Baby Doll just glowed in a recently acquired sage-green dress. Her slim figure was accentuated by the narrow cut of the waist. It was so flattering on her. Doll's green eyes stood out, shining with contentment and lightheartedness. She had dabbed rosemary and lemon oil about her, giving her an uplifting scent; it also helped keep the mosquitoes at bay.

Hentie and her team had been out in the field for a while distributing the midday food for the enslaved workers when Hentie heard the rattle of the buckboard wagon as it shuddered along the dirt path out to the fields.

The master pulled his wagon up to Big John and Hentie as he said, "Hello, Big John. Hentie." He dipped his head in greeting. He shoved back a picnic basket tucked under the seat that had slid forward when he pulled the rig to a stop. On top of it was a neatly folded colorful quilt.

"Afternoon, Master." Big John respectfully snapped his head downward and lowered his eyes. With a broad smile he said, "Sure is a fine day, Master. This sunny day makes my soul feel good!"

"Well put, Big John. I plan to enjoy the day as well." He turned his head briefly toward Baby Doll and smiled. As he did so, Big John and Hentie exchanged a glance. Hentie then turned her head away as she looked toward the skies in displeasure.

As Big John and the master spoke, the master turned briefly to Doll, touching her leg to point out an eagle he spotted. Their eyes locked as they shared the moment and took in the scene of the eagle soaring through the bright-blue sky. Big John changed the subject to one involving the harvest and the great progress the workers were making in pulling in the crops. In the distance they heard the singing of the field hands, the distinctive tenor voice of Cuffee blending in with harmony. As the gang of workers sang, they worked in unison.

"They doing good out here, Master. They are working hard and pulling in the crop. McBride had big numbers on the chalkboard in the barn. When we weighed the gathering baskets last night, everyone met quota. Most gone over it! This year's crop heartier than anything we ever had before."

"I know. I checked the board first thing this morning. I was happy with the numbers. We're going to have a good year." The master smiled broadly. He looked happy and more relaxed than usual. Things were going well for him. The plantation was humming along with productivity, and he had a beautiful young woman sitting attentively by his side.

"You have a fine day, Baby Doll. You too, Master." Hentie raised her hand and waved to the two.

The master waved as he pulled off, but by now his eyes were locked on Doll. He had already forgotten his conversation with Big John.

"Let's get back to the Big House. Lots going on there. We best not waste time." Big John put his hand gently on Hentie's lower back and guided her to the wagon.

As Big John pulled off in his wagon with Hentie beside him, he said, "Hmm. I hope that Doll don't get into no trouble with the master. He sure do have his eye on her. He's acting like a schoolboy."

At week's end the work was done. Hentie thought the day would never come. Everyone was drained. This year Mr. Langdon decided to be particularly generous due to the abundant harvest and Baby Doll's influence, giving three days off and an outing to the beachfront. Oh my! Hentie could hardly believe it.

Back in the kitchen house, the building hummed with excitement. Everyone was jubilant and in good humor. Nellie was thrilled to be planning the food for this event. They could grill shrimp, fish, and oysters caught in the nearby waters. There were plenty of vegetables and fruits that could be taken to the beach. There were peaches, watermelons, blackberries, cantaloupe, okra, corn, peas, and tomatoes. It would be a feast like no other.

The kitchen-house staff had to gather up baskets and old crates to carry the food in and wooden bowls to eat with at the beachfront. Everyone pitched in. During the flurry of work, Juba crossed paths with Cuffee. They both smiled and blushed. At one point they happened to be loading items at the same time and touched. They paused and longingly looked at one another. Standing so close, she could feel the heat of his body and smell his scent. With all her might, she wished Cuffee would draw her close and hold her against his strong body. She yearned for it with a fierce desire, trembling briefly at the thought as her heart hurled itself against her ribcage. Because of the work at hand, not much more than a nod and a word of acknowledgment could be shared. Nonetheless, it carried Juba throughout the day. She was sure that Cuffee must have feelings for her, or he would not look at her so.

⌣

On another end of the plantation, workers prepared the harvested goods for shipment to the city of Charleston. Gathering crops from all over the expansive grounds was a huge undertaking. All the workers were out in the field or in the barn where the cotton was checked in, even some of the enslaved workers who ordinarily had other duties elsewhere on the plantation.

Hentie noted one woman, usually assigned to the laundry, toiling in and around the barn, receiving bags and baskets of cotton. She had a baby slung on her back. The sling she had crafted for the infant was made of sackcloth in which she tied the child into a snug little cocoon near her shoulder blades. The baby would press her chubby cheek on her mother's back and then fall into a wakeful stupor, watching the goings-on about her. Eventually the constant movement set the tired infant's eyes to slow, gradual, long blinks until they fell shut. Hentie smiled at the sight of it, remembering how her own daughter, Amahle, would slumber in her arms as an infant.

At long last, the grounds of Twin Oaks had started to cool a bit. The humid days of summer pressed into autumn. Hentie looked skyward and saw the dark iron of swollen clouds with their foreboding dank blanket of air.

The plantation had access to wetlands, creeks, and ponds. It was fortunate to have a freshwater source and be located on a navigable waterway which led to the Atlantic Ocean, thus giving access to fresh and salt water. There was a large dock where boats were loaded to take cotton and other products down to the city, a relatively short distance away. The dock had an upper and lower deck. The platform on the lower level was where the stevedores and shipmen loaded goods and jumped to board the boat. Immediately adjacent to it was a cavernous storage area, bigger than a barn, where goods were stored pending shipment. It was surrounded by spartina grass and cattails, and seagulls flew overhead. Unfortunately, there were also flying insects; the dockhands had to bat aside scrims of sandflies and mosquitos while they worked.

Sometimes Hentie took food and water down to the men loading the boat. She liked to go to the docks, as the surroundings by the water were so different from the rest of the grounds. It felt cooler there because of the sea breeze. The birds were different, too. She saw sandpipers hop around on the beach. With their long legs and tapered beaks, they probed the sand for food. Down in the marshland Hentie heard the high-pitched cry of the osprey and saw the beautiful black-winged raptor circle while looking for prey. With its wings extended, Hentie could see the white underbelly and underwings contrasting with its brown wrists and strongly barred flight feathers. In a single swoop it could pluck a fish from the water, the great fish hawk at work.

The marsh grasses were vibrant with their new, emerald growth. There was a sudden puff of air, and Hentie turned to identify the source of the sound. Hentie glimpsed the silver back of a mother porpoise and her baby undulating through the grasses at the water's edge.

Hentie looked up and saw the ducks starting their southward migration along their long-established flyway. As they wheeled across the sky, they moved in a single veil, honking as they soared. It was another sign that the growing season had already climaxed, and the fall harvest was nearly complete. Yet another year had passed. As she pondered what she was thankful for, she stretched and straightened her dress.

The sunrises here were striking. The shimmering sun over the water was always breathtaking. Hentie found it an ethereal and inspiring experience. It made her feel close to God there, for only he could design such beauty. Hentie felt small in the presence of a view so profound. She felt connected to it. The Gullah Geechee people had always lived close to the water and fished it. The waters abounded with a variety of fish and shrimp. There was tuna, mahi-mahi, grouper, red snapper, flounder, sea bass, and swordfish. Empowered to be part of this godlike circle of life, Hentie felt the glistening light enter her soul to fill her with hope. Perhaps one day she would be free and no longer the slave of another man.

Her life had taken so many turns since her capture in Africa. She had lost her family and come to a strange land, had to learn a new language and new customs. But she had adjusted over time. Now her days were imbued with renewed energy and purpose. She had made good friends here whom she cared deeply for and they for her. Big John was always so kind and protective. She felt safer with him around. The circle of enslaved workers here on the plantation was her new family. They were bonded for life.

As Hentie lingered on that thought, she saw the master's buggy. She turned toward it and enjoyed the coming fall coolness cloaked in the wind that caressed her face. She thought, *Lord, what does that man want now?* But as she looked back to the rig, she saw Doll sitting next to the master, giggling about something. Pulling the wagon near, the master said, "We're going into town to get some paregoric and other supplies. Nellie told me to get flour and salt. Is there anything else we need for the main house?"

Hentie gave a quick curtsy and said, "No, sir, I think we're doing just fine. Thank you for asking."

Hentie noticed the nice blue calico dress Doll was wearing. She glanced down in embarrassment at her own soiled gingham dress and felt the heat in her cheeks rise.

Hentie waved them off and said, "Enjoy your trip!"

Boy, the master sure is in a good mood. I'm surprised he stopped to talk to me. Must be because he's with Doll, Hentie thought.

The master and Doll nodded and waved, then turned the buggy around to the main road. The two looked happy. Hentie noted how they leaned into one another as they spoke. Doll's belly was looking round and swollen. *The missus is going to throw a fit when she finds out Doll having the master's baby.*

The following day the jubilant crowd of enslaved workers prepared themselves for the festivities. Several field hands jumped in two wagons typically used to haul crops from the field. Some were on horseback; others went on foot. It was an hour's journey to the beachfront on the Isle of Palms. Everyone grew calm and tranquil as they approached the great expanse of the Atlantic Ocean. It was soothing just to stand in the cool breeze of the ocean and take in the scent of the salt water. The waves rolled in rhythmically. Seagulls squawked as they flew overhead. They had felt these sensations before, but today it was as if they felt them anew. The relief from the grueling work in this calm environment seemed to quell the soul.

As more of the enslaved workers gathered on the beach, the mood shifted. It was over an hour's journey to the beachfront on the Isle of Palms and involved a brief ferry ride. Having been restored by the salty air, everyone was ready to celebrate. Voices grew louder; laughter was more boisterous and frequent. The ebullient mood cascaded over the crowd. Children and young adults went down to play in the waves. One child ran down the beach with a streaming piece of linen on a stick, watching it wave in the wind like a kite. Others looked for shells and starfish in the sand along the water. Women unpacked food and supplies to organize for the big feast.

It was a beautiful day full of sun and pale-blue skies. The temperatures were moderate. The air itself felt nourishing. Most people wore garments made of the oatmeal-colored Negro cloth, especially the dresses and shirts. These neutral colors were highlighted by some brightly colored fabrics. Some had been dyed blue with remnants of indigo, while others were made of fabric scraps of red or gold.

People clustered all over the beach. Some were reclining, while others sat on large pieces of driftwood or rocks. The mood was light, and it seemed like the group was one large family. People shared fruits and nuts while imparting stories about their lives. Each person had a different background and history of how they got to Twin Oaks.

At one point, Juba took a brief respite from her duties as a kitchen-house worker to look around at the gathering. Without meaning to, her eyes were drawn to Cuffee. He sat on the sand in a semicircle with some other young men. He turned to see Juba looking at him. It jarred her to be discovered. At first, she jerked and tried to look away. But Cuffee flushed as he looked at her and smiled broadly. His acknowledgment soothed her. She smiled back and nodded. *Good,* she thought. *We've had some connection. Maybe I can talk with him later.* With that, Juba returned to her duties.

She then noticed that Nellie had watched the whole exchange and was smiling at her with a knowing look.

"So, you like that Mr. Cuffee, huh? He a good man." Nellie winked and nodded.

Juba was caught off guard and helpless to do anything but smile and shyly look down.

"Maybe so," she replied. She felt the heat rise to her cheeks.

The day wore on, and a large fire was built to cook the day's catch. The men had a good morning on the waters and brought back sea bass, crab, kingfish, and flounder. The kitchen-house crew fileted the fish and prepared it for the fire. There were three men charged with overseeing that the seafood and other items were properly cooked.

As the sun started to set, all the food was ready at last. It was laid out on blankets and large cloths. The crowd gasped at the plentiful spread. Nellie announced, "Come on now! Eat!" The eager crowd moved through in an orderly manner. People were patient with those too young or too old to make quick decisions and move swiftly. Eventually everyone had a bowl or square cloth with food. Children ate from their usual food trough.

For a time, the crowd grew quiet as they looked down upon their savory feast.

Rosa called out, "Let us praise God for our bounty. For he is good to us. Amen!"

Nellie replied, "God is good. He provides for us. We enjoy his plenty!"

The crowd rumbled back, "Thanks be to God!" "God is good!"

The good mood of the crowd continued. People dug in to all the plentiful food, then lingered over their tasty fare and continued to chatter. After a while, the kitchen-house women started to collect used bowls and platters. While Juba was stacking the dishware, she felt someone touch her elbow.

"Excuse me," Cuffee mumbled as he cleared his throat. "I

wondered if you might want to go for a walk on the beach?"

Juba, at first taken aback, locked eyes with Nellie. She didn't know what to say.

Nellie jumped in and came to Juba's rescue. "Young man, Juba would looove to go on a walk."

Juba first gave Nellie a hard look, then turned to Cuffee with a smile.

"Yes, I'd love to," Juba confirmed. Cuffee beamed.

"I'll be back in just a little while," she assured Nellie.

"Take your time, darlin'. Take your time." Nellie gleamed as she spoke.

As the couple sauntered off, they walked together closely. Juba casually brushed against Cuffee. He warmed to their closeness. As Juba looked into Cuffee's eyes, she tripped over a piece of driftwood that had washed onto the beach. Cuffee swiftly reached across her back and took hold of her in a sort of sideways hug.

"Whoops!" Juba yelped.

"Steady there! What would I tell Nellie if I brought you back injured?" Cuffee joked.

Once Juba was stable on her feet and the way was clear, Cuffee let his arm fall away, but the echo of his touch lingered. Juba found herself caught up in the current of sensation that hummed under her skin. She sighed softly. Then she shook off her reverie. He seemed to sense her mood and smiled. Cuffee couldn't help but add a small jump and an awkward skip as they neared the water's edge. He was beside himself with happiness. Juba glowed as she basked in Cuffee's presence. She never thought she would be so fortunate as to enjoy a big feast followed by a walk with Cuffee.

The two continued to walk and talk with one another the remainder of the night. They shared stories and laughed. They hardly payed attention to anyone else; they only had eyes for each other. It was hard to say goodbye at the end of the evening. Before walking back to join the crowd on the beach, Cuffee grabbed a quick kiss.

Juba initially jerked back, but then grabbed Cuffee's arms. Suddenly, she was staring into his eyes, lost in the deep chestnut abyss, the imprint of his kiss still lingering on her lips. She simply nodded and smiled, her throat too dry to speak. Their fingertips lingered as they pulled away. Juba watched as Cuffee walked to join the other field workers. Juba was momentarily locked in place, still dazed by the encounter. *Yes, God is good*, she thought. *God is good.*

Chapter 18
Southern Rights Clubs

Juba was working in the kitchen house as she reflected on how much love she had for her man, Cuffee. Their love was still new and exciting. Unfortunately, their workdays were spent on opposite ends of the plantation. Juba worked in the kitchen and main house, while Cuffee labored in the fields. Their paths crossed infrequently. It was very hard for them to find privacy on the plantation since their activity was always under the careful scrutiny of a driver or household member.

Cuffee continued to live in the dormitory-style slave quarters at the rear of the plantation grounds, and Juba slept on the floor of Hentie's shack. They hoped to marry and live in the same cabin, but that day was a long way off. As a result, they had to meet surreptitiously after darkness fell.

Juba had approached the missus about being permitted to marry, but Mrs. Langdon just waved off the matter, saying, "It's none of my affair. It's up to my husband to decide such matters. You know you can't legally marry him anyway. It's against the law for a slave to marry. A wedding would be a mere form without any legal value."

It was hard to catch the missus in a moment when she wasn't under the influence of her "friend." The doctor had prescribed opium for Mrs. Langdon to assist her with her fits, but she was far too fond of the remedy. She lay days on end in her bed, demanding more drops as she felt a fit coming on.

She kept one of the enslaved children in her room with her to assist her in getting around the house and to run errands for her. The child was supposed to sleep on a pallet on the floor in her room but was often found up on her bed beside the missus. She seemed to treat the child more like a pet dog than a human being.

As lunchtime approached, Juba asked to carry out water, bread, and a bit of fruit for the workers. Nellie agreed that would be fine but warned her not to linger too long in the fields with her sweetheart. Juba smiled and agreed. She snapped up a wagon for the food and a few water jugs. She grabbed one of the more responsible children to accompany her. While only five years old, the child had been drafted into doing daily labors more suited for an adolescent or teen. He removed his specially crafted tool belt, which had been tailored to fit a small child, and jumped onto the wagon.

The skies were a bit cloudy, but that was alright with Juba as it brought down the temperature a bit. She took in the smells around her, the moisture in the air enhancing the fragrance of the oak trees and the large magnolias. Their leathery leaves looked rather dull compared to their usual shine on sunny days. As she progressed from the kitchen house, she caught a whiff of the honeysuckle, heady, strong, and sweet. It grew all along the side of the wash house where the laundry was done.

She saw Doll and Rosa look out from the infirmary adjacent to the laundry house. Juba greeted them with a warm smile and waved.

"It's a fine day," Juba hollered. Her face shone bright with excitement, and there was a delightful lilt to her voice.

"What are you so happy about? The master promise to set you free or somethin'?" Rosa asked as she took in Juba's exuberance.

"No, just taking some water and food out to the field hands. Maybe see Cuffee out there." Juba hopped a step as she said his name.

"Oh, that explains why you actin' like it's Christmas or something," Doll said while waving her hand and laughing.

"That be it," a chuckling Rosa agreed. "It brightens the day to see your man. Uh-huh, dat's for true!"

Once she was out in the fields where they were working, she hollered to Duke, the plantation's black driver, that she was there to give the field hands water and peaches if they were ready for a break. They rarely permitted such indulgences, but the enslaved workers labored in the subtropical heat long hours. Duke paused, saying, "Well, I'm not sure they deserve it. Two of the men were caught talking when they should have been working." Then he looked away briefly to make sure McBride, the overseer, wasn't around. "Well, okay. We'll take a short one." He hollered at the men and they came running.

Juba eagerly searched the crowd for her Cuffee. She didn't see him initially and started to worry. Then suddenly he came bounding out of a wooded area. She thought maybe he had to make water and wanted the privacy.

Cuffee came up to her smiling. He leaned in and said, "I've been stashing some things out in the woods. Maybe one day we can run away together and live as man and wife, the way things should be for us."

Juba's eyes grew large as shock overtook her. "What, are you crazy? We'd never make it out on our own. They would just set the bloodhounds after us. Have you seen what them dogs do to a man? They rip the flesh right off him! They train the dogs to kill a black man!"

Juba went on, "At the very least, they cut your heel strings to prevent you from running away. Once they do that, you can barely walk, let alone run again. Can't do that. No! Can't do that!"

Juba looked deep into Cuffee's eyes and said, "Now, you get those crazy ideas out of your head, hear me? We can meet up later tonight. Maybe after dinner when the master's family gets settled in. We can meet around the old storage barn. Look for me there."

Cuffee nodded and grinned. "I'll be there, sugar pie!"

The day passed quickly, knowing that she would be able to meet up with Cuffee and hold him. After the evening meal, Juba made sure she had every bit of food properly tucked away and all the dishes were washed. The workspaces were cleaned and everything was in good order. She did not want to give anyone a reason to come looking for her.

Once she felt confident that she was no longer needed, she asked Nellie if she could leave. Nellie agreed and told her to have a good evening. Juba's chest burst with excitement. *At last I can go!* She ran back by her shack, tidied herself, then left for the old storage barn.

Dusk had fallen. The full heat of the day dissipated. Sounds of the night started to percolate. Katydids, cicadas, and crickets provided a soothing melody to the evening. Their singing, kind of a pulsating sound, was a calming and familiar hum. All was as it should be. Every creature in God's kingdom at rest. The early nightfall gently shrouded the plantation.

As Juba came around the back of the barn, Cuffee reached out and grabbed her, taking her by surprise. Then Juba felt the warmth of Cuffee's body and familiar frame, so she threw her arms around him. It was so good to be in his embrace. At first, they just held each other tight, savoring the moment, but then Cuffee started to give Juba warm, passionate kisses. Juba's ardor unleashed, and she became uninhibited. Soon they found themselves enjoying each other's passions. They snuck into the barn so no one would see them.

They scrambled up the ladder to the upper level of the barn. They had just tumbled into the soft hay stored in the loft when they heard someone approaching. This was a secondary outbuilding; no one ever came out this way, at least not in the evening. This was where they stored old furniture, empty barrels, worktables and such.

Juba's eyes grew wide. "Maybe they put a hex on us. If we sneak away, a hag will get us!"

"Don't be silly. Why would they do such a thing? We work hard all day. We don't neglect the master or his wife." Cuffee waved off the suggestion.

But then the two heard a creaking noise. Not quite sure what it was, they thought perhaps it was otherworldly. Small droplets of perspiration formed as they tried to adjust their eyes to the darkness, listening carefully. Frozen in fear, they heard only their own rapid breathing.

Then they heard footsteps, slow in measure, first dragging on the grass, then shuffling through the dirt path. Labored breathing accompanied it. Now fully alert, the two lovers strained to hear the hag's approach. What would she look like? Undoubtedly a vile-looking wench.

Cuffee thought of confronting the malevolent spirit. He wanted to call out, "Who's there?" Perhaps if they showed a strong front, the boo hag wouldn't think they were easy prey. Or perhaps it was better to stay put and remain quiet, lie waiting, secreted away under the cloak of darkness. But a hag could find them no matter what they did. It was not easy to outsmart a hag; she knew where you hid and what you thought. She was pure evil.

The slow, labored movement of this creature gave the impression that she must be carrying something burdensome. But what could that be? The creaking suggested a wheelbarrow. The loathsome vixen must be carrying a large bag of tricks.

Suddenly, the hag kicked the door open. The young lovers pulled back, alarmed, so terrified they could hardly move. Cuffee's mind raced. Should he jump on the hag and try to surprise her? *No*, he thought. *We are caught.* They might meet their maker this very day.

Juba wanted to scream but found no voice. They sat waiting to see the silhouette of the hag, expecting long unruly hair and a crooked nose.

The hag rifled through her large bag of tricks nestled in the tub of the wheelbarrow. Not surprisingly, she pulled out a candle and a match. *Oh God, we are about to see the true face of evil.* She lit the candle, and the flame illuminated the creature's face. It was not a hag but Mr. Langdon holding the candle. The two lovers looked at each other in shock. *Mr. Langdon? What's he doing here?* They slowly and quietly scooted back from the edge of the hayloft.

"What we do now? We caught. He will whip us until we're dead." Juba looked at Cuffee with her eyes wide. "We dead. That's it. We dead," she muttered.

"No, we just stay here. Be quiet and see what he does," Cuffee whispered, trying to calm himself and Juba.

A few minutes later they heard voices approaching.

"Man, we are really dead now. The master will have others to help him kill us!" Juba moaned.

Two men walked into the barn talking about how many were expected at the meeting that night. Mr. Langdon got some items out of the bag—a cloth to cover an old table and some more candles. They draped a banner of sorts on the wall. Langdon changed his jacket and put on a vestment and a white apron, both with embellishments.

As more men joined, Cuffee and Juba recognized some of the other participants; they were planters from the area who had been to Twin Oaks. A few were members of the elite society of the Charleston peninsula, those who lived in grand mansions. The men spoke about the importance of raising funds and munitions to keep their efforts moving forward. Their club, the Knights of the Golden Circle, was founded to ensure that slavery remained intact in the Southern states and throughout the nations situated south of the US. It was one of many Southern rights clubs that had sprung up since the early 1800s.

The young lovers huddled in fear. Once the meeting got started, they felt helpless to do anything but keep their surreptitious presence hidden.

As the discussion progressed, they learned that the Knights of the Golden Circle was a secret society, founded in Lexington, Kentucky, by a young ne'er-do-well schemer named George Washington Lafayette Bickley. It was a men's invitation-only group. Many rituals and protocols borrowed from the Masons were integrated into the group's traditions. Clandestine meetings in support of the organization were being held throughout the South.

The Knights of the Golden Circle wished to curtail the powers of the federal government and strengthen states' rights. Their objective was to annex a golden circle of territories from the Confederate States of America, Mexico, Central America, and the Caribbean as declared slave provinces. They hoped that the newly created federation would be led by Maximilian I of Mexico. If those states south of the Mason-Dixon line could join with others south of them, this swath of jurisdictions could form their own country. Slavery could be perpetuated, and the great wealth gained from slave labor could go on. The group was also devoted to reviving the African slave trade. Their ideals were founded on the philosophy promoted by John C. Calhoun.

Many Southerners supported this movement, even some Northerners. Over time, they would experience a great deal of success. The Knights of the Golden Circle had a well-armed army of around 14,000 men. Membership numbers of the group itself were large, well over 50,000. Some of the smaller associations had merged with them. They were prepared to do battle, but would eventually step back, allowing Confederate troops to do the work.

After the US Supreme Court's Dred Scott decision, the South feared abolitionism would grow. The court had decided that Dred Scott, an enslaved African American, did not have standing as a citizen of the United States and therefore could not bring a legal suit in a court of law. The court thought it would settle the slavery question. However, its effect was just the opposite and would prove to be a catalyst triggering an expansion of the abolitionist movement.

The meeting wore on. Juba and Cuffee scooted closer to the edge of the hayloft to get a better look. They saw some of the men standing erect in odd white aprons and one in a grand robe—such strange dressings.

"What's that?" Juba hissed.

A few pieces of straw trickled down to the room below. One of the planters caught the motion out of the corner of his eye and looked suspiciously behind him and upward to the loft. Juba and Cuffee froze. They would probably be killed for watching this clandestine meeting. The man continued to look around the room with a scowl on his face, watching and waiting for another movement, another sign.

But at that moment the fervor of the speaker intensified, and the man jerked back to the speaker, engrossed in his heated words. "It's critical that we keep the institution of slavery! It allows us to keep our economy going and our very way of life! Fight with every ounce of your being to keep our peculiar institution intact! It enables us to continue, as well as our children! Where would we all be without their labor? Slavery *must* be perpetuated!"

At long last, one of the men announced the meeting had concluded. He told the attendees the next meeting date and time. He reminded the men to bring their fee to pay at the door and to be prepared to share their special password or watchword, handshakes, and grips. One might also need to give a special crisp knock on the exterior door and show "the claw" by raising his arm to jaw level and coiling his fingers inward, thereby imitating a claw. There was a whole array of secret signs, and, depending on one's level within the society, he would need to display these esoteric gestures. If a member forgot how to show these signs and all else failed, he could flash a special token carved with the seal of the Golden Circle, an item distributed to every member following an elaborate initiation. The token had a variety of symbols, including the name of the man, Bickley, who had founded the organization and designed the token.

All the men acknowledged the admonishments, nodded at Mr. Langdon, and shook his hand. As they filed out, Juba and Cuffee took a deep breath. The highly charged evening was coming to an end.

They waited as Langdon packed up all the trinkets, robes, and table coverings. Juba, in particular, was still pulsating with fear, worried that the master might feel their presence, sense their energy, maybe even smell them. They continued to hold their breath as Langdon loaded up his wheelbarrow. He took off his apron and robe, folding them on top of the pile, then covered the stack with a sheet. He propped open the door and slowly wheeled his wares out.

"Whew!" Cuffee exhaled and looked over at Juba, smiling. "We survived, baby. It's over. Let's just wait a bit, then scamper outta here."

"I can't move. My muscles are all locked up." Her eyebrows furrowed together.

Cuffee soothed her. "Don't worry, baby. As you start to believe it's over and the master is gone, you'll relax. It will be okay."

Juba slowly breathed in and out, trying to calm herself. Suddenly, a loud thud rang out. "Oh God! What was that?"

"I think a branch just hit the roof. It's okay, Juba. We gonna be okay. Let me look out. I'll signal you to come down, alright?"

"No, don't go! What if they catch you? They will kill you, Cuffee!"

"We have to try to get outta here, honey. Get back home. Now, you stay here."

Cuffee quietly scampered down the ladder and looked out. He waited for a minute or two. Nothing. "Baby, it's okay. Come on down."

At first Juba's muscles were still locked up. She couldn't move. She said a short prayer to God to help her down from the loft and felt her muscles loosen; she rose and clambered down the ladder. In a few moments she was at Cuffee's side.

The two paused at the doorway to the outbuilding and listened carefully to the night. The crickets chirped and the cicadas hummed. They looked up to the oak trees surrounding the building and took in the woodsy smell of the air. Then, turning to one another and nodding, they jumped onto the dirt path. In a few moments they sprang through the fields and the work yard, all the way home. Cuffee dropped off Juba at her shack, then went on to the slave quarters. Thank God, they were home. Thank God.

Chapter 19
Juba and Cuffee Jump the Broom

At long last, the master agreed to allow Juba and Cuffee to get married and celebrate the occasion with a symbolic wedding ceremony by jumping the broom together. They would be permitted to live together in a shack that had recently been vacated. Some grumbled that it only behooved the master to encourage them to marry and have children together, as it created more slaves for the buckra, but for the most part everyone was delighted and happy for the young couple.

It was like God and all his angels were smiling down on them. They enjoyed a brilliant autumn day. The air was crisp and cool, the sky clear and a brilliant azure. The offensive heat and humidity of the summer had fully abated. The lighter air made the mood joyful.

Doll and Mimba were busy putting the finishing touches on a special wedding outfit for Juba. The dress was a vibrant blue with colorful trimmings. The seamstresses had carefully crafted a colorful head wrap to match Juba's dress. Since most of the enslaved workers only received new garments, or fabric to make new garments, at Christmas, the enslaved community had to come up with wedding clothes made from already existing pieces. They had thought of asking the mistress of the household for one of her cast-off dresses, but she was too self-centered and mean-spirited to contribute to such an event. Moreover, her dear friend opium seemed to be controlling her life again.

At this point, the master had been buying Doll store-bought dresses and bolts of fabric for quite some time. He had a few favorite dresses he liked to see her in, but for the most part her clothes had started to blend together for him. He just wanted her to look well groomed and cheery. As a result, the group decided they could take a dress of Doll's and an unused bolt of fabric to create a new garment. Mimba, the seamstress and servant in the main house, was a wizard with thread and needle. Doll used her way with the master to get him to relent and allow the women to make Juba a wedding outfit.

The women likewise made a special outfit for Cuffee. An ivory shirt made of Negro cloth, brown trousers, and a special belt. Men didn't usually wear anything grand for their weddings, but this outfit fit Cuffee well.

On the plantation, most ceremonies involved a celebration in which the couple jumped a broom. The actual words used and steps within the process varied from plantation to plantation. Some farms required two brooms; others had the couple jump backward rather than forward. But in Juba and Cuffee's instance, they would use only one broom. Big John helped to secure someone to officiate the celebration. Their ceremony would be more informal. Formal wedding ceremonies with clergy involved were generally reserved for house servants, particularly those who worked for the wealthy families in the city of Charleston. In such cases, a white minister would perform the service. Any ceremony had no legally binding effect as chattel slaves were considered property, not people, so the union could be annulled at any time. Nonetheless, the master could choose to allow the service and treat the servants as a married couple.

As the hour approached, the two lovers became more and more excited. They had hoped for this day a long time. Their love for one another was strong, and they were committed to a life together.

Big John stayed in the slave quarters with Cuffee to keep him calm and to attend to his needs. Cuffee was giddy with delight.

"Boy, you need to calm down. You're about to pee yourself with excitement. You don't want to be doing such things on your wedding day." Big John shook his head as he spoke.

"Big John, I just can't believe this day has finally come and Juba and I get to be together. I can lay with her at night. We can be with each other. No more catching her whenever we can get away." The enthusiasm poured from Cuffee. His excitement was electric.

"Yes, God must have blessed you the day the master said he would allow you to marry. Not like that man to show kindness. You best remember that. Don't do anything that might anger him. He can take all this away in a heartbeat." Big John pointed his finger at Cuffee and shook it.

"No, we won't trip up. Me and Juba work hard for the master. We are loyal to him. Nothing going to go wrong, you'll see. Before you know it, we'll be having a baby boy and name him after you." Cuffee chuckled and gently poked Big John in the shoulder.

"You best do that. Work hard and don't trip up." Big John looked deep into Cuffee's eyes. Then he reached over and pulled the nervous groom into a big bear hug.

"Thank you, Big John. I will do my best; I'll keep things right."

While Big John worked to soothe Cuffee's nerves, Hentie, Doll, and Mimba prepared the bride. Juba was full of hope; it seemed her life had taken a positive turn. The thought of being with Cuffee every day made Juba ecstatic. His touch always calmed her and helped her stayed anchored. Juba still carried physical and mental scars from her time with her previous master. She would still jump at loud noises and get overwhelmed when the master or missus started yelling. But her friends and Cuffee helped to soothe and reassure her.

"Doll, thank you so much for giving me your dress and this fabric. It's all just beautiful. I love this blue fabric." Juba beamed at Doll.

"Well, I'm glad you were able to wear it. You can't have no fine gown like the missus would have, but what you have is a nice, proper dress. You make a pretty bride for Cuffee," Doll said.

Juba glanced out the door of the kitchen house and saw folks starting to gather for the ceremony. Preacher Elisha had arrived from a neighboring plantation and was pacing back and forth in the work yard. Although ceremonies of this kind were rare at their plantation, they had happened before. Elisha had also officiated at prior weddings.

Rosa stood in the middle of the yard glancing about her, nervously tapping her leg, waiting for things to start. Amazingly enough, the master had allowed everyone to take the late afternoon and evening off to be present at the gathering. The ceremony was to be held at the end of the workday just before sunset, or first dark, so as not to dramatically interrupt their labors. The big fall harvest had already concluded, and the main cash crop, cotton, had gone off to market, so the pressure to produce had subsided.

A platform for the ritual stood on the edge of the work yard. It was left over from an event the missus had held for the family quite some time ago when Mr. Langdon's kin came for a visit. The ceremony was to be held in an open space closer to the main house and the missus's special gardens. This was a special privilege; thank goodness it was Big John who approached Mr. Langdon about it. He convinced the master to allow it this one time. Tables had been set up. The animals were secured in barns and pens.

As the minutes ticked away, other enslaved workers trickled into the area. Cuffee and Big John walked out from the slave quarters to join the other men. Big John kept a knowing hand on Cuffee's shoulder to keep him steady. He was as nervous as a cat in a room full of rocking chairs. Juba paced between the kitchen house and infirmary while encircled by her close friends.

The preacher thought it was time to get started, gave the nod, and the word pulsated through the crowd.

Rosa said, "It's time now. It's time."

Juba squealed with delight. As she hopped from one foot to the other, she made two fists and started pumping them.

"Now, girl, you calm down. This is your weddin' day," Rosa scolded her.

The rest of the women darted a glance at Rosa and waved her off. They were all excited. After quieting their nerves, the group walked out. There was an audible gasp as Juba appeared before the crowd. While her garments were not made of great finery, they were bold and flattering. Juba's face glowed, and her eyes were fixed on Cuffee. Likewise, he only had eyes for her.

As the couple took their places, the preacher said a few words about the couple and their commitment to one another.

Then he said to Cuffee, "Do you want this woman?"

Cuffee was so excited, he spit out the word, "Yes!"

Then the preacher asked Juba, "Do you want this boy?"

Juba smiling with joy and answered, "Oh yes. Yes."

The preacher then looked to Big John and said, "Fetch me the broom."

John was such a big man that the broom looked like a little stick in his enormous hands. The preacher took it from him and waved it over the couple's heads.

"I ask all the evil and dark spirits to leave us. Do not pester this good couple. Before you jump this broom, Juba, I want you to know that it symbolizes your commitment and willingness to maintain a household for Cuffee. You agree to rear any children you may have. Jumping the broom symbolizes your bond to your husband and to your home."

Juba nodded her understanding, then said, "Yes, sir."

"Now, whoever jumps higher over this broom gets to be the decision-maker in your household, so, Cuffee, you best jump high." He then laid the broom on the ground.

Everyone chuckled at the preacher's words. And with that, the two looked at each other, joined hands, and jumped over the broom.

Laughter and cheers erupted as the ritual concluded. The two seemed to jump at about the same height, so the rest of the evening was spent on good-natured arguments concerning who got to rule the house.

The workers encircled the couple. Big John and a few others sang songs of joy. This was a special day for the couple and everyone on the grounds. Food was laid out on the tables for the feast that was about to commence. Some wild game had been cooked over an open pit, as well as a few chickens. Sweet potatoes had been baked in the ashes of the fire. There was cooked okra with onions and tomatoes. Heavenly biscuits. Fresh cut-up watermelon, peaches, and strawberries.

Because it was September, the guests were able to enjoy a particular treat most waited all year for—the savory red drum fish. A big fish, often fifty to sixty pounds, it had an eye-like spot near its tail. Rosa knew how to cook it to perfection.

The laughter and happy voices carried throughout the plantation. Juba brightened at the gaiety of the evening. She sang an old lively song, then twirled around once, then twice, until she was laughing with a wide-open smile. Her sweet musical voice filled the air as her laughter accompanied it. Hentie was heartened by the sight of Juba's unbridled happiness. Her feet began to tap the ground and her hand bounced off the side of her skirt. She shot a smile to Big John and gently touched his sleeve. He looked down on her warmly and nodded, his eyes twinkling.

The missus peered down on the happy crowd from her bedroom window with disgust. *Why did William allow these goings-on? Those darkies are nothing but ignorant beasts. Savages that could not survive without our care and supervision. Allowing them to marry is just foolishness.* Mistress Langdon then shook her head and returned to take a few more drops of opium. *I can't worry about these matters. I will let William deal with the outcome of his actions.*

And so, the merriment carried on below, partygoers oblivious to the scowling Mistress Langdon. Song and dance were accompanied by hand-clapping and laughter. It was a good day. Even the master stopped by for a little while. He sat for a spell and enjoyed a cigar while eyeing Doll most of the time. Doll acknowledged and walked to him. His eyes flared as she approached, perhaps a step closer than propriety should allow. Doll suppressed the urge to kiss him. She looked around for observers, then continued to hold the master's eyes. She reached out a hand to rest on his forearm. Her fingers landed on his warm skin and she inhaled involuntarily. His eyes flickered to her. Doll put one hand on her round belly, and with the other she squeezed his forearm. They stood for long moments staring into each other's eyes, knowing they could not take their actions further with all those around them. The master then shook Doll's hand loose from his forearm. The air started to move again between them. He nodded at her, then stood to walk away, departing the festivities. He would see her again later that evening.

Later on, Rosa presented the newlyweds with a special quilt she and others on the plantation had made as a wedding gift. It was a beautiful, brightly colored blanket. Rosa pulled the couple aside to speak to them in hushed tones about the quilt.

"May you and Cuffee enjoy this quilt all the days of your life," she said as she handed it to Juba. "Someday you may rely on this quilt to act as your special guide to point you to safety. It is full of symbols and signs that may direct you to landmarks along the way to freedom. The master can never find out about the importance of the symbols. When you are ready, I can teach you what they mean."

With lifted eyebrows, Juba asked, "What do the symbols mean? Why are they so special?"

Rosa looked around her, then motioned for the newlyweds to step closer. "What we have given you is a sampler of several patterns in the code of the Underground Railroad. Right here is the monkey wrench, there are the tumbling blocks, and that is the evening star. You may never go on the Underground Railroad yourself, but your children may, or you may help someone."

"Oh God! Oh my Lord!" Juba whispered.

Cuffee lit up and said, "What a special gift! Why thank you, Rosa! This is beautiful. We will always remember what you done for us." Then he gave Rosa a big hug around the neck.

Juba, still trying to recover, said, "Thank you, Miss Rosa. This is so kind of you and all the women who helped you. Bless you for your kindness."

As the evening drew to a close, people wandered off to their slave cabins and the large slave dorm at the rear of the property. Only a core handful of people remained, held together by a special bond. Big John, Hentie, Doll, Rosa, Juba, and Cuffee felt like family and enjoyed the warmth they shared with each other. They spoke in hushed tones and gestures. Sometimes they didn't need to utter a word, their thoughts already understood by the others. Finally, the group decided to bring the evening to a close and wish each other good night. They shared hugs, then everyone turned to go their separate directions. Juba and Cuffee walked to their new shack, Juba wrapping her hand around Cuffee's arm. He looked to Juba with the moonlight shining into his eyes. Softly he said, "I'm the luckiest man on earth. I get to be loved by a wonderful woman like you. I would give my life for you, Juba. I hope we'll be together until the day I die."

"So do I, Cuffee. So do I," replied Juba as she gave Cuffee a squeeze.

They walked close together, knowing that in a few moments they would be in each other's arms as man and wife.

Juba got a sparkle in her eye, then quipped, "I still say I jumped higher than you!" She poked him in the ribs and ran off ahead of him.

"That Juba, she gonna be a handful," he muttered, then smiled at the notion that she was his wife.

⌣

It was early the following morning, at dayclean, just past daybreak, when all the commotion started. Juba and Cuffee stirred. Juba had been snuggled up against her new husband, taking in his scent and feeling his chest rise and fall as he breathed. But now they were both alert from the noise outside. Cuffee jerked to an upright position. Outside a couple of slave trackers and a posse from the slave patrol were apparently in pursuit of a runaway slave.

It looked like the men in the slave patrol weren't from the militia but were cadets from the Citadel. In this case, a freelancing slave catcher joined them. Their role was to enforce the laws impacting blacks, whether free people of color or enslaved. South Carolina was the first state to come up with the notion of slave patrols. The federal law that helped to fortify the state statute was the Fugitive Slave Act.

The trackers were knocking over barrels and crates, scaring chickens away, and tearing down laundry. Hens were clucking and goats were bleating. The men were oblivious to being on someone else's property, disrupting daily life. Moreover, they were blind to the destruction they caused. They didn't care as long as they got their man.

It was later confirmed that an enslaved man had run away and was on the property. The desperate fugitive was just a young teenage boy. He thought his younger brother was somewhere on Twin Oaks. He risked his life to take his little brother north with him so he wouldn't have to live his life as a slave.

The lead slave hunter called out, "Just catch him. I get the pleasure of carvin' 'em up!" He turned his head and unapologetically spit a long stream of dark-brown juice out the side of his mouth, nodding as he wiped the remaining tobacco adhering to his lip with his already soiled sleeve.

This dark-bearded man was the epitome of evil. He was unkempt and wore dark clothes; stains of food and chewing tobacco marred his shirt. His discolored teeth betrayed years of tobacco use, the love of red wine, and a persistent hankering for whiskey. His dirty hair and scraggly beard bore bits of his last meal. Around his neck he proudly displayed a necklace of human ears taken from unfortunate runaway slaves he had captured. His name was Chamas, and he learned to make a living tracking the woeful souls who could no longer endure the tortures of slavery.

Typically, Chamas's goal was to track recalcitrant slaves, capture them, and turn them over to their proper owners for a fee. However, at times the owners were so infuriated that their slave had run from their dominion that they gave Chamas the choice of bringing the slave back dead or alive. Often in such instances, he and his fellow slave trackers would publicly torture their victims so as to dissuade others, particularly after the law had been fortified with the second Fugitive Slave Act. Chamas took great pride in his work and appeared to enjoy watching others suffer. Ice ran through his veins.

A posting had been distributed about this young man, as with other runaway slaves. It listed where the boy had previously lived, near the Ashley River, and gave all the details about him, such as his height, build, manner of speech, complexion, scars, the plantation brand, even the clothing he had been wearing when he fled. A disguise was impossible for this young man, as he only had one set of clothes. Since fleeing, he had been forced to stay mainly in wooded areas and swamps, dodging snakes, gators and other wild animals.

For a couple of nights, the youth joined with a band of other runaway slaves supported by some local Native Americans. He was able to eat, drink, and rest, then pushed onward. It was grueling and treacherous traveling. But he had become weary over the miles: he was desperate and making mistakes.

This boy had not made any connections with the circuit of abolitionists who dotted the area. Sometimes those who lent assistance were ministers or church folk; others were just merciful souls. They might allow someone to stay in a cellar or shed or offer transportation in boats or large carts. The crucial comfort offered by such people was the food and water they gave and their ability to treat any injuries sustained along the way. He didn't have that support. This poor fugitive soul appeared to have gone off without a plan in place, much less coordination of stops along the Underground Railroad. He was running blind. Unfortunately, the slave hunters planned to utilize that to their advantage.

The commotion awoke everyone in the area. The enslaved workers watched the slave catchers from a distance. Hentie and Octavia joined the crowd, at first keeping a safe distance. Hentie grabbed her friend's elbow, fearful of what was about to happen. They prayed for that poor boy that he could go on and enjoy freedom up north. But it didn't appear to be his day for freedom or redemption. The slave trackers finally cornered the boy in a barn, put a pitchfork to his neck, and got him to come out. When the noise temporarily abated, some of the enslaved workers began to filter out of the main house, then the kitchen house and then the barn. They had no idea what this man Chamas was about to do.

Initially, all anyone could hear was the occasional wet slap of tobacco juice and spittle against the ground as the men eyed one another, trying to decide what to do next. Then Chamas smiled broadly, exposing his rotting, bark-brown teeth. He leered at the boy as a dastardly idea sparked inside him. He grabbed hold of the boy, and his breath blew rancid in the captive's face. The boy looked for any means of escape. Seeing none, terror pummeled the hapless victim.

God himself could not have predicted the evil about to unfold, for only the devil could engender such acts. Chamas caught the eye of a cohort and winked, then said, "Let's teach these niggers to never think of running." With that he ordered that the boy be held stomach down in the middle of the work yard. He was slammed into the earth. His face hit the ground and a flurry of dust rose. Chamas hefted his mud-caked boot and clamped it down on the boy's leg. A sickening sound of the bone shattering folded into the boy's scream of pain, his cry echoing over the work yard. Chamas shouted for heavy wooden beams to be dragged out and a hefty slave catcher to assist in holding him down.

"Now get me a hatchet! This boy will never run again!"

Everyone drew in a breath as trepidation gripped those surrounding the spectacle. Those watching were terrified of what he was preparing to do. The boy hollered that he would go back to his master and never think of leaving him again, but it was too late. In an instant, they had hacked his heel strings. Blood spurted out, and a wail pierced the air, rattling in the chests of those looking upon the gory scene. The boy continued to scream, sensing the doom that was about to happen. The slave catcher's minions pulled him up, but unable to stand, he dropped to the ground.

As the blood flowed, the slave hunter said, "Get that nigger up. I want him on the ground spread eagle! I'm not done yet! I want y'all to see what we do with runaways!"

The man's assistant and the patrol carried the boy to an open spot on the work yard. They put four stakes in the ground and tied the boy's hands and feet to posts so he couldn't move. The enslaved workers were horrified.

"Oh, my Lord, what are they fixing to do to that boy?"

"Lord protect him. Save him from this evil man."

Chamas chuckled. "Now we got ya, boy! You ain't a man, and you never will be. You'll never have any nigger children. I'll see to that!" He directed his minions, "Tear off this nigger's clothes. I want him naked as the day he was born!"

Chamas reached down and held out the boy's ears. One at a time, he severed them from his head. The boy screamed in pain as the knife sliced through his flesh. Chamas held them up for all to see, saying, "More trophies for my necklace. I got me some more nigger ears to wear round my neck!"

He then bent down and lifted the boy's genitals and sliced right through them with a razor-sharp knife. He held up the severed appendage for all to see. "There you go, boy! You're no longer a man!" Blood spewed from the gaping hole between the boy's legs. Some of the womenfolk had to leave. Hentie knees gave out. Her chest felt twisted, leaving her weak and sickened. *Animal! How can he treat a human being like this?* Octavia turned from the sight, sobbing. This was too much.

Chamas, not thinking this was enough torture, turned to Big John and said, "Fetch me a flask of oil from the kitchen house."

Hentie froze, not knowing what would happen next.

As Big John returned, Chamas grabbed the flask and poured the oil all over the agonized boy. Then the slave hunter struck a flame and threw it. In moments, the flames covered the boy's body. He shrieked in terror and excruciating pain, his mouth gaping open as he gasped. His eyes were terrified as the flames overcame him. His voice was shrill and full of agony. His piercing cries went on for a couple of long minutes. He then either passed out or died.

No one would ever forget the boy's shrieks. Grown men cried as the horror overcame them. Women covered their mouths with their aprons or their hands, aghast at the sight. The smell of burning flesh permeated the air.

Nellie could not handle the sight any longer; she turned her head and retched. Then she ran from the scene and dropped to the ground, passed out, overwhelmed from seeing the boy tortured, mutilated, then burned to death.

Chamas, reveling in his handywork, said, "There. We cooked us a nigger." He turned and looked into the crowd of enslaved workers. "We will find you no matter where you try to hide. And once we hunt you down, you can expect the same. You best remain in your quarters and mind your master. It is where you belong."

Most had already turned from the scene, grief-stricken, unable to watch anymore. Their chests ached with the anguish at having watched such malevolence. How could these men behave this way in a civilized society under the code of law? But in fact it was a federal law, codified by American lawmakers, that permitted such acts. And, so, the inhumanity went on unabated.

A group of the womenfolk went into the kitchen house to collect themselves and recover from what they had just seen. A few sat, unable to stand any longer. Finally Rosa spoke. "I'm a God-loving Christian woman. I understand all kinds of things about God. How he has a plan and his mysteries and such. But I am gonna tell you this. Lightning may strike me down right here. Some things that happen in this world are not the hand of God. It is not his actions. That man was the devil himself. Sometimes white folks are just doing the work of Satan, and this is one of them. God could not have intended an innocent boy to get hurt like that and go through such terrible suffering; it was some demon. This gruesome act just don't make no sense. No sense, no how."

Nellie nodded. "You're right. What we witnessed was the work of the devil. This whole thing should never have come to pass. Uh-huh. Never should have come to pass, not here."

The group nodded in agreement.

Rosa lifted her hand skyward and said, "We send up our sufferings to God. We hope that someday we will understand why a man acted so cruelly. One day we live in God's glory and no longer feel any pain. God will wipe away all our tears and wrap us in His love. There will be no more suffering like what we saw today."

Hentie added, "What we saw today was pure evil. God don't do such things. Only evil white men who act with hatred in their heart. Only the evil white buckra."

⁓

According to the Fugitive Slave Act, runaway slaves had to be returned to their owners. From that, a cottage industry had sprung up of brutal slave hunters who hunted human beings like wild animals, returning beleaguered slaves back to their original dire circumstances. Chamas was just the human manifestation that sprang from the law; he did not act alone. Unfortunately, there were many who made a living this way, at the cost of other lives.

After Chamas finished his acts at Twin Oaks, he went into town. Later that night in a local tavern, the burly slave hunter and townspeople swilled beer and choked down strong whiskey. Chamas proudly recounted his acts. The white men assured themselves that what was done earlier in the day was the right thing to do.

Eventually, the slave hunter cleared his throat, stood, and blew out his old, rotted breath as he spoke, causing a nearby observer to turn away.

"We have to keep the darkies scared, afraid to run and afraid to rebel against their masters. They outnumber us. If they turn on us, we're doomed."

The slave hunter held up his necklace of ears.

"I cut off all of these ears from niggers I tracked down. I wear this necklace proudly, to scare them, keep 'em in their place. We have to treat them like the dogs they are, or they might turn on us. I hear that uprisings have occurred all over. The one in the Caribbean ended up with nearly all the white people dead."

A rumble went through the crowd; people gasped in horror, and a few shifted uneasily in their seats. An older man, lanky and pale, sat tight-lipped. He raked his fingers through his thinning hair and snatched glances at the others around him.

A husky man in a dark-red shirt and tattered vest shouted out, "Yeah, we're only doing what's right. We have to do this. Got to keep 'em in line. It's the only way we can keep the natural order of things."

The crowd nodded in agreement, taking comfort in the notion that this was not what they wanted to do but what they had to do to keep order and their very way of life, soothing any sense of guilt.

Chapter 20
Doll Confronts the Master for a House

Spring bloomed in the Lowcountry. The air grew warm but was not yet full of the humidity one waded through in summer. It made Doll feel renewed.

Doll stood by the fountain looking out to the vibrant green grasses and the formal gardens that rolled out before her. The fountain pool rose to her waist and was nearly six feet wide. In the distance she saw the chapel-of-ease that sat on the outskirts of the property. Doll ran her hand across the cool water in the fountain, contemplating her plight. She absentmindedly raised her hand and gently fingered the blue beaded necklace on her throat.

The chapel-of-ease was a handsome but small building. The master's father had permitted the low-lying chapel to be erected on the very edge of the property decades ago. It had been constructed in concert with the Church Act of 1706, which established the Anglican Church of England as the colony's official religion. Roughly a dozen separate parishes were established around the Charleston area, each with a church and chapel-of-ease, a smaller, satellite house of worship erected to service congregants living in more remote areas. At the time, Mount Pleasant, lying at some distance from the peninsula of the city of Charles Town and across the Cooper River, was considered an outpost.

The chapel, a tender shade of white, had an understated exterior with a jerkinhead roof and stucco exterior. It had doors on three sides, the north, south, and west, with bull's-eye windows decorating either end of the gabled roof. The underlying brick was carefully crafted Flemish bonded and tooled mortar joints. Doll had heard the master say it was an impressive piece of work and that his family had contributed to its construction. Some of the enslaved plantation workers had helped to build it along with other buildings on the grounds.

Doll thought about how the master bragged about his family's generosity in contributing to the chapel, but the master would not tender the home in the city of Charleston he had promised her for months now. She walked toward the chapel, taking in the fragrant smells around her. The mighty oak trees formed a protective archway around her and a verdant green canopy above her. Doll lost herself in thought. She passed the graveyard that surrounded the modest holy place. She glanced at the headstones, thinking of all the landowners who had lived there before. As she got closer to the chapel, she noted the colorful plantings. Four-foot rectangular walls made of tabby, a cement-like mixture of oyster shells, lime, water, and sand, enclosed the cemetery. While some of the stucco coating had started to chip a bit, the tabby wall still made the cemetery look neat and tidy.

Doll thought of how best to solve her dilemma. She had been daydreaming about the home the master had promised her, something that would be her very own and that she could live in forever. It would be a haven for her and her son—or, more accurately, their son. Doll was still a young woman. She was tall and slender with a sturdy frame. Her brown hair had flecks of blonde in it. Her captivating eyes were a light green.

On this day she wore a pale-blue calico dress with little peach and pink flowers. The master had given it to her following his travels to Philadelphia on business. While she contemplated her circumstances, she stroked the beaded choker necklace that her grandmother had once worn. It carried her grandmother's spirit and helped to comfort and protect her.

Doll had a lighter complexion; she had been told she was a mulatto. However, her dah contended she was not half Negro, but one-eighth, an octoroon. Her son, Jeremiah, was nearly all white and could easily pass as such with his curly blond hair and blue eyes. His angular face and dimpled chin looked nearly identical to his father, the master. While everyone on the plantation knew that Jeremiah was the master's son, it was never discussed with those outside the grounds. In fact, his son was not openly discussed with the master's family or the master himself. As the laws of South Carolina mandated, Doll was not permitted to name her child's father. To even hint at his identity could result in a brutal whipping at the Work House in downtown Charleston.

Although Jeremiah could pass as white, he was nonetheless enslaved. Pursuant to the doctrine of partus sequitur ventrem ("that which is brought forth from the womb"), Jeremiah was born into the status of the mother. Doll had hoped that her son could be designated a free person of color by her master, but the gesture did not appear to be forthcoming.

More recently, the census bureau had designated mulatto as a new category of race. Three other categories, black, white, and Indian, already existed. Although the term had been in use for hundreds of years, it was not defined in the census form. Over time, this would be further clarified and explained. Doll only knew that she and her son fell into this classification; the significance didn't matter.

In addition to better educational opportunities, mixed-race or "brown" children often became the more elite among people of color. While lighter-skinned Negroes had greater opportunities, they were often scorned or excluded by other blacks and castigated by whites. Most were the illegitimate children of slave-owning white masters. Nonetheless, they could own local businesses, participate in exclusive social clubs and mutual aid societies, and own property. Doll hoped that she and her son could enjoy these privileges should the master set them up in a comfortable house in the city.

Charleston had many mixed-race or mulatto people. Two-thirds of mixed-race Charlestonians were not enslaved but rather known as "free people of color." Those designated as free people of color had to wear a badge, similar to the badges used to rent out slaves. However, this metal badge had *FREE* stamped on it along with the city's name and an assigned registration number.

The master held the power to grant manumission to not only his son, but to Doll as well. She had hoped he would grant her freedom and a home while she carried their child, but the master never acted on it. And now, even if he acted on it posthumously in his will, South Carolina's most recent statute would render it ineffective. Charlestonians and white planters elsewhere in the state had complained too strongly to the statehouse about their land going to less worthy Negroes.

While Doll contemplated what she might do to gain her freedom, she became lost in thought. If she was rented out, perhaps she could save enough to buy her freedom and that of her son. Doll thought she could talk the master into allowing her to be hired at a fine home in Charleston, perhaps one around the Battery where wealthy families lived. Doll was bright and hardworking; she had even taught herself to read some with the unwitting assistance of the master. She could care for ill or elderly household members and serve as a nursemaid.

One time, Doll saw the master's ledger sitting out on the desk in his office. She glanced at one of the pages where he listed his inventory of valuable property.

Rum	22 bottles
Madeira Wine	15 bottles
Beer	4 barrels
Salt	2 bushels
Pine timber	140 boards
Cedar boards	75 boards

Negroes: 195

Full Field Hands	94 @$800/each
Three-quarter	50 @ $600/each
Half hands	25 @ $400/each
Quarter hands	15 @ $200/each
Carpenters	3 (Thomas $1,500;
	Samuel $1,200;
	Lucius $1,100)
Butler, Gentleman's Servant (Amos)	1 @ $900
Head cook (Nellie)	1 @ $1,000
Kitchen girls (Hentie)	3 @ 700/each
Ladies Maid (Octavia)	1 @ $800
House maids	3 @ 600/each
Infirmary Workers	(Rosa) @ $1,000; (Doll) @ $800

Suddenly, Doll was jolted from her thoughts.

"Good morning! What are you doing out here, my dear? I didn't think I would be so fortunate as to see you out on the grounds." The master glowed at the sight of Doll as he took a few long strides toward her.

"Oh, Master, I was hoping I might see you. I wanted to talk to you." She felt the pull of his magnetism and drew in his familiar scent as she approached. He must have just recently bathed and shaved; she smelled the freshness of the soap. He took a step to face her, then cradled Doll in his arms. His soft lips brushed against her forehead as he looked into her loving eyes. She relished his touch. While she had some awareness of how he treated other enslaved workers on the plantation, she was able to push those thoughts to the back of her mind. She loved the master and enjoyed taking in his manliness.

As they talked, they walked back to the fountain.

"What is it you wish to speak to me about? What is in your heart?" he said, his eyes carefully reviewing her face. Her pale-green eyes appeared lighter than usual. They gleamed with a thousand emotions, but it was her smooth brown skin and perfectly symmetrical features that now captivated the master. He lowered his view to her sleek figure. Desire whirled through him. Recognizing her beauty, he was momentarily intimidated, but then he reminded himself of their relative stations.

The master wore a full suit of clothing: a fine white shirt, a dark waistcoat, and a morning coat over it. He must have had a meeting with another businessman that morning.

Doll's breath hung high in her chest and tension crossed her face. "Well, Master, I have been wondering when I might be able to move with my son into a house elsewhere off the plantation." A curious sense of foreboding rippled over Doll as the master paused and gave her a quizzical look. Doll bit her bottom lip, wishing she could take the words back. Her voice caught, and she choked on her words, not able to go on with her query. She struggled to read his eyes, but he masked his feelings for her, only allowing himself to ponder the business consequences. He took a step toward her, and Doll raised her face toward his, hopeful that his lips would meet hers.

Instead he looked at her with shadowed eyes, his emotions seeming to shift. "I cannot," he whispered. Hoping that would satisfy Doll, he turned away.

At first, shock rendered her mute, unable to speak. Doll's heart thumped heavily in her throat. For a moment she forgot how to utter a sound. She was unable to form the right words, even in her mind. No breath moved through her.

At last Doll let out a long shuddering exhale; her stomach churned as she searched for the right words. Finding her voice, she stubbornly pressed on.

"But there have been so many nights that I have cried myself to sleep, longing for a time when I could feel you in the bed next to me, away from this place, knowing our son was safe and near us. I would wake up those desolate nights with a pillow sodden with my tears for you, for us. I would reach out, hoping to feel your warmth, only to feel the cold emptiness of the space beside me. Let's change that. Let's have a house away from here. I feel like my life is a constant current of restlessness. I have a sense that something more is waiting for me somewhere else."

Doll's eyes begged him to change his mind. Her breath came in gasps. The binding bodice of her dress and the growing heat of the day threatened to stop her breathing altogether.

The air between them became thick with emotion, unspoken words dangling. He sighed, a sound of pain mixed with desire. He gently placed the palm of his hand on Doll's check and bent to kiss her. With all her will, she turned away. His lips brushed her cheek. He lingered there for a moment, his heated breath teasing her neck. It took all of Doll's determination not to reach for his warm lips. Instead, she took a step away. No matter that she was in bondage, it was as if her spirit would not submit to the reality of her position in life. She held her power the only way she knew how. Gripping hard to her conviction, she stared into his eyes.

Eventually, the master straightened and comported himself with greater dignity. He whispered her name as he brushed a finger on her jawline. Doll remained impassive.

His temper flared to a new heat in the core of his chest. The master was not in the mood to hear a servant's demands. His ire having been provoked, he said, "You'll get the house when I am good and ready to give it to you. How dare a Negress make demands to me!"

She closed her eyes, unable to look at him for fear of collapsing, and urged, "I am not making demands, Master. I am merely inquiring about the house you promised me long ago."

Doll opened her eyes and gazed upon her master, her lover, and the father of her child. Hurt and pain percolated inside her; Doll battled not to give in to the tears of frustration welling up inside. His inscrutable eyes stared back at her. Doll sobered quickly; the blood drained from her head. Nausea rose in her throat and she worked to calm herself. Tasting bile eking its way up, she grimaced and swallowed it down.

The master's face flushed deep red at Doll's reminder. He had only suggested the house to soothe her while he carried out his trysts with her. Although he had once shown her a document noting his intention to give her a house he owned, he had only done so to further his ruse. Back in that moment, his mendacious behavior had worked as he had hoped, but now it seemed to be backfiring.

When the master first targeted Doll to address his sexual desires, she was reluctant. She was very young. But he wooed her with gifts and special treatment, and at times became aggressive. Doll grew to only see the good in him and languished in his affections.

Doll sat on the long limb of a live oak snaking along the ground and tried to regain control of herself, then said, "But, Master, we have a son now." She nodded in the direction of their son, Jeremiah. "I know we can never marry since the law won't allow it, but we have had a special relationship for years now. Don't I deserve something as your mistress?"

Doll was well aware that pursuant to law the interbreeding of people from different races was forbidden and there was a bar to transracial unions. It would be another hundred years before miscegenation laws were ruled unconstitutional by the US Supreme Court.

The child looked much like the master and his family. He had shiny hair with golden, curly locks. His happy face smiled up at them with a flash of deep-blue eyes. Doll's eyes left her beautiful son and returned to the master's stern face.

"If I had a house in the city, you could come visit me there. We wouldn't have to wait for night to fall. Perhaps you could have me work for a mistress along the Battery. Most of my income would go to you."

The master stiffened.

"Most?" the master snapped. His skin blazed with heat from the temper leaching out from under his flesh. "I own you, girl. Don't forget that! If I ever give you freedom, it will be because it pleases me. You will rue the day you made demands of me."

Doll swallowed her disappointment and focused on the ground before her. She was trying to cling to all that mattered to her: her son, her lover, and the hope for her own house. Her ambitions, her hopes, and all her dreams—she felt they were slipping through her fingers. She needed to take a dramatic step.

"Well, Master, you wouldn't want me to share our secret, would you? I am sure Mrs. Langdon would be gravely disappointed in you should she discover that we have lain together and now have a son."

Doll had misjudged the impact of her words.

The master roiled at her threat. He lunged toward her and slapped her face hard, knocking her to the ground. Doll held her hand to her stinging cheek. She thought, *I have him. He is cornered and can't get out of this. He has to give me the house.*

"Yes, Master. Give me the house and my freedom, or I'll let everyone know, starting with your wife!"

In his rage, the master unleashed his brutality and slammed Doll against the fountain.

"Bitch, you will never force me to do anything. You are a slave girl. I own you! You do not own me."

He grabbed a fistful of her hair and shoved her face into the water of the fountain. As he plunged her face down, he felt the full force of his savagery. It electrified him. He held her head under the water as she struggled and spewed. Doll's arms flailed, but she could not fight off the master. His rage added to his strength. Her neck hit the side of the pool, and her grandmother's necklace broke, the beads cascading down into the water. Her grandmother's spirit could no longer protect her from her master's demonic urges.

Doll struggled to rise back into the air she desperately needed. But to no avail. After a few minutes, her body went limp. The master let her body fall to the ground.

Langdon stepped back, horrified at what he had done. *Oh my God! I've killed her!*

Panic took hold. He took a deep breath; then his vengeance kicked in: *She deserved that! How dare a Negress tell me what to do! How dare she threaten me!*

Langdon stepped back, looking around and seeing no one. *Good,* he thought. But he struggled with what to do next. *Do I hide her body? Do I leave her here?*

Guilt enveloped him like a dark veil. *She is just a slave; I need not do anything!* But she had been his longtime lover and companion. How could he just leave her body there?

Their son started to wail. Though barely more than a toddler, he had instinctively realized his mother's demise and that her spirit was leaving him.

Langdon panicked and bolted from the scene. He ran across the well-manicured lawns until he reached a storage house. He sat down on a crate until he could catch his breath.

How shall I explain what has happened? Even if I confess to drowning her, what shall be my reason for doing so?

The dark side of him countered, *I don't have to explain anything to anyone. I have the right to treat my slaves however I want. I shall simply refuse to discuss it with anyone.*

Then he thought of their son. *Will one of his other enslaved workers hear his wailing and come rescue him? Shall I summon someone to fetch him? Would that merely point out that I knew he was there with his mother's dead body?* Perplexed and frightened, he sat and pondered it all.

Then two enslaved workers abruptly entered the storage shed while speaking loudly with one another, not expecting anyone to be in there. In shear surprise, Langdon jumped to his feet.

Shocked to see the master in the storage shed, one of them blurted out, "Oh, sorry, Master, we didn't mean to frighten you. We didn't know you was in here."

The master, trying to regain his composure, modulated his voice through an unexpectedly strangled throat. "Oh, I was just checking to see how much rice was stored in here, confirming it against my ledger."

Doubtful of this, the enslaved worker answered, "Oh, good, Master. I hope it's all right."

Langdon, still shaky, responded, "Yes, yes. All good."

Seizing control of the moment, he nodded at the two enslaved workers and left. He tried to regain his composure and walk with authority to the main house. Still overwrought with guilt, he worried about Doll's body and the distressed child.

As he entered the main house, he heard the panicked voices of the house staff. They had retrieved the child and were calming him. The master overheard that some of the male enslaved workers had recovered Doll's body and carried her to the dispensary.

When Doll was carried in and laid on a bed, Rosa begged the Lord to bring her Baby Doll back to her. Finally, Nellie put her gentle hand on Rosa's shoulder and said, "She's gone, Rosa. She's gone. Ain't nothin' we can do to bring her back."

Rosa's sobs grew. A few moments later, Big John helped lift her to her feet.

"Nellie's right, Rosa. She's gone. She's gone home to the Lord."

Rosa started to wail; her sorrow ran deep. Rosa couldn't believe that the baby she brought into this world and raised as her own was gone. Overwhelmed by the weight of her grief, she simply collapsed in a heap on the floor. Her strength left her. Others encircled her to help soothe her, their efforts futile.

Some of the other women in the room started to focus on Doll's body and preparations for burial. They laid a cloth over her head and upper body. The team of women made plans to bury her later that same day, before nightfall. The men would help carry her body out to the black cemetery at the rear of the plantation.

Meanwhile, in the main house, the master was holed up in his office. He walked back and forth on the wooden floors, his buckled shoes clicking with each step. For several minutes he paced incessantly, as if some solution would present itself to undo the tragedy.

Nellie tapped lightly on his door, fearful of his mood. After he barked for her to enter, she approached with a tray of scones and biscuits. Along with the treats, she had a steeping pot of tea and his favorite china cup. She hoped to ease the master's tension and appraise the situation, still unaware of all that had transpired.

The master strode to the other side of the room to receive his tea. He walked behind his fine, polished mahogany desk purchased from an English importer up on King Street. He lowered himself into his ornate leather chair and tried to make it appear that he was focused on business matters.

"Oh, set it over there." He pointed to a small table near the window, then turned back to papers on his desk.

Nellie said, "Enjoy your tea, Master." She curtsied and nodded in his direction. The master responded with a grunt as he absentmindedly shuffled papers on his desk.

As Nellie quietly pulled the door shut and he heard the clasp engaged, he thought, *Good, no questions. No accusations. It's all been taken care of. I shall remain here in my office and let the rest of the house sort things out. I am now free of this matter. She was a mere slave.*

"Humph," he said as he exhaled and cleansed his mind of the matter. With that, he began to review his ledger and the list of enslaved workers. He drew a line through Doll's name and slammed the book shut.

Chapter 21
Sale of Juba

It had been an ordinary day in the kitchen house as Nellie and Juba went about their duties. Nellie stood at the worktable with a mixing bowl and stirred the batter for the master's special cinnamon muffins. A seasoned pork tenderloin was stretched out on a board in front of her; it was to be her next task. The door burst open and the master came blustering in, full of rage. He yelled about the food, which he ordinarily loved, but on that day, he hated it. Nellie was at a loss for what to say.

The master roared, "What is this slop? It isn't fit for a dog!"

"Master, you usually love our pork and red rice. You don't feel like eating that today? Can I make you something else?"

"Pork and red rice. Pork and red rice. We have it all the time. Why not duck or chicken or something intended for humans?"

Nellie, still taken aback by Mister Langdon's brutish behavior, said, "I can make some fresh corn bread and a pie if you like."

The master started throwing things and cursing. Cookware and dishes flew as he unleashed his venom. He was much like a young child having a temper tantrum. It became more and more apparent that his frustration had nothing to do with Nellie's cooking and everything to do with his guilt over murdering Doll.

"Nothing is right. I can't eat. I'm hungry, but nothing satisfies me. It must be the food. What else could it be?"

He looked upon Nellie as if daring her to speak of his sadistic actions. He crossed the kitchen house in two strides and locked eyes with her. "What do *you* think it is?"

"I don't know, Master. Maybe you just feelin' poorly," she said.

At that moment, Juba burst in carrying a jug of milk from the barn. She had heard all the commotion and the pots and pans being thrown. In her haste she bumped into Mister Langdon. The milk spilled all down the master's suit.

"Idiot! You stupid wench! How could you ruin my clothes this way?" Mister Langdon was incensed at her clumsiness. He glared at her, his face streaked with anger.

"Why, Master, I didn't mean to. I just heard all the yelling and came right away."

The master exploded and unleashed his oceanic rage on Juba, shouting at her and degrading her with his words. She was careful to look down and remain motionless no matter how demeaning he became. Powerless to react, all she could do was take the master's berating.

"I want this girl whipped for her incompetence. How can a house girl pour milk on her master?"

Juba fell to her knees and begged the master to change his mind. "It was only an accident, Master! I'm so sorry!" She started crying and continued to beg him.

Nevertheless, Mister Langdon was in a foul mood. He was of a mind that all of a slave's misfortune was brought on by their own actions. *They are stupid, ignorant dogs.* The master had become like a snake consuming its own tail and all that was important to him.

Shortly thereafter, Duke came for Juba. She was dragged off and tossed over to Simon McBride, the overseer. He was ready for her; he had a bullwhip wound up and tied to his belt. McBride lashed Juba's hands to a post and said, "There you go, nigger."

Juba, dreading what was about to befall her, let her eyelids fall shut on the world. The back of her dress was torn open, fully exposing her flesh. Juba kept screaming and pleading for mercy. "I'm sorry, Master! I didn't mean to do it! I'm sorry!"

The master turned his head away and said again, "Stupid wench!"

Juba tried to prepare herself for the first blow and block the pain of the lash, but she was unable to do so. The pain shot through to her bones. With each strike, the razor-sharp whip cut her skin and tore off bits of flesh. The velocity of the lash also had the punch to knock Juba several inches each time it struck. She grimaced in agony as she pitched forward with each blow. The bright-red blood pulsed onto her light-blue dress, darkening it as it flowed. Gradually, the dress turned a midnight blue. It was totally saturated with blood. After several minutes, she hung limp from the trauma, passed out. It was probably better that way; her pain was temporarily suspended.

Big John came to untie Juba from the whipping post. He unfastened the leather straps from her wrists and saw the ligature marks rising from her flesh. As Juba fell, he caught her and carried her off to the infirmary. He tenderly cradled her in his big arms, careful not to pull on her injuries. Her blood smeared onto his chest. Tears rolled down Big John's face. It hurt him so to see Juba in this condition. As he passed others in the work yard, they teared up as well. How could the master do this to poor Juba? She was always polite, always cheerful, and such a hard worker. Everyone loved her.

Big John stepped into the infirmary with Juba, ducking his head as he stepped through the doorway. Rosa gasped. "Juba?"

Rosa almost didn't recognize her. The lash had not only hit Juba's back but also sliced through part of her face, which was now swollen.

"Did it put her eye out?" Big John asked tentatively.

"Lay her on this bed here and let me take a look. What's wrong with the master? Why he do this to her?"

"You know what's wrong. He done in Doll. He feeling guilty about killing her."

"Well, let me see what I can do. Can you help me make up a poultice and start tearing some strips of cloth for her back? Lord God. Cuffee is going to lose his mind over this!"

The two worked feverishly to help ease Juba's pain. Rosa put the poultice on the lacerated, swollen side of her face. The poultice was a warm, moist cloth soaked with special plant elements and selected oils. Juba's back was so raw and chewed up that muscle was exposed. Rosa put down spiderwebs where the flesh was completely gone and gently applied salve to the wounds. She put liniment oil on her cheek. Then the two tried to cover those areas with bandages and improvise as best they could to cover her wounds.

The next day everyone was talking about the master's actions. Even Mrs. Langdon was outraged that Juba had been so brutally whipped. She was such a competent worker and polite to everyone. The master continued to verbally upbraid the enslaved servants and his family members. He erupted into rages that frightened the whole family. He napped in the afternoon, exhausted from his constant tirades. His family and the house staff were too scared to wake him from his sacrosanct nap, fearing his wrath. His persistent curmudgeonliness contrasted with his typical regal style. He had become a brute through and through.

Mrs. Langdon knew the man who lay beneath his fair skin. While seemingly reserved in manner and thoughtful in nature, he hid a tempest inside. "William! Why did you have that poor girl whipped? She's one of the best servants we have here. You caused all that commotion yesterday. Not her."

"I can damn well do whatever I want. I own these darkies, and I can treat them however I wish. I have half a mind to sell the wench so I never have to hear about this again. Our slaves are property, not people. God himself put them into these circumstances." A violent orchestra of rage and anger poured forth from him.

"So, God did this to her? Not you?" his wife queried.

In an intemperate outburst, Mister Langdon rose to his full size so he towered over his wife; then he leveled her with his gaze. "No, God set the order of things. He made the Negroes into slaves. He made them less than whites. It has always been that way and always will be. We are just the beneficiary of God's good graces."

"Oh, William, even I realize that it was man that made the Negroes slaves."

"No, God did it. Not us. It's God's plan and his order of life."

Mister Langdon left the room and went out. Still in a foul mood, he decided he didn't like being challenged about his decisions, particularly when it came to the discipline of a mere slave. He approached his overseer and told him he wanted Juba sold. The master directed him to give her about a week in the infirmary so that her back could start to heal, then to take her to Charleston to be sold.

Several days later, Juba was taken to Charleston. She begged and pleaded all the way not to be sold, but she was ignored. Cuffee had been working out in the fields and was completely unaware of her removal from the estate. After Juba arrived where the slave sale was being held, she was placed in a holding pen to await her fate. Hours later, she was sold to a wealthy man from Beaufort, some fifty miles south of Charleston. Helpless to change the outcome, her vitality and upbeat spirit left her. The bedraggled Juba was carried in the back of a wagon to a new life in another town. Mr. Langdon, with Big John at his side, was later informed of the outcome of the transaction. The former owner was given 800 dollars for the sale of a human being.

Word of Juba's fate traveled like wildfire across the plantation. When Cuffee heard the news, he was struck numb. He fought just to stand; it was like an iron rod had hit him. He retreated to his cabin, shut the door and dropped onto a stool. Cuffee felt strange and hollow, still stunned by the news. How could he go on living without Juba? He felt nothing but a grave sense of loss, an empty, extinguished place in the pit of his stomach. He had to do something. He pulled out the quilt Rosa had given them on their wedding day.

Cuffee ran to Rosa and said, "Show me! Show me what the symbols mean! How can I travel to see Juba? We need to run to where we can be free and together. No more whips! No more being sold off!"

Rosa told him to lower his voice. She walked to the door and carefully closed it behind him, making sure it was shut tight. "I will show you, but you must be patient. Setting things up so you can travel will take time. Don't go rushing off, or you'll be killed. If you run off with nothing in place, they will just set the bloodhounds on you, to catch you and rip you to shreds. You hear me?" She narrowed her eyes at him to confirm his understanding.

"Okay," Cuffee agreed and took a deep breath. "I just gotta get my Juba back. We need to be free."

"Now, what you have there on your quilt is a sampler of patterns. Each one means something. One tells you to prepare. One tells you to pack those things you'll need for your travels. Watch for quilts being aired out. The display of a quilt is actually a signal. The symbols shown on a hanging quilt will tell you what to do. Even the knots on your quilt are important. They are important for their message and for the power given to you. Sometimes there are charms tucked inside, things that will protect you, in the batting or hidden under an applique.

"Once you start on your travels, you need to go to places that have been especially chosen. They are chosen because we have a friend there. May be a free person of color. May be a white man. You have to keep the directions in your head and then look for a signal. That signal could be anything, but usually it is something you can see from a distance. It might even be something as simple as a small painted black coachman figure used as a hitching post. If the lantern is lighted it means that you have reached a safe haven. You'll know in advance what to look for. Understand?" Rosa tipped her head down to confirm that Cuffee grasped what she was saying.

"Yeah. Yeah." Cuffee nodded anxiously.

"You won't always have a safe house or station to go to. Sometimes you have to make do outside. Maybe you hide in the woods or in a graveyard. People don't like to look in cemeteries searching for runaway slaves, so you're pretty safe there."

"I will want to go to Beaufort first, which is south, to get Juba, but then we want to go north. I hear some folks go all the way to Canada."

"That's true. Many people go to Ontario, but some stop in other places, like towns in Ohio, such as Oberlin. Cleveland, Ohio, is a big crossroad too; so is nearby Detroit, Michigan. You might stay there or go on further north. Lake Erie is there, and you can cross it to another city or over to Canada. It depends on how you travel. If you travel on foot, it can be slow going. You might only go five miles in a day. Maybe at times you get to hide in a wagon and can get farther in one day.

"You might be really lucky and travel on a ship. Traveling on water is safer and can take you farther faster. There are ways to travel by sea, lakes, rivers, and canals. Sometimes there are ships that go all the way up the East Coast. There are black seamen that transport fugitives over the water all the way up to New England. The whalers, fishermen, and tradesmen sail up and down the coast. Some hide fugitives aboard ships. Those black sailors can be pretty smart, too. They have to learn about geography, dangerous waters, languages, and customs of people. They not only offer transport to enslaved black men, but also take information back and forth through the network of folks who help the runaways.

"You need to listen to the songs folks are singing. They have a special hidden meaning. You know how out in the fields the overseer has you sing so he knows just where you at? Well, we outsmart him. We sing for him, but we use the songs to tell folks what's about to happen. The master thinks we are making joyful noise unto the Lord when we actually telling each other somebody fixing to run. Hearing the songs helps gird you for the journey you are about to take. Master thinks we singing about the Land of Canaan when we actually singing about goin' up to Canada. When you head that way, you'll be following the Canadian geese. You watch how they fly and where they land to drink.

"Sometime you may see a cooking pot turned upside down outside the kitchen house. That means a meeting planned for that night. You watch for it. Most time folks run during the springtime. That's when we have lots of thunderstorms. Big storms for three or four days. The storm washes away your scent so the bloodhounds can't follow you. It also washes away your footprints so they can't track you. Don't know which way they will send you, but maybe through those mountains, the Appalachians. Maybe by the port of Charleston.

"The word to go will probably come first from our blacksmith. He a smart man. He is the one who tell us when it's time to go. We're not allowed to use drums because they outlawed, but we can use an anvil and hammer. He rings out the message.

"You should first look for the monkey wrench on a quilt being aired out. That's the symbol here. It tells you to start to prepare. But you never say nothing, you hear?" Rosa looked Cuffee dead in the eye. She knew he was anxious, but he had to be patient until it was time to run.

Cuffee was so wound up he was shuffling his feet like a little boy waiting for Christmas. He wanted to get to his Juba right then, but he paused, took a deep breath and said, "Okay. I'll be patient. I'll wait until they tell me to go. What kind of things should I take on this trip?"

"Try to take a compass, something to defend yourself, like a knife, something to eat, something to drink, and a few coins to help you on your journey. We'll see if we can get you some good walking shoes. You'll have so many miles to cover. You'll be given a change of clothes once you get to where you going. It will probably be a black man who meets you and gives you the clothes, then takes you to a safe place, probably his own house. It's safer to keep a fugitive with people of your own color. Then you don't stand out. People not suspecting."

The word rippled through the plantation. As the other enslaved workers heard about what happened, they all thought of how they might support Cuffee. Word also spread by the waterway; trusted contacts were given a heads-up. Their support was solicited, and everyone had a role.

Later in the day, Mimba, the plantation's root doctor who practiced conjure medicine, walked up to Cuffee and grabbed him by the arm. She locked eyes with him while she stuffed a small bag into his hand.

"How you doin', boy?" she said really loud as if she were just greeting him. She then lowered her voice and said, "This here root is a 'hand' you need to wear around your neck. It has some powerful herbs in it. It's special charm, a mojo, a gris-gris. It will protect you in your travels."

Cuffee looked down and saw a small flannel bag packed tight. The contents felt kind of crunchy. Mimba said it held dried leaves, ashes, small frog bones, snakeskin and powdery dirt. Part of a small feather protruded. It had been sewn onto a long, circular piece of twine.

"Boy, I put special conjure medicine in this bag for you. It will protect you. I spoke the magic words of unknown tongues over it. As you go on your travels, remember to stop the flow of evil. Evil travels in straight lines. Make sure you mix up your path so evil don't touch you and avoid the white buckra who may be hunting you. Follow the drunkard's path, just like the quilt show you. You hear?"

"Yes, ma'am. I thank you for the root bag. I know your conjure is powerful," said Cuffee as he smiled and nodded at Mimba.

Mimba's conjure bag made Cuffee feel as though he had some protection and a better chance of reaching Juba. He was anxious to get on the road, but he understood it would be dangerous and he would be hunted by white men. Slave catchers and the slave patrol would have dogs. If they caught his scent, they would be unleashed on him. Bloodhounds were known to tear the flesh from a man while he stood there living and breathing. If Cuffee were captured and brought back to the plantation, he could face tortures even worse. But Cuffee knew he couldn't go on in this state. He longed to see Juba. The long days working in the fields became nearly unbearable. Only thoughts of Juba made them tolerable. It was hard to stay steady and not lose his mind.

A couple of weeks later, Cuffee walked over to the infirmary to see Rosa and find out if she had any news. She had a sewing circle going. About five women seemed to be feverishly engaged in piecing together a quilt.

"What y'all doin?" Cuffee asked.

The women looked up from their work and in a quiet voice Rosa said, "We're making a special 'follow the stars' quilt. It has the drinkin' gourd or Big Dipper. Once we done sewing this here quilt, you need to memorize it."

Then an older enslaved woman started to quietly sing:

When the sun come back,
When the firs' quail call,
Then the time is come,
Foller the drinkin gou'd

Foller the drinkin' gou'd,
Foller the drinkin' gou'd
For the ole man say,
Foller the drinkin' gou'd.

He wondered what the women were talking about, but then he looked down at their work. Their quilt depicted the heavens above and the constellations. Prominent on the quilt was the North Star.

While Cuffee prepared for his journey to freedom, Juba was adjusting to her new life down in Beaufort. They lived in a large home on Prince Street. Her new master owned multiple properties in the area. She was heartbroken at having been ripped away from her home and loved ones for a second time in her life. She lamented, *How can there be a just God?*

Juba found comfort with some of the folks in the house and others nearby. She was a house servant, so her life was far better than had she been working in the fields. Another enslaved house servant named Eliza was kind and seemed bright. She helped Juba understand the household's workings and the preferences of their master, Henry McKee. He and his wife, Jane, were considered somewhat akin to royalty in that small community. They were very wealthy, owning a house in town and a nearby plantation named Ashdale, a large Sea Island cotton plantation on nearby Lady's Island. He owned well over fifty slaves, including Juba and Eliza.

While Juba transitioned to her new life, Cuffee's plans to run away to join his wife fell into place; everyone was working to make the plan successful. Nellie had sewn for Cuffee little pouches stuffed with ground-up Indian turnip. He would tie them to his feet when he ran. The root smelled like strong pepper and would keep the bloodhounds from picking up his scent.

Weeks of waiting passed. Cuffee started to lose heart. It had been so long since he had seen Juba. All he did was work in the field all day and pine for his sweetheart. He got to the point he didn't think he could take it any longer. Then he heard a chorus from the spiritual "Go Down, Moses."

When Israel was in Egypt land,
Let my people go;
Oppressed so hard they could not stand.
Let my people go.

"Thus saith the Lord," bold Moses said,
"Let my people go;

If not, I'll smite your firstborn dead,
Let my people go!"

Oh go down, Moses
Away down to Egypt's land
And tell King Pharaoh
To let my people go!

At first Cuffee was annoyed at the noise, but then he paused and reflected. *Maybe this is a sign. Maybe my time for freedom has come!*

At the end of the day, he sprinted back to his cabin. On the way, he saw an overturned pot on a porch, then heard the blacksmith striking his anvil, sounding out the message: time to go.

When he got back to his cabin, Big John was there. Cuffee wondered what he wanted. He hoped he wasn't there to discourage him from running. But once he got closer to Big John, he saw the spark in his eyes. Cuffee knew he was there to help.

"Gots some planting seeds for you, Cuffee. I got them from a man I trade with at the water's edge. I give him meat and vegetables. He gives me things I need."

Cuffee thought it odd. Puzzled, he took the burlap seed sack from Big John. It was rather heavy and uneven for seeds. He sat down and opened it up. He recognized the kindness Big John had just bestowed on him. It was a pair of boots. Tucked inside were socks.

"Thank you, Big John! I can't tell you how grateful I am! I never expected seeds like these!"

"They might not be just the right fit for your garden, but I done the best I could fetch for you."

Cuffee jumped from his seat and hugged Big John with such enthusiasm that he forced the air out of him. "I know I'll make it, Big John. I know I can make it now."

The following day all the signs were there. A quilt with a monkey wrench was being aired out and displayed on a slave cabin. On another shack was a quilt with a constellation of stars. Cuffee started to collect up things he would need for his travels and stash them in a special spot inside a hollow tree by the cotton fields. He would later sneak them to his cabin.

Most importantly, Cuffee had managed to acquire a compass. The careless overseer, McBride, had left it inside the barn one day when he had been drinking too much ale. Cuffee managed to scoop it up while McBride bumbled around in his drunken state. That same night, Cuffee was able to take a couple of coins from McBride's pocket as he helped him to his feet and into his cabin. McBride thought he had spent the money at the tavern and waved off the missing coins.

What Cuffee really needed was a good knife. He managed to get one from a trusted slave who worked in the barn with the horses and tack. When the barn assistant silently passed the knife to him, Cuffee couldn't believe his good fortune. As Cuffee walked away from the barn, he was stopped by Christmas Luke, the man who maintained the praise house.

"Here you go, Cuffee," Christmas Luke said as he passed a small object to him. "God been watching over you."

Cuffee held a small, handcrafted cross made of twigs and twine. He smiled and nodded at Christmas Luke and said, "Thank you kindly. I know I'll be needing this. I'll keep it in my pocket and hold it when I say my prayers. I appreciate your thinking of me."

Later that day, Nellie took food down to the tables where the field hands were seated. She walked over to Cuffee with a plate of chicken. "This here is a special treat for you, Cuffee. I made it special for you."

As she passed the plate to him, he noticed she had a napkin under it. He thought it must be hot and took it carefully from Nellie. He glanced at the napkin and noticed that a map had been drawn on it, along with a man's name, a reverend down in Beaufort. Big John had written it out for him, but it was Nellie who passed it along.

Nellie whispered, "Ask for that reverend. He will help you once you get down to Beaufort. He will help you on your way." She also told him about his first contact, a man who would be waiting for him by the Cooper River. With that, she smiled, turned her back, and walked away, acting as if she had merely passed food for dinner to the weary workers.

A special colorful quilt was hung out on Rosa's cabin. It signaled the others that someone was going to run soon. As the night approached, they sang a special song that likewise signaled the plans of an enslaved worker to run. Acknowledging the signal, Cuffee approached Rosa later that night. She filled him in on the other helpers he would come into contact with as he made his way down to Beaufort. She quickly went over his travel plans. As she looked into his eyes for understanding, she also clasped his hand, as if she hoped to convey her plans and her energy through her touch as well as her words. Cuffee nodded that he understood and burned her words into his memory. He knew that he had to remember her directions in order to survive and safely make his way to Juba.

That night, Cuffee filled an animal skin bladder at the water spigot, hoping he could take enough water to sustain him on his trip. While there, Hentie casually walked up to him, pulled something from her pocket, looked about, then said, "Here, Cuffee, I want you to have this. It is a special lodestone, a talisman that can protect you on your travels. It will help you journey safely to find your freedom. It's a very powerful thing. A while back, it protected me and Big John traveling on the dirt roads near here.

"We had been caught in a storm along with Octavia. Our horse reared up, scared by a huge snake. Big John got down to soothe the animal. I was afraid that viper would lash out at the horse and Big John. Black folks not allowed to carry a sidearm, so we had no way to protect ourselves. I felt that lodestone spark and sizzle like it was electric. It was throwing heat, then suddenly its power jumped out of it. The stone's power brought down a branch that pierced that serpent like a pitchfork. Never seen anything like it. Must be special conjure. I want you to carry it with you; it will protect you on your travels."

"Oh my, Hentie, I can't take your special lodestone. You'll need it for yourself, protect you from the Langdons and their hateful ways. You need it for yourself, I mean it," insisted Cuffee.

Hentie grabbed Cuffee's forearm and stuffed the special stone into his hand. "Cuffee, you need to find your wife. There will be many things you must overcome on your travels. You and Juba need this far more than I do. I want you to have it." Hentie locked eyes with Cuffee, pressing her point.

"Okay then, I thank you for your kindness. You don't know how much this means to me."

That night, Cuffee sat on his bed and prayed out loud: "Dear God, it's me, Cuffee. I know I don't talk to you very often, but today I need your help. I need you to help me reach my girl, Juba. I can't live without her; she my lifeblood. Please watch over her and keep her safe. And please watch over me as I try to get to her. Guide me, Lord; help me find my Juba. Help me find my way down to Beaufort. Protect me, Lord. Let me be safe from the white man. Thank you for listening to me. Amen."

He reached under his bed for the old burlap seed sack that Big John had given him. He pulled the socks on. They felt good; they would help protect the feet that had to carry him to Juba. He then reached for the boots and loosened the laces. These boots were far better than the shoes he had. He'd had to cut out the toes of his current shoes to make them fit. The newly acquired boots fit perfectly fine—a bit loose, a bit worn, but good.

Cuffee pulled out the special bags Nellie had made for him and took a deep sniff. "Whew! This does smell like pepper! Surely this will throw off the dogs!" Cuffee tied the bags around his ankles. He thought about how lucky he was to have everyone on the plantation backing him, helping to ensure his safe travels.

To the empty sack he added some dried meat, a few carrots, a turnip, a hunk of bread, a bladder of water, the compass, the knife, and a blue rag that Juba used to tie on her head. He stuck the coins into his pants pocket. He took the cloth with the map on it and glanced at the name again: Reverend Samuel Taylor. He carefully squirreled the cloth into his jacket. He clutched Hentie's lodestone in his hand, its protection being critical to his safe travels.

That's it, he thought. *I'm ready.* He stood and took a last glance around his cabin. With hesitation and much trepidation in his heart, he said to himself, "There is nothing in here I need; the only thing I need in life is Juba."

He walked across the cabin floor, taking in a deep breath. It was an arduous task he was about to undertake. He could only hope God was on his side. He rubbed the lodestone in his hand, feeling a warm glow of protection emanate from it. Tonight was the night.

"I best go now," Cuffee said to himself. He listened carefully before he cracked open the door to his cabin. Thank God, the moon was shining down on him to show him the way. Round and white, it loomed large at the top of the sky. Cuffee cautiously slipped out the door and quietly pulled it shut. He tugged on the conjure bag to ensure it was still around his neck. *Mimba makes good conjure; please let it protect me*, he thought. *And I have my special lodestone. If it can kill a snake, it can throw off bloodhounds searching for me. Keep me safe. Please keep me safe.*

It happened then that a protective blanket of white light fell over him, seeming to ensure his safety. Feeling the warmth, Cuffee sucked in a big breath, then bolted across the open area surrounding the slave cabins toward the woods, crouching as he ran.

Chapter 22
Cuffee Runs Away

Having committed himself to the journey, Cuffee ran from the slave cabins, springing into a cluster of loblolly pines where he had a great deal of cover. From there he went into the belly of the woods. His anxiety rose as leaves crunched under him and dead twigs cracked; he hoped no one would hear the subtle sounds of someone running through the woods. At one point he stumbled in a hole that sent him sprawling on the ground. It frightened some large birds who suddenly took flight. In his forward momentum, Cuffee flung his bag some distance away and panicked. Terror paralyzed him when he lost sight of it. *Oh God, what will I do without the compass and knife? What about my lodestone? I need it to protect me.*

For a moment, Cuffee thought all the sounds around him ceased. It was like the whole world waited for a few beats. There was a vacuum. The cicadas stopped humming and frogs stopped croaking. Even the sound of the chirping crickets had vanished. Cuffee looked about him into the dark earth, molted leaves, rotting logs, and crawling moss. He saw the pine saplings rising up from the floor of the forest and was pulled deeper into his panic. What was he to do?

He looked up to the thick canopy of trees and started to feel the pain from the scrapes he sustained on his palms when he had sprawled onto the hard dirt. With his fingers splayed, he quietly pushed himself off the ground and looked around. He heard a twig snap. Cuffee stopped and choked, catching a glimpse of what looked to be a haint. Perhaps it was playing tricks on him. Cuffee drew in a deep breath when he saw no other movement, he decided he must move on. *I gotta keep going. Gotta get to Juba. I just have to see her.*

He forced himself to recall which hand had carried the bag and in which direction his momentum had carried him. He ventured cautiously in that direction. As he took tentative steps, his boot kicked something soft. He looked down and saw the precious bag under the toe of his boot.

"Praise God!" he softly uttered. He bent down and snatched up the parcel. "Thank you, God! Thank you!" Feeling renewed, he continued to search for the lodestone that had been in his hand when he fell, but after searching frantically for several minutes, he was unable to find it. Feeling that to delay any longer was the greater risk, he decided to move on.

He had to cross water and was thankful he had on his new boots as he waded through the stream for nearly a mile before climbing out on the opposite side. He pulled himself up the embankment on a branch sticking out. He gashed his fingers but ignored the pain and entered another wooded area. He went on for nearly half a mile, then backtracked to the stream. He remembered that he should not run in a straight line since that was how evil flowed, so he tried to jog this way, then that, to mix up the pattern. He hoped this would divert the flow of evil and confuse the hounds that would undoubtedly be sent after him.

Once safely into the darkness of the dense forest, he followed the signs he saw along the way, heading toward the river where he would cross. His heart pounded in his chest until he thought it was safe to stop. After climbing into the branches of an old oak tree, he waited and listened. Waiting was a hard but essential part of the journey. Silently, Cuffee prayed and gently rocked, hoping to see a small light or some other signal in the hours to come. He imagined himself holding Juba again and them laughing like they used to. Cuffee tried to think of where he was going, not of getting caught. When thoughts of hounds tracking him or white men with torches and knives coming toward him intruded, he quickly pushed those thoughts out of his mind.

I need to cover a good distance, and quickly. Then he heard the loud snort of a horse. Cuffee peered through the trees into a clearing where a wooden fence enclosed a large pasture. He made his way through the fog-drenched forest, not stopping until he saw smoke curling from a chimney. It was still dark, and Cuffee shivered in the moist air, partly from the temperature and partly from nerves. Dawn was just beginning to break. The early-morning breeze carried the pungent aroma of horse manure and the scent of incoming rain, of summer grass, and of the various farm animals. Fat, billowing black clouds moved toward him. He needed to make a quick getaway before the rain rolled in. This horse might be the trick to quickly cover the miles. Cuffee peered into the gray skies, then at a saddleless horse some distance from him. The horse, a chestnut-colored stallion with a black mane, sauntered by some tall grass, gently pulling out blades to munch on.

As Cuffee advanced toward the fence where the gate was latched, he saw a woman in a patched blue skirt come out of a barn. The farmer woman laid her long gun on the side of the building and walked toward a worn storage bin. She then dipped a shallow bowl into the bin for feed. She pushed back a wisp of hair that had fallen into her face; somehow it had escaped all the hair pins that held her mousy brown hair in a taut bun. Straightening, she then turned to face the brood of chickens. Fortunately, her back was to Cuffee.

She began to shout, calling out to the hens. Then, with a thrusting motion, she spread the feed onto the ground for the birds. As she slowly moved through the barnyard, she muttered, "Here, chickie, chickie."

Cuffee crawled on his stomach, hoping that neither the farm woman nor the horse would sense his approach. As he inched forward, he looked up to the latch. *Just a little farther, just a little farther*—then the horse caught Cuffee's scent.

Oh God, please let this turn out good. I need your help, God. Don't let that farmer woman see me!

Cuffee heard a soft nicker from the nearby horse. Out of curiosity, the horse clomped his way toward Cuffee. Cuffee sucked in a breath, feeling raw and exposed. "Good horsey. Good boy." He kept his voice low and steady. A knot in Cuffee's belly rose in his throat like bile. The horse regarded Cuffee with lazy eyes and continued to chomp on the tender blades of grass.

"Here, I have something even better," Cuffee whispered and drew from his bag one of the carrots he had stashed.

This meant less for Cuffee to eat, but a horseback ride was just what he needed. Cuffee reached up and unfastened the latch. Crouching, he approached the mild-mannered horse. The horse showed only gentle curiosity as he raised his head. Cuffee lifted the carrot, the point of it raised heavenward, hoping the horse would recognize the shape. Cuffee heard the sounds of the clucking hens and the farm woman's voice in the distance. He started to back up, drawing the horse in toward him.

There was a pause in the sounds from the barnyard. He saw the farm woman look about her as she laid the bowl down on the storage bin. "Damn!" Cuffee stiffened and his skin tingled. "That woman might have seen me! God protect me! Don't let that farm woman shoot me!"

Cuffee continued to back up, faster now, until he bumped against the pole at the gate. He swung it open and it squeaked. Cuffee glanced at the woman walking toward a pail to feed the hogs. She broke her stride as she bent down to pet an old hound that suddenly appeared in the yard. *Good, she's distracted.* Cuffee snapped the carrot in half. He stuffed half of it in his pocket and held out the other half to the horse. He lured him with his open hand, offering it to the horse, who quickly devoured it. Cuffee adroitly jumped to the second rung of the fence and leapt onto the horse's back. Cuffee pulled down his hat, dug in his heels and clucked. The horse stalled, so he slapped the horse on the hindquarters, then shouted a bold "Yah!" As he did so, a flock of birds frightened by the sound flew up from a tree. This captured the ambling farm woman's attention, and her head jerked up toward the birds. An instant later she caught the movement of Cuffee on the horse and dropped the pail. She looked about, wildly spreading her arms and legs in the process.

"Damn, where's my gun?" She scrambled to seize the rifle and aimed it at the escaping culprit. The farm woman fired off a round. Cuffee felt a ripple of air to his left and the resounding report of the rifle behind him. There was a pause; then Cuffee heard the singing of the second bullet right before it hit a tree near him with a burst of bark. The stallion lurched forward, nearly catapulting Cuffee. Fortunately, the horse had on a bridle, which Cuffee seized tightly. He maintained a tenacious hold on the animal. *Damn! That was close!*

Cuffee pumped his arms and dug his heels into the horse as they galloped away. Cuffee threw one last look at the woman and saw her standing in the middle of the pasture, her arms loose at her sides, as she stared forlornly at Cuffee, who was getting away at breakneck speed. Cuffee urged the horse to intensify his gallop as they approached a low fence. The fence was no obstacle for the stallion, who flew up, up, and over with ease. Cuffee was so terror-struck and winded that he knocked his chest to steal his breath back and restart his heart. He laughed at the thrill of overcoming the obstacle so readily. The horse galloped on, and they disappeared into the woods. Since Cuffee was at some distance and the skies were dark, the farm woman could not determine who the man had been or whether he had been white or black. She only knew a man had stolen her favorite horse.

"Thank you, Lord! Thank you. I know you have smiled down on me this day!"

As Cuffee galloped off, he saw a flash of lightning in the sky. There was a pause, then the rumble of thunder. *Oh Lord, just what I need, a thunderstorm.* Fat drops of rain began to fall, pounding the ground below him. A few moments later a torrent of rain was unleashed. The wind blew with such force that the trees bowed. A loud clap of thunder rang out, startling Cuffee, but he hurried on.

While Cuffee initially resented the rain, after a moment's thought, he was soothed by the notion. The rain would make it harder to track him, washing out his scent and his tracks. "Thank you, Lord! You are on my side today!"

Cuffee and the chestnut horse galloped into a landscape erupting with the same wildness he felt inside. The skies appeared malevolent, teeming with ferocious winds and pelting rain. His blood continued to surge; his skin prickled with heat as a coat of sweat formed on his chest. He panted for breath. Cuffee wiped the perspiration from his brow and noticed for the first time the mud spattered across his face. Cuffee continued two miles north to the Wando River along a hard-packed road, now wet with the heavy rain. He made good time on the horse. The stallion was slick with sweat with froth on his lips. Cuffee had ridden him hard. Fortunately, the horse continued at a steady trot in the rain, apparently used to traveling in such conditions.

Cuffee slowed the horse, and at the reduced pace the stallion's hooves thudded against the wet ground, and he occasionally emitted a low nicker. The trees creaked under the deluge of rain. Cuffee pulled the horse to a halt. After a few minutes of waiting, the rain started to dissipate and turned to a mist. Branches hung heavy, water dripping off them. Cuffee wiped droplets from his face and narrowed his eyes and focused. He looked for the sign, a small light of a lantern.

It was to be carried by his first contact. He would be a man with a neckerchief and a scarlet shirt.

As Cuffee approached the river, his gaze flickered over the perimeter. He adjusted his sweat-soaked, rain-beaten hat and gingerly slid down from the horse. He held on to the animal's halter, drawing the horse near him. They entered an area with a few trees and some bushes. He crouched and surveyed his surroundings. The place seemed to be deserted. He heard only the sound of crickets and gently lapping water. Then Cuffee heard a horse's strangled whinny and a rustling in nearby bushes. Straining to listen, he peered out and saw movement. Uncertain who or what it was, Cuffee remained hidden. He heard the creaking of leather, perhaps a saddle, then saw a man dismount his horse and set a lantern by his feet. It was his contact; he recognized him by his scarf and red shirt. Cuffee tossed a pebble at the man.

The man jerked his head in Cuffee's direction and quietly said, "You can come out. It's safe now."

Cuffee's contact was a white abolitionist and a member of the Underground Railroad. His eyes looked sorrowful as he took in Cuffee's countenance. Cuffee's face was a grotesque mask of burrs, mud, and blood; it was reddened and cut in several places, as if he had been whipped by every branch in the woods during his frantic ride. Cuffee was gasping and wild-eyed, his pulse still racing. The scalp of the sympathetic aide prickled with fear, wondering what poor Cuffee had been through and what he had yet to endure. But the man knew he needed to present himself as calm and steady so as to reassure this scared and injured man.

He drew in a deep breath, smiled, and waved Cuffee over to where he stood. Cuffee slowly crept out while looking all around him, afraid his new comrade might have deceived him. As he approached the man, he could see his kind face and warm eyes. It was clear he meant him no harm. Cuffee relaxed a bit.

"Get in," the man said as he motioned to his small boat.

With that, the two hopped into the bantu boat and looked to the other side of the river. As the man paddled, the bantu glided silently across the water. It only took a matter of minutes, but Cuffee was apprehensive the entire time they were on open water.

When they reached the other side, the man said, "God be with you. Travel safe."

"Thank you. Thank you kindly. I wish I could repay you," Cuffee said.

"Live a good life; that is repayment enough," said the man. "I hope you find the freedom you seek."

"Bless you." Cuffee nodded and waved to the man, grateful for his kindness.

Then Cuffee entered the woods on the other side and began his trek toward the city of Charleston. Eventually, he came into sight of some of the city's buildings. He needed to look for a man connected to the Cigar Factory; he was supposed to have a wagon. The word "cigar" had been included on the cloth Nellie had slipped to him with his dinner. Cuffee moved silently as he edged down to the meeting point. It was late at night and few people were out. Fortunately, the rain had almost ceased completely. His cold, damp clothing was as icy as a corpse's fingers. Cuffee knew he had to be careful to avoid the slave patrol. If caught by them, his quest would be over. He would be mercilessly beaten, if not killed.

Eventually, a man, a sort of rube, trundled by in a wagon loaded with crates and boxes. Cuffee noticed the marking of *Cigars* on the side of a box. The old white man driving the wagon carefully looked around him, searching for any movement. He was rather small, with a worn hat and a tattered jacket. *Thank you, Jesus! This must be the man!*

The man removed his hat and began to tap his leg with it. Each smack grew louder and more impatient. He kept looking about as he slowly rolled forward in his wagon.

Cuffee heard the noise of an owl, a sign that this was his

connection. His eyes flitted to the tattered man with the dark, soiled hat. As the wagon approached, Cuffee lined himself up with it so that he could quickly bolt out and jump in.

The man did not make eye contact, but muttered, "Hey ya. Get in."

Cuffee climbed into the back of the wagon and pulled a tarp over his head while the driver maintained his vigilance. Hunger squeezed his belly, and thirst clawed at Cuffee's throat. Cuffee tried to push thoughts of bread and cool water from his mind. Sweat beaded on his scalp and trickled down his back. He worked to refocus on the arduous journey ahead. *I just need to think of the safe house. They will have food and water for me there. I just have to make it to the safe house; then everything will be okay.*

The rain was now a fine mist and nothing more than a mere annoyance. They rolled along in the wagon for what seemed like a long time, but Cuffee knew it would only be minutes until he was delivered to the waterfront. He was to be dropped off at the harbor. As the wagon rolled to the lower peninsula of Charleston, Cuffee saw the gaslights overhead on the street. He started to count, thinking that it would help him count the streets to the harbor, but he heard someone on the street shout. It startled him and he lost count. Cuffee heard voices around him and the sounds of activity. Someone scampered across the street, but he dared not peek to see who it was. His heart pounded. He feared that at any moment someone would throw back the tarp and he would be revealed. Cuffee wanted the driver to speed up and get to the harbor quickly; instead the wagon moved slowly, just quietly rolling along. The driver was doing his best not to draw attention. Cuffee heard feminine laughter followed by what sounded like the hushed sounds of a young couple sprinting home.

At last the wagon reached the harbor, and they rolled down to Adger's Wharf. *Thank you, Jesus!* Cuffee thought. He heard the voices of the dockhands and longshoremen, the occasional ringing of a ship's bell as the wind knocked against it, and the soft sounds of the waves lapping against the wharf. The wagon pulled up to the loading dock.

The man quietly whispered, "We're here now. When I tap the side of the wagon, you hop down. After you jump down, you head to a boat marked *Planter*. It's the second one down there. About a hundred and fifty feet long with two side-wheels. You'll see a young black man in a white shirt. His name is Robert Smalls."

Little did Cuffee know the fame that the ship and the man would later acquire as a hero in the War Between the States. Smalls would commandeer the ship and navigate it, along with several enslaved passengers, to freedom. Wearing Captain Charles Relyea's familiar wide-brimmed straw hat and jacket, Smalls took the wheel of the ship in the wee hours of the morning of May 13, 1862, then navigated the ship past numerous checkpoints into the Charleston Harbor where it was surrendered to the Federals, along with its cannons, guns and ammunition. His sixteen Negro passengers were free for the first time in their lives. This event would be the most spectacular coup of the Civil War. Charleston's symbolism as the cradle of the Confederacy and one of the largest ports in the South made this military stroke of luck something not only renowned up and down the East Coast but across the Atlantic as well.

Cuffee thanked the man and quickly made his way down to the sidewheel steamer. The briny scent of marshes swept across the harbor. In the frothing water by the wharf, debris drifted by—palm leaves, algae, sea lettuce, and sargassum seaweed—plunging, disappearing under the surface, then rising again. The deadened vegetation was trapped and hopelessly caught in the current, much as Cuffee had become in this unfolding foray. As he gazed into the waters, he felt the vertiginous sensation of being sucked up into darkness. Cuffee shook that sensation loose and jerked forward. He would grab hold of his destiny and hop on board the *Planter*, finding his way to Juba and their destined life in freedom. With that notion, he vaulted down onto the landing dock and searched for a white shirt.

Cuffee saw a nearby whitewashed building with a sign over the door listing the shipping company's name. A man stood under a gaslight and nervously paced back and forth. He pulled out a timepiece from under his coat and glanced down at the watch that dangled from a silver chain. Pressing down on its pumpkin crown, the latch released and the filigree case opened. The man stared down at the black hands on the porcelain dial, then snapped it shut and stuffed it back into his coat pocket. Apparently, he was waiting for a delivery.

Cuffee hesitated at the gangplank, but was then met by Robert Smalls, a man short in stature and sporting a sullied, rain-soaked white shirt. Smalls waved him on board and guided him down into the hull of the ship. There, Cuffee was hidden with the cargo and covered by a tarp. Cuffee slinked down and sat on the floor, making himself as small as possible.

Robert Smalls told him that he was familiar with Beaufort and had a contact down there that would help Cuffee once he got there. Fortunately, a lot of information traveled up and down the waterfront, some of which helped the Underground Railroad.

While the journey would have been considered short by some, to Cuffee it seemed like an eternity. He anxiously waited, tucked in between crates and barrels, fearful that somehow he might be discovered by the white crew hands on the ship and killed. He waited and prayed to reach his next stop. As he heard the voices of two white sailors approach, goosebumps spread across his arms and down his spine. Feeling doomed, he wondered what tortures they might devise. His anxiety rose and his heart fluttered as beads of sweat ran down his forehead.

Dear God, I wish I had that lodestone to protect me. Who knows what they will do to me if they find me? Dear God, help me. Help me now! Cuffee tried to control his breathing so they would not hear him but continued to take in short puffs of air, his heart racing.

"Why did the damn captain send us down here to find his stinkin' booze?"

"Because the lazy bastard would rather have his crew do it for him. What's the whiskey in? A burlap bag?"

"Yeah, I think that's what he said. He wrapped it up in a bag and tucked it in a corner. That damn thing could be anywhere."

As the sailors rifled around, Cuffee heard them approach his side of the storage room. He closed his eyes tightly and tried to hold his breath. His skin tingled with pinpricks of sweat and goosebumps. He froze still as a statue, afraid to move or make a sound.

As the two men moved around crates and parcels, he heard the scampering of mice. Afraid that one might suddenly drop onto him, he ducked his head and cupped his hands over his scalp.

"Here it is," shouted one of the ship's hands. "Damn that bastard. Why did we have to dig around down here? God only knows what rats and vermin are crawling around."

"Thank God! Let's get out of here. It makes my skin crawl."

With the whiskey in hand, the two departed and returned to the deck of the ship. Relieved by his good fortune, Cuffee quietly sighed. *Thank you, God!*

Finally, the crew prepared for departure. They added wood to the fires, which they had banked when they moored the ship the previous night. Cuffee nervously waited for the water of the steamer's boilers to heat up. Above, Smalls paced the deck, willing the steam to build. Finally, a plume of smoke wafted up. Smalls remained alert, but no suspicious crew or guards appeared. Relieved at their luck, Smalls returned to his duties and notified the steamer's captain that they were ready to depart. He made a special effort to bark out that the ship was ready for departure to allay Cuffee's anxieties. As the steamboat left the dock, the paddles began thundering, the smokestack began blowing, and the crew moved busily about the ship.

Slowly, the ship entered the Charleston harbor. Following the coastline, the steamer made its way south and at last landed at

Beaufort. The deckhands readied the ship and hollered out their approach. The scampering of the ship's crew on deck and the clicking of their heels was sweet music to Cuffee's ears. He was approaching the town where Juba lived. He would see her once again.

Despite Cuffee's excitement, he had a long wait before him. He was put off until they were docked in Beaufort and all the white ship hands, along with the captain, had left the ship.

As the white crew started to clear out, Smalls came down to the hull and whispered to Cuffee, "I have some clothes for you here. They are clothes worn by stevedores. Put them on. People will think that you work for one of the ships or the dock itself. Then put your old clothes in this sack. I'll get rid of them."

All Cuffee could say was, "Thank you!" and he whispered those two words quietly, careful not to tip off anyone.

Cuffee quietly and carefully changed his clothes. He discovered a new pair of socks in the bag. What a stroke of luck! Dry feet again. He stuffed the old clothes into the sack. As he cautiously came from behind the crates, he heard the captain's voice up on deck. Struck with terror, Cuffee ducked. The captain was pacing, shouting about a missing crate. There was someone arguing and then crates being slammed around. Cuffee's heart pounded. What would he do if they started to tear through the stowage in the hull? He had nowhere to hide.

"Oh, here it is!" shouted one of the deckhands. "I found it!"

"Good. Then all is well, Captain," said Smalls.

"Alright then, I'm going to Clancy's for a hot meal, then on to the boarding house for a rest. You take care of things here, Smalls."

"Yes, sir," Smalls sharply replied.

Cuffee continued to wait in the hull for a signal or word from Smalls. Eventually, Smalls came down and said, "It's safe now. You can come out. Most everyone has left the dock. A man in a black coat and a black hat will be waiting for you. Watch for him. He will take you to the next station. Be careful."

"Thank you, sir. Thank you." With that, Cuffee bounded to the end of the dock and tried to blend in with passersby on the street above. Cuffee was vigilant, his eyes darting about, looking carefully for his contact. He spotted a man in a black coat made of light wool and a dark felt hat. The man also wore a pectoral cross around his neck and the familiar white detachable clergyman collar.

Cuffee crossed the street to meet the man in black. The contact introduced himself as the reverend at a local church, and he said he was active with local efforts to assist Negroes; his name was Samuel Taylor. Reverend Taylor told Cuffee to follow him and they would depart in his wagon. They turned the corner and climbed onto his rig. Reverend Taylor said he was taking Cuffee to his property outside town where he would be safe. While Cuffee's anxiety started to diminish, he knew almost anything could still happen to him.

The man moved slowly and cautiously looked around as he traveled down the street. They made some small talk, but both were far more concerned with their surroundings. While they periodically turned to one another to make a comment, they otherwise canvassed the streets and potential hiding places a slave catcher might be lurking. A coach turned onto the street, and Cuffee made an audible gasp. He temporarily froze, arrested by the *clomp* of the horses' hooves and the way their high strides made eddies in the leaves. But the other wagon turned down an alley and disappeared from sight. They both breathed a little easier when the sound of the wagon faded. As they made their way out of Beaufort and started out to the man's home, their vigilance subsided a bit. The man said his home was on the outskirts of town and he felt things would be safer out there.

Then the man said, "I suppose you know that there is talk of a war starting between the states sometime soon. People's emotions are going strong about the slavery issue. Most of us abolitionists are afraid to say a word for fear of being harmed. I've heard talk of people being beaten or their homes being burned down just for speaking favorably about black folks. It's got white people and black people all churned up."

As a worried look crossed his face, Cuffee replied, "My friend Big John tells me the people down on the docks talk about a tenseness in Charleston. There has been a fear of South Carolina leaving the Union for a long time. There are federal soldiers at Fort Sumter in case something happens."

The reverend nodded, saying, "The Federalists seem to be preparing for a fight and are desperately trying to bring in supplies. Secession seems inevitable. We hope there will be no confrontation, but of course anything could happen. While President Buchanan wants to avoid a war, it seems the Carolinians are set on executing their plan to break away from the Union. Who knows who will be president next and what may happen?"

Stunned by all that the man had said, Cuffee replied. " Us black folks hope we can be free. We pray for it all the time, nearly every day."

"Well, son, let's hope our peculiar institution of slavery comes to an end. All we can do is hope and pray. I do what I can helping folks like you," said the man.

The man pulled the wagon into the lane adjacent to a house. He looked deeply into Cuffee's eyes and in a quiet voice said, "Okay, keep your voice down. We will be going into the house. Only my wife will be in there. You can greet her, and then we will proceed upstairs. We will be taking you to a storage area in the attic of our house."

Cuffee nodded and said, "Thank you, sir. Thank you. I appreciate your kindness. I know this is a great risk to you and your kin."

With that the two men quietly entered the house. The man's wife had been moving about the kitchen. She was facing the door when they entered and seemed to anticipate Cuffee's appearance. She nodded and smiled when she saw him. She was a kindly looking woman, her brown hair combed back tightly into a bun. She wore a modest, deep-green dress that emphasized her sage-green eyes.

"Thank you, ma'am, thank you for allowing me to come into your home. This is a great kindness you are doing for me. I miss my wife, and I hope to find her here in Beaufort. I thank you for allowing me to join you here."

"You're welcome, son. You know it is very dangerous what we are doing. I hope you appreciate our risks. You need to follow our rules. You need to be as quiet as you possibly can while you are here. We have a hiding place up in our attic. I will bring you food once a day, twice a day if I can. I will give you a basin of water to clean with and another can to relieve yourself in. We will exchange cans every day. Here, I have made a small basket for you. It has some dried meat, a sliced apple, and bread. I also put in a flask of water."

Cuffee nodded and bowed at the waist. "Thank you. Thank you. I don't know how I can repay you."

"Well, we believe this is how God wants us to act and to show such kindness," said the wife. "In the fullness of time we will be rewarded by God, and you shall find the freedom you so sorely seek."

The three of them ascended the steps to the attic. When they got to the attic space, the husband moved out a large dresser. It covered a half door and a storage space under the roofline; there were no windows in it.

"You will have to keep everything with you in this storage space. We hope that there will be certain times of the day we can move the dresser and let you walk upright in the attic, maybe even peer out the window. We will have to be very careful that no one ever sees you or any light up here. Do you understand?" Both the husband and wife regarded Cuffee seriously. They needed to make sure there was a tacit understanding.

"Yes, sir. Yes, ma'am. I understand. Again, I realize you are doing me a great kindness. I will not jeopardize your safety, or mine." Cuffee continued to nod and shuffle back and forth as he looked to the couple. "By the way, I am Cuffee. May I have your name, ma'am?"

"Oh yes, dear. My Christian name is Sarah, and my husband here is Samuel. You may already know our last name is Taylor. We help run a local church, and our time is tied up with that a great deal. We have no children, which helps make it easier for us to assist others. We think that it was part of God's plan." Her husband flushed a bit and nodded in agreement.

"Yes, ma'am. My wife, her name is Juba. She a pretty girl. She was sold to a master down here in Beaufort. I need to find her."

"We'll see what we can find out. In the meantime, you need to hole up now. I have blankets and a homemade mattress for you in your space. I put in a couple of prayer books and small things for you to look at. I figured you probably don't know how to read but might want to feel God close to you with those books. Maybe we can teach you to read over time. Perhaps we can start by teaching you your letters."

"That would be wonderful, ma'am. You know, we are not allowed to read, but I would love to learn so I can be independent one day. Thank you for your kindness."

"Yes, perhaps one day things will change for black folks. Until then we'll have to make do as we are here."

They exchanged pleasantries and said good night. Cuffee was able to get a bit of light from a small gap in the roofline. He looked out and saw a portion of the sky and leaves on trees, but that was about all. He tried to settle in. Cuffee stared at the dark plank of the rafter over his head and felt some sense of safety here. A wave of calm fell over him.

Little did Cuffee know that this little town and nearby Port Royal would later play a critical role as a stronghold for the Federalists. It would also become a haven for the many Negroes who became freemen with nowhere to go and no means to support themselves. The Port Royal Experiment, as it was known, would take hold there, with an organized effort to educate and enable the newly freed slaves with the direct support of missionaries, sometimes dubbed Gideon's Band. Over a thousand recently freed Negroes would be housed at Port Royal and nearby Hilton Head. This surge in support of this revolutionary program would be done with the approval and consent of General Sherman and a group of black leaders, as well as the American Missionary Association.

Cuffee just knew he was safe for the moment and Juba was within arm's reach, out there somewhere close by. A memory flashed through his mind of holding her and taking in her scent. *That will happen again for me, and we will be free. Freemen, no more whippings, no more beatings; free to live our own lives.*

Chapter 23
Cuffee Waits to Find Juba Down in Beaufort

The days turned into weeks of hiding at the pastor's house and seemed to drag on forever. Cuffee knew he was close to Juba but didn't know where she was or how he could contact her. The tension was sometimes unbearable. Longing to hold Juba in his arms again, he had no power to control his life, no autonomy or right to self-determination. Having committed no crime, nor performed any wrongdoing, he was unable to direct the course of events. He had to wait to be told when he could see his wife. The pastor at this station told him to be patient, that things would happen in time. The pastor promised that he would try to find Juba and somehow bring the two together. Cuffee needed to sit tight and be content that he had a safe haven in the underground network.

In the meantime, the pastor's wife would let him come down from the attic space to a room on the second floor for about an hour at a time. She shared church lessons with him and started the process of teaching him to read. Cuffee was frustrated at first, as he had never had any kind of book learning. He had to make his brain work in new ways. But the church lady was kind and very patient with Cuffee, encouraging him by praising even the smallest of successes. When they were through each day, she would hand him a piece of paper to study up in his attic space. Cuffee drilled himself again and again, trying to memorize what he learned each day as best he could.

Most of the time Cuffee had to lie on his back and stare at the boards in the ceiling. The room was tiny, very narrow with a height of about three feet. Sometimes he found himself anxiously tapping his leg or rubbing the fabric of his linsey-woolsey breeches. Other times he was lost in thoughts of Juba and the tenderness of her touch. If he was lucky and had daylight, he could look about. When darkness fell, all he could do was listen to the sounds around him. Since the pastor's house was outside the city, for long periods all he heard were birds and other wildlife. At other times he overheard people talking downstairs. He tried to make out what the conversations were about, if for no other reason than to keep his mind active. Sometimes he caught bits of information from those chatting downstairs about fears of war, South Carolina's debate about leaving the Union, or what was going on with the Lowcountry's key crop, Sea Island cotton.

⌒

Meanwhile, back in the Charleston area, the master had posted signs for his runaway slave. He had the signs tacked to pillars, posts, and boards all over Mount Pleasant and Charleston. Master Langdon was offering a reward of 100 dollars for Cuffee. The poster described Cuffee's height, weight, and general characteristics. The master even mentioned the manner in which Cuffee walked. The master was infuriated that such a good slave would have the nerve to run off from him. Langdon told the slave catchers that he would accept Cuffee dead or alive, he didn't care, so long as they carried him back home. The master was seething with anger and offered a bonus if they found him within the month. He told the slave catchers that Cuffee was likely running to Beaufort to find his wife.

"Keep an eye on Juba. She was sold to a family that lives in the town of Beaufort. I think the owner's name starts with the letter *M*. Watch that house, for surely Cuffee will try to reconnect with his wife. They're young and were just married a short while ago."

The following morning, Hentie was thrown from her deep sleep by the morning bell. People started to move outside. She overheard one worker complain about the soreness he still had in his back and hands, even after a partial night of sleep. Hentie glanced over toward Juba's empty pallet. *I hope Juba is doing alright. She has had so many bad things happen to her. I wonder if her new master a kind man or a brute like so many? I hope Cuffee found her. I hope so, for both their sakes.*

Hentie shook herself from her thoughts and threw off her tattered quilt. She needed to get moving. The master and missus would want their breakfast. She quickly readied herself.

As she stepped onto the path outside her slave cabin, she heard someone walking. She turned and saw Big John, who just happened to be nearby.

"Mornin', Hentie." His eyes sparkled as he stopped and moved toward her.

"Morning, Big John. Sure is a pretty day, isn't it?" She paused and looked into his large round eyes as she spoke. He stood so close she could feel his warmth. Big John appeared lost for a moment, just staring back into Hentie's eyes. For the first time Hentie noticed flecks of gray in his hair and new creases near his eyes. *I guess we're both getting older.*

"John, you okay?"

Snapping out of it, he blurted, "Oh no, I'm fine. I mean the sunlight was hitting your eyes just so . . . and I . . . I . . . well, I best get a move on. Master will lash me for sure if he catches me wasting time." Big John started to pull away, then stopped, paused and turned back to Hentie.

"Hentie, maybe we go for a walk down by the water after suppertime?"

Hentie's face lit up as she broke out into wide smile. "Why, Big John, I'd love to walk with you. I'll look for you at suppertime out here at the tables."

Big John bobbed his head up and down and said, "Good, that's wonderful, Hentie. I'll look forward to it all day."

And so will I. And so will I.

The two turned from one another, the energy sizzling between them.

Hentie floated away from the exchange. *Big John sure is a nice man. He's been kind to me since the first day I landed in Charleston. Always so gentle and caring. He's just a good soul. And smart, too, real smart. He knows his letters, how to read. He could run this plantation if the master had a notion to allow him. I bet he'd be a good husband to a woman; take real good care of her. I wonder if he might feel that way about me.*

As Hentie reached the threshold of the kitchen house, she glanced back toward Big John. She stared as she watched Big John's large frame move with vitality and athleticism. *Those broad shoulders sure are something. I bet it would feel good to be held in those arms.* Hentie emitted a soft sigh.

She was pulled from her musings when she heard Nellie's loud belly laugh. She had been standing in the doorway watching the whole exchange.

"What you looking so lovesick about?" She leaned out and looked over to Big John. He was standing at the end of the work yard talking to the overseer.

"Girl! I wondered when you were going to wake up and realize what a good man Big John is. He's been sweet on you for ages!"

"Really? You really think so? You wouldn't joke about something like that, now, would you?" Hentie's eyes were so serious and penetrating, looking for any clue of Nellie's true thoughts, that Nellie burst out laughing again.

"Honey, you got it worse than you know!" Nellie chuckled to herself as she walked back into the kitchen house toward the food preparation table.

"Big John and Hentie. Um, um, um. Now there's a couple for you. Two good folks."

"Nellie, don't say such things. He just asked me to go on a walk, that's all." Hentie turned her head and flushed like a woman half her age.

"Girl, that poor man has been waitin' on you for years; you just too blind to see it."

"He's so big and strong." Hentie broke into a smile just thinking about him.

"Well, I'd watch yourself for a while. Never know how the master feel about you being with Big John. He's the master's right-hand man. I'm sure he'll be protective of him."

"Never thought about whether the master would approve. Can't even love a man without the master's say-so." Hentie shook her head.

"Well, Hentie, just be careful. The master is a moody man. Never know how somethin' gonna hit him. He could sell you off if he don't approve. White folks do things like that, especially the master."

"You right, I best watch myself. I was going to walk with Big John down by the water tonight. We best sneak down there separate-like, so that master don't know," Hentie whispered in a cautious tone.

"I can let Big John know if you want me to. I talk with him now and again during the daytime."

"That would be good, Nellie. Thank you. That's very kind of you." Hentie nodded in appreciation.

Hentie took a step to the side to start her work, looked down for a moment and smoothed her hands on the coarse fabric of her skirt, then moaned as she pulled out a mixing bowl to make a batch of biscuits.

Lord God, why do it have to be so hard? Can't even love a man without white folks controlling you. Isn't it enough that white folks already took my family? Can't I just be loved again?

⌒

Down in Beaufort, Cuffee persevered in his lonesome waiting. One day he noticed a gimlet left on a ledge. He treasured the device and used it to hold open a small trapdoor hidden among the stacked boxes and crates in the attic. It seemed the pastor had created the door so the confinement wouldn't be as suffocating. Cuffee also discovered a small round opening between the boards that allowed him to look out. A knothole had been knocked out, creating a modest-sized hole for him to peer through unnoticed. These small niceties made all the difference in Cuffee's small world. Never did he think the fresh scent of out-of-doors and the grass beneath one's feet could be as alluring as a whole side of ham.

Time rolled on, and eventually the weeks became a matter of a few months. The weather took on a cold rawness. The attic space had no protection against the chilling winds. At times rain leaked in so badly that Cuffee was soaked to the bone, unable to stand, dry off, or change his clothing. He merely lay on his soaked pad and prayed that God was watching over him and knew of his suffering.

The pastor and his wife were kind people. They never did anything to harm him, but he could sense that they wished he was gone. He must have been a perpetual source of anxiety to them. They would surely be killed if it was discovered they were hiding a runaway slave. Cuffee didn't wish to cause them distress, but he wanted to see Juba again. He had to wait this out.

The pastor's wife continued with Cuffee's reading lessons. She carefully and patiently coached him on how to form his letters. Eventually, Cuffee was able to do a rudimentary job in writing his name. He was thrilled the first time he formed all the letters for both words, Cuffee Langdon. The missus also was persistent in her Bible lessons. Many of the words were far beyond Cuffee, but he did his best to listen intently and show his appreciation when she was done.

One night the constable and a slave catcher were at the house. They said they were trying to locate a fugitive slave. They questioned the pastor and his wife at some length about their beliefs and whether they might stoop to helping a darkie. Fortunately, the man in question was someone other than Cuffee who had run away from a plantation near Savannah. The couple genuinely knew nothing about him. The constable and his cohort eventually left the house, angry at the outcome and still suspicious of the pastor.

On occasion, the pastor held prayer meetings at his house, particularly if someone was seriously ill or a parishioner had died. On these nights, Cuffee might hear the people downstairs singing hymns. He held the cross that was given to him before his travels and silently prayed along with those pious souls downstairs, hoping their petitions would be lifted up to the Lord. And, perhaps, that God would look down on him and help him in his plight.

Finally, one day the pastor brought up a bit of news for Cuffee with his evening meal. He said that they might have found Juba working for a white family in town, but they weren't sure yet. The family had a large two-story white house with a double piazza. It sat on a corner at New and Prince Streets. They only knew the enslaved servant was a young woman who had been with the family a couple of months. The servant girl had mentioned that she came from somewhere near Charleston. It might not be Juba.

Thank God! Cuffee had to believe it was her. He just had to! His loving Juba was within his grasp.

That night Cuffee lay on his cushion and dreamed of what it was like when he and Juba had lived together and were able to hold each other at night. He thought of her smile and having her body close to his, the two melding into one another. He hoped that she thought of him too and missed him like he missed her. He hoped her new master was kind to her and kept her warm and fed. He prayed to God that He would watch over Juba and take care of her. He begged God not to let any harm come to Juba because she was all he had in life, the only one who mattered. *Please, Lord, keep her safe.*

Then, one evening a few weeks later, Cuffee decided to take matters into his own hands. He couldn't take pining for Juba any longer. He chose to sneak out of the house. He had thought about his plan for days. He waited until darkness had just fallen and before the slave patrols made their rounds. He pushed open the door to the storage place, using all his might to move the trunk out of the way. It inched forward until he was able to squeeze out.

He slowly and softly tread down the steps. When he got to the bottom, he listened to the quietness of the house. Standing in the fading sunlight, Cuffee hesitated before moving forward on his quest. Questions invaded his thoughts. What if Juba did not want to see him? What if she did not want to take the risks of running north? But Cuffee was desperate to see his wife. He resolved that he would accept whatever she chose to do.

He slowly but surely made his way, sliding his feet across the floor. The floor softly creaked. The ticking of the hall clock quietly meted out the time. It appeared that the pastor and his wife had gone into town for a prayer meeting at the church. That was just what Cuffee had hoped and suspected was the case. He had carefully tracked the days with scratches on the wall.

Soundlessly, he slipped out of the house.

Once outside, he tried to orient himself to what he recalled about the lane leading to the house and its location outside of town. Keeping low to the ground, he crossed a field and moved into the nearby woods where he blindly made his way through the foliage, trying to head in the same direction so he would continue toward town.

After a bit, the trees started to thin. Hearing someone on horseback, he ducked down close to the ground. His heart skipped a beat as he realized there was more than one man. Undoubtedly, they were armed. The blood rushed from his head, making it difficult to focus on the sounds and determine their proximity. A hot, nauseous wave swept through Cuffee, and he started to perspire. Fearful that it was the constable and his men, or perhaps the slave catchers, his breathing became rapid and shallow. If they discovered him, they would release the dogs on him and he would be ripped to shreds.

He remained there in agony for over an hour, afraid to move. Suddenly, a reptile of some sort seized his leg. In his fright, he lifted a large jagged rock and struck a hard blow to it. The cold, slimy reptile, whatever it was, loosened its hold. The pain he felt indicated that it was poisonous. *Oh, why did I lose that lodestone!? It would have protected me from this serpent like it did Hentie and Big John. The stone could have protected me against the snake and the white lawmen out there. I wouldn't have to fear the slave catchers. Why, God, why?*

Cuffee knew he had to turn around immediately. The pain became intense, but he groped and dragged himself back to the pastor's house. He hoped he could make the long trek.

As he crawled up the back steps to the house, he managed to open a door leading to the rear. He heard voices inside. *God, let it be someone who will help me,* Cuffee thought.

Once inside, he staggered, working to hold himself up. His legs buckled, and he landed on the floor with a thud.

Within moments, the pastor and his wife hurried down the steps from upstairs with a lamp in hand, curious to discover the intruder. Fortunately, there were no visitors at the house that night.

"I'm sorry. I'm so sorry, I tried to make it out to find Juba. I just want to see my wife again, to hold her. I'm sorry—" he called out before he blacked out.

Stunned by Cuffee's look of anguish, they glanced at each other in shock, not sure what to do next. The pastor bent down over Cuffee and saw his torn pant leg. He moved back the fabric and inspected the bite mark on his swollen and inflamed leg. He looked up to his wife in despair.

"Looks like a snakebite. Must have been venomous. This man is half dead. What do we do?" said the pastor.

Sensing the gravity of the situation, the pastor's wife said, "I'll make up a warm poultice of ashes and vinegar. You steep a dozen coppers in vinegar. Later, we'll apply the cankered vinegar to the swelling."

Already his affected leg was much bigger than normal. Hopefully they weren't too late. The application of the poultice gave some relief from the pain, but the swelling did not abate. The possibility of his being disabled or dying became likely. Cuffee quaked and came in and out of consciousness.

"What shall we do? We can't have him lying on our floor. We need to get him out of here!" the wife hissed.

The horror in his wife's eyes jarred the pastor into action. He said, "I will just have to carry him upstairs. He must lie on a bed and recover, at least for a bit. We must help this poor man if he is to live."

"This is a big, solid man. Are you sure you can do it?"

"Well, this isn't a matter of whether I can; I simply must," he said with determination as he locked eyes with her and held a firm look for a few beats.

Thankfully, the pastor was sturdy, with hearty farmer blood in him. He still ran a small farm that he, his wife, and a few hands managed.

With a deep breath, the pastor hoisted Cuffee over his shoulder in one smooth motion. His fear of being discovered pushed him through all his straining, and his benevolent desire to keep Cuffee alive bolstered him.

The two managed to settle Cuffee on a bed in a guest room. The wife brought spare blankets and continued with their homemade remedies. God in his mercy had found Cuffee a friend indeed. They did their best to keep him conscious and able to respond, despite the risks. The pastor and his wife took turns throughout the night nursing Cuffee and his wound. By late the following morning, he seemed to be coming around.

The pastor's wife eventually brought broth for Cuffee to sip. Though he had difficulty at first, he was finally able to get some of the hot concoction down. He seemed to turn the corner. Over the next few days he continued to rest, sleeping for long periods of time. Fearful of being discovered, the pastor was compelled to move Cuffee.

"Friend, I hate to urge you to move, but I think we must. I have changed out the blankets in your hiding place. We must get you back upstairs and concealed," the pastor urged.

"Yes, yes. I know I must go back. I thank you for giving me the time that you have in this fine bed. Let's try to make the move." Cuffee nodded and lifted his body.

Leaning heavily into the pastor, and hopping at first, the more they progressed, the greater movement Cuffee seemed to gain as his body became more lubricated and limber. Nonetheless, it was a dismal moment when Cuffee looked into the small, confined space that had become his new home. Despite the pain of the previous evening, for a few brief moments he felt like a human being again, one able to determine his own destiny, free to move in the open air, not cowering like a dog. Now he had to go back into that darkened hole.

"Sorry, friend. We will get you out and on your way to your wife as soon as we can. In the meantime, you rest up and get well." The kind pastor gave a gentle smile and urged Cuffee onward.

Cuffee crawled back into the small space and nodded at the pastor. "Thank you so much for helping me and getting me through this. I will always be grateful to you and your wife."

The pastor nodded again and slowly closed the door on Cuffee. He felt a sense of guilt in closing the door on him, but at the same time a sense of relief at having him hidden away.

Cuffee returned to his bleak life, tucked under the small crevices of the roofline. He continued to mark his time with this pocketknife on the wall. He knew that the holidays would be coming soon. He hoped that maybe, just maybe, he would be blessed with finding Juba before Christmas Day.

Juba was outside beating a rug on a line when a panicked voice whispered her name. "Psst. Psst. Juba, come here," the speaker said.

Looking about the work yard, Juba didn't see anyone and thought she must have imagined the voice. But it called to her once again. "Juba! Come here!"

Juba looked carefully in the direction of the voice, then discerned the figure of a man concealed behind an expansive magnolia. The man signaled to her, and she cautiously strolled over. He stepped out from the hedge. The man appeared to be a light-skinned mulatto with a chestnut tarpaulin hat and brown trousers. His concern seemed genuine and his countenance sincere.

"There is a man named Cuffee who has made it to the pastor's home on the edge of town. We will arrange a meeting. It will have to occur around dusk before the slave patrol starts to move through the city. It will be your opportunity to flee this place. We have helpers all along the coast, up into Philadelphia and New York. They will help you in your travels to freedom in the North. When it is time, I will tie a red piece of cloth to this magnolia. Watch for it every day. That will be your signal to leave at sunset. Head toward the waterfront and wait there for Cuffee."

With that, the man turned and sprang from the bushes toward town. Juba had no idea who the man was, but he seemed to want to help. She felt like she could trust him.

As his words sank in, a happiness unknown to her for so long tiptoed up her spine, then burst forth in sheer delight. Cuffee was here! At last they could be together again. She never thought she would see this day come. *God is good!* She could catch up with him after their months apart and share the good news about her recent discovery.

Meanwhile, Cuffee shivered in his small space. The cold nights became nearly insufferable. He tried to remain positive and be thankful for the haven he had been given, no matter how grim. He would daydream about Juba and the possibility of their reunion. Through the knothole he saw that the grounds had turned brown and the garden was nearly barren. As the wind and rain continued to seep in, Cuffee filled in gaps with chinks of oakum torn from a rope he found in the attic. Nonetheless, the chill was bitter, and at times almost unbearable. At one point, Cuffee had a very painful sensation of coldness in his head. His face and tongue stiffened, and he feared he had lost the power of speech.

When the evening meal was brought to him, Cuffee was unable to speak. He made gestures to communicate. Lethargic and weak, he did his best to convey to the pastor his dire circumstances. After initial confusion, the pastor realized the gravity of the situation and took immediate action. He gave Cuffee a dry shirt and extra blankets. The missus made up a hot metal bed warmer filled with hot coals. The cylinder was tucked into the blankets to help him stay warm. Under the circumstances, it was impossible to summon a physician to check on his condition. They had to warm him up as best they could, then watch and wait.

Finally, a meeting date was planned for Juba and Cuffee. They would connect while others were preoccupied with holiday festivities. Many of the townspeople were to attend a Christmas party. Key people such as the constable and other town leaders would be there. The holiday gala was being held in the home of Robert Barnwell Rhett. He maintained two residences, one in Charleston near his newspaper, and the second in Beaufort, where his wife and children resided. This second was a sprawling home near the river with scenic vistas intended to enthrall visitors.

Juba began her preparation to flee. She collected her clothing and personal belongings, neatly folding her drab calico dress, a brown, loose, coarse-cotton dress, and a shift made of Negro cloth. She piled them in a stack. Juba added a few other items such as a small beaded cross, a red handkerchief, and a button from Cuffee's shirt. There were so few possessions she did not have to think much about packing. She could place everything she owned in the whole world inside a handled basket she used for the market. She tucked it carefully into a corner of the kitchen and covered it with a linen cloth.

When she saw the strip of red cloth tied to the magnolia, she burst with excitement. Today was the day. Her sense of giddiness was exhilarating. At last she would get to hold Cuffee again.

At dusk, Juba slipped out of the house and headed to the side streets near the wharf. She casually strolled as she looked about. She sometimes glanced into her basket, just to reassure herself everything was still there. There were her few possessions, but she also stole some food for the trip, including bread, nuts, and beef jerky.

After a bit, she heard a voice. "Juba, come here!" It was a man speaking in hushed tones. Upon hearing her husband's voice, her body suddenly became electrified.

Cuffee jumped out from behind some storage crates. His face was jubilant, his body alert. At first Juba was hesitant, almost disbelieving who she was seeing, but Cuffee was already in a trot toward her. She gulped in breaths of relief. At last, Cuffee was with her again. Just as Juba readied herself to fall into Cuffee's arms, a shot rang out. Stunned, she looked toward the sound of the blast, then glanced at Cuffee. He had a puzzled look, but then his eyes grew wide as if in shock. He paused momentarily, then dragged one foot, but kept his forward momentum. *The lodestone; I need the lodestone.* He took a few steps more, then another shot rang out. It struck him in the back of the head. She saw matter spew from his skull. Juba was almost upon him. He fell forward, and she lurched to catch him in her arms. She fell to the ground with Cuffee's sagging body.

"Oh no! God help us! How can this happen? Save him, God, please save him!" Juba gasped.

But as she looked down, she saw the blood pouring from the back of his head. He was unable to speak or move. Juba clung to his torso with one hand, while the other grasped the side of his head. His dark curls rose up over her fingertips. She continued to clutch him by the back of his woolen jacket.

"Oh, Cuffee," she cried, "don't leave me. I want to tell you about your child that I'm carrying. He will want to meet his daddy. Don't leave us!"

But then the shudder of life left his body, and he fell limp from her grasp. Juba looked up to see the approaching slave catcher, a broad smile on his face. He was the demon who had just killed her husband. Dressed in dark, soiled clothing, he had a knife in its sheath tucked into his belt and a heavy pistol in his hand. No circle of hell would be horrible enough for this monster. She stared at the vile white man, repulsed by his appearance, fury beaming from her eyes. Tears welled up, and her chest tightened in anger.

Then she looked again on Cuffee's face and saw the pallor of his skin and blue emerging on his lips. Realizing he was truly gone, she pressed her hand to her quivering chest, sobs surging up in her. She struggled to draw breath. The pain started as a sting in her loving heart and burned its way out of her body until she bent over, wailing in pain.

The slave catcher strode before her to drag off Cuffee's body as evidence of capture. His arms were crossed, and he looked upon her dispassionately, rolling his eyes.

With the man standing before her, Juba regained control of her emotions. Then she glanced down and gently rubbed her swollen belly. "I promise, Cuffee, this child will make you proud."

She stepped back from Cuffee. Rage burned on her face, and she glared at Cuffee's murderer. Her entire being seethed with anger and hate as the savage brute picked up Cuffee's lifeless body and threw him up over his broad shoulder. At the top of the levy, he dumped the body onto a cart where his comrade stood. The two erupted in laughter and progressed toward the city.

Juba stiffened at the sight, and rage smoldered within her. With clenched fists, she said, "You will pay for your actions, you cruel bastard, if I must go after you the rest of my days. I will avenge this murder!"

Touching her pregnant belly again, she pledged, "Cuffee, I promise you, your child and I will fight with every bone in our bodies. As God is my witness, this boy will someday know freedom. He will never suffer the pain we have. He will glorify your name and the name of God. I give you my word! He will live to right this terrible wrong!"

Those back at Twin Oaks waited for word about Cuffee. Everyone hoped he found Juba and that the two were together heading to freedom in the North.

Hentie and Big John had met by the plantation's waterway the evening before and Hentie was still glowing from the encounter. She had gone down first and waited; then Big John quietly advanced down to meet her. When Hentie turned to look at Big John, an electric wave pulsed through her. She knew he was there because he wanted to be there with her, not for an errand for the master or because he stumbled on her by mistake. As he came near, the two fell into each other's arms. They had waited so long for this moment. Hentie sunk her head into Big John's broad chest. His large frame enveloped her. Their spirits seem to mesh. Even a day later, she could still feel the imprint of him. She savored the warmth she continued to feel from their rendezvous as her mind drifted to their moments together.

As Hentie carried out her duties around the grounds at the kitchen house and nearby gardens, she was suddenly struck by an odd feeling, which rolled into horrific agony. She had been strolling across the work yard to fetch some herbs for cooking when a stabbing twinge hit her back; it was so intense that she yelped. Moments later an explosive pain erupted in the back of her head. Hentie staggered, then slumped to the ground.

"She must be having some sort of attack. Go get help!" Octavia shouted. "Get Big John. There is something bad wrong with Hentie."

As Octavia gently held Hentie's head and patted her check, Rosa scampered over.

"What happened here? What's wrong?"

"I don't know. She just dropped to the ground like she'd been shot. Never seen anything like this before. Don't know what caused it."

As the two exchanged worried glances, Hentie started to make sounds and roll her head.

"What is it? What happened? I just had the strangest feeling. I felt such a horrible pain in my head, and I felt so afraid, like something bad just happened. Don't know what it could be. It just crawled up in my insides, and I had a picture of Juba and Cuffee cross my mind. It was almost like I was there. I thought I heard Juba say, '*He's gone. He's really gone now.*' But that's crazy. I must just have them on my mind. That's it. Just worrying too much."

"Yep, that must be it. Just your nerves actin' up. Too much worry," Rosa said. "I'm sure the Lord is caring for our Juba and Cuffee. They cradled in his hands. The good Lord watches over us and them two as well. It's all within the power of the Lord God. He will make things right and wipe away all our tears."

Acknowledgments

Over the past handful of years I have been on a journey of discovery led by a vision. I thank God for choosing me to tell this story of pain, love and tragedy. One of the exciting aspects of writing this book has been the opportunity to speak with and learn from a wide variety of people. I am deeply indebted to those whose generosity and support helped me along this path. These people's positions and disciplines ranged from Gullah culture interpreter to archival specialist, from museum curator to sweetgrass basket maker. There were local historians, docents, and tour guides who showed me historical sites throughout Charleston and the Lowcountry region. They all spent many hours researching, reading, and committing to memory the many interesting facts about the area.

I would like to acknowledge particular people who were instrumental in formulating the breadth and depth of my research and the material I used in creating this novel. At the top of this list would be the conscientious resource librarians in the South Carolina Room of the Charleston County Library, particularly Malcolm Hale. I am particularly indebted to Brandee R. Worsham, reference librarian in the archival library of the National African American Museum of History and Culture in Washington, DC, and the "Gullah Lady" from Charleston, Jacqueline Odom-Mickell, presenter and true Gullah descendent. Hands down the best researching experience I had on this journey was at the Citadel. I was put in the capable hands of Tessa Updike, a diligent and knowledgeable archivist who patiently answered all my questions. I am eternally grateful for the insight and guidance of these people and their colleagues.

I have shared these past several years with the love and support of family and friends who generously lent me their wisdom, unflagging support, and reassurance as this book took shape. In particular, my husband, Mark Niccum, and daughter, Allie Moorman, who have reviewed manuscript drafts and gone along with me on this journey to tell the truth about slavery in the Lowcountry. I am truly grateful to you both as your support was instrumental in ensuring that this book materialized. I am forever indebted to my dear friends Jo Ellen Layne, Beth Tuttle Denny, and Susan Brasier, who selflessly devoted their time to reading and critiquing the countless drafts of my ever-changing manuscript. I will always appreciate your enthusiasm and loving critiques that helped guide me along the way. Most importantly, my deepest gratitude goes to David Larkin, my insightful and talented editor, for helping to make this a much better book and me a better writer along the way. Thank you! This project would not have come to fruition without all y'all!

Appendix

"Those who fail to learn from history are doomed to repeat it."
Sir Winston Churchill, House of Commons, 1948

A Brief History of the Gullah/Geechee People and Slavery in America

In writing this book, I hoped to enlighten the reader about the history of slavery as it occurred in Charleston, South Carolina. I sought to tell the truth about the horrors of human trafficking and the "peculiar institution" of slavery. I believe there are a number of good books about the Lowcountry during the antebellum period, but some writers have softened the gravity of what occurred. I hope through this book to reveal the harsh realities of what people of color endured and continue to endure due to America's history. For, you see, the past history of slavery manifests in our present.

At the time of the Civil War, the institution of slavery had proliferated throughout the country, and four million enslaved people of color lived in the United States. South Carolina, although settled primarily by settlers from the British Isles and their descendants, some via the Caribbean, became a state densely populated by people of color. African Americans, both enslaved and free, made up 57 percent of the state's population. Charleston was the country's largest port of slave trade, the city where many of the enslaved people first landed. Nearly half of all enslaved African Americans came through this port of entry. It is estimated that over 75 percent of all black Americans can trace their heritage to South Carolina, many to the port of Charleston. While many of the ships were registered to Newport, Rhode Island, and other New England ports where they were built, the slaver ships brought the majority of their human cargo to Charleston. Many of the deep pockets financing the human trafficking were investors from Northern cities such as New York and Boston.

Any history of slavery in America begins with Charleston. This may not be where the first slave landed, but it certainly is where slavery saw its greatest proliferation. It is also the heart of where the proslavery movement and the idea of a separate nation, first as a collection of nation-states in the Golden Circle, then later as the Confederacy, took hold.

Charleston was built on slave labor and, for nearly 200 years, thrived under a slave economy. Founded by white planters from the English colony of Barbados, they transferred many of the practices they developed on their sugar plantations to Charleston. King Charles of England awarded generous land grants of 150 acres to each white planter and an additional 150 acres for each servant transported by the planter. This critical factor of the head count brought to the region encouraged planters to acquire enslaved workers as they came to the Charleston area. The first ship, the *Carolina*, backed by eight royal proprietors, arrived with the men of the Corporation of Barbados Adventurers. With them they brought the first slave, a man unnamed.

The slave owners of Barbados were known as "hard masters"; this island nation was where the gang labor system was first introduced, and slaves worked long hours of intense labor in the sun. Their methods were brought to Charleston. African enslaved laborers were subjected to frequent floggings, brandings, and mutilations. This later included blinding, castration, and splitting (or hacking off) the nose from the face. These practices were specifically included in Charleston's Slave Law of the 1700s, taken nearly word for word from Barbados's statute on managing black enslaved workers. The wealthy sugarcane plantation owners also brought an opulent lifestyle and display of wealth, marked by extravagant consumption, fine clothing, and lavishly furnished homes. These men were known not only for enslaving black Africans, but Native Americans too.

The history of the Gullah people goes back over 300 years on the southeast coast of America. As the slaves imported from the Caribbean or enslaved from local Native American tribes died out, Charlestonians began to show a preference for "saltwater blacks" brought directly from Africa. Many of these slaves came from the west coast of Africa, where they had similar languages and customs. This cohesive group of people formed a culture and a language known as the Gullah or Geechee, now descendants of those formerly enslaved. Generally, North Carolina and South Carolina use the term Gullah; southward toward Georgia and Florida, the term Geechee is more commonly used. The recognized region they inhabit extends at its most northern point from Cape Fear and Wilmington, North Carolina, south to Northern Florida near Jacksonville. It encompasses all of the Sea Islands and approximately thirty-five miles inland to the St. John's River. This region has been identified by the federal government as the Gullah/Geechee Corridor.

There are numerous islands in and around Charleston and Beaufort, South Carolina, most of which were only accessible by ferry or boat. It was not until after the early twentieth century and the rollout of the Works Progress/Projects Administration ("WPA") programs that bridges were built and traveling between the islands and the mainland increased. Then later around the 1960s outside developers began to purchase large areas of land, most notably Hilton Head. Most of the Gullah who had lived on the islands for generations were forced out so that hotels and resorts could be built.

The language and manner of speaking which evolved among the Gullah was a mixture of African terms, melody of the language, movement and nature of expression coupled with British English. At first it was referred to as "bad English," but over time it has become recognized as its own dialect. It is a creole language. This, however, took decades to be realized.

While the newly enslaved were unable to bring personal possessions, they had memories. They could practice their arts, language, agricultural know-how, culinary skills, oral tradition, and spirituality. These elements streamed into the Gullah culture and enabled it to flourish. When we think of "Southern cooking," much of it is an amalgamation of American elements such as butter and crème along with African foods such as okra, rice, watermelon, sorghum, black-eyed peas, and yams.

The African slave trade flourished for hundreds of years. The early Europeans who voyaged to the Americas were mostly from Spain and Portugal. They brought Africans to the Caribbean in the 1500s. Some of those Africans eventually migrated to North America. Slavery in the Deep South of the United States did not occur overnight. This "peculiar institution" was one that evolved over time.

In Colonial times most of the servants were white indentured servants. They had come to America by way of an agreement. Generally, what they were offered was passage to the New World in exchange for a contract of servitude for a defined period of time, typically two to seven years in duration. Once the period of time had expired, the indebted party was freed. Initially, most of the servants were English. By the 1700s many were Irish, Scottish, Scotch-Irish, German or Swiss. While in theory this system seemed to be a viable alternative to a young lad with no education and few options who could receive an apprenticeship from a tradesman such as a blacksmith, it was rife with pitfalls. There was no child welfare system in those days, nor child labor laws. Orphans often fell victim to mercenary tradesmen seeking free labor. Hence, the period of service turned from seven years to ten or twenty or even a lifetime.

Over the centuries black resistance persisted. Sometimes it was more overt, with acts such as running away or participating in an uprising, while at other times it was more covert. Although Southern masters sometimes believed their slaves adored them and were happy with their circumstances, this could not be further from the truth. Their quiet resistance took many forms of subversion, from reluctance to work, feigned illness, and labor slowdowns to breaking tools and destroying property. The enslaved always knew this peculiar institution was wrong and that their masters were ruthless; they just had limited means to oppose it. The layers of oppression for Negroes was extensive, starting with drivers, overseers, masters, the City Guard, slave hunters, the militia, and the Work House. Of those limited numbers who did grow to feel affection for their masters, particularly enslaved house servants, it is now thought to have been a form of Stockholm Syndrome known to exist among other kidnapping or human-trafficking victims—a condition in which hostages develop a bond or alliance with their oppressors. Being unable to flee, they bond with their capturer.

Historians, linguists, and anthropologists have collaborated to identify the area from which these African descendants originated. Through painstaking work, a particular area of Sierra Leone has been uncovered as the likely region that at least some of the Gullah emerged from. A tremendous number of African slaves were captured in this territory of the Rice Coast of Western Africa. Moreover, the Krio language of Sierra Leone is remarkably similar to Gullah. While the origin of the term *Gullah* is uncertain, it is believed to be a variation on the African word Gora or Gola, which are the names of African tribes in and around Sierra Leone. Some theorize it could also be a reference to Angola.

The author with the mayor of Freetown, Sierra Leone, Yvonne Aki-Sawyerr

The slaves brought to America were skilled in growing rice, a difficult and complicated crop with its differing requirements in planting and cultivation. African rice is related to Asian rice, yet it is a distinct species. Once it was discovered that it could grow in the American South, slaves knowledgeable about rice were actively sought out. Rice had been grown in Africa for over 2,000 years, so a reliable body of knowledge evolved for the Gullah people. They knew how to develop and build irrigation systems, dams, and earthworks, something previously unknown to plantation owners of European descent.

Over time, the principal crops of rice and indigo gave way to the even more lucrative crop of cotton, which came to dominate

American and global markets and was tremendously profitable. Some argue that the tremendous wealth and lavish lifestyles that cotton afforded spurred the intrinsic dependency on slave labor which led to the Civil War.

Setting the Stage for the Civil War

While most of us were taught that the drafting of America's Constitution was a watershed moment and a happy occasion in our history, many of us are unaware of all the tensions and finagling that went on behind the scenes because of slavery. Although there was a significant proliferation of human bondage going on in our country at the time the Constitution was signed, mention of it is curiously absent from the document. That was not due to oversight, but rather to compromise. This "imperfect" document was signed by our country's leaders, who were fully aware that slaves and people of color were noticeably absent from the landmark document. Certain Southerners were adamant that the Constitution had to be proslavery. George Mason of Virginia, who owned more than 200 slaves, was insistent. From South Carolina, Charles Pinckney, Charles Cotesworth, and John Rutledge were all forceful proponents of slavery. John Rutledge famously highlighted the differences between the North and South by noting that they were as "different as the interests of Russia and Turkey."

The census figures of 1790 show the dependence on slave labor and its importance to the economy of the South. Of the approximately 700,000 slaves living in America at the time, 642,000 resided in the South and 42,000 in the North. South Carolina's population was 249,073. Of that, 107,094 were slaves, and 1,801 were free people of color. Slaves made up 43 percent of South Carolina's population.

Due to the staunch position of certain Southerners, it was believed that a Constitution was only possible if compromises were made. It was genuinely believed by some that slavery would wither away. As the market price of certain cash crops dropped, so did the value of slaves. It was known that tobacco depleted the soil, and it was believed to be dropping in value. At that time, rice and indigo were also small markets. If these crops withered away, so would the need for slaves to work the land.

Hence, it was believed to be better to have an imperfect union, thereby avoiding anarchy. The need to create an effective national government was paramount. So, although those present knew that "they had thrown equality to the winds[,] . . . the sacrifice purchased the continuation of the union and made possible a national government. At that moment, those objectives seemed to be worth the price."

But as we know, slavery did not fade out on its own. Instead it began to proliferate. The cash crops of the South were modified. In South Carolina it went from indigo and rice to Sea Island or black seed cotton. This commodity was one of the most desired types of cotton in the world. It was used not so much for American markets but for British and European markets. At first what was produced in the South was meager, as the seed had to be separated by hand from the cotton fiber. A man doing it by hand could only clean one pound a day. With the cotton gin developed by Eli Whitney, fifty pounds of cotton could be cleaned in a day. This dramatic boost in production changed the game. Unfortunately, it, along with other factors, perpetuated slavery and the antebellum way of life.

Fashion also played a factor in this, particularly among royals and Napoleon, given the Greco-Roman revival of the early nineteenth century. The white-cotton muslin gowns worn during the Regency period by the French and English were born, including the empire waistline. There were also a number of wars going throughout the world, including the Napoleonic Wars and the War of 1812. It was also the first time that comfortable undergarments came into being. This was curtailed around the 1830s when hoop skirts and corsets were introduced.

It would seem that the coalescence of a handful of factors

perpetuated slavery and spurred the War Between the States:

- Large American farms or plantations capable of cotton cultivation
- Black enslaved labor
- The invention and incorporation of the cotton gin into American plantations
- Revolutionary technology developed in the British textile industry

These factors, along with fervent greed and intense racial prejudice, kept the cotton plantation churning for decades. It led to one of the most heinous wars this country has ever seen. Not only was it American against American, but sometimes kin fighting against kin. At the time of the Civil War, battle was close up and personal. You saw the whites of the enemy's eyes. Even though he was your brother, you fired your musket at him and saw part of his face blown off just feet away from you. Because of the implications of slave-produced cotton, 700,000 Americans died. Hundreds of thousands were permanently maimed or injured.

Defense of the South's Peculiar Institution

After the African slave trade commenced and the Middle Passage took hold, slaveholders began to argue that the institution of slavery was a necessity to perpetuate their way of life. Some slaveholders promoted the ideas of certain Southern doctors, scientists, and paraprofessionals who argued that the innate characteristics enslaved blacks possessed stemmed from their dark skin tones. Some contended that not only was their skin better suited for the hot summers and humid heat, but so were their muscles, membranes, and tendons. Some even included the Africans' brain and nerves. Dr. Josiah C. Nott of Mobile, Alabama, took this notion to the extreme, contending that Negroes and whites did not belong to the same species.

Confederate currency promoting this notion was distributed

throughout the South in the early and mid-nineteenth century. Images were used to glorify and justify an inhumane institution. Scenes of agricultural labor being performed by enslaved black workers typified the engravings. In this propaganda blitz, most of the scenes involved King Cotton and the faces of happy, healthy bondsmen performing work related to the cultivation of cotton. Sometimes other crops were shown. On one North Carolina currency, enslaved workers were shown happily working in a factory.

Even after 1900, there were well-educated men who contended that African Americans were innately suited to slavery. Professor Ulrich B. Phillips, born in LaGrange, Georgia, was an American historian who largely defined the field of the social and economic history of the Antebellum American South and of slavery. He premised a study of slavery on the notion that "Negroes by racial quality are submissive, lighted hearted, amiable, ingratiating and imitative." He contended that the plantation system of the South helped to civilize the slaves. He touted that the plantations acted as a school, constantly training and controlling pupils who were in a backward state of civilization. He contended that the plantations were the best schools for the mass training of that sort of inert and backward people, which the bulk of the American Negroes represented to him. Such thinking dovetailed with notable Charlestonians such as John C. Calhoun, statesman and former vice president of the United States.

As late as 1953, a distinguished biochemist suggested that races of men, like breeds of dogs, may possess distinctive emotional characteristics, and that the Negro's "inborn temperament" may have made his enslavement feasible. Others countered these arguments, noting that since the first colonization in the American Southeast, white men had toiled in the South's hot and sunny conditions and performed heavy labor. In the 1850s, Frederick Law Olmsted, the famous landscape architect, journalist, and social critic who designed Central Park in Manhattan and Golden Gate Park in San Francisco, saw numerous white women in Mississippi and Alabama at work in the hottest sunshine "in the regular cultivation of cotton."

Often overlooked is that much of Charleston, the White House, and the US Capitol Building were built on the backs of enslaved people of color. Of particular note, in Charleston, the stately homes on Rainbow Row were built with slave labor. Their pastel colors were influenced by the palette used in Barbados and other Caribbean islands. The foundation of American historical institutions ushers in the thorny question of how to deal with the painful reality that neither the thousands of enslaved workers who played a role in building our country, nor their descendants, have ever been recognized or compensated for their arduous labors. The sensitive question of reparations is something we shall explore below.

Reparations

Some have suggested that the federal government should somehow reimburse or give recompense to African Americans for the horrors they endured during slavery and the years that followed. The reparations could take the form of financial compensation but would more likely take the form of a special social program. Human trafficking was sanctioned by the federal government for nearly 250 years, and the use of slaves was protected up until the Civil War. Congress, although aware of lynching and other acts of terror perpetrated against blacks that occurred well into the twentieth century, knowingly failed to act, blocking any legislation to prohibit this behavior. Hundreds of murders and acts of violence occurred during this time.

The United States has paid reparations to many around the globe. In 1988, President Reagan signed the Civil Liberties Act to compensate more than a hundred thousand people of Japanese descent who were incarcerated in internment camps during World War II. The legislation offered a formal apology and paid out $20,000 in compensation to each surviving victim.

Reparations is a notion debated by advocates as something we have traditionally done for foreign countries we invade and annihilate, but not for our own people. The exception to this, of course, is the white slave owners who were compensated following the Civil War for their loss of chattel property. President Abraham Lincoln paid white Union loyalists up to 300 dollars for every enslaved person who was freed. It is reported that the largest payout under the District of Columbia Emancipation Act was 18,000 dollars for sixty-nine slaves. If we could render such a large cash payment, could we not even look at recompense or acknowledgment of the loss and hardship suffered by enslaved workers?

Recent Racial Turmoil

What does the past tell us about the present? The struggle for racial equality grinds on, and relentless eruptions of racial violence continue to roil the United States. While racial violence seemingly peaked in the riots of the 1960s, it has taken on a new life in the second decade of the new millennium, resulting in countless deaths. One would think that after 300 years, a civil war, and the enactment of many laws which call for equal treatment, our peoples would have seamlessly blended, but they have not. Animosity and resentment still linger. Some feel the need to display hurtful symbols such as the Confederate flag, which continues to send a chill down the spines of many, both black and white. It reminds us of a lawless time when lynching was commonplace, well into the twentieth century, and lawmen turned a blind eye. Even now, in the twenty-first century, the Confederate flag is often displayed while acts of terrorism are perpetrated. In Charleston, South Carolina, it is a common phenomenon for white supremacists to mount large Confederate flags on poles in the beds of their pickup trucks, then drive through black neighborhoods shouting racial epithets. Sometimes they fire guns while doing so. This was such a problem in the Charleston metro area that multiple police jurisdictions were called together to address the issue.

Recently, the Confederate flag serves as a rallying cry for white supremacy and bigotry, as we have learned with confessed killer Dylann Roof, who massacred nine members of the Emanuel Mother African Methodist Episcopal Church on June 17, 2015. Mother Emanuel, as it is commonly known, is in downtown Charleston and is the oldest standing AME church in the city, if not the state. It was the same church where Denmark Vesey, who planned the famous 1822 uprising, was a member. On that day when Roof entered the church, good, God-fearing people were holding Bible study classes in the basement. They invited Roof to join them when he entered the building. Despite their warm welcome, Roof would later open fire on the group.

Roof contended that he had not been raised in a racist household; it was something he learned online, apparently from white supremacists who spewed racial hatred. He spent an inordinate amount of time developing his plan, researching it, and visiting historical sites throughout Charleston and the state. He developed a handwritten list of churches he targeted for attack. All were black churches situated in the Lowcountry.

On the day he perpetrated the horrifying carnage, Roof sat in the church with the Bible study group for an hour. They discussed the teachings of the selected passages. While conversing, Roof had time to gain an impression of the band of church members around him and to abort his plan. There were children in the group. Nonetheless, Dylan Roof went on to perpetrate one of the most heinous crimes in recent history, carried out in a cold and calculated manner. How did he get to be that hateful? How did the Confederate symbolism he connected with play a role? How does propaganda entice such acts? Consider its role with Hitler and the Nazi party. In Germany, symbols including the flag of the Third Reich and the Nazi salute have been banned because of their emotionally charged and offensive nature.

A national outpouring of sympathy occurred after the 2015 Mother Emanuel massacre, and a torrent of grief and anger over the slaughter of innocent churchgoers reverberated around the world.

Meanwhile, white supremacists continue to promote racial hatred.

In 2018, a white South Carolinian man sought to imitate Roof's heinous crime. Benjamin McDowell, a resident of Conway, a small town in Horry County north of Charleston, reportedly formed bonds with other white supremacists while in prison. Upon his release, he contacted such believers over the internet. Although in violation of his release from prison, he acquired firearms in furtherance of his plan. Online, McDowell expressed his desire to imitate the 2015 massacre by executing an attack "in the spirit of Dylann Roof." He was frustrated with other white supremacists and their failure to take deliberate action in furtherance of their beliefs. McDowell contended it was not enough to scream "white power'"; it "was not getting the job done."

In North Charleston, a white police officer, Michael Slager, murdered a black man, Walter Scott, over a failure-to-appear warrant, meaning he failed to comply with a summons to attend a hearing. During this incident, Patrolman Slager stopped a vehicle with a black occupant for a taillight that was out. The driver, Walter Scott, knew he had an active bench warrant due to his failure to appear for a court hearing regarding back-due child support in the amount of $18,000. Rather than risk apprehension and potential jail time, the driver chose to run away from the officer. In a struggle with the police officer, a taser was used. Walter Scott managed to free himself from the officer and run a short distance. While only a few feet away, the patrolman drew his gun and fired eight rounds. Scott was struck five times; a bullet which entered his back, then his lungs, was fatal. Why was deadly forced used in this situation? Do white officers sometimes treat black suspects differently?

On August 8, 2014, in Ferguson, Missouri, a suburb of St. Louis, Officer Darren Wilson, white, shot and killed a suspect of color, Michael Brown, an unarmed eighteen-year-old. Missouri had been a slave state pursuant to the Missouri Compromise. The facts of this case are not clear, but an argument ensued that led to a physical confrontation in which the officer and Brown fought over the officer's service revolver. The revolver apparently discharged twice during the struggle, during which the officer had remained in his vehicle. Following this, the officer pursued Brown and shot him multiple times. There was a dispute as to whether Brown had already surrendered with his arms raised when the officer fired. This event spurred weeks of unrest and protests. In response to this and similar events, white officers were gunned down in various spots throughout the United States for no apparent reason except retribution. Since the Ferguson occurrence even more heinous acts of police violence have been perpetrated, such as the Minnesota incident with George Floyd's throat compression by an officer's knee, then the Rayshard Brooks killing in Atlanta in which the victim had fallen asleep while waiting in a Wendy's drive-thru.

There is a state statute affecting Confederate flags and monuments codified in South Carolina law. This law, enacted in 2000, is designed to make it more difficult to remove or replace Confederate symbols. The law thwarts local citizens as well as municipal or county governments from deciding what is appropriate for their communities. If local residents find Confederate statues or other memorabilia to be too offensive or hurtful, they are powerless to have them removed. Only legislatures from outside their communities are able to decide such matters. Decision-making on these matters has been taken from their hands. A handful of other Southern states have similar statutes.

Over the past few years, President Trump has been criticized for inciting racial hatred. In early August 2019, two mass shootings occurred within forty-eight hours, in El Paso, Texas, and in Dayton, Ohio. Many claim that President Trump promotes this kind of behavior. He had told four congresswomen to go back to where they came from, even though three were born in America. White nationalists have reportedly found great comfort in his rhetoric and have been energized by his tirades. Allegedly his tone was set when he sympathized with white supremacists at a Charlottesville, Virginia, rally and the murder of a counterdemonstrator who was promoting tolerance of others. President Trump said, "There are good people on both sides." White supremacists have used those words as a rallying cry: "We now have a president who believes in us and supports our cause." The FBI has documented that white nationalism has gone up dramatically since President Trump took office. When asked about this, he demurred. Is he a demagogue? Do federal senators and congressmen play a part? What should Americans do to stop this violence?

More recently Americans have begun to call for the removal of statues and memorials honoring Confederates. Does this mean the death of the Lost Cause mythology? It took hold near the end of the Civil War, but later flourished after Reconstruction near the end of the nineteenth century. It served to aggrandize the notions of white supremacy and was a push back on the rights of African Americans.

Due to COVID-19, Americans were cloistered at home and able to watch incidences such as George Floyd's killing. While Americans initially became alarmed following the Ferguson, Missouri, 2014 riots, followed by the 2015 Charleston Mother Emanuel massacre and then the 2017 Charlottesville killing, it seemed to come to a head in 2020. Some contended that President Trump had developed toxic politics which spurred a burst of rage across the American landscape. This anger was manifested as demonstrations, riots and general racial unrest. How does American heal from this and bring about the vision held by Martin Luther King, Jr.?

Select Bibliography

(Not listing interviewees, original documents and information gained during site visits)

Albert, Octavia V. Rogers. *The House of Bondage or Charlotte Brooks and Other Slaves.* New York & Oxford: Oxford University Press, 1988

Ashton, Susanna. *I Belong to South Carolina, South Carolina Slave Narratives.* Columbia, South Carolina: University of South Carolina Press, 2010

Bailey, Cornelia Walker with Christina Bledsoe. *God, Dr. Buzzard, and the Bolito Man; A Saltwater Geechee Talks About Life on Sapelo Island, Georgia.* New York: Anchor Books, 2000

Ball, Edward. *Slaves in the Family.* New York: Farrar, Straus and Giroux, 1998

Ball, Edward. *The Sweet Hell Inside.* New York, New York: Harper Collins Publishers, 2001

Bartlett, Irving H. *John C. Calhoun, A Biography.* New York: W. W. Norton & Company, 1993.

Blain, Keisha N., Chad Williams and Kidada E. Williams, *Charleston Syllabus,* Athens, Georgia. The University of Georgia Press, 2016

Boyer Lewis, Charlene M. *Ladies and Gentlemen on Display, Planter Society at the Virginia Springs, 1790-1860.* Charlottesville, Virginia: University Press of Virginia, 2001

Brown, Alphonso. *A Gullah Guide to Charleston, Walking Through Black History.* Charleston, SC. The History Press, 2008

Burton, Orville Vernon with Wilbur Cross. *Penn Center, A History Preserved.* Athens, Georgia: University of Georgia Press, 2014.

Campbell, Emory S., *Gullah Cultural Legacies,* 3rd Edition. San Bernardino, CA: Self-published. 2008

Chandler, Genevieve W. *Coming Through, Voices of a South Carolina Gullah Community from WPA Oral Histories.* Columbia, South Carolina: University of South Carolina Press, 2008

Charles River Editors. *The Knights of the Golden Circle; The History and Legacy of One of 19th Century America's Most Notorious Secret Societies.* Middletown, Delaware: Charles River Editors, 2017

Coakley, Joyce V. *Sweetgrass Baskets and* the *Gullah Tradition.* Charleston, South Carolina: Arcadia Publishing, 2005

Conte, Robert S. *The History of the Greenbrier, America's Resort.* Charleston West Virginia: Pictorial Histories Publishing Co., 1989

Creel, Margaret Washington, *A Peculiar People. Slave Religion and Community-Culture Among the Gullahs,* New York, New York University, 1988.

Cross, Wilbur. *Gullah Culture in America.* Winston-Salem, North Carolina: John F. Blair Publisher, 2008.

Daise, Ronald. *Gullah Branches, West African Roots.* Orangeburg, South Carolina: Sandpiper Publishing, 2007

Dataw Historic Foundation, *Dataw, No Ordinary Place,* Hilton Head Island, SC: Lydia Inglett Ltd. Publishing, 2015

Dattel, Gene. *Cotton and Race in The Making of America, The Human Costs of Economic Power.* Plymouth, UK: Ivan R. Dee, Publisher, 2009

Dickey, Christopher. *Our Man in Charleston: Britain's Secret Agent In the Civil War South,* New York, New York, Broadway Books, 2015

Drago, Edmund L. *Charleston's Avery Center: From Education and Civil Rights to Preserving the African American Experience.* Charleston, S.C.: History Press, 2015

Fordham, Damon L. *True Stories of Black South Carolina.* Charleston, S.C.: The History Press, 2008.

Franklin, John Hope and Alfred A. Moss, Jr. *From Slavery to Freedom, A History of African Americans, Volume One.* New York: The McGraw-Hill Companies, 1947

Fraser, Jr., Walter J. *Charleston! Charleston! The History of a Southern City.* Columbia, South Carolina: University of South Carolina, 1989

Frazer, Herb. *Behind God's Back, Gullah Memories.* Charleston, SC: Evening Post Books, 2011.

Gates, Jr., Henry Louis & Donald Yacovone. *The African Americans, Many Rivers to Cross.* India: Hay House Publishers India, 2013

Gonzales, Ambrose E., *The Black Border, Gullah Stories of the Carolina Coast,* Columbia, S.C. The State Company, 1922.

Greene, Harlan, Harry S. Hutchings, Jr. and Brian E. Hutchins. *Slave Badges and the Slave-Hire System in Charleston, South Carolina, 1783-1865.* Jefferson, North Carolina: McFarland & Company, 2004

Hadden, Sally E. *Slave Patrols, Law and Violence in Virginia and the Carolinas,* Cambridge, Massachusetts: Harvard University Press, 2003

Hammond, Pearce W. *The Gullahs of South Carolina.* Okatie, South Carolina: Halftide Publishing, 2011

Jacobs, Harriet, *Incidents in the Life of a Slave Girl.* Mineola, New York: Dover Publications, Inc., 2001

Jones, John W. and Gretchen Barbatsis. *Confederate Currency, The Color of Money, Images of Slavery in Confederate and Southern States.* China: New Directions Publishing, 2004

Keckley, Elizabeth. *Behind the Scenes, or, Thirty Years a Slave, And Four Years in the White House.* New York: G.W. Carleton & Co., 1868

Kemble, Frances Anne. *A Witness to Slavery, Journal of a Residence on a Georgian Plantation 1838-1839,* Self-Published, Middletown, Delaware 2017

Littlefield, Daniel C., *Rice and Slaves, Ethnicity and the Slave Trade in Colonial South Carolina*, Urbana & Chicago, Illinois, University of Illinois Press, 1991.

McInnis, Maurie D., *The Politics of Taste in Antebellum Charleston*, Chapel Hill, NC, The University of North Carolina Press, 2005.

Michelsohn, Lynn. *Gullah Ghosts, Roswell, New Mexico, Cleannan Press, 2009.*

Morris, J. Brent. *Yes, Lord, I Know the Road: A Documentary History of African Americans in South Carolina, 1526-2008.* Columbia, South Carolina: University of South Carolina Press, 2017

Opala, Joseph A. *The Gullah: Rice, Slavery and the Sierra Leone-American Connection.* United States Information Services, distributed through the National Park Service, 1987

Perry, Lee Davis and J. Michael McLaughlin. *It Happened in South Carolina, Remarkable Events That Shaped History.* Guilford, Connecticut: Morris Book Publishing, 2003

Pinckney, Roger. *Blue Roots, African-American Folk Magic of the Gullah People, 2nd Ed.* Orangeburg, South Carolina: Sandlapper Publishing Co., 2003

Pollitzer, William S. *The Gullah People and Their African Heritage.* Athens, Georgia: The University of Georgia Press. 1999

Powers, Bernard E. *Black Charlestonians, A Social History, 1822-1885.* Fayetteville, Arkansas: University of Arkansas Press, 1994

Pyatt, Thomas. *Gullah History Along the Carolina Lowcountry, Self-publication, San Bernardino, California, 2006*

Raven, Margot Theis. Night Boat to Freedom. New York: Square Fish, 2006

Robertson, David, Denmark Vesey, The Buried Story of America's Largest Slave Rebellion and the Man Who Led It. New York, NY: Vintage Books, 1999

Rosengarten, *Tombee Portrait of a Cotton Planter.* New York, New York, William Morrow & Co. 1986

Schwartz, Marie Jenkins. *Born in Bondage, Growing Up Enslaved in the Antebellum South.* Cambridge, MA & London, England, Harvard University Press, 2000.

Stampp, Kenneth M. *The Peculiar Institution, Slavery in the Ante-Bellum South.* New York, New York: Vintage Books, 1956.

Stubbs, Tristan. *Masters of Violence, The Plantation Overseers of Eighteenth-Century Virginia, South Carolina and Georgia,* University of South Carolina Press, 2018

Tobin, Jacqueline L and Raymond G. Dobard, *Hidden in Plain View, A Secret Story of Quilts and the Underground Railroad,* New York, Random House, 1999.

Whitehead, Colson. *The Underground Railroad.* New York, New York: Random House, 2016

Williamson, Joel After Slavery, *The Negro in South Carolina During Reconstruction, 1861-1877,* Hanover, NH and New York, University Press of New England. 1965

Wood, Peter H. Black Majority, *Negroes in Colonial South Carolina From 1670 Through the Stono Rebellion,* New York, New York, W.W. Norton & Company, 1974

Works Progress Administration (WPA) interviewers; 34 former slave interviewees. Edited by Norman R. Yetman. *When I Was A Slave; Memoirs from the Slave Narrative Collection.* Mineola, New York: Dover Publications, Inc., 1941

Beyond the Big House, Tour and Storytelling (of Charleston buildings used by enslaved African Americans) The Slave Dwelling Project & Historic Charleston Foundation, September 16, 2017.

Questions for Discussion

Book Clubs:

- What did you learn about the Gullah culture? Had you previously been aware of this group of people? What was most interesting to you? Burial practices? Beliefs about haints and boo hags? Blending of African and Christian traditions? Importance of symbols used in quilts?

- Do you think there are other Gullah customs and traditions that have become integrated into Southern living? Sweetgrass baskets? Herbal remedies?

- Do you think African foods and Gullah cooking have influenced Southern cooking?

- What was it like for you to read about Hentie's capture, trip to American in the Middle Passage, and her sale in downtown Charleston? Had you previously been aware of the practices on slaver ships?

- What are your takeaway thoughts about Doll and William Langdon's relationship? What were the dynamics of a white slave master who kept an enslaved Negro for a lover? Can you draw parallels to modern-day relationships, or even historic ones, such as Thomas Jefferson and Sally Hemings?

College-Level Course Discussion Questions:

- What have you learned about the Gullah culture? What was most interesting to you?

- Were you previously aware of what "harsh discipline" of slaves entailed? Was it surprising to hear about an institution such as the Work House, which was something more akin to a medieval torture chamber, where blacks were beaten and tortured?

- Cuffee was rented out on New Year's Day as was the practice on "Hiring Day" prior to the Civil War. This day was also known as

"Heartbreak Day" where families were often torn apart as family members were rented or sold to other plantation owners. In one slave account, a mother saw all seven of her children go onto the auction block, then sold. How might such an event affect you and your family?

- Was the Civil War unavoidable, or could it have been resolved through peaceful discussions? How might our country be different if a new country, a "Golden Circle," had formed? (Such as the group portrayed in Chapter 18, Southern Rights Groups) Were you aware that this group was still active?

- Do you think today's prejudices are rooted in the claims of people like John C. Calhoun and Robert Barnwell Rhett about African Americans?

- Do you think we should respect the perspectives of secessionist and Confederate groups? Is there a need to better understand "The Lost Cause"?

- Confederate memorials were not displayed until well after the end of the Civil War, most around the late 1800s or 1900 when Southerners became disgruntled about rights having been given to blacks. It was done to promote white supremacy. Knowing this, how does it impact your beliefs?

- Now holding a better understanding of some of the roots of our prejudices, why do you think racial prejudice still occurs ?

- According to historians, the Confederate flag was rarely displayed after the Civil War except for military reunions until the onset of the civil rights movement of the late 1950s and '60s. It was then used as a pushback to promoting racial equality. Does this alter your view on the Confederate flag?

- As we know from recent national events, white supremist groups still exist and are very active. Consider the massacre of the nine Mother Emanuel AME Church members by convicted mass murderer and white supremist Dylann Roof that occurred in Charleston, South Carolina, in June 2015. This was followed by the murder of a woman in Charlottesville, Virginia, who opposed white supremacists. Should we continue to display Confederate flags and Confederate military statues even though they might be hurtful to others? Consider what has happened in Germany where the swastika and all Third Reich symbols have been banned, including the salute.

- Is there an argument for reparations to slave descendants? The US has paid reparations to foreign countries we have conquered and to Japanese Americans who were sent to internment camps during World War II. Legal terrorism of black Americans continued long after the Civil War, well into the new millennium. Should there be recompense?

- How has the information in this book altered your point of view?

- It is estimated that current human trafficking is about four times as prevalent as the African slave trade was in the 1800s. Currently, human trafficking affects foreign-born citizens and Americans. What lessons have we learned over the past 300 years, if any?

- Do you agree or disagree with the author's perspective?

Author's Notes

Several years ago, when I first decided to take on the project of writing a book about the Gullah culture and the history of race-based slavery in the Lowcountry, I found the notion overwhelming. I felt called to write a book about the history of the Deep South after a series of vivid dreams. I wanted to tell the truth about the gravity of what happened in a moving and enlightening way. I caution the reader that the facts and historical events within this novel are accurate; however, the timeline is hazy. I needed to truncate the story to fit it all within the main character's lifetime. I chose to go with authenticity of culture and events over accuracy of dates. I tried my best to compress the timeline of fifty-five years or longer with defensible creative license. Thus, the places and activities described actually took place around 1800 to 1859. I took out references to actual dates so that the characters' slow aging process would not be so apparent.

Nearly all the scenes in the book are based on actual events, many of them taken from the WPA's Writer's Project slave narratives.

However, I also used many other primary source materials such as letters, journals, plantation ledgers, bills of sale, newspaper articles, flyers, billets, pamphlets, and the like. My years of experience doing legal research by hand as a law clerk, then attorney, proved beneficial. All of the physically violent and harsher depictions in the novel were garnered this way. I also used many secondary sources amounting to dozens of books. These authors were consistent with what I found in my own personal research. Along with this, I personally interviewed a number of Gullah women, wherever they were willing to meet with me: in their homes, on plantations, at local libraries, in the historic Charleston City Market, at Gullah festivals, and even at sweetgrass basket huts along Route 17 in Mount Pleasant.

After nearly six years of careful research I learned so much that had previously been completely unknown to me; I would say well over three-quarters of it was new information. I'm a well-educated person with multiple degrees, and still I had no idea about practices on slave ships, the significance of Charleston as a port for human trafficking (Gadsden's Wharf), the existence of a Black Code, or the de facto caste system that existed in Charleston for generations. I was horrified to learn of the Work House, also known as the Sugar House, and its medieval torture methods, which included a dungeon where poor enslaved souls were stretched, whipped, and tortured. Almost without exception, white Charlestonians I spoke to informally reported being unaware of the notorious institution. I found this puzzling. Do we choose to repress the more unsavory parts of our own history?

I had no prior experience as a writer, other than a few journal articles, before I moved to Charleston and began my research. I only knew I needed to tell this story and share the truth of what happened here. As time has gone on, the story has become more and more vital to our present-day race relations. The thwarted slave uprising planned by Denmark Vesey who helped establish the Mother Emanuel AME Church has a direct link to the 2015 massacre perpetrated by Dylann

Roof. He chose that church because of that historical link. Southern Rights groups, include the Knights of the Golden Circle, still exist, as well as other White Supremacists organizations. Thus, to better address our present, we must understand our past.

About the Author

Josie is a new Southern author who lives outside Charleston, South Carolina. Prior to commencing her writing life, Josie was an attorney and social worker who spent her career addressing child abuse, domestic violence, and sexual assault. Her call to service was spurred by early life experiences growing up in poverty in the inner city with hardship, strife, and violence. Josie initially gained a bachelor's degree in social work, then provided services to troubled youth and their families, many of whom suffered from mental illness and disabilities. Following this, she returned to a university setting to gain a master's degree in social work. After a period of time in the field, she decided to pursue additional training in Europe and attended the London School of Economics where she engaged in graduate studies in public administration and public policy. In order to bring about real change for those she served, she then decided to pursue legal studies in New York where she gained a law degree from Hofstra University. Josie worked for over thirty years as a public servant and advocate. In the twilight of her career, Josie chose to serve on a statewide committee to combat human trafficking in her home state of Ohio. This professional background has served her well in her current pursuits.

After moving to the South from the Midwest, she became deeply interested in the Gullah culture and race-based slavery. Leveraging her legal research skills, she began to interview Gullah slave descendants, conduct site visits, and research archival records. In early 2020 she released her first book, *Growing Up Gullah in the Lowcountry*, a children's picture book about the Gullah culture, heirs' property, and the history of Charleston. *Gullah Tears* is Josie's debut historical fiction novel, the first in a series.

Printed in the USA
CPSIA information can be obtained
at www.ICGtesting.com
LVHW101311130823
755092LV00002B/186